The ALCHEMISTS Of L⚒OM

keymaster press

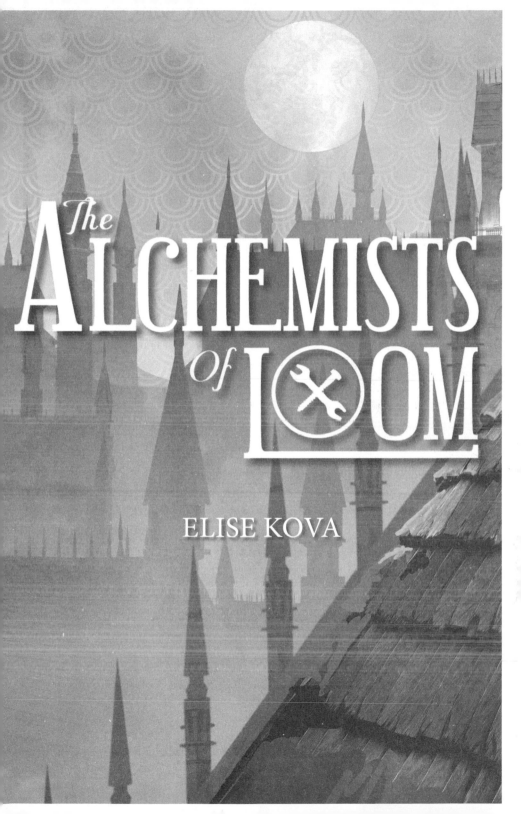

The ALCHEMISTS of LOOM

ELISE KOVA

Published by Keymaster Press
3971 Hoover Rd. Suite 77
Columbus, OH 43123-2839

Edited by: Rebecca Faith Heyman
Cover Design by: Nick D. Grey
Proofreading by: Christine Herman
Layout Design by: Mr. Merwin D. Loquias

ISBN: 9781619844414
eISBN: 9781619844421

Library of Congress Control Number: 2016932412

Printed in the United States of America

Also by Elise Kova

LOOM SAGA
The Alchemists of Loom
The Dragons of Nova

AIR AWAKENS SERIES
Air Awakens
Fire Falling
Earth's End
Water's Wrath
Crystal Crowned

GOLDEN GUARD TRILOGY
The Crown's Dog

for grandpa
the man who taught me the beauty in science

Contents

ARIANNA

Arianna had a bomb, three bullets, two refined daggers, a mental map of her heist, and a magic winch-box. All she waited for now was darkness.

The refinery she stared down upon had been coughing up only wisps of smog from its spiraling smokestacks since sunset. Ari had been watching it dwindle for weeks until it finally all but wrote *"Tonight is the night, oh White Wraith"* in the sky. She'd been eager for this job; the pay was astounding. But that hadn't been what drew her to it. No, she loved the challenge of it, the way it dredged up patience and planning and calculation from her like rare minerals from a mine.

Weeks of preparation—listening in on grunts describing their rotations, lifting papers from refinery manager's homes, studying the logic behind the blackened, mammoth skeleton of steel and iron that was known as the refinery had come down to this night. She looped her line through the stonework next to her and clipped it to itself. Dortam's infamous White Wraith was so very ready for what was coming next.

Moonlight streamed bright enough to cut her shape into the ground far below, making her presence known to any who bothered to take note. But Ari stood with relaxed shoulders and a slack posture. The grunts would be called into the refinery's core to provide extra protection when the reagents were switched. They wouldn't know they were a glint in her eye until it was far too late.

The refinery belched up a sudden stream of smoke. Thick, inky, *oppressive*. It sizzled across Ari's nose with the uncomfortable tang of magic turned sour. The reagents had been exhausted.

The moon's annoyingly attentive stare finally faltered in the clouding sky, and Ari stepped forward into welcoming blackness. The winch box on her hip sang as it funneled golden cabling from spools attached to her belt and through the harness strapped across her waist and chest. Seconds ticked by in her mind, sharp and precise. Ari knew how fast she would fall, and the exact height of the building where she'd perched just a moment ago. After that it was basic arithmetic to determine how long it'd take to reach the top of the iron-spiked wall that bordered the refinery.

Magic pulsed from her fingertips as she tapped the winch box. The gears within clicked smoothly, slowing her descent at her behest. Ari reached down and felt the top of one of the spikes just beneath her, exactly where she had expected. Vaulting off the wall, she pulled the linchpin of her line and tumbled onto the barren ground below.

Ari rested a hand on one of the two crossed daggers at the small of her back and summoned the line back into the spool on her hip. The metal cord shuddered and sprang to life at her silent magical command, slithering back to its home like a snake to its den. She turned on her heel and strode through the murky darkness without need of a light. The refined goggles that served to enhance her already-above-average eyesight made easy work of navigating the night.

A giant, ineffective padlock attempted to bar her entry. She'd taken apart her first Rivet lock when she was a toddler; the satisfying weight of the tumblers engaging with the soft *click* that followed filled her with a familiar delight.

Numbers remained consistent. Numbers and facts attempted to bring order from a chaotic world, to make sense of the impossible. They were the foundation for colossal structures and the tiniest of clockwork machines alike. Ari loved numbers, and not just because they saved her life by keeping her alert in her surroundings.

She knew that each of her long strides were about a peca. She knew the dimly lit workers' passage she went through was about twenty pecas long. And just for fun, she knew—based on the foreman's old schematics that she lifted from his home office a week earlier—that they placed tiny bioluminescent scones about every two pecas.

She moved with the ease and purposefulness that came from being unafraid and unhindered by the concerns that clouded the emotional mind. It all vanished the moment she became the White Wraith. Like this, she was an extension of the will of her benefactors, an enemy to all Dragons, and more than just a Fenthri. She cast aside the mortal coil to become something...*more*. When Ari felt the tattered flaps at the bottom of her white coat hit her booted calves, she felt like a bloody god.

The slow beats of mechanical hearts grinding to a halt echoed up to her from deep within the refinery. Mechanisms that spun molten steel for final refining grew still. The room would cool, then Revo grunts would guard the Alchemists as they replenished the reagent chambers anew. Which meant that right now, two floors above her, they were preparing the next batch of reagents for refining. They had been taken from a chilled stasis locker and were waiting, ripe for the taking. Ari's fingers twitched.

With impeccable timing, Ari reached the grated door of one of the refinery's four supply elevators. The New Dortam refinery could process four separate chambers of reagents, but the smokestacks on the north end had been cool for over a month. As expected, the elevator was still and silent, just waiting for her.

The motor glinted high above, at the top of the shaft. Its large wheels nearly glowed through the filter of her goggles. Ari focused on it carefully, willing it to life. The cogs obeyed, slowly churning in the darkness. She stepped onto the roof of the elevator as it eased by, and rode it two landings up.

When heists were this easy, it almost felt like she hadn't done anything to earn her infamy. The "impenetrable fortress" of New Dortam had presented a challenge no greater than the one posed by a standard bank vault.

The elevator put her just where she expected: a dark wing of Alchemist laboratories. Magic hung heavy in the air, nearly suffocating. It made her skin crawl with the sensation of *rot*. Experiments they had been working for far too long were locked away in some of these chambers.

She stopped at the twelfth door, spinning the map of the refinery in her head. Each room was five pecas wide. On the diagonal heading she'd made after entry, she should be just above the reagent preparation room.

The door lock was plain iron—not a trace of gold about it. Ari clicked her tongue against her teeth. *Unrefined and nonmagical.* She'd have to open it manually. It was trickier than the Rivet padlock, but just slightly, and equally ineffective at barring her entry.

The room was thick with the nearly visible haze of magic and chemicals. Worktables stood littered with records and research. Beakers sat out, some full, some empty. Ari reached into her inner breast pocket and pulled out the metal disk that had been digging into her chest all night beneath the straps of her harness. She tossed it into the center of the room haphazardly before strolling back out.

Some Alchemist was about to have a *really* bad morning.

With a thought, the gold at the center of the disk turned molten and the heat activated the powder packed around it. The bomb exploded with a *BANG* of satisfyingly epic proportions. With it, Ari's relatively quiet heist was thrown full steam ahead.

She started to run.

She clipped her line to the handle of the door that had just failed to keep her out, jumping through the now gaping hole in the floor. She landed on rubble and the remnants of half the reagent preparation room. The blood of an Alchemist oozed from underneath the pile, and Ari was careful not to step in it. Blood left tracks that were too easy to follow by Fenthri, Chimera, and Dragon alike. The other Alchemists were still reeling, coughing, wheezing trying to figure out what was happening.

"Th-the reagents..." one wheezed.

"Have been so beautifully prepared," Ari praised brightly. "Still cold and encapsulated, their magic preserved just so... Perfection!"

She grabbed the three golden tubes from the floor where they'd landed after the explosion. Her prizes had been destined for refining, but now she would whisk them away from the hands of Dragon dogs.

"White Wraith, die!" one of the Alchemists shouted.

Ari scrutinized the woman. Her hands were long and bright red, a thin scar around her wrists where they met pale grey flesh. Ari's eyes fell on the woman's face. Two triangles—one pointing up and the other down, connected by a line that intersected their off-set points—were tattooed in black ink on the woman's cheek. A bold circle encased them. "You're young for a circle. Don't throw your life away."

The woman charged with a cry.

"I warned you," Ari sighed dramatically. In one swift movement, she stepped to the side, drew her dagger, and plunged it to the hilt in the woman's gut. Ari hated murdering talent; the world had such precious little of it. But the woman had been warned. Ari pulled her magic back, only lacing her dagger with enough to make the wound difficult to heal but not impossible. The Alchemist was a Chimera and, if her Dragon blood was strong enough, she'd manage to survive such a wound.

The doors to the room burst open, the grunts behind it freezing at the sight before them. Ari grinned wildly. Their cheeks bore the tattooed symbol of a revolver chamber, with one of the six holes filled. *Revo grunts.*

"Too late!" Ari gleefully withdrew her dagger from where it still nestled in the woman's gut. The winch box on her hip sprang to life with a thought and she sprang upward, back through the hole and up onto the floor above.

Gunfire pelted the opening she'd just traversed, leaving singed and pitted marks.

"Incendiary rounds, for little old me? You shouldn't have." Ari pulled her head away just in time for another volley of shots to light up the ceiling above her. *Barely marked Revos.* It took nothing to goad them into wasting a precious canister on her taunting.

"Get her!" someone cried, rather unhelpfully.

Ari would've been nervous or scared by the proclamation if anyone actually competent was on her tail. She bounded down the hall, each long stride of her muscled legs carrying her toward freedom, success, and a tidy sum of dunca. She threw her shoulder into a door as she opened it, letting the momentum swing her around a corner to another access hall.

Footsteps were incoming from the left, but Ari was too fast. She ran with her life on the line and, instead of fear, she felt elation at the fact. Blood pumped through every inch of her, racing as fast as her feet. Her skin tingled with the magic that mended the tiny tears from exertion in her muscles as soon as they formed.

Ari bounded through a door at the end of the hall and was met with the early light of a gray dawn. With near mechanical precision, she clipped onto, and leapt from, the railing surrounding the suspended walkway. Ari fell harmlessly, slowing just before the ground rose to greet her.

"It won't work," she called up to the grunts trying to cut through her clip. "For working at a refinery, you're certainly imbecilic about gold."

With a touch that was befitting of the White Wraith's reputation, Ari snapped her fingers at the clip high above her. It unclipped itself and reared back before slapping across the grunts' faces like a barbed whip, leaving a sharp crimson line across their tattoos in its wake. She swung her arm and watched with curt satisfaction as the clip soared to a balcony on the other side of the refinery wall. The winch on her hip couldn't have moved faster; Ari didn't have time to properly brace herself and her head shot back with the force of the pull. It wiped the smug grin off her face.

Magic was electric in the air, sending tiny daggers prickling against her exposed skin.

The seconds she took to move her line were almost too long. The ground rattled right where Ari had been standing, imploding inward in what should have been a lethal attack. *Bloody, steaming, Chimera, circled Revo.*

This was not like the Chimera Alchemist Ari had encountered in the reagent preparation chamber. *This* Chimera was a hulking creature whose skin was a scarred patchwork of a dark Fenthri gray and Dragon rainbow. Ari turned, straining her neck in spite of the pain to get a good look at him. If he had been chasing her from the onset, she would've been in trouble. *He* hadn't been in any of her notes.

She braced herself, slammed into the balcony railing she'd chosen, and flipped over it. The Chimera roared, foaming at the mouth. *Imperfect, poor soul.* The powers that were at the refinery had taken a circled Revo—a master of his craft—and stuffed as many Dragon parts as they could into him. He was a Chimera in the worst of ways, and he wasn't long for the world now. No matter how many organs or how much blood the Alchemists pumped into that "experiment" of a creature, his core was still Fenthri. And that much magic was breaking down his body, starting with his brain.

Ari thought he might not see more than another dawn, but that was enough time to make trouble for her.

The Chimera raised a hulking weapon. A crackle of magic filled the air and Ari was off with barely enough time to fill her lungs again. She wasn't there to slay any forsaken Chimera—that was *way* above the pay-grade for this job, even at the insane amount she'd been contracted for. Ari was proud, but she wasn't stupid. She didn't fight battles she had a slim chance of winning if there wasn't a reward on the line.

The creature gave chase the second Ari was on the move. She bounded from rooftop to rooftop as more grunts poured out from the refinery. The stone and concrete skeleton of a building under construction had her skidding to a halt over roof shingles. She pulled a small canister from her belt, three notches marring the otherwise flawless exterior. Ari drew her revolver from its holster on her left leg and popped the canister into one of its open chambers.

Malice.

It surged through her, the will to destroy—the desire to burn and crash. The *want* to explode things into a million tiny pieces that could never have any hope of being put back together. Alchemical runes on the outside of her gun shone white as she pulled the trigger, and let go of it all.

Florence hadn't been lying. The girl had outdone herself with the canister, which demanded an exhausting amount of magic, but in turn shot a beam of pure power to the structure Ari had chosen. The explosion was as bright as sunlight and nearly blinded her with the magnification of her goggles.

The building shuddered and groaned, coming to life. Ari pushed herself as hard as she could, the Revos from the refinery still hot on her tail. But she was several steps ahead, literally and figuratively. She knew how the building would sway and fall. She knew the way to run to narrowly miss the first colossal beam collapsing. Once more, it all came down to numbers: the number of load-bearing pillars, the weight distribution of the structure, the probability of how the collapse would occur.

The second she crossed onto the other side of the smoke and chaos, Ari dropped down into an alleyway. She'd had her grand finale. Now it was time for her to do as her namesake and disappear like a wraith with the dawn.

Ari didn't have any safe houses in New Dortam. She could never feel safe in an area that worked so closely with the Dragons, their Royuk language was used as commonly as Fennish. Even if her eyes could make sense of the rectangles, lines, and dots, she avoided reading the Dragon notices and advertisements plastered on buildings.

Well, almost.

"That looks nothing like me." Ari squinted at the drawing of a lithe and long-haired woman on a wanted poster that had *White Wraith* written in bold Royuk below, along with an impressive sum of dunca. The reward for her head had gone up, Ari noted with pride. She tore the notice off the wall. Florence would find amusement in it as well.

An unnatural scream tore through the sky, followed by a fast *zip*. Wind rushed through the alleyways and fluttered the mostly folded paper in her hands. Ari scowled at the rainbow trail glittering through the pale morning clouds.

Bloody Dragon Rider. What in the Five Guilds was going on to get a Rider involved? Ari felt in her bag for the three tubes she'd swiped from the refinery. It was a capital offense to engage in the illegal transport or harvesting of reagents, but that shouldn't merit the *King's* Riders.

A second time, the heavens themselves sounded like they were being torn apart as a Dragon descended from the sky world of Nova. The Dragon's mechanical gliders swept arcs of magic across the impenetrable clouds that separated Loom and Nova as they darted over the city. Ari pressed the wanted poster into her breast pocket. She'd stick to the original plan. Now was not the time for panic or over-calculation.

The sewer systems of New Dortam funneled together into the older, original system in Old Dortam. Ari headed in a straight line, sticking to alleyways and hastening across the slowly crowding streets she couldn't avoid. Eventually, she knew she'd hit a main line access, or she'd run into Old Dortam. She'd lost the Revo grunts from the refineries. So long as she moved quickly and confidently, people wouldn't notice the unorthodox clockwork gearbox and chest harness she wore. People only ever saw what they expected, rarely what was actually there.

Ari rounded the corner of a back alley near her expected sewer entry, and came to a dead stop.

Shingles littered the ground, scattered underneath a prone Dragon. Ari's breathing quickened, her goggles flaring brightly with the Dragon's magical presence. Slowly, she reached for the sharper of her daggers.

The Dragon's steel blue flesh was covered in the shining glow of a corona. It looked like the scales of a sea serpent, sparkling with its own unnatural brightness, and would render even her sharpest golden dagger useless no matter how much magic she put behind it. Ari inched around the opposite wall, her eyes tracking the Dragon the entire time.

He didn't move. She couldn't even tell if he was breathing despite being only a short peca away. Ari dared to creep forward, and luck rewarded her.

Exhausted, the Dragon's corona flashed and disappeared as the golden bracers that sustained the protective magic cracked and fell from around his wrists. Still, the Dragon did not stir. His head and heart were intact, so no matter what state he appeared to be in, he was certainly going to wake soon. His Dragon blood was quickly pulsing through his body, healing him. When his mind caught up from the blackness his fall had created, he would be as well as if nothing had ever happened.

Ari passed the dagger hand to hand.

She didn't have time to harvest the body properly of all its useful parts. She had to be prepared for the Dragon to wake the second she began trying—if she tried at all. Ari slid her feet over until she was standing next to him. She'd have to cut out his heart in one motion.

It was reckless to the point of idiocy. Ari's mouth curled into a sinister smile. *Florence would scold her for it later.* But perhaps the tidy sum a Dragon heart could fetch would be enough to sway the girl.

Kneeling down beside the rainbow-colored eyesore, Ari raised her golden dagger. It was refined steel, and tempered to her magic and her will. It'd slow him if he woke. Ari could only imagine what a fresh Dragon heart was going to fetch in the seedy underground market of Old Dortam.

She plunged her weapon down.

In the same instant, the Dragon's hand shot up and caught her wrist, stopping her just short of his chest. He stared at her in surprise.

Ari snarled and bore her teeth in rage. *She'd been set up.* It was certainly too good to be true. A prone Dragon without his corona? Never.

Ari pulled one hand from the dagger and reached for her other. She sliced at the Dragon's wrist, cutting deep, but the blade was the duller of the two and it stuck in his hardened bones, turning into a spigot for golden blood to pour onto her knees.

The Dragon didn't move. He held her in place and stared through her attacks and her snarls. The black slit of his yellow eyes roved over her face.

Was this a ploy by the Riders to find out what she looked like?

Ari pushed off the ground with her feet, rotating in place. The Dragon was strong and could hold the sharp point of her dagger off its mark even with all her weight above it. But it took two hands for him to do so, which meant when Ari twisted, she was able to bring her feet down, *hard*, onto his unprotected face.

He finally let her go and she flipped backward, landing on the balls of her feet, a dagger in each hand. The Dragon stood, contemplating the wound on his arm. It was as though he'd never been cut by anything other than unrefined steel. His broken nose was already resetting itself and would be healed well in advance of the gash in his wrist.

She had a choice. On one shoulder, there was a very sensible little version of herself reminding her that this was not her prey or her job. She'd done what she came into the land of Dragon dogs to do. She should leave and collect her handsome pay. In short, she should stick to the plan.

On the other shoulder was a different tiny version of herself. This version was screaming bloody murder. *Cut out his heart!* It demanded over and over. It cried for her to do what she was made to do: slay Dragons.

It wasn't hard to pick which one to listen to. Ari darted forward. First stepping with her right foot, she drew his attention in one direction before jumping onto her left and bringing her right heel across his face.

The Dragon half-dodged, reaching out his foot to hook behind the heel of Ari's supporting leg. She bent backwards, releasing the duller of her two daggers to tumble with one unarmed hand.

"I don't want to fight you." The Dragon held up his palms as though any gesture of his could be nonthreatening. Despite his words, his claws were out—wicked sharp and extending past the end of his fingers in points.

"So don't, and let me cut out your heart." Ari set in for another string of attacks. The Dragon dodged about half of them.

"Fenthri—" He side-stepped, narrowly missing a dagger point in his throat. "Listen to me!"

"Not a chance!" she almost sang, pushing him against the wall. His head hit hard and he was dazed a moment. "I have a very strong 'no negotiating with the enemy' policy."

Ari rotated her grip on the knife to an icepick hold and pulled back. His eyes regained clarity as she once more attempted to plunge the dagger into his chest. He grabbed her wrist again, but *still* didn't attack. His claws had retracted.

The magical *zing* of a Dragon Rider flying overhead piqued both their attentions. Fenthri and Dragon alike looked up as the Rider slowed not far from where they'd been brawling.

"I can give you something better than my heart." The Dragon's voice had taken on a thrumming intensity that burned with a fire Ari hadn't heard there previously. But if her feverish attacks hadn't inspired the change…what had?

"Something better than the satisfaction of killing a Dragon and the reward of a fresh heart?" She hummed. "I doubt it."

"I'll give you a boon."

Ari paused, considering this. She'd heard of boons before, but oh, they *were* rare. A Dragon rarely lowered himself to the point of giving a boon, and especially not to a Fenthri.

Dragons saw the Fenthri as the servant, not the other way around. A boon would make him *hers*.

"Any one wish of me." The Dragon's eyes kept darting skyward. "You can demand anything of me as the terms of the boon."

"For letting you keep your heart?"

"For taking me to the Alchemists' Guild."

It really didn't matter to Ari what she had to do for the boon. *A wish.* There were so many things she could wish for. So many old wrongs she could right with the unquestioned help of a Dragon and his magic. It could be a chance for redemption—for vengeance.

Or, at the very least, she could always wish for him to cut out his own heart and give it to her. Then she'd get the satisfaction of watching him do it.

"*Fine*, Dragon." The agreement was an ugly smear of magic across her tongue as the boon was formed. It tasted of disgust peppered with loathing. "You have your deal."

CVAREH

"W e're not going in there, are we?" Cvareh made a scene of squinting into the dark manhole. He could actually see perfectly fine.

The woman shot him a dull look and pointed into the hole. "Go."

"It smells rancid." He scrunched his nose. He'd known he'd need a Fenthri's knowledge of Loom to escape the King's Riders, but he'd hoped for something or someone a little more... elegant.

"So don't breathe."

"You must be—" Cvareh never finished his statement. Her legs felt dense as lead and the sharp kick to his lower back had him pin-wheeling his arms to avoid falling forward.

He landed nearly headfirst, choosing to crack a few bones in his wrists over taking yet another assault on his face. The ground was covered in a thin, cold film that had him frantically rubbing his hands over the walls—no cleaner—the moment he stood. *Filthy, filthy, filthy.*

The woman pulled the manhole cover back into place and slowly descended the metal ladder cemented into the portal wall.

"Do you have a light?" he asked, massaging the newly knitted bones in each of his wrists.

"Afraid of the dark?" she called over her shoulder. She'd begun walking confidently along the narrow path that was the only thing keeping them from the flowing sludge of the sewer.

"Ah, my darling—"

"I am not your darling." She wheeled and the dagger point pressed into his neck, attempting to pop the words from his throat.

"Will you ever talk to me without brandishing a weapon?" Cvareh sighed. They both knew the dagger would do nothing more than annoy him, even refined. Pointing it at his chest was at least threatening. The only way his neck would be a cause for worry was if she somehow planned to cut his head clean off.

"I'd rather not talk to you at all," she ground out through her flat teeth.

"Where are you from?" He tried a different question, trying to ease the ever-increasing tensions between them. She had no guild mark on her face. *An illegal.*

The woman twirled the dagger in her hand, slicing up his mouth. He licked his lips, tasting his blood and then the flavor of the magic on her blade. He didn't recognize it; whatever Dragon had given parts of their body to refine that steel was one Cvareh didn't know personally.

But the weapon wasn't just refined; it was tempered. There was a layer of her power embedded above the original Dragon's magic that told him the weapon would only respond to her will. He wouldn't be able to command it no matter how much magic he exhausted.

And that wasn't all he learned. Cvareh pulled his lower lip between his teeth, his sharper canines nearly drawing blood, and ran his tongue over it. He tasted *her*, and wasn't that the most interesting of flavors…

"What did you do that for?" He narrowed his eyes.

"A threat."

"Of what sort?" Dragons smeared blood as warnings. They communicated through trace amounts of magic left behind. Had she been intentionally communicating with him as a Dragon would?

"That I will cut you every time you show idiocy."

"You wouldn—"

He didn't finish before she had him slammed against the wall again, her dagger half into his mouth. He'd have to cut through his cheek to move, or cut his tongue to speak. This woman was really starting to annoy him.

"Listen, Dragon, I will not repeat myself." Her words were level and calm, but they had a wild timbre at their edges, like chaos was trying to pull them apart into raw cries of rage. "You set the terms of the boon. I didn't ask why you need me to take you to the Alchemists' Guild because I don't give a bloody cog about who you are or why you want to go there. I won't pretend to enjoy this. So do us both a favor and don't make this something it's not."

He stared through the darkness at the Fenthri's face. It was round, like a loaf of bread, or a pork rump. The goggles pressed over her eyes, leaving small indents on her ashen-colored cheeks at their edges. Scraggly-cut white hair fell over her ears in messy parts. Fenthri were hideous creatures, really.

Finally, she withdrew her blade, wiping it on her covered leg before sheathing it and starting forward again. Cvareh followed in her steps through the winding sewer passages. The path became even narrower, and the walls changed from stone and steel to red clay bricks.

"Where are we headed now?" He decided his options were to go crazy from silence or risk her stabbing him again.

She didn't answer.

"Have we left New Dortam?"

"We're headed for the Alchemists' Guild."

Whoever this woman was, she certainly harbored a deep hatred for Dragons. Cvareh knew he'd never come across her before, so it wasn't as though she could resent him personally. In fact, she was the first Fenthri he'd ever met in person, and what an impression she was making for her entire race.

"Yes but—"

"Dragon, how was I unclear?" she sighed.

"Cvareh Xin'Ryu Soh," he persisted. "If we're going to be traveling together we should at least know each other's names, don't you think?"

"Not really." She paused. "Cva."

Cvareh curled and uncurled his long fingers one at a time, resisting the urge to unsheathe his claws. "Cvareh Xin'Ryu Soh."

"You can't possibly expect me to say the whole thing," she drawled with an annoying little smirk. "It's such a mouthful."

"It's actually quite important on Nova." *Patience*, Cvareh reminded himself. The Fenthri had likely never left the ground of Loom. She didn't know what was important above the clouds.

"Oh, I know it is." She smiled, and he barely contained a cringe at how her flat teeth made a perfect line in her mouth. "Come now, Cva, we're going to be late," she chided.

"You may call me just Cvareh Soh," he insisted.

"*Mmm*, Cva is easier."

"I must insist—"

"Don't push your luck, Dragon." A hand curled around one of the crossed blades at the small of her back. He was getting rather tired of seeing that golden steel. "We could always go back to the heart-cutting."

Cvareh looked her in the eyes, or, well, the goggles. She didn't tense and didn't shy away. Whoever this woman was, she certainly had no love for Dragons—and no fear of them either.

"I don't think you will." He took a step closer to her. "You want your boon."

"Ah, yes, a boon." Rather than shrinking away, the woman met his step with her own. She was almost as tall as he, and Cvareh was of average height for Dragon standards. He'd always been told the Fenthri were a smaller race. "They're quite rare for Dragons to give out. What could you possibly want at the Alchemists' Guild so badly that you'd surrender yourself to my whims?"

"You think I'll tell you?" He took another step toward her. His blood rushed at the feeling of her magic: wild and varying, a blend of many Dragons' powers combined into something all her own.

"I could make you." Her chest, flat and strapped under what appeared to be a harness, touched his.

Cvareh paused. *A harness.* Why did his mind tell him that was important?

She clicked her tongue against her teeth then stepped away when he didn't rise to her challenge. His failure to respond to her banter had disappointed her. So his options seemed to be allowing himself to be annoyed at her very apparent efforts, or pleasing her. Or swallowing his pride and letting her say what she wanted but not giving her the satisfaction of taking the bait.

He was growing to hate this hideous wench with every second.

Somehow, Cvareh managed silence. He followed her through the rank passage for what seemed like forever until the sewer vomited its sludge into a slime-covered river. The woman paused, glancing outside and back at his hands.

"Dragon, can you make illusions?"

"Not a skill I possess." Though he was glad she asked. The look of consideration she gave his clawed fingers let Cvareh know she was well aware of what Dragon parts held what magic. It further confirmed that, whoever she was, she truly knew about Dragons beyond the value of a heart.

"Of course you can't. That would be far too easy." She let out a sigh of utter disappointment. The woman thought for another long moment. "Very well, stay here."

"Wait, where are you going?"

"If you walk around Old Dortam looking like—" Her head moved up and down as her eyes raked over him. "*You*, you're going to cause a scene. Or someone else will harvest you. And then I'm out a Dragon heart as well as a boon."

Cvareh would appreciate it if she'd stop discussing cutting out his heart, but he knew better than to say so. He also knew she was right. Cvareh adjusted the wide sash around his waist, heavy with the beads and embellishments of his station. His shirt was done in a dark navy that highlighted the color of his powder blue skin just so. Its capped sleeves showed the strength in his arms—his physical ability to assert dominance. Dragons took note of the feature, which had helped ward off challenges for years.

He looked back at the woman in her heavy leather coat and worker's trousers. She was unfashionable and plain, a continued source of vexation for him. Certainly, she was poor and couldn't afford more than basic clothing. But why would anyone choose to wear white in this industrial wasteland?

"I suppose you're right," he admitted.

"Of course I am," she agreed confidently. "Now stay here like a good little Dragon and don't move."

Cvareh did as he was told.

Time was hard for him to tell on Loom and the seconds smeared into tedious minutes. The thick layer of clouds above hid the progression of the sun, filtering it into a bleak and neutral light. Cvareh cursed himself for forgetting his timepiece back on Nova. He hadn't really had time to pack anything.

He opened a small pouch at his waist and pulled the folded papers from it. They were old, or had been through a lot to find their way up to Nova. He expected the latter was more likely. The parchment was weathered and already delicate, the leaves beginning to tear at the folds. He didn't dare spend longer than a moment making sure all were accounted for.

The delicate lines made up schematics that meant little to Cvareh, but they would mean something to a Rivet. However, he wasn't headed for the Rivets' Guildhall. The engineers of Loom had long been under the close eye of the Dragon King and, seeing as how Cvareh had stolen the documents from under said King's nose, he didn't think heading toward anyone or anything that was notorious for being under his thumb was a good idea.

The woman reappeared.

"You actually made a line in the slime." She appraised where he'd been pacing. "That bored?"

"Well—" Cvareh didn't know why he tried to answer. She interrupted him by tossing the cloak she'd had folded over her arm at his face, leaving Cvareh scrambling to catch it before it fell onto the grime-coated path.

"Put that on, pull the hood, and keep your head down."

Cvareh did as instructed and followed her without needing to be told.

She led him up the hard dirt of the river's embankment and into soot-covered streets. Welders worked in a nearby factory, their torches lighting up the cobblestones under his feet. He heard the occasional crackle of magic, but the world on Loom was quiet compared to the splendor of Nova. Mostly normal, un-augmented Fenthri surrounded him.

It made the woman in front of him stand out all the more. She seared his senses as wildly as the strongest Dragon Rider he'd ever met. Why would someone who hated Dragons so much choose to become a Chimera?

He dared a glance up at her back. She didn't turn or slow, ignorant of his study. She may have been a Chimera, but she looked very much Fenthri. Her shoulder-length white hair, gray skin, broad shoulders, and dingy clothes fit in with the iron, brass, and sepia tones of the world around her. It was as though Loom itself had given birth to the woman.

He followed her down a side street and up a flight of stairs to a shut down, boarded up shop. She glanced at him from the corners of her eyes, wedging her body between him and the intricate door lock. Metal slid on metal and the door swung open.

"Welcome back." Another Fenthri woman—barely more than a girl, really—jumped over a sofa in a haste to meet them. She skidded to a halt as the Fenthri in white closed the door behind Cvareh. "Is this the one?"

"Would I be around a Dragon if it wasn't?" The woman who held his boon and still hadn't told him her name unclipped her high boots and dropped them on the entryway tile.

Cvareh took in the room and was surprised to find it well styled, given his earlier assessments of the person he was now keeping company with. The floors were smoothed from being walked on for years—uneven in a way that seemed perfectly imperfect. Dark leather furniture was accented with heavy knit blankets around a crackling iron stove. Steam and water piping ran through the barren beams overhead, keeping the room warm and glinting in the midday sunlight let in by two tall, iron-framed windows.

"Did you draw the bath?" His boon-holder started for a side door.

"I did," the younger Fenthri replied.

"Lovely."

"Wait, what am I to do?" Cvareh asked, hovering uncertainly. "I'm filthy."

The woman in white paused in the tall doorframe, unclasping the harness and shrugging out of her white coat. She wore a loose cotton shirt with ruffles at the collar under a tight black vest.

"Why don't you just stand there, Dragon?" She pulled her goggles over her forehead.

The woman's eyes were bright purple, a dark slit that matched his own instead of the usual rounded Fenthri iris. If Cvareh had needed any further proof that she was a Chimera, there it was.

"Your magic already stinks. I don't want you dragging sewer sludge into my home too." The woman threw the verbal jab at him before disappearing into the side room, working on the first button of her vest as she disappeared.

Cvareh looked at the remaining Fenthri, who was failing to hide her amusement behind a dark gray palm. Rolling his eyes, he started for one of the sofas.

"I wouldn't do that." The woman's black eyes focused on where Cvareh's still-booted feet crossed onto the wood. "If you track mud into the house after she made her proclamation, I fear she really will kill you."

"Not if she wants her boon." Cvareh was getting tired of repeating the fact, but he couldn't take his offer back. She'd agreed; the magical contract was formed between them. He was at the mercy of this Fenthri woman until she delivered him to the Alchemists or willingly relinquished her contract with him.

"Then I may kill you, because I'm the one who cleans the floors."

"Are you her servant?" Cvareh didn't think Fenthri kept households. Judging by the woman's laugh, he was right.

"Grind my gears, of course not." She shook her rounded face, her boxy shoulders slowing from her mirth. "I'm her initiate."

"Initiate?" Cvareh frowned. The outline of a raven had been tattooed on her cheek in black, almost blending in with her granite-colored skin. "You're both Ravens then?"

"No." Her demeanor changed completely. The girl regarded him coolly when she had been almost welcoming prior. "I am a Revolver. And my master is a Rivet."

Now *that* made no sense. One of them was an unmarked illegal, out of place in the world, and the other was claiming to be something other than what she had been marked. "Assuming that's true, a Rivet couldn't teach a Revolver."

"Indeed she can. And she is certain to get me help when her knowledge has gaps. We're in the heart of the Revolvers' Guild, after all." The woman grinned. Cvareh continued to be unnerved by the image of flat teeth making a perfect line.

"It is against Dragon law to be taught outside your guild. Any marked who desert their duty could be punished by death. Going unmarked is no better." Cvareh didn't actually care. He was hardly about to uphold the laws when he was the one seeking out the Fenthri rebels at the Alchemists' Guild.

"No one in Old Dortam would turn either of us in," the girl hummed. "And people in New Dortam have more important things to worry about when the White Wraith shows up than the fact that she isn't marked."

The sun fell from Cvareh's sky at three words. "The White Wraith?"

The young woman paused her ministrations at a back table. "Who did you think you were traveling with?"

Cvareh honestly hadn't a clue. But his guess wouldn't have been New Dortam's most infamous criminal.

FLORENCE

I'm Florence, by the way," she introduced herself to the yet-hovering Dragon. "Take off your shoes and sit at the table. It'll be the easiest to wipe down."

The walking rainbow twisted off his ankle-length patent black boots and crossed over to the table in the corner of their flat by the small kitchen. At least he did as he was told. That would increase his chances of Ari not killing him before she got that boon.

Florence's master had stormed into their home like an engine off its tracks, demanding the largest cloak they owned and rambling something about a boon. It wasn't too long until Florence pieced together what exactly had her in such a tizzy. But by the time Ari had ranted off enough facts for her to do so, she had already left. Florence hadn't had much time to inquire deeply about the nature of this agreement, but whatever it was, she trusted her teacher implicitly. Ari always knew what she was doing.

Florence finished hanging Ari's harness and coat then crossed to the kitchen. She felt the Dragon's eyes on her as she rummaged through the upper cupboard.

"Here."

"What is it?" The Dragon inspected her peace offering skeptically.

"A cookie." Florence shoved one in her mouth for show. And then a second one, just because the first tasted so good.

"Why are you giving it to me?"

"Who questions a cookie?" She laughed, placing the confection on the table for the Dragon to decide if he wanted it or not. "But we will no longer be friends if you waste it."

"Are we friends?" There was genuine surprise in his inflection.

"That's your choice, Dragon," she called back. Florence left the truth of it—that if he did anything to hurt her Ari, all bets were off—unsaid.

"I'm Cvareh Xin'Ryu Soh," he replied quickly.

Florence glanced over her shoulder, looking at the man with the unreasonably long name. He wasn't so different from a Fenthri, really. Instead of gray, black, and white, he was colorful. Like the paintings she had seen of the foliage called flowers. There was his color, then, and his pointed ears, elongated canines, talons, *and* slits for eyes.

But he had two arms, two legs, and one head. He spoke with the same sounds they did and moved in similar ways. She gave him a small smile of acknowledgment.

Florence eased the bedroom door shut behind her. A giant bed greeted her, still a mess from when she'd woken not long ago. Florence turned right and focused on the footed copper bath that stood steaming under a large window.

Ari was submerged up to her neck, her white hair slicked back and shining in the light. Florence smiled, tiptoeing over.

"I hear you."

"I know you do." Florence laughed brightly.

"What is the Dragon doing?"

"Eating a cookie."

"You gave him a cookie?" Ari opened one eye. "That's generous of you."

"Is it?"

"You barely share your cookies with me," Ari muttered, closing her eyes again. "I'm going to think you like Dragons more than me."

"But you don't like cookies at all." Florence scooped salt scrub into her palms. She plucked Ari's hand from the bathwater and massaged it over her skin, soothing the calluses created by her gold lines.

Florence loved everything about the woman known as the White Wraith. Ari was sharp and witty. Her skin was the most lovely shade of gray and her face had a beautifully healthy curve to it. Arianna wasn't just pretty—she was strong too, broad shouldered and wonderfully stocky. Florence was of average build for a Fenthri, if a little too thin. Ari was perfect.

Florence kneaded stress out of the strong muscles that cut out from under Ari's skin. "So how did this all come to pass?" she asked.

"I was on my grand escape from the refinery and ran into a Dragon, unconscious, with an exhausted corona." Ari remained focused on the ceiling as she spoke. Florence could tell the woman was still debating with herself over the course of events that led them to having a Dragon in their home. The tension wasn't giving up on her shoulders. "So I decided to cut out his heart. He woke up and offered me a boon instead."

"You couldn't just leave him be?" she hummed playfully.

"If you want enough dunca to keep affording sugar for your confections, you don't want me to leave prone Dragons with all their organs intact."

"Wasn't that what the refinery job was for?" Florence waited with a drying cloth as Ari emerged from the bath.

"A little extra never hurts," her teacher reminded her.

"A little extra will get you killed." There was a heavy note to Florence's words, one she couldn't stop because it stemmed from a genuine fear of her master meeting an ill fate during one of her many dangerous jobs.

"Florence, look at me." Ari placed her fingertips under Florence's chin, guiding her gaze and giving her no other choice. Florence studied Ari's eyes, the unnatural purple striking an odd contrast with her skin. They had unnerved her at first, but she had learned to see past them. They may have been harvested from a Dragon, but they were Ari's now. "You know it would take a lot to kill me."

"I know," Florence mumbled, trying to look away.

Ari held her chin fast. "After all, I have some of the best canisters and explosives in Loom looking after me."

"Oh, what did you use? The bomb of course, but a canister? I saw number three was missing. It was number three, right?" Florence ran over to the bed, jumping on it as Ari began to rummage through her wardrobe, dropping clothes she decided against into a pile on the floor that Florence would likely be the one to tidy later.

"It was number three, and it was one of your best yet." Ari placed a tight-fitting white shirt onto the bed before returning to the wardrobe. "The disk had a nice blast radius. Incredibly effective but contained. Impressive destructive power."

"Tell me about it?" Florence dreamed of someday watching Ari on one of her little missions. She had no interest in actually fighting herself. But just once, she wanted to see one of her explosions in person, not just as calculations on paper.

"The canister? Flash of white, red at the edges, and then it turned yellow when it hit the target. There was black smoke too." Ari was awful at painting descriptions with words—she'd have had more success drawing it—but Florence hung on her every syllable all the same. "But it took a lot of energy and had a slow fire."

"If you want explosive canisters that large, it will." Florence picked at the white vest and silver necktie Ari had placed on the bed.

"You can do better, Flor. Make a canister like that, but designed for use with a refined gun by someone who isn't a Chimera, and you'll be a rich woman."

"I know, I know." Ari was right, as usual.

It had been two years since Florence had met Ari during her escape from the Ravens Guild and somehow convinced the woman to agree to be her teacher. In that time, Florence had been given ample opportunities to experiment with different ways to combine gunpowder, chemicals, refined metals, and even alchemical runes to create some of the best explosives Ari had ever seen. At least, that's what Ari told her. But the woman wouldn't lie, not even to spare her initiate's feelings.

Their life was unconventional and mostly outside the law, but it was a life Florence had come to love. Ari was an acolyte of the old ways, unmarked on her cheeks and firm in her belief that every guild was connected. That overlap between fields of study was essential. She let Florence explore, create, question for the sake of it. It had all made the terror of escaping the guild worthwhile.

"Speaking of." Ari adjusted the necktie, pinning it with a crossed wrench and bolt done in black iron—the symbol of a master in the Rivets' Guild. "How many canisters do we have in stock?"

"I think I have thirteen made. Why?"

"We may need more for the journey." Ari strapped the belt with her daggers and winch box high around her waist. "It's a three-day train ride to Ter.5.2. Then a week-long airship ride to Keel."

"We're going to ride an airship?" Florence bounced to sit at the edge of the bed.

"Fastest way to get to the Alchemists' Guild."

"I'll pick up materials in Mercury Town. But you better not blow up the first airship I ride on," Florence mock-scolded.

"You never know what wrench could get thrown into the machine along the way, Flor." Ari's grin was playful, but her words were serious. "Use the dunca from the reagents to get what we'll need for the trip. I trust your judgment. I'll fill in the Dragon on the plan and the rules for travel."

"He doesn't seem bad." Florence tried to smooth over the kinks she foresaw in their journey. After all the stories she'd heard of Dragons, she expected a horrible monster. While she wouldn't call the Dragon handsome by any stretch—his colors were borderline headache-inducing—she wouldn't call him evil incarnate, either.

Ari stilled. She crossed back to the bed and, with both hands, cradled Florence's face delicately.

"Listen to me," Arianna whispered. "None of them seem bad. But they are not what they seem. It's that thinking that killed Loom, Flor. *Don't trust him*. He will turn on you and kill you in a second if it suits him."

Florence swallowed. She knew Arianna had real memories of the time before the Dragons, when the Five Guilds were free and the world was run by the Vicar tribunal; when Fenthri didn't have to be marked—when they were free to study and learn as they wanted.

There was a terrifying lust for that time in Ari's heart.

"Do you understand?"

"I do." Florence nodded.

"Good." Ari let go of her face and started for the door again. "Now, get to Mercury Town before it gets too busy. The 'king' will want his reagents before they get warm."

Florence heard the muffled sounds of Ari and the Dragon talking on the other side of the door. She wondered if what her master said was true: if every Dragon was like the ones who had enslaved Loom and, if they were, why Ari had agreed to help one at all. But Ari would remain an enigma, and Florence knew better than to dig too deeply under her ashen skin. Florence said only quick goodbyes as she donned her favorite feathered top hat and grabbed Ari's bag, heading out for Mercury Town.

Old Dortam had woken and the streets were busy with men and women going about their business. Lace parasols shaded faces and pearl pins adorned ties. Storefronts glistened, freshly washed and still dripping. The air smelled sweetly of welding torches and gunpowder, creating a welcoming potpourri to complement the sounds of metal on metal that echoed over the conversation in the streets.

It was as perfect as a schematic.

Mercury Town, on the other hand, was a schematic of a very different sort. The narrow alleyways and curtained windows created a heavy atmosphere that only grew weightier every time someone opened a door to a parlor and released thick clouds of scented smoke on the backs of jacket-clad patrons. Men in long frock coats stood at some doors, watching those who passed warily, casting a careful eye over the street for any who might feel bold enough to try to put an end to the shadowy dealings that occurred in this tiny pocket of Old Dortam.

Florence wasn't uncomfortable. She'd been coming here for years now and most of the door guards gave her a nod as she passed. Two streets later, Florence stopped before a man with a shaved head.

"Ralph." She smiled. "Here for King Louie."

"Don't tell me the White Wraith actually did it."

"If you doubted she would, you shouldn't have sent her." Florence proudly flashed him the contents of Ari's bag. Long enough to tease, never long enough to give away the goods.

"Well, I'll be greased. Wait here."

The man disappeared by side-stepping into a narrow door. Florence rocked from her heels to the balls of her feet impatiently, spending the time by making a mental list of the supplies she'd need. She was only ten items down when Ralph reappeared, motioning for her to enter.

Louie was a scrawny, anemic Fenthri who positioned himself chiefly against the Dragons and at the head of Old Dortam's underworld by adopting the ironic title of "King". His patent velvet jacket was cutaway, set over another heavy velvet vest underneath. Long black hair, teased into ropes, pulled back tautly and tugged at the skin of his face, making his piercing black eyes look even sharper and more angular. It was all in stark contrast to the white of his skin, not a trace of gray on him.

Florence didn't let herself be intimidated. The man had more connections with powerful people than a refinery did slag, but that wasn't going to dissuade her. If this little man was the King of Old Dortam's underworld, then Ari was his champion knight—and that made Florence her page. The one thing that kings in stories never did was kill their champion's second.

"I have a delivery from the White Wraith." Florence slipped the bag off her shoulder, holding it out.

"Let's see what presents you bring me today." Louie hooked a bony finger and two men retrieved the bag from Florence. They placed at the foot of Louie's wing-backed chair. With the toe of his pointed boots, he flipped open the satchel. His eyes lit up like sodium metal in water.

Louie reached forward, swooping down like a bird of prey. He held up one of the three gold canisters, still so cold it wafted mist into the dim and smoky air of his parlor.

"Aren't you a pretty thing?" He turned the canister before handing it to another one of his lackeys. The man had crimson eyes and the black symbol of two triangles, connected by a line, on his cheek—an Alchemist. "Well?"

"Prime reagents, in healthy condition," the man affirmed.

"Did you have any doubt?" Florence folded her arms over her chest.

"In my line of work, one must always check." Louie chuckled at her haughtiness. "I have another job for your master."

"My master has already accepted something."

He gasped in mock offense. At least, Florence *hoped* it was pretend. "Who is the White Wraith cheating on me with?"

"I didn't realize you two had become so serious," Florence replied in kind.

"Name this other upstart's price. I will double it." Louie settled back in his chair as the Alchemists ushered the reagents out of the room. It unnerved Florence, letting them out of her sight before they were paid for.

"I'm afraid that's something you can't do."

"Girl, do you know who I am?" He gripped the armrests of his chair as slowly and tightly as he enunciated his words.

"Louie, we've only been working together for a year now," Florence said brightly, so sweet it could give the man cavities. "I know well who you are. But this job is personal for the Wraith."

"I've never heard of a Wraith having feelings before." Louie squinted his eyes. "So Dortam's infamous thieving ghost is flesh and blood after all."

Florence needed to tread lightly now. Arianna was strict that no one should know her identity, or anything about her. The few times someone had decided to get cheeky and tail Florence back to the flat, Ari had intercepted them and quickly flayed them with her daggers, leaving the body in Mercury Town as a warning.

In truth, even Florence didn't know much about her benefactor. She couldn't say with confidence that "Arianna" was the White Wraith's real name. But unlike everyone else, the truth didn't matter to Florence. She wasn't trying to play detective. She was happy with her life, content to learn what the woman had to teach her. The only thing a person got when they stirred up a river was muck; Florence preferred clean hands.

"Ralph," Louie called across the room. "Have you heard of a Wraith needing to tend to personal matters?"

"I can't say I have," Ralph obliged. He knew who paid his checks, and that meant he had to play along.

"How interesting. So the Wraith really is Fenthri after all."

Florence didn't say anything, waiting for Louie to exhaust himself with his futile discourse.

"Perhaps, if he could come himself, we could strike a deal that would put him on my retainer." Louie hadn't tried this for a few weeks.

"I don't think the Wraith will be working for any one man or woman anytime soon," Florence responded, as she did almost every time. "Now, the three-hundred dunca?"

"I can see why the Wraith chooses you, Florence; you're quite stony when it comes to giving away his truths." Louie waved a hand with a smug little smirk. Florence didn't drive any bargains and they both knew it.

"My Master has taught me well." Florence watched as Louie's lackeys filled Ari's satchel with three paper wads. She knew fairly well what a stack of one-hundred dunca looked like, and she didn't think Louie would screw them. It wasn't in his best interest. And if there was one thing King Louie didn't do, it was anything that didn't directly benefit him in some way. "I'm afraid I can't be bought."

"That's the first rule, Florence: every man can be bought. What does he give you that I cannot?" Louie smiled, a somewhat sinister curve of the lips. There was an overtly sexual nature to the question.

Florence paid it no mind. Let them think she was the Wraith's lover. It made no difference to her and it helped maintain Louie's illusion that the Wraith was a man. The further he was from the truth, the better. Plus, her and Ari shared a bed anyway. "A certain type of knowledge."

She smirked and excused herself, focusing once more on giant explosions and guns. Louie was likely thinking of explosions of a different sort, judging by the look on his face. Ralph saw her out and the transaction was done. Overall, she liked working with King Louie the best of all Ari's patrons, and Florence had no doubt that helped Ari decide between jobs when it came down to choices.

It was as pleasant to look at Louie as it was a hairless anorexic cat, almost as bad as looking at a Dragon, and he had an equally appealing sense of humor. But the man paid on time, never backed out, and never wavered on the terms of the job. It made everyone's lives easier when Ari didn't have to go on any collection trips. The woman could hold a grudge.

Florence rested her hand on the pistol in her arm holster as she passed by some shady characters—and shady by Mercury Town's standards was saying a lot. The regular patrons gave her no cause to worry. They knew her, and they wouldn't risk the White Wraith's ire by harming Florence. It was the new lot that would set up shop in the dark overhangs and grimy alleys she needed to be wary of, those beneath King Louie who had yet to ingrain themselves in Old Dortam's illegal economy.

She made her way toward her favorite shop, the one that always had the things that made the biggest boom. This time, Ari had given her free permission to use the dunca as Florence saw fit to prepare for their trip, and she planned to see fit for quite a few things she'd been drooling over.

She was halfway to the shop when she heard the first Dragon Rider's glider scream through the sky.

ARIANNA

"I'm sure she's fine," the Dragon said again.

In less than twelve hours he had managed to find Ari's last nerve, rip it out, step on it, throw it from the window, light it on fire, and bring it back to life, only to repeat the process twice over. She was half a breath away from telling the Dragon that his boon be damned, he had the choice of lying quietly while she tore out his heart…or struggling while she tore out his heart. And oh, how she hoped he picked the struggling if it came to that.

"Three Riders. There are *three* Riders now. There were two this morning—other than you. Now there are three, *here*, in Old Dortam." Ari peered out at the sky. The rainbow trails that tore through the clouds behind their gliders were still etched in her memory. The foreboding colors had long since vanished, glittering on the wind, but they remained burned into her eyes.

She'd cracked the window and stretched her Dragon sight, but the Riders were too far to be seen, even with her augmented goggles. And Ari couldn't make out their smell over the heavy aroma of oil, welders' tools, explosives, and the Dragon she had let into her home.

"Again, I'm sure she's—"

"Cva," Ari interrupted him with the grace of a gear falling off its axle. His eyes narrowed at her insistence on using a shortened version of his name. "Tell me something." She turned her gaze inward from the direction of Mercury Town, pulling off her goggles. The Dragon met her stare; he seemed more disturbed when she smiled than when she addressed him with outright malice. "These Riders, they wouldn't be looking for you, would they?"

"Why would you think that?" He sat back in his chair.

"Don't play me for a fool," Ari spat. "We can go a year without having Riders descend once, even in New Dortam. Now, suddenly, we have two descents in one day? Or perhaps the same descent, and they haven't left yet? And that just so happens to be on the same day you seek passage to the Alchemists' Guild for some inexplicable reason."

Ari didn't remember crossing the room, but she now loomed over the Dragon. He looked up at her and she could almost smell his fearlessness. The man was confident in his ability to beat her, nearly to the point of arrogance. It was almost enough to make her scream. Almost enough to make her throw him down onto the floor and rip off an ear just to show him she could. Just to show him why he should be afraid.

"You didn't seem interested in asking me these questions before you accepted my offer of a boon." The blacks of his eyes narrowed to slits, his body responding to the challenge just as hers did.

"That was before Florence was gone for far too long."

"If you wish to relinquish the boon, perhaps you should get on with it so we can both move on." Where Ari's voice grew louder when faced with a confrontation, his lowered. It was the auditory equivalent of the velvet of his shirt. It was a contradiction that Ari couldn't explain. One that shouldn't be but was—something gentle and dangerous.

"No." She spoke the word like a curse. "No, I am not letting you go. You are going to be mine, Dragon. You are going to hang on the fact that I can call you at any time, on my whim, until I see fit to give you whatever command pleases me."

A low growl rumbled in the back of his throat. His magic spiked and brought Ari's up with it. The terms of the boon were only that she had to get him to the Alchemists' Guild. He'd said nothing about doing so without causing bodily harm in the process.

Magic cracked, strong enough to nearly be heard, and the rumble of an implosion followed. Ari raced to the window, her heart in her throat. Dust plumed up from Mercury Town, marring the horizon.

"We're leaving." She raced for her coat and harness, and grabbed the emergency satchel of basic supplies and weaponry she always left on a peg by the door.

Mercury Town was nearly two thousand peca away. It was close enough that if she used her winch box to propel her along her golden cords, she could cross the distance in a few breaths. Ari looked over the rooftops of Old Dortam, the buildings crumbling together to form a skyline of stone sentries no longer needed at their posts.

She could use her winch box *if* she could find places to loop her line. *If* she could do so without being noticed, or noticed as more than a blur. Her eyes turned inward and narrowed. *If* she didn't have a Dragon in tow.

Ari's mind whirred faster than a freshly struck flywheel. Eighty greca—or eight thousand peca—separated her from Flor and the Dragon Riders. She could run just under six hundred peca a minute, if she pushed and wasn't held up anywhere. Which meant, at best, it would take her just shy of fourteen minutes to reach Mercury Town.

A powerful Chimera could recharge an implosion gun in less than seven minutes. Ari suspected a Rider could do it in less than five. And all that was ignoring the havoc they could wreak with their claws and teeth in the meantime.

Every second she wasted was another second Flor was out there alone. The *one time* she hadn't trailed the girl into Mercury Town, and this happened. Arianna had no idea if Florence could take care of herself. Sure, she carried a revolver, but Ari had never seen her shoot it. She didn't even know if it was loaded or if Flor carried extra rounds. The girl had decent enough instinct, but no practice to back it up.

She needed time to get to Florence. Time she didn't have. Unless...

"Dragon." Arianna swallowed hard. It took two tries to get her pride down her throat and out of the way of her words. "Cvareh." Using his name got his attention, the sort of attention that implied he might actually be willing to listen to her. "Where does your power lie?"

He hesitated. The bloody Dragon wasted precious seconds as he sized up her inquiry.

"You infuriating monster, tell me!" Ari snarled.

"Going to sell my organs?" he replied, level. He'd known what she carried earlier. If she could sense the magic off the reagents, a Dragon would certainly be able to.

"If I wanted to turn you into a reagent farm, you'd already be in chains," she pointed out.

He considered this.

"Knowing what magic you wield will only help me fulfill your request."

"I have the ability to heal. To control minds and see long distances. To persuade others…"

Blood, eyes, tongue. Ari mentally listed off the parts where each of the magics resided in his body. He had nothing really special about him thus far. Rusty cogs, she was saddled with the most inept Dragon of them all. What was even the point of a boon if the Dragon delivering it barely had magic to speak of?

"And to slow time."

"What?" Ari focused on him with the attention of a wild dog on a bone. "Your lungs?" She was honestly surprised he'd confessed it to her.

"Yes, I can slow time." The Dragon was clearly uncomfortable with her naming off what body part the magic lived in.

No matter, she suddenly had the time she needed. "We're going to run for Mercury Town." Ari was talking even faster than she was moving. She grabbed an extra empty bag from the bedroom and a long frock coat that would cover up the Dragon's ghastly clothing. The former was slung over her shoulders and the latter she tossed to him. "I need you to stop time along the way. I want to get there in under five minutes."

"But that much magic—"

"Imbibe from me if you must."

His eyes widened and surprise stilled them both. The Dragon looked at her in shock as Ari once more swallowed down that sickening feeling she got from the prospect of working with a creature like him. Of helping him. Of doing anything that could make a Dragon stronger, not weaker.

It betrayed everything she stood for, and everything she worked for. But Ari had learned, the hard way, that fighting for an ideal meant nothing if the people it was meant to benefit died in the process. She was not a proud creature. She was a creature that did what must be done. Her coat was on now, and she was again the White Wraith. A wraith was above nothing.

Shouts drifted up from the streets as Old Dortam continued to descend into chaos at the hands of the Dragon Riders, who were no doubt taking the opportunity to "impose the King's law" on the side of the city that was less than friendly toward their kind. Ari couldn't waste any more time. Nearly two minutes had passed since her count began. At this rate, they wouldn't make it there before there was another implosion.

She grabbed for the door handle. With or without the Dragon, she was leaving. Flor was more important than his indecision.

His hand closed around hers, and Ari felt his magic slipping over her skin. It wrapped itself around her like sentient, invisible ropes, tightening until she wondered how she was even breathing. She felt the magic build as pressure behind her eyes and a swarming in her ears like a thousand gnats. He remained focused on something beyond the physical world before them, oblivious to the discomfort he was causing her.

"Don't break contact," the Dragon whispered.

The world slowed, sand sliding through an hourglass underneath her feet and threatening to pull her down with it. Ari clutched onto his hand as though it were a lifeline thrown to her in a riptide. She fought against the current of time, fought for air, fought to break the bonds that chained her within space and time.

You are the White Wraith, Ari reminded herself. This would not stop her. Time itself would not stop her! Least of all when she was on a mission for Florence's sake. She was invincible, and she would be damned if something as small as magic and minutes got the better of her.

As though she were freeing her feet from mud, Ari pushed forward. She held onto the Dragon—onto her lifeline— and charged out the door. She threw herself into motion like a boulder down a hill. Time slowing had stunted her momentum, her world, but she had regained it with sheer will. Now she was like a locomotive, speeding weightlessly through the chaotic streets.

Men and women moved slowly, sounds were muffled; the fire from a welder's torch barely flickered. They were like the gradually turning pages of a flip-book, tiny shifts and changes only visible if one stared too closely. Ari darted through them, pulling the Dragon in tow. She may have been breaking the bones in his hand with how hard she was holding onto it, but she didn't care. Florence was out there alone, still.

A rumble shuddered through the world, rippling outward from the man at her side. The Dragon was quivering, his focus wavering. Ari pulled them into a side alley, then down a smaller, narrower walk. She got them out of sight before he lost his fragile control of time.

The Dragon collapsed against the wall as every clock crashed back into motion around them. Sound assaulted her senses as though it were the first time she'd heard it. Smells were sharper, light was brighter.

He slumped, coughing. Golden blood splattered the ground. *It was going to mark*, Ari noted, willing her senses back under her control. The Riders would know where they'd come from. Magic strong enough to send an organ into failure from one use would leave a trail, and the blood would set the Riders in the right direction. There was no going back now. They had to find Florence and get out of Dortam.

"Here!" Ari thrust her hand into his mouth. It raked against his teeth, their razor points cutting into her flesh and drawing blood. The Dragon shook his head in protest. *Arrogant beast,* he didn't even want her magic when he was so exhausted that his own was struggling to keep up the healing his body required. "The Riders will come. They will sense this magic. You knew that from the start." Gold streamed down over her wrist and onto the ground from his mouth. "We have no choice now but to get to Mercury Town so we can get Flor and leave. *So imbibe.*"

And he did. The lump in the Dragon's throat bobbed as he finally swallowed the blood that had been filling his mouth— her blood. Ari felt her magic leaving her, flowing into him. She felt it being leeched from her body, fading before it became his.

She'd understood the principle of imbibing before, but she'd never done it. His hand went up to hers, holding it to his mouth ravenously. His tongue was smoother than she expected as it lapped against the side of her thumb. His eyes met hers, seeking out validation for the understanding she was giving him—an understanding of her that was raw and base, impossible to gain from any other method.

Ari wrenched her hand away, covering it with her other palm. Golden blood still trailed down his chin as the Dragon panted softly, staring at her. The wound under Ari's fingers healed, leaving no remnant of his teeth on her flesh.

"Let's go," she whispered. A threat lay under the words that warned if he were to speak about what they'd just done, she would make sure it was the last thing he would ever say.

The Dragon wiped his face with the back of his hand, smearing away the blood that evaporated quickly in contact with the air. He stared at her with eyes the same color as that blood. Eyes that now seemed to look through her.

Ari felt exposed, mortal—even in her white coat and harness. It was terrible, and she hated him all the more for it.

There was that same slipping sensation as he took her hand again. This time, Ari was ready for it. She let the world pass through her fingers as the seconds slowed and everything stilled. Cvareh had that same faraway look on his face, one of brow-furrowing focus. Ari only waited long enough to know he had the magic under control before they were off again.

Just shy of eight minutes had passed when Arianna and Cvareh stepped into Mercury Town. They collapsed once more against a wall in some forsaken storage area packed with crates and barrels. She waited cautiously, until he coughed blood again, before shoving her hand into his mouth. The Dragon was no longer shy. Like a babe to a nipple he latched on, drawing life and magic alike from her veins.

Ari bit the insides of her cheeks, keeping herself focused when her eyes met his again and that same sensation took over. A sensation of seeing him as more than a Dragon, as more than a person—of seeing more than blue, and gold, and orange. It was as if skin and eyes and hair were blending together to make someone with as much will and heart as she possessed herself.

She would never let him imbibe from her again.

Footsteps, faster than a Fenthri's and closing in, echoed in her ears. Ari ripped her hand from Cvareh's bloody mouth and quickly hid it behind her back, grabbing a dagger while the marks from his teeth healed.

"Found you." A mint-skinned Dragon skidded to a stop at the entrance to their alley. He grinned wildly, flashing every one of his teeth.

Ari returned the expression, pushing her goggles over her eyes. Almost nonchalantly, she pulled cabling through her gearbox, clipping the end to a small loop at the end of the hilt of her dagger. "Yes, you did."

Her blood and half her organs might have been stolen from Dragons, but when Ari moved, it was like they had never belonged to anyone but her. The dagger flew out toward the leafy-colored monster at her mental behest. The Rider jumped, anticipating her attack.

Vaulting through the air, he swiped for her face and neck. Ari ducked and reached for her other dagger, then spun upward, slashing in reply. The gold of her dagger rang out against a bracer over his wrist as he twisted and fell behind her.

Bloody corona.

The Dragon's skin shone brightly as his magic was transformed into a barrier atop his flesh, keeping out her attacks. The one benefit of him activating a corona was that he could no longer expend mass amounts of energy on anything else. But when it came to removing it... There were only two options when a Dragon activated a corona: wait for it to exhaust on its own, or force it to exhaust with attacks.

Ari wasn't the most innately patient of women.

Her dagger flew back toward her as the cord retracted. She arced it through the air and it rang harmlessly against the Rider's shoulder as he continued to advance on her. Ari flipped her grip on her other dagger, crouching for a flurry of small attacks designed to tire her opponent.

With a growl, Cvareh lunged past her. The two Dragons tumbled on the ground, blue and green. They were a jumble of claws and teeth, like two wolves fighting for the alpha position in the pack. There was no regard for etiquette or honor. Only the base desire to dominate.

Cvareh recovered on all fours, his claws scraping against the ground as the two broke apart.

"Cvareh Xin'Ryu Soh." The Rider's voice had gone deep and harsh, guttural. A heavy Royuk accent that wasn't there before bled into his vowels as he spoke. "More like Cvareh Xin."

Arianna only knew the overview of why titles were important on Nova. She had chosen to study other things than the hierarchy of Dragon nobility and the suffixes attached to every rank. She knew enough to know that it would annoy the Dragon when she'd dropped the ranks.

But Cvareh had clearly been making allowances for her as a Fenthri. When another Dragon chose to do the same, the rage was sudden. He roared and attacked faster than Ari's eyes could process. Golden blood exploded as Cvareh's hand plunged into the other man's chest and straight through the corona her steel had been useless against moments earlier.

The Rider coughed and sputtered, but Cvareh was more ruthless than Arianna had ever imagined—more than she had given the Dragon credit for after their first encounter. His hand closed, twisted, and pulled. In one motion, he ripped out the Rider's still beating heart, raised it to his mouth, and bit down with a snarl.

The Dragon Rider died instantly, the gaping wound in his chest still oozing gold that glittered and faded in the air. Cvareh stood and threw down the chewed remnants of the heart. "Dan *Tam*." He spit on the Rider's corpse. "All things were not made equal this day."

As if suddenly remembering she was there, Cvareh turned. This was the creature she had been expecting all along.

Golden blood glistened on his face from where he had feasted on the heart of his fallen foe. He stood over the corpse like it was a prize—a trophy that illustrated what he was capable of. He was finally the monster she had been expecting.

But expectations had shifted, and they both looked at each other with new eyes. The Wraith and the Dragon had shared blood. It was a step toward something she hadn't expected—and certainly didn't want.

FLORENCE

Instinctively, she pressed herself into the nearest doorway and glanced up to see the rainbow of color arcing down toward the other end of Mercury Town. Florence felt like she'd sprinted a hundred peca. Her heart raced and her breathing quickened.

Fight or flight. Ari had explained the instinctual response time and again, but Florence hadn't felt it much. Now, her mind was already clouding with the choice to stay or run. A glider landed on a rooftop in the wake of her indecision.

The irony of Dragon gliders had never been lost on Florence. Dragon magic, inherently, couldn't be used to manipulate anything tangible. But the moment the Alchemists and Rivets had expanded the refining process for steel, the whole world turned differently. Everything focused on the importance of gold: steel refined a final time with the presence of reagents—Dragon organs and blood. Steel transformed into gold was magic given form, and could be manipulated by Dragons and Chimera alike. It wasn't long after that discovery that steam engines were replaced with magic ones, and the first of the Dragons' gliders began to traverse the clouds.

The gliders were shaped to give Dragons the wings of their namesakes, a surprisingly poetic choice by Loom's standards. True, the Dragons themselves looked nothing like the mythical creatures in storybooks of old. They weren't much different than the Fenthri in general form. But their gliders had wide, fixed, pointed wings like a bat's, connected by a platform upon which the rider could stand and steer the mechanical monster with a combination of handles and mental—magical—commands.

Harnessing enough magic to use a glider was something not every Dragon could do. Even Chimera—Fenthri outfitted with Dragon blood and organs—stood no chance of using them; too much magic was required. That fact had been one of many that kept the Fenthri effectively grounded in the land below the clouds, solidly underneath the oppression of Dragon rule.

Florence was inclined to believe that even the strongest Chimera stood no chance of piloting a glider when the first Dragon Rider dismounted. Sparks of raw magic glittered into the air from underneath the contraption, fading into the haze that was Mercury Town's omnipresent tenant. Pure power seemed to ripple under every sculpted muscle.

It was easy to assess the Rider's physical prowess, as the woman hardly wore clothes. Her breasts were wrapped with a sash tied from shoulder to waist. Her midsection was on display for the world, the same bright vermilion as the rest of her. More wrappings around her legs disappeared under a short skirt made of fur that left little to curiosity other than wondering what animal had died for her to have it.

Her eyes shone like sapphires as they surveyed Mercury Town through her long bangs. A thick braid ran down her back and a single beaded strand dangled by her right ear. As if sensing Florence's stare, she turned suddenly; Florence pressed closer into the alcove.

The Rider issued some commands to the companion who landed next to her in the guttural sounds of Royuk. Florence leaned out once more and watched them with careful regard. They began walking along the rooftops with their long Dragon strides. She'd thought Cvareh had been a large creature, but these Dragons were virtual giants, nearly two times her size.

Fight or flight. She had never been in a scrap before and she didn't want her first experience to be with a Dragon Rider. She might be able to threaten some alleyway scum into leaving her alone, but a Dragon Rider would skin her alive. Florence stepped down out of the alcove and began to hurry for the nearest side alley that would lead out of Mercury Town. She wished she'd worn a shorter top hat.

"Fen." The Rider spoke the shortened slur for Fenthri with her thick Dragon accent to the assembled masses beneath her. "At the request of the Dragon King, we are looking for any who have knowledge of a Dragon that descended to Loom illegally earlier this morning. Those with information leading to his capture will be rewarded handsomely."

She's talking about the Dragon Ari brought home. He was on the run from the Dragon King? He didn't seem half as intimidating as the woman who addressed the alley beneath her. If it were true, it was no wonder he needed Ari's help.

The street slowed. Florence was forced to stop her flight so she didn't draw attention to herself as the only one not gawking at the Dragon addressing them from the rooftop.

"Permit me to rephrase." The Dragon tensed her hands, claws shooting from her fingertips. "Come forward with information, or I will extract it from you with necessary force."

Mercury Town was the lowest rung in Dortam, a small corner serving the necessities of many, though only a few would admit to traversing it. It would be a playground for the Riders, a place where they could reap whatever havoc they so chose without consequence. No one would come to the aid of illegals and dealers. The Riders could be as vicious as they wanted and hide behind the curtain of self-defense or upholding the law should any try to call them to task on the matter. They all knew it, and the Dragon wasted no time as a result.

The woman leapt from the rooftop, landing heavily on the ground. Crimson waterfalls poured from her fingertips, from the hearts she had ripped out of the two nearest Fenthri. Shocked onlookers wore masks of fight or flight for a brief moment, instinct surpassing all training. Half turned tail, fleeing. For the other half, conditioning won out as they boldly stood their ground.

Men and women reached for weapons concealed underneath their frock coats. Gun-barrels of varying sizes were hoisted parallel to the ground, aimed at the Dragon. The rider brought her wrists together, banging them with a sharp metallic noise.

The volleys would be useless against a corona. Florence knew it, and everyone else must have known it, too. But that didn't stop them from firing anyway.

Gunshots echoed over her hasty footsteps. She ignored the fighting and Dragons, focusing instead on turning down one narrow street, then another. Out of the flow of people, Florence tried to catch her breath and figure out her next move. She didn't want to risk going home. The chances of a Dragon actually following her specifically out of Mercury Town were infinitesimally small—a number Florence had no doubt Ari would have calculated in an instant and told her not to worry over. But any risk that would put Ari in needless danger as a direct result of her actions was too much for Florence. That woman was way too good at finding her own danger—she didn't need Florence's help.

The Dragon Ari had brought home didn't seem evil, not in the way Ari had painted him. Florence was willing to give him the benefit of the doubt, which meant these Riders were likely hunting him for some nefarious purpose. Florence constructed the story in her head and found it supported her decision not to go home.

That meant she had to head to the bunker.

The ground rumbled and the buildings shook with the crack of an implosion. The way the mortar and stone groaned was a symphony to Florence's ears, destruction of an epic nature the likes of which only pure Dragon magic could reap. It conveyed a clear message: the Riders had no qualms about leveling Mercury Town on their hunt for Cvareh.

Judging from the echo of the sound, Florence would have ranked it among one of the best implosions she'd ever heard. She was so enamored by it that she had to remind herself to be afraid. Her mental reminders were only partly successful, as she now harbored a secret desire to see one such implosion before they were done.

Florence pushed off, her breath nearly caught.

Ari had only taken her to their tiny safe room in Mercury Town once. It had been late at night, a time when oil burnt low and most seedy occupants were high on whatever the substance of the day was. Florence didn't have Ari's photographic memory; her muscles didn't remember every twist and turn as Ari's could.

But her mentor knew how Florence's mind worked. She had taken care to describe every step as they were taking it, utter every street name and point out every building flanking the alleyways on the way to the small room known to them as the bunker. The chaos and noise faded away and Florence focused only on where she was and where she was going. There was enough distance between her and the Dragons now that she didn't need to be worried.

Or so she thought.

An emerald-skinned Dragon seemed to fall from the sky just before her. Men and women scattered in all directions like rats from a flame. Florence skidded to a stop, shifting her weight from foot to foot to prevent herself from taking one more step closer to the Dragon or falling backwards.

Her hand found the grip of her pistol as her heart raced. The option of flight had been taken from her. Now she could only fight or roll over for the Rider—and Florence, student of Arianna the White Wraith, would never roll over. Not for a Dragon, not for anyone.

"You're the one." The Dragon looked right at her with a sinister sort of smile. Even though he had the same elongated canines Cvareh had, they looked ten times sharper and more malicious in the Rider's mouth. "Girl—"

"I am not a girl." Her palm was too slick to get a good grip on her pistol.

The Dragon laughed. "You smell like Dragon."

He inhaled deeply, his eyes fluttering closed. Florence toed a step away before they opened again. The Dragon's eyes drifted to Ari's bag, so recently occupied by reagents.

"At least, *that* does…"

Florence finally got a grip on her pistol as another implosion rang out from afar.

"But whatever you had there wasn't *his*. Yet you still have that pungent scent of House Xin on you." The Dragon inhaled deeply. "Little organ trader, tell me, you wouldn't happen to know of the Dragon we're seeking, would you?"

"I don't know what you're talking about." That much was true. She didn't know anything about a House Xin. "But I wouldn't take another step closer."

Florence drew her pistol and targeted the man. She held it out with both hands, the skin on her fingers straining with the tightness of her grip. She wished her arms would stop shaking long enough for her to make a convincing threat.

But the truth was, Florence had never put the explosive end of a weapon toward any living creature before. For everything Ari had said, for all the Dragons had done, Florence couldn't help but wonder if it was right to kill the man before her. No, she'd be able to kill him to protect herself. What set her muscles to trembling was the idea of living with herself after.

"What do you think that'll do to me?" He roared with laughter. "You people are certainly determined little gnats."

"I'll shoot," she threatened.

"By all means, do. I'll even stand here and give you to three to do it."

Florence's forehead was dotted with sweat and her chest burned. She gulped down shallow breaths of air.

"One..."

Her eyes darted around for help. Everyone else had taken the Dragon's attention on her as an opportunity to clear the area. She would've done the same.

"Two..."

This was it. The clock had run out and it was time for her to make a stand. Even if the Dragon was about to tear her limb from limb, she couldn't go down without a fight—she wouldn't.

"Th—" The Dragon stopped himself short. His nostrils flared and his head jerked to attention over Florence's shoulder.

She instinctively glanced in the same direction, but saw nothing. The Dragon didn't lunge for her while she was distracted. Whatever he was seeing, it was something important—and something she could not.

With a roar and a triumphant flash of teeth, the Dragon bolted in the opposite direction. He led with his nose, pushing his feet into the ground as though pulled along by an invisible tether. Florence was completely forgotten. She spun, watching him go.

He was halfway down the alley when she lifted her gun again. Her finger ghosted over the trigger…but didn't squeeze. She returned the pistol to its holster. She'd been lucky the Dragon had been distracted by something and forgot about his quarrel with her. She didn't need to shoot him in the back just to prove that she could. Ari would never forgive her for taking a risk like that.

Florence continued her run in the direction opposite the Dragon. The bunker wasn't far and, if anything, she could be thankful that the Dragon's presence helped clear the streets of any potential witnesses. Through a narrow passage between two buildings, over a low wall, and down a decrepit flight of stairs, Florence found herself face to face with a soot-covered iron door.

Built into the door, in place of a knob, was a sort of circular lock. She had no confirmation, but likewise no doubt, that Arianna had been the one behind its design. Ari didn't like keys if she could avoid them. They were a security threat, too easy to replicate. No, Ari's locks were always a combination of numbers and shapes, turning wheels and timing sequences. They were numerical codes given shape in steel.

Florence spun the wheels until the shape Ari had shown her was made. The inner mechanisms of the door clicked in release and she pushed the portal open. The bunker got its name from being beneath a basement of a gambling hall. It was another flight of stairs down that would have been pitch black were it not for the electric lighting.

Only a building with as much money as a gambling hall would have the funds to outfit itself with electricity. The hum of the few solitary bulbs fascinated Florence every time. Rivets boasted that the lightning channeled through copper wire would be the future of Loom.

First steam had been 'the future of Loom.' Then the Dragons came, and magic was to be the future of Loom. Then, when magic could make machines accomplish things far beyond steam ever could, electricity was to be the future of Loom. In Florence's short life she'd heard people boast of three different futures. But no matter what future came, there'd always be something in it to blow up– which was what initially drew Florence to the studies of the Revolvers over the Ravens.

There was another door, and another lock, before she was in the actual bunker. One room, not much to consider by any stretch. It looked like more of a storeroom than any kind of living space. Shelves lined every wall and heavy boxes were piled on them, making the long planks sag in the middle. One bulb cast the room in a ghostly light, shadows haunting the corners of the various effects Ari had squirreled away here.

It was more than Florence had seen the first time, which meant Ari had been adding to it in secret. Florence sat herself on one of the boxes in the back corner, resting her timepiece next to her. Ari had told her to retreat here if ever there was a crisis. She'd wait for a good few hours before heading home.

Either Ari would meet her here, or she had no idea what was happening in Mercury Town and would be waiting at home when Florence returned.

Florence pushed off the boxes, already unable to handle the boredom. She began poking around, looking for something to occupy her time. She had a sneaking suspicion she was waiting for Ari to come. There was no way an implosion of that size had gone unnoticed. And, if Florence knew anything about her mentor, it was that she wouldn't be physically able to keep herself from running head-first into certain danger.

CVAREH

The King's Rider still lingered in Cvareh's mouth. The man tasted like a rose, sickeningly floral. Cvareh clicked his tongue, trying to dislodge the flavor.

"How did you do that?" Arianna demanded from over her shoulder. She led him through the winding alleyways of what he could now only assume was the infamous Mercury Town. It was filthier than the regular streets had been and he had no idea how living creatures could willingly choose to live in such squalor.

"Do what?"

"Break through a corona," she clarified, turning sharply and running backward a step or two for emphasis.

A man ahead of them froze in his tracks as they came barreling down the alley. Arianna didn't say anything, just shoved him out of the way as they tore past. The man blubbered, trying to find his thoughts. By the time he could even form the word "Dragon" they were already far enough away that the shout only echoed to them faintly.

"Corona are meant to keep out steel, bullets, blades, weak Chimera magic... My claws are none of those things."

"I see." It was the first time he'd witnessed her mind put to action when prejudice wasn't hindering the winds behind her mental sails. Arianna squinted at him thoughtfully. She kept using new eyes to give him looks he didn't yet comprehend.

"The other Riders will catch up soon," he warned.

"How soon?"

"I can't tell. I can sense their magic growing, but not how near or far." If they'd been bleeding, he would've been able to catch the smell or get a true taste of their power on the wind. But he wasn't exactly surprised that they had yet to be wounded. The only Fenthri whom Cvareh could see standing a chance against a Rider stood before him.

"Then I must assume the same is true of them and you?" He was surprised when her voice rose slightly on the last word, indicating a question. *She was actually asking him things.* Quite the sudden change from a few hours earlier.

"As long as we stay ahead of them. And I'm not coughing up more blood anytime soon." Cvareh wasn't pleased about her abuse of his powers. He should have known from the moment he told her about it that she would demand he use the ability for her ends, and it'd only taken her a minute to back him into a corner until he felt there was no other option. *Why had he told her?*

"I won't need you to stop time again." She vaulted over a railing and down into a tiny side stair. Cvareh walked around as she whirred dials on a strange looking lock built into the doorway. "We're here." Arianna paused, considering him for a long moment. "And you best hope that Florence is too."

Cvareh knew the outcome of her threat before he could respond. Arianna contained her emotions well. Her face remained impassive, swathed in the unnatural, terrible light of the electric bulbs that lined the tiny stairwell. But he could feel the relief about her, standing so close.

This was one of the many reasons why imbibing from the living was so taboo. If every person's mind was a locked chest, then their magic was the key. It was the way into a carefully guarded and illogical system, unique to each individual. Letting someone imbibe was allowing them to make a copy of that key. They could open you up and understand you without effort for a length of time after the imbibing. And really, once that understanding was imprinted on the mind, could it ever be forgotten?

Cvareh vowed to himself that he had no interest in understanding this woman as she opened the lock on the second door. She was equal parts intolerable, brash, harsh, improper, and—worst of all—unfashionable. But there was a counterweight to her heart. Something in her magic shone as brightly as starlight as she swept up her ward into a tight embrace. Something about it made the gray skinned Fenthri woman almost... glow.

"Flor! You had me more worried than a Harvester who can't find their mining pick."

"You know I can take care of myself." The girl patted the pistol that sat just under her arm for show. The motion was brave—false, but brave. "It's not like you to be so worried."

"There are Dragon Riders about and we're hiding in the bunker. This isn't normal. I think my worry is justified."

"Speaking of..." Florence's eyes drifted over to him. "They're looking for you, I think."

Cvareh wasn't surprised. His hand went to the folio strapped around his waist, checking to make sure the clasp hadn't come undone. The Dragon King would know what he'd stolen, and Cvareh had been expecting that he'd go to any measure to retrieve it.

"Yes... I don't believe we ever finished that conversation." Arianna stared at him with her stolen eyes. Cvareh wondered what Dragon had given them up. Had they been killed? Or were they harvested and left to suffer as the organs grew back in their empty sockets?

"I thought we had." He sighed, leaning against some of the boxes. The room was horribly dusty, but his clothes were already soiled past hope. Cvareh was distracted long enough to inwardly cringe at the notion of eventually being forced into some coverings like those they wore here on Loom.

"Dragons barely *lower themselves*—" her tone was sarcastic "—to come to Loom. Never Old Dortam and even less Mercury Town."

"Didn't you hear the doomsayers in the streets? They say Dragons are going to start raining from the sky and finally torch the gods' forsaken rock known as Loom." He returned her sarcasm with some of his own. Cvareh was tired of her mood swings, but could only seem to succeed in drawing them out.

She crossed the room in two long steps, almost as wide as his own. Her hands twisted around his collar as she pulled him onto his feet again. Cvareh met her halfway and kept his lips closed, resisting the urge to curl them back in a snarl.

"You're going to rip my shirt, and I quite like this shirt." So what if he'd already decided one of his favorite garments was forfeit? He'd already kicked the hornet's nest that was Arianna again; he may as well stomp on it too.

"I don't give a damn about your shirt." For a Fenthri, this woman could act like quite the Dragon.

"Then give no more care to who exactly I am, where I'm going, why I need to get there, or why the Riders want me." He narrowed his eyes, ignoring the hideous line of her teeth. "Care about getting me to the Alchemists' Guild hall. You think I'm any more thrilled at the idea of traveling with the White Wraith?"

Her eyebrows rose.

"Yes, I know you. Many have heard of you on Nova. The White Wraith is infamous for making organs disappear and helping traffic Dragons into illegal harvesting rings." *That's right*, he reminded himself, *I should hate this woman.* Whatever sparkle she had for her ward was overshadowed by the cloud of guilt she should bear for all the lives she had submitted to the torture of the harvesters. "Why do you think Dragons never— how did you put it?—*grace* Dortam?"

"Then it seems like I've done my job."

"Enough, both of you." The black-haired girl pushed herself between them, pulling Arianna away. "What's done is done. You said you'd get him to the Alchemists' Guild, Ari. There are King's Riders outside our door. I think we have more pressing matters than tallying up who's who and who's done what."

He didn't expect to find sense from the youngest among the three of them, but that was where it lay.

"Fine." Arianna pointed in his face, close enough that he could've bitten her finger clean off if he wanted. "Florence is right. It doesn't matter who we are. But I cannot take you to the Alchemists' Guild if you don't tell me what else I may be up against in getting you there."

"You seem to have the overview." He held out his palms in a 'nothing up my sleeves' gesture that was only half true. Cvarch still had the entire deck squirreled away. She just didn't need to know that.

"You're not being helpful." She pulled her hand from his face and began tearing through the room. Wood chips and shavings flew as she rummaged through crates. "Will I need a large revolver, or a small cannon?" Arianna stacked weaponry of varying shapes on the boxes as she continued her tirade. "Am I to assume they'll leave when they're done demolishing Mercury Town?"

"They could be at it for a while." The Riders would toy with Loom for a bit just because they could.

"Dragon—"

"They said they were after you because you descended illegally," Florence interjected before the argument spiraled out of control again.

"Flor." Arianna's voice audibly shifted when she addressed the girl. She went from ice to restorative broth within the space of a breath. "Descending illegally is a matter for their constabulary, not the King's Riders," she thought aloud. When she returned her attentions to him, the warmth completely vanished once more. "Why does the Dragon King want *you*?"

She continued to handle herself with an utter absence of grace and tact, but the question was sincere. She'd again put aside whatever grudge fueled her. Cvareh closed his eyes with a sigh.

He could have answered with a hundred things. He could've made up a lie, told a half truth, concocted almost any reason and—from what he knew of her—Arianna would've accepted it at face value just for the sake of ending the conversation. But Cvareh did none of those things. He told the truth.

"Because I want to help overthrow him."

"What?" The entire spectrum of color exploded across her magic.

"The Riders want me because I am working to overthrow the Dragon King."

"You lie," she whispered.

"Why else would the Riders be after me?" He sighed again, growing even more tired of the woman. He avoided her questions, and she throttled him. He was smart with her, and she drew her blades. He told her the truth, and she acted like he'd told the most boldfaced lie she'd ever heard. There was literally nothing he could say or do around her that didn't end with her maiming or insulting him.

"I could think of a number of reasons."

"And none are better than the explanation I just gave you," he insisted.

"Why would a Dragon want to overthrow his King?"

His cheek tensed as he struggled to keep his mouth from curving into a condescending smile. A Fenthri could never understand the plight of the Dragon houses. They saw all Dragons as one—one enemy, one overseer, one force to overtake. Even the most enlightened Fenthri would grapple with understanding nearly two thousand years of infighting and power struggles.

"Why are you the White Wraith?" Answering her question with a question annoyed her all the more.

Ari opened her mouth, rising to his challenge as he knew she would. And then her lips clamped shut, smothering the words she'd been about to say. She chewed them over and swallowed them along with every expectation he had for her reaction. Her face was as stony as her skin when she spoke, "Fine, we'll go with your earlier assessment, Dragon. We don't need to know anything real about each other."

Arianna stalked over to him. The woman was almost tall enough to look him in the eyes. She'd be average height for a Dragon, making her unnaturally tall among Fenthri. "But if you have some knowledge that will interfere with my ability to fulfill this boon…"

Cvareh took a sharp inhale, overwhelmed by her scent as she took one step closer and crossed the threshold into his personal space. Her magic assaulted his. It made him hungry for her. He'd had a taste of this woman and now all he could think of when she was so close was the feeling of her, the rush of power as her magic encapsulated his. Yes, there were so many reasons why imbibing from the living was an awful idea.

"If it's something that's going to put Flor in harm's way again…" She was talking. Cvareh struggled to focus on her words, to focus on anything other than the urge to grab her and sink his teeth into her flesh again. "I expect to know."

Every muscle in his body held him frozen with tension. Arianna was challenging his dominance, trying to overwhelm him, to stay in control of the unorthodox relationship they were forming. She was under his skin. In her he suddenly saw Petra in the most wonderful and heartbreaking way. He loathed it. He *loved* it.

"Well, now that that's settled…" Florence summoned both of their attentions once more, snapping them back to reality. She had an amused little glint to her eyes, as though they were more delightful than frightening to watch.

The woman eased away from him, and her magic with her. The powder kegs around them stacked taller, but for now remained dry and cool. Eventually, the only way out would be to forfeit everything they were and strike flint.

"Obviously I didn't have a chance to go shopping, but I still have the dunca."

"We have enough supplies here to get to Ter.5.2.," Arianna muttered. She seemed to look anywhere but him for the first few seconds following their confrontation.

"We're not going home, are we?" The girl seemed more intrigued than disappointed by the idea.

"Not until we've unsaddled ourselves from this one." Arianna's particular breed of tact had returned as she motioned rudely to him. "Speaking of..." She resumed rummaging through things, tossing rags in the shape of clothing his way. "You should change."

"You don't honestly expect me to wear *this*, do you?" He poked at the fabric with his toe as though the offending plain trousers were likely to attack him.

"We can't have you strolling around like a giant blueberry," Arianna drawled.

"My clothes are quite fashionable," he defended before he could stop himself. No doubt he'd just given her extra ammunition to attack him with later.

"I fail to see how *that*—" Ari stole his inflection on the word as she raked him up and down with her eyes, "could be construed as fashionable by anyone in their right mind."

The desire to rip out her throat was certainly more natural than whatever had been happening earlier.

"Come now, we don't have all day." She waved him on as though he were a lowly unranked. "We have a train to catch."

Cvareh scooped up the clothes along with the remnants of his pride. He waited for them to avert their eyes. "Are you going to turn around?"

"Oh he's modest," Arianna quipped to Florence. "Who knew? I didn't think anyone who could wear something so gaudy and revealing could have real modesty."

He was right. She had used the knowledge of his love of fashion against him at the first opportunity. But the two women finally obliged.

"If you think you can attack me while my back is turned, I'll—"

"I know, you'll cut me," he finished dryly.

Cvareh begrudgingly pulled the clothes from his frame, dressing instead in the dull rags that had been forced upon him. This was going to be a long trip to the Alchemists' Guild hall. A very, *very* long trip.

LEONA

Incense hung heavy in the air. Perfumed tendrils of smoke curled through beams of light like the tentacles of a hungry octopus. The windows were shades of blue, folded against splashes of gold and curves of iron. No two were alike. The stone arched over them like waves against a boat and cut each into a slightly different shape. Between them, mosaic was laid in abstract patches of color that had always reminded Leona of fish scales.

"Petra Xin'Oji To will arrive within the hour, Yveun Dono," a little man reported from her side of a large, circular screen. Wood the same shade as the floor outlined it, a base mirrored at the top and bottom creating the imagery of a sun rising through the clouds.

"See her to the red room," the Dragon King answered from the other side.

"Understood." The man gave a low bow before walking briskly from the room.

Leona narrowed her eyes to slits at the man's back, cautiously regarding him as he left. His skin was the standard jade of House Tam. They were loyal to the King—and generally smart enough not to challenge the fact. But she was always on alert when anyone was around her sovereign. It had been two decades since the last duel against the Yveun Dono, and she would see it to a third.

"Leona." The King's strong voice echoed across the space to her. Every time it formed her name, the muscles around Leona's pointed ears tensed, ever so slightly.

"Yveun Dono?" She bowed at the waist, holding the low pose of respect as he rounded the screen.

"Ease, Leona."

She stood straight at his command, retracting the claws that had been out on alert the entire time the man had been in her King's presence.

"Have you any word from your sister?"

She shook her head, a long strand of hair that extended past her bound breast clinking softly as the beads shifted.

"How many hours has it been?" The King walked over to the windows, near where she stood. Near enough that she could smell his skin as much as his magic. Near enough that he could strike her if he so chose.

"Since the theft it has been six, Dono." Leona stripped all emotion from her voice. She would betray no favoritism, no concern. She had been trained better. She had fought and killed and clawed her way up for twenty of her forty-six years to be the King's personal guard, and she would not let anything separate her from her lord for the remaining eighty her life should hold.

"Six hours, and three Riders." The sun lit fire in the King's red eyes as he studied its progression through the sky.

The Dono was a handsome man. His wine-colored skin brought out the purple tones of his hair that, in turn, contrasted with the brilliant fury of his eyes. He was over sixty-five, Leona knew that much. She suspected he could even be pushing eighty. But he looked not a day past fifty, a man still well in his prime.

"It seems too much to track down one lowly Xin Soh." He looked over to her, his stare ablaze with the same sort of quiet danger as lightning. Beautiful, enchanting even, from a distance. But it would strike and kill without warning.

"It does, Dono," Leona had to agree. Her sister or no, the fact was a fact.

"Your sister, Sybil, isn't it?"

She hated the way her sister's name rumbled the back of his throat. "Sybil Rok'Anh Soh," Leona specified for him.

They were both of house Rok, but Leona had the luck to be born of a Soh and a To, an upper common woman and a high noble. Her half-sister had not been so lucky. Their mother had chosen a life-mate who was also a Soh. Acceptable for their stature, but not so much in the way of getting Sybil ahead.

Leona didn't know who her father was. Her and her sister had both inherited their mother's crimson tinted skin, as the woman had been the alpha in both relationships. But, whoever he was, Leona thanked her sire silently most mornings as she stood next to the King.

"She seeks to be Sybil Rok'Anh Veh."

"She does." Leona couldn't deny it. Having a sister who was two ranks higher in society had been a strain on Sybil for many years. Leona didn't bother hiding her shadow; she cast it long and proud. Sybil would rise up and find her own light, or she would wither like a flower under the shade of a stronger tree.

"I gave her this as an opportunity to show me why she should be of my chosen nobility, to earn her rank." Yveun started for the door and Leona followed.

"That is most generous of you, Yveun Dono." It *was* generous. Sybil had no doubt been given the chance because of Leona's track record. If she squandered it, that was entirely on her, and she'd find no sympathy from Leona on the matter.

"I am quite generous, aren't I?" He was amused.

"Without a doubt. It is why we are so joyful to bend completely before you." They walked through a long hall. Glass arched over top like sailcloth ballooned with wind. Wood and metal made a ribcage at irregular intervals to support it. The Rok estate in Lysip spared no expense in its crafting. The unnatural borrowed from the natural world as stones morphed from uncut to elegant sculptures supporting metalwork that could only be completed by a master craftsman. There were many who fought to rise high enough in society to spend a night on the magnificent grounds. And this was the place Leona called home.

"No half measures." The King recited the motto of House Rok. He paused, making a show of inspecting a carving he had seen hundreds of times.

"Something House Xin would be best to learn," Leona muttered.

"The Xin'Oji is our guest today," the King cautioned against her transparent insult.

"Of course, Dono." Leona bowed and held the position.

A hand floated under her chin. Leona lifted her face at the unspoken command, his fingertips hovering just over her skin—never touching. She should be thankful he avoided making contact. His hallowed flesh was above hers.

And yet, by every God in the pantheon, she yearned for it. He owned her mind with his decree. He owned her soul with his very presence. She had nothing more to give him if he gave her his touch as well.

He looked down at her, and she up at him. Leona reveled in the silence, in the feeling of his attention on her. It was that feeling that pushed her to victory in every duel she'd ever fought as the King watched on. She lived for him and silently affirmed it every time she thought he might be asking without words.

The King dropped his hand and departed. She waited a few steps before following behind. They were never seen walking side by side before anyone of importance. That spot was reserved for his life-mate, the Rok'Ryu. But Coletta'Ryu was rarely seen outside of her quarters.

The red room was aptly named. Wood stained in various shades of the color alternated in a pattern on the floor and up the walls, even on the ceiling. It was sparse compared to the other adornments in the Rok manner, and made the single, golden chair look all the more important.

A child turned away from inspecting the Dono's throne a little too closely. Petra Xin'Oji To was younger than fifty, and already the Oji of a Dragon house. No, Leona knew better than to underestimate the *woman* before them. She had challenged her eldest brother to a duel at twenty and won. Her mother fell before her when Petra turned twenty-three. The woman had challenged her own father at thirty and consumed his heart in its entirety to gain his rank and title. They said she didn't even flinch as she imbibed her sire's still-beating strength.

Petra may look a child. But her gold eyes shared the same qualities as the Yveun Dono's. This was a woman on a mission. And those eyes looked right through their King to the chair upon which he sat. Everyone knew Petra's lust for the throne, and it was that desire that had turned House Xin from the annoyance it had been under Petra's father, to a threat.

"Petra'Oji," the King said after he had settled in his throne.

The woman with midnight blue skin crossed over and knelt before her King. "Yveun Dono, you honor me by this invitation."

"Do I?" The King rested his chin on the back of his hand. Leona remained poised at his side.

"I suppose only you can confirm that." Petra stood before she was given leave to do so. It made the muscles around Leona's claws strain against the skin, pushing out the razor sharp talons as far as they would go. "It isn't every day I am summoned to House Rok's most noble of estates."

"Indeed it is not." The King wasn't handing Petra anything.

"Stunning, really. I can't imagine how long its construction took." Petra folded her hands before her. The woman clearly had no interest in the construction of the estate and its trimmings. The two House leaders were digging in their claws and waiting for someone to push hard enough to tear flesh.

"With a House as noble and established as House Rok, we can afford to take our time on things." Yveun Dono's lips curled into a snarling smile. "And how is your estate faring, Petra'Oji?"

"The latest revisions are coming along nicely, thank you." She smiled widely, showing her teeth.

The edges of Leona's lips parted, just enough to flash her elongated canines. She did not *want* to tolerate this eager upstart's encroachment on her King's honor. But she *did* tolerate it, only as long as Yveun Dono did.

"That is most excellent to hear." Silence filled the room following the King's statement. Leona watched it settle over Petra. It crept under the other woman's skin, multiplying and manifesting until she had to speak.

"But that is not why you invited me here today."

"It isn't?" Yveun Dono rested his elbow on the armrest of the throne, looking bored.

"A letter, or a whisper, would have sufficed if you wanted to talk about remodeling." Petra squinted her eyes, barely.

"Speaking of whispers, have you heard from your brother?" The King finally began to circle around his point like a carrion bird.

"You likely have more recently than I. Is he not your counsel on matters of treasury?"

Petulant child. Leona kept the thought to herself, barely.

"That is not the brother I am asking for." The King sat straighter in his chair. It was a fraction of movement, but it betrayed his increasing impatience with Petra's obstinacy.

"I didn't even realize you knew I had a younger brother, Dono. You honor House Xin with this interest you have taken in us." Petra lied through her teeth—teeth Leona fantasized about smashing with a variety of instruments.

"Where is Cvareh?"

"I believe he is still at the Temple of Lord Xin, praying to the Death-giver for wisdom of the ends."

Yveun Dono was no more convinced by Petra's lie than Leona was. "Does he pray often?"

"Only when he thinks he needs our House Patron's wisdom."

"And how often does Cvareh need the guidance of the Death-giver?" Yveun Dono tilted his head to the side, just barely. "He isn't renowned as being particularly ambitious."

"Yveun Dono, do take care; that is my brother of whom you speak."

"'Take care', Petra?" The King dropped all formality from her title. It was a pointed and successful jab on the King's part, judging from the expression on the Oji's face. "What exactly must I 'take care' of? I already care for our people, for Nova, for the misplaced masses in the land below the clouds. I take care of an astronomically large yet finite amount of resources to ensure there is more than enough to go around for both us and the Fen. I am mindful of the tax their irresponsibility has put on a world we now know we share. I oversee their guilds to ensure proper teachings. Am I not taking care of enough?"

Petra was silent, the most sense the girl had shown since the encounter began.

"Or must I also take care of your family's fragile sensibilities as well?"

"I will look after House Xin." There was almost a growl to Petra's words.

"Will you, Petra? Or will your willing lack of ideals lead them to ruin?" The woman's lesser experience compared to Yveun Dono's was telling. A few words twisted around her House's motto—*ends before ideals*—and she wound up so tightly that Leona could almost smell the quiver in her muscles. House Xin was too proud, too bold. "This is not about House Xin, Petra. This is about the good of our people, the longevity of our traditions, the eternity of our ways, the future of our world. A future we must pursue with no half measures."

"No half measures," Petra repeated the motto of House Rok. "It must be easy to say from where you sit when any half measure does not come off Rok's measuring stick."

The fruity taste of blood laced Leona's mouth as she bit her tongue to keep from speaking. The King could defend himself; he didn't need her to step forward and give Petra a verbal or physical lashing. But she still hoped he would ask.

"Careful, Petra." The King would give no more caution than that. No matter how badly Leona suspected he wanted to be off with Petra as well, they couldn't just kill another House's Oji. There were rules to be followed when it came to duels. If they cast aside the foundation of their society's hierarchy, they'd be left with the anarchy Loom experienced before Yveun Dono had begun to restructure it. "Now, I will ask you again. Where is Cvareh?"

"Then I will tell you again, he is high in the mountains at the Temple of Lord Xin."

The problem was, even though they all knew it to be a lie, there was no *proof.* So Petra and the whole underbelly of Dragon society called House Xin would continue to unfurl whatever plot they were playing at. At least until Yveun Dono had enough evidence of treason to bring down even an Oji.

"Then it should be no problem for him to attend my summons."

"Actually, it is." Petra's triumphant smile returned. She knew she had the upper hand. If they'd had anything they would've been out with it, and she was going to stick to her idiotic story until they did, it seemed. "He is in solitary meditation, and will not leave until he has heard the guiding words of our Lord. I'm sure you understand the importance of seeking the will of our House patron, Dono."

"Quite."

"Why the sudden interest in Cvareh? Would you like to employ him as well?" Petra asked.

"I believe him to be involved in a crime." One would expect such a claim from their supreme leader to silence Petra and wipe the smug grin off her face, but she just kept smiling.

"How ghastly. But I'm sure my dearest Cvareh has not had any part in it."

The King leaned back in his throne. "We will see, won't we? If you are lying, there will be grave consequences on your whole House."

"Your glory is all ends House Xin seeks." Petra's words were poetic, pretty, and utterly insincere.

"I'm sure." The King waved a long-fingered hand.

Petra bowed, heeding the dismissal with grace. She spun like a dancer and strode out the room with long, measured steps. Leona watched the young Oji go, boring holes in the door with her eyes long after she left.

"Ease, Leona," the King reminded her again as he stood.

"She's lying to you, Dono."

"I am aware." He started for the door himself, trusting Leona to fall into step.

"Cvareh stayed with his brother here. He could've easily uncovered what we had. It had to have been him; only a Xin would take the schematics," Leona insisted, trying to persuade someone who was already of her mind.

"And he is no doubt carrying them to Loom to find someone who can finish the engineering of the Philosopher's Box."

"Should we increase our efforts in watching the Rivet's Guild? Even the best watchmen close their eyes to sleep." It would make sense for Cvareh to head there. The engineers of Loom would be the ones to finish what the last resistance had started.

"I trust you to it," the King agreed, starting for a different set of council rooms.

"I bend to your will." Leona bowed.

"However, even more so, I want your sister to bring me back what is rightfully mine." The King paused, giving Leona a long stare.

"I will see that she does," Leona vowed. "Personally, if I must."

"Very good." He nodded and continued on his way.

Leona didn't know what was holding up Sybil beneath the clouds. But frankly, she didn't care. In Leona's world, there was only success or failure. There was no 'almost', or 'close enough'. Leona had given Yveun Dono her word now. If she had to, she would raze Loom to the ground to avoid failing him.

ARIANNA

S team billowed over the platform, curling in opaque clouds from underneath the train and casting halos around the dim lighting of the Old Dortam station. It was the last train of the day to embark along the winding trail that curved through the mountain range to the south of Dortam and out toward the coast.

Florence's inability to spend the dunca from Ari's mission proved a favorable happenstance. It was handier to have the money in notes that were easy to exchange for three tickets on a sleeper car. Ari had initially been thinking of stowing away, but she wanted to eliminate the number of things that could go wrong. They were already traveling with a Dragon; the last thing they wanted to do was engage in any activity that could raise suspicion.

Ari stood with Cvareh as Florence approached the ticket counter. Iron gates extended on either side, and train staff waited at each of the small entrances. It was the only thing that stood between them and finally getting out of Dortam, and Ari was holding her breath at the thought.

Their disguises were simple but effective. The three of them would be medical travelers, seeking out the colder air of

Keel—conveniently where the Alchemists' Guild was located—
to help with their highly contagious, skin-rotting affliction.
Florence had thought of it from something she'd read in a book,
and Arianna was content to not question. Flor was playing the
nurse—the only one among them who could show her face.

Arianna and Cvareh each covered their faces with
cloth medical masks and large goggles that hid their eyes. Ari
kept her hood down to avoid too much suspicion, but Cvareh's
was raised. Luckily, his skin was a shade of steely blue that
could almost pass for gray in the right light. It was the best
they could hope for when the bloody Dragon couldn't even
make an illusion.

Then again, he *could* stop time.

His face became the sole object of her focus. Her
hand tingled from where it had raked against his teeth. The
ghost of his tongue ran along her skin. She wondered how her
power stood up to his. He would know now, since he knew
how much magic he expended to stop time and how much
hers replenished. Were they well matched? Or could he indeed
overpower her? Ari had never imbibed from a living host, and
the notion suddenly fascinated her.

"I have our tickets." Florence's cheer was almost
believable. Arianna stepped first, Cvareh half a step after as
she'd instructed. They both fell into place behind the youngest
among them as they approached the gate. "For the three of us."

The ticket-taker tore all three tickets in half at once,
passing one part back to Florence.

"Step widely, you two," she instructed, waving them
around the man and onto the platform. The train staff didn't
look twice. Between the mask, the goggles, the hood, the haze,
and the darkness—Cvareh was passing as a Fenthri. A large

Fenthri. But Arianna suspected that her standing next to him helped. "Don't get anywhere near this nice gentleman. You don't want him to catch your sick."

Others on the platform took heed of Florence's loud cautioning to the ticket man and gave them a wide radius. Ari smiled proudly under her mask. She'd helped raise quite the cunning little sneak these past two years.

"Let's see… Our car is…" Florence led them down the long platform, continually checking the tickets. "Right here."

Arianna had traveled by train a couple times in her life, but she was quick to forget how little traveling Florence had done. The young woman stared in wonder at the plush red carpet and patterned metals, embellished with fabric, of the sleeper car. Cabins lined one side of the hall, windows on the other.

Florence was so taken by it all that she momentarily forgot where they were going—a distraction quickly remedied with a small cough from Ari. Their cabin was small, as most were in second class. It would be tight, but manageable for the few days they would be on the train. This was a trip for business, not pleasure, and Ari was certainly *not* going to spend more than she had to on the Dragon.

One long sofa was on the right, a low bar for basic effects on the left. Over the sofa was a second bed that could be folded down from the wall. It was cramped with the three of them and Ari was stuck awkwardly shuffling around Florence and the Dragon to pull the curtains over their window and lock the door behind them.

"Flor, you did a great job."

"I was so nervous, I thought I'd be ill!" The girl fell onto the sofa with a dramatic sigh and began rummaging through her bag for a foil-wrapped chocolate.

"It didn't show." Arianna pulled the mask down from her face and rested her goggles atop her head. Her eyes fell on the Dragon as he carefully inspected the metalwork with one of his bandaged hands. "Well, Lord Dragon, fashionable enough for you?"

"And how long have you been waiting to use that quip?"

Arianna was dangerously close to appreciating the Dragon's adaptability in managing her sarcasm.

"But yes, it is quite fashionable. We would use wood on Nova for something like this. I'd never thought metal could look so... soft."

The compliment caught her off-guard. Her immediate reaction was to probe for falsehood. But she could see none in the way he delicately traced the star-like shapes the intersecting diamonds of raised metal made. That sent her mentally pinwheeling in the opposite direction. If this Dragon thought he could win her over with a more delicate approach to her world and people, he was certainly wrong. Ari sat heavily on the sofa, stretching her legs as long as they could go in the narrow compartment.

"Look, Flor, he admits the whole of Loom shouldn't be burnt to the ground." Arianna closed her eyes, satisfied at having the last word.

"I don't think he ever said he thought it should be."

Arianna cracked one eye open. Florence had the audacity to grin at her. *Traitor.*

Cvareh lowered his hood, his blood orange hair spilling around his head like a halo in all directions. In about thirty seconds he went from being a narrowly passable Fenthri to looking entirely Dragon. It soured Arianna's stomach with the sobering reminder of why they were on the train.

"Don't take too much off," she cautioned him. "Never know when a stray conductor could decide to poke a head in."

"That happens?"

"Sure, looking for stowaways or people who have overshot their tickets." Florence gave Arianna a pointed look at the end of the statement, which Arianna held knowingly. It was their second time traveling by train together. The first time, they had been those stowaways in hiding from the conductors and train workers.

Yet another reason for Ari to be silently glad they'd had the money in cash to buy the tickets—she had the opportunity to take the girl on a train properly.

With a sharp whistle and some calls from the platform, the train ground to life. Florence pressed herself up to the window, pulling back the curtains just enough to peer out. Arianna watched the hazy lights illuminate the fabric in increasing frequency until they zoomed by in a race to meet the impending blackness that awaited them at the city's edge.

Arianna stood. The gentle sway of the train was making her tired, and she wasn't ready to be lulled to sleep just yet. She wouldn't feel comfortable until more space was placed between them and Dortam. They'd never found out what happened with the Dragon Riders. They'd overheard whispers and hushed conversations on their way to the station, but no one spoke too loudly and no one knew if the Riders had truly left Dortam to return to Nova, or just left the area. The further they got from the city without incident, the more relaxed she'd let herself feel.

"I'm going to go to the dining car. It's late, but they may still be serving something since the train didn't get moving until just now. Flor, do you have a preference?" Arianna made it a point not to ask Cvareh.

"No, anything is fine." She was entranced by the outside world blurring by as the train steadily gained speed. "Actually, should I go?"

Arianna's mask was halfway on when her student recalled the illusion they were working to uphold. She considered this, weighing the options. "We can both go."

"Why are you unmarked?" Cvareh's attention hadn't wavered from the cheek she had just covered with her mask.

"Because I was in the guilds before *your kind*." Her skin prickled at the retort—at the memory of the time before the Dragons.

"Florence said you're a Rivet." Arianna glared at her student for imparting such information to the Dragon. He continued, "Why not just get the mark? Then you wouldn't have to hide your face. Wouldn't it be easier?"

"Because I do not want the mark." There would be no way a Dragon could ever understand. It was like asking a Revolver to fix an engine, or a Harvester to use just enough medicine to save rather than kill. Even if she believed he wanted to understand—which Arianna *didn't* believe—he still couldn't.

"But you wear it anyway."

The iron of her pin was cool under her fingertips. "I can remove this." The man was infuriating, and she wasn't going to defend herself to him. "Tattoos should be choices, not brands."

Cvareh was silenced and seemed to heed to her words. The tattoos Arianna did bear burned underneath her clothing. They reaffirmed her position.

"Now, we are going to find food. Stay here, and don't get into trouble. If you do I'll—"

"I know, you'll cut me. Or kill me. Or have me kill myself." He flopped into the corner by the window and pulled back the curtain a sliver, just enough to watch the gray world slip further into darkness.

Arianna concealed a smirk under her mask. He was fun to toy with, more fun than she'd had in a long time. Sure, her jobs kept her satisfied enough knowing she was bringing a measure of harm to the Dragons' system. But seeing an actual Dragon caused any measure of pain by her actions? It was an unparalleled joy.

"Are we going to make it to Keel in one piece?" Florence asked as the door closed behind her.

"That's mostly up to him." Arianna lowered her voice as they walked through the corridor. It was dim now that they no longer had the light from Old Dortam's platform. Small sconces filled with bioluminescent bacteria in water rocked with the sway of the train, bathing the passage in a dim glow.

"Why did you take the boon?" Florence was still mastering the skill of intimidation. Her penetrating stare was nothing more than a harmless reflection of Ari's own insistent looks.

"Because I want the wish." She rewarded her apprentice's efforts with a real response. The easy way out would've been to hide behind her hate for the Dragons. But Ari would give Florence more than that. She'd earned it with her boldness, and with the risk she was willing to take.

"*Why* though?"

Ari had carefully built her walls over the years. She'd made them thick and tall around her most guarded truths, and were constructed along the lines she'd drawn when she'd first met Flor. The lines kept the other woman just far enough away that Arianna could sleep at night with some small assurance that her student would be safe, from even her. They were the same lines that showed Arianna where the edge to oblivion was. It was the only thing that kept her plunging into the madness revenge begot.

These walls, her guards, were oddly shaped, however, and they let Florence see a picture that Arianna knew didn't quite make sense. Ari had told Florence of her hatred for the Dragons and everything that the wretched creatures wrought. Flor was smart enough to also know that Ari was a woman on a mission. She'd likely figured that much out from their first meeting.

Not a single day had gone by in the two years she'd been around Florence that Arianna wasn't silently haunted by the ghost of her failed mission. The banner had fallen upon her shoulders, weighted by guilt amid the winds of change that swept across Loom. It was the only thing that still truly mattered in her world—or would have been, if she hadn't met Flor. It was an unfinished portrait that would now be the masterpiece of her revenge. And it was missing one brush stroke—a stroke a Dragon could give.

They had stopped walking and by the way Florence was staring at her, it had been Arianna who had halted their forward progress. Arianna reached out and laced her fingers with the girl's. She looked at her apprentice in the way she reserved to signal the imminent announcement of the final word on a matter.

"I need this boon, Flor, because there is something he can give me. I will never be free until I finish what I made myself for. And, as much as I abhor the fact, it's something he can provide."

CVAREH

The train had become a moving tomb, the compartment his coffin. Cvareh had never had much of an opinion on the mechanical boxes that whizzed around Loom like hornets on unknown missions, but he was quickly finding one. He was about to go mad—or maybe he already had. For on the third morning, he found himself debating the fact with his favorite diamond shape in the corner of the ceiling.

There had been no magic whatsoever on the trip. That was a strong and fast rule from the great and always correct Arianna. Sarcasm and eye rolling aside, Cvareh didn't actually disagree with the mandate. They seemed to have managed to give the Riders the slip by some miracle, and using any magic would only increase their chances of discovery.

He glanced over at the woman known as the White Wraith and wondered if the magic he'd imbibed from her helped mask his own. Or perhaps she had treated the inside of that bunker with some unknown substance and the Riders lost the trail. Cvareh was learning that his traveling companion had a knack for being two steps ahead and one calculation over-planned.

She also had a knack for being more annoying than a no-title upstart determined to gain rank through a back-alley duel. There wasn't a thing Cvareh could say that wasn't countered in some way. Honest questions were responded to with bitter retorts. It had him seriously wondering if he had somehow hurt this woman in a past life.

He rested his temple back on the wood by the window. He hadn't changed his clothes in days—days! And he hadn't left the room for more than the call of nature, and even that was with an escort. He felt like a prisoner on the run. Which, when he considered it, was almost exactly what he was. Though if he was caught, he'd be killed on sight rather than imprisoned.

The world outside the window had changed dramatically. Dortam was land-locked, nestled in a valley in the center of mountains. For a day and a half, they'd wound around narrow tracks high above sheer cliff faces. Overnight, however, the land had flattened and the train picked up speed as it shot out of tall hills and toward the flattening coast.

They passed towns and small villages that crept up out of nowhere and went running away toward the horizon as soon as the train passed. One or two times, they stopped at a small platform and a few people got off—fewer got on. But everything went as smoothly as butter gliding across a hot pan.

In his moments of frustration, Cvareh bemoaned Ari's existence. But the farther he got from Dortam, the more he realized his spur of the moment decision to ask her to take him to the Alchemists was a wise one. He knew nothing of this world or its people. He didn't know why the thin grasses grew so feebly, a pale yellow gray color rather than the vibrant viridescent to which he was accustomed. He didn't know why men and women buttoned and bundled themselves like swaddled babes, barely showing any skin—often times not even their hands.

He couldn't tell the highborn from the low. And it was difficult to discern who had wealth and power from those who didn't. Everything looked much the same as everything else. Ornamentation on rooftops and windows was fine, but not outdone. Nothing stood out, nothing fell apart. New Dortam had been a world away from Nova, and even that was more similar to the cities he was accustomed to than these rural towns.

It was small wonder the Dragon King demanded all Fenthri be marked with their guild rank. Without it, there would be no way to tell them all apart or make sense of their backwards society. He kept such thoughts to himself, of course, as they were certain to upset his present company.

"Four hours to Ter.5.2," a conductor called from the thin hall outside their cabin. "Four hours to terminal."

Arianna stood and reached above them for one of the bags. She stacked paper money in perpendicular bundles, counting to herself. Cvareh watched her hands as they flipped through the bills, sequestering out batches before repeating the process. Her fingers didn't joint exactly the same as his. Cvareh flexed his fingers, unsheathing his claws momentarily.

"What happens if it rips?" He should have known better than to ask the question by now, but silence and boredom had him in their hold.

"Then the bill is void," Arianna answered as though the fact was obvious.

"So why make the money paper?" It seemed ill advised.

"What else would it be made of?"

"Metal?" *Like on Nova.*

Arianna paused her counting and looked at him like he was stupid. Cvareh was many things, but he was not stupid and the look made him bristle. "We have more important things to use our metals for than money."

He stared as she returned to counting, wondering if he had actually said the comparison to Nova rather than thought it.

"Flor, we'll barely have enough to buy passage on the airship, I think." Arianna went back to ignoring Cvareh.

"*Barely.*" Florence picked up on the key word in Ari's statement.

"I may need to do some work while we're waiting to get on." Arianna began laying out the belt and harness he had only seen her remove yesterday.

Cvareh had taken it as a good sign when the woman felt comfortable enough with him being in her presence to remove her weaponry. Though it could've just begun to chafe. He shifted to scratch an itch. Gods knew he had reached that point as well.

"Not as the White Wraith, I take it?"

"No," Arianna affirmed. "I don't want people to know I've left Dortam. Plus, I won't have time for a job of that scale."

"People will find out you've left Dortam if you do *any* work." Florence leaned back into the sofa with a small grin. "Subtlety isn't your strong suit."

Arianna glared in the girl's direction. But unlike the ones she regularly cast Cvareh's way, this look was light and playful. He'd begun to wonder as the nights slipped on what the real relationship between the two women was. They shared the narrow sofa while he took the upper bunk at night. Florence was too old to be Arianna's daughter. Sisters, perhaps?

"I'm going to heed my needs before I get all strapped in," Arianna announced, donning her mask and slipping out the room—careful to not let the door open wide enough that Cvareh would be visible.

"What will she do?" Cvareh asked. Florence looked at him, confused. He'd found a friend in the girl—that was undeniable. She listened to his questions and did her best to answer them. As a result, Cvareh picking her brain had become a quickly adopted ritual whenever Arianna left the room. "For work."

Florence made a noise of comprehension. "If we're lucky, just some pick-pocketing. But I don't think Ari has limited her skills to just that in ages, if ever. I'm sure there will be whispers of the White Wraith expanding her hunting grounds before we board for Keel."

Cvareh waited a long moment for Florence to expand in more detail, but she didn't. For once, he decided against probing further on the topic. There was a worried cloud hanging over the girl's head as she engaged in a staring battle with the tools of Arianna's trade. It was as though she silently accused them for the habits of their master. While Cvareh found the woman abrasive, rude, and hideous, Florence saw beauty. He wondered where he'd have to stand to make sense of the White Wraith the way the young Fenthri did.

"You two are close." His observation wasn't a question, so Florence didn't answer more than nod. "How did you two meet?"

"I was running." Florence didn't pull her eyes away from where they had fallen on Arianna's gear, but she was no longer seeing anything in the small compartment. "There was a group of us...we all decided we would leave the Ravens together. We would strike out for freedom. But we were caught. Most were killed, some imprisoned." The girl's knuckles turned white from where they gripped the seat. Cvareh could hear her heartbeat quickening, the tension in her breath. She was nervous saying just that much. "I happened along Ari on the way and I begged her to take me with her. She agreed."

Florence pulled herself from her thoughts and looked at him with a forcefully brave smile. The crawling unease he felt at the sight of flat Fenthri teeth was beginning to subside. He stared at Florence's rounded cheeks and delicate nose, her small ears and dark gray skin. She wasn't pretty by any stretch of Dragon logic. But a little kindness was helping him no longer find her repulsive.

"I guess she has a habit of helping people who need to get places."

Cvareh snorted at the girl and flopped back into his prior spot, knowing the woman in question would return shortly. "She's helping me because she wants her boon."

Ari returned before another word could be said on the matter. Cvareh watched her work as she began to don her harness once more. He was beginning to have more questions than answers when it came to his boon holder. And, while Cvareh usually found unknowns challenging and thrilling, he looked at Arianna and only saw danger. Judging by the woman's glares, she didn't want him looking at her at all.

Ter.5.2 had surprising splendor despite its uninspired moniker. Trains created a patchwork of raised rails across the condensed city. Smaller city tracks bumbled along, weaving in and out with open-style boxes filled to the brim with people. Busy streets hummed below them, their occupants unconcerned with the new travelers the vessel was going to impart upon them.

Women wore corsets, tight around their torsos, which accentuated billowing blouses. Fitted jackets adorned with intricate embroidery and rope embellishments matched plumed hats and wide skirts. Overall, it was a sea of muted colors and industrial practicality. But Cvareh caught glimpses of brightness here and there. A crimson feather, a sky-blue lapel, a bright mint under-sleeve ruffle. Against the demure palette, these snatches of color seemed to shine like jewels in a mine.

"You should begin wrapping up," Florence reminded him.

Under the weight of Arianna's disapproving stare, Cvareh obliged.

The train steadily lost speed and the station engulfed them. Metal ribs stretched glass between them, supported by stone columns on each platform. Men and women bustled along the stretches of concrete between trains, heading to and from their destinations.

Cvareh stared in wonder. It felt like the apex of a world he had never so much as considered in all his years of life above the clouds. Six trains were lined up, two more platforms vacant. Conductors shouted and soot-covered workers hastily moved all the necessities required to maintain and fuel the metallic creatures. These were the vessels carrying the lifeblood of the Fenthri to and fro.

"Stay with us." A hand closed around his forearm.

Cvareh followed the gray fingers up to Arianna's covered face, cast in a plum shade as a result of the goggles he wore.

"And keep your head down," she commanded.

He obliged, letting her lead him in tow. Cvareh swallowed his pride, reminding himself that this was not the time to worry about his rank and dominance compared to hers. There weren't any Dragons to witness him deferring to a Fenthri, at least.

Or so he thought.

"Bloody cogs," Arianna hissed. "Florence, stop."

Cvareh looked ahead, where the crowd thinned enough between them and the station's exit to see what gave Arianna such cause for concern. Four Riders lined up along the exit. Each of them had a long strand of hair falling over their ears, every bead signifying a victory in a duel for their position. The shortest was ten beads long, which was nine beads more than Cvareh could boast had he decided to become a Rider at that moment.

They were all shades of red—elite of House Rok, he had no doubt. He snarled instinctively under the tightly bound mask over his face. It was nepotism at its finest and a statement of where House Rok stood. *No half measures*, they said; Dragons were either for the House or against it. Those against didn't last long.

"Get yourself under control." Arianna tightened her grip on his forearm, startling him back to reality.

Cvareh relaxed his face and his magic with it. He would give them away with his hatred for the Dragon King's House and it would no doubt play into Yveun Dono's ploy with sending all his own.

"Florence!" Arianna had taken her eyes off the girl only for a moment, but it was too late. Florence had approached the customs line with them a few steps behind.

"Tickets," one of the Riders demanded of her. Florence produced them—Cvareh watched as they quivered in her outstretched hand before the Rider snatched them away. "From Dortam? Your traveling companions?"

"Are here." Florence motioned to Cvareh and Arianna. "Though, I wouldn't get too close. They have the onset of Necrotizing Fasciitis. I wouldn't want you to catch it."

"Do they?" The Rider seemed unconvinced. Cvareh's heart pounded. "Where are you headed?"

"To Keel."

"Home of the Alchemists?" The Rider's scowl deepened. He seemed to look only at Cvareh.

Other travelers continued to go through the line of Riders without problem, a couple questions and they were off. The rider before them was suspicious. Cvareh could practically smell it on him.

"If anyone can help the condition, it will be an Alchemist." Florence took a step forward and the Rider blocked her path.

"You smell like Dragon blood." He looked straight over Florence at Cvareh.

"Likely my fault." Arianna lifted her goggles without missing a beat, showing her magenta eyes.

"Chimera." The Rider spat. "Filthy thief."

The Rider had no idea how right he was. Chimeras had a poor reputation on Nova, especially since half of them got the required organs through illicit trade. Trade that Arianna engaged in and clearly took pride in, as her smile was nearly visible from under her mask.

"Get out of my sight." The rider waved them on in disgust and Florence took an eager step away.

One of the other Riders called over to the man who had been interrogating them, asking what the holdup had been. The words were likely lost on his companions, but Cvareh understood the Royuk clearly.

"Invalids and Chimera," the Rider answered. "That's what reeks of foul blood."

"How can you be sure it isn't Cvareh, then?" the other Rider jested back in Royuk.

Cvareh ground his teeth together at the use of his name without any titles. He could learn to live with the slight from

Arianna, who hated everything, and Florence, who meant well but didn't know anything. But these were Dragons. This was intentional. *It was personal.*

"Inept and dirty blooded, sounds like House Xin all right." The first Rider roared with laughter.

Cvareh twisted and Arianna grabbed for him. But he was too far gone mentally and physically. No one would slight his House like that to his face, not while he drew breath.

The satisfaction of ripping out the Rider's throat was deep and true, but short-lived. Golden blood poured between Cvareh's fingers, his magic preventing the rider from healing. The heart would die shortly, from lack of air and blood-loss, but by then the other three Riders would have Cvareh on the ground and vivisected.

He could see Petra's face, he could hear her words scolding him as though she already knew what he'd done and was magically whispering across worlds to him. His pride had blinded him and he'd lost sight of the long game. In defending House Xin's honor now, he'd thrown away the possibility for his family's glorious future.

A dull *thunk* reverberated up through the Rider's body and into Cvareh's hand as a dagger plunged into the man's heart. Cvareh felt Ari's magic pulse through the Rider; the dagger twisted, pulverizing the heart before it retracted into her waiting palm. It was the first time he had ever been relieved to see one of those blades.

"You idiot," Arianna muttered, before she started on one of the other Riders.

ARIANNA

D ragons could not be trusted.

She'd known this much to be true all her life. When the first Fenthri broke through the clouds of Loom and uncovered the Dragon homeland, it began a chain of events that proved Dragons were opportunists and liars. From the Dragon King promising equality between Loom and Nova, then enslaving her people, to the Guilds being overthrown and turned into a mockery of their former glory, to what happened the last time a resistance stood against them. At every opportunity, Dragons acted in their own self-interest, pursuing their own goals at the expense of others.

Dragons could not be trusted.

Arianna's magic pulsed through her fingertips as she commanded the dagger at the end of her line like a barbed whip. It cut through the air with a sharp whizzing sound that rang louder and more true to her ears than the cries of the other Fenthri at the fight that had broken out among them. She managed it like a cat and a tail. It was part of her, but moved seemingly with its own mind.

Her other dagger in hand, she launched at one of the remaining three Riders. Three Riders, and two of them—Florence wouldn't be much help. Arianna loved numbers, but she hated those odds.

Cvareh moved for the third Rider. His claws flashed in the sunlight that flowed unfiltered through the glass ceiling above. Her ears picked up the sound as they locked against the Rider's, bone grating on bone.

They had been through the line when he attacked. It made absolutely no sense. They were free and clear and there had been no reason for it. He had willingly endangered them all for nothing. If they made it out of this scrap alive he would have some serious explaining to do—assuming Arianna didn't just get on the next train back to Dortam and leave him to fend for himself.

That was an appealing thought, the idea of taking Florence and running from the fight. But Arianna didn't give it too much heed. There was no time to think that plan through and besides, she was already committed to the struggle. At the very least, she'd get to slay some Dragons, and it was always a good day when that happened.

The Rider before Arianna spun, kicking through the air. He moved with deft precision and a speed that spoke of no movement wasted. Arianna turned and ducked, the kick passing over her head. With an outstretched leg she tried to hook the heel that still supported the majority of the Dragon's weight.

The Rider hopped, shifting weight to the foot he was previously kicking with and—in one motion—bringing up his other foot into Arianna's face. Her nose sounded like celery snapping; Arianna thanked every stroke of luck she'd ever had for the thick cotton covering her face, hiding the blood that no doubt exploded from it. She tumbled back, twisting the dagger in her hand to a saber grip, then lunged forward again, targeting the Dragon's chest.

A swipe of her dagger, a parry from the Dragon's claws or a twist for Arianna's blade to hit a shoulder, a forearm, a hand. The Rider took all forms of punishment in order to protect his heart—the one organ whose destruction would prove a fatal injury. The Rider caught one of the jabs of her blade and with a swift motion, snapped Arianna's wrist with ease.

Arianna cried out and retreated. She switched the dagger from one hand to the other, giving the bones in her right wrist time to knit. The Dragon didn't want to relinquish the hard-earned upper hand and continued to strike. A blow to the chest knocked the wind from Arianna, almost rendering her twist to avoid the talons closing in for her throat useless.

The hits racked up. Arianna struggled to avoid any significant blows. Punches she could take, but there were too many people around to take a hit that broke skin. As loath as she was to admit it, Arianna was outclassed. Her eyes wildly scanned the room, looking for alternative solutions, trying to formulate a plan.

A familiar explosion burst out from behind her shoulder. It was the worst thing she had ever felt. It meant Florence had joined the fight.

With a cry of rage, she ducked under the Rider's open palmed jab. A claw caught on her shoulder, tearing through the white fabric and nicking Arianna's skin. The Rider's eyes widened, looking at the superficial wound that was already quickly healing itself. Arianna took the distraction as an opportunity and plunged her dagger into his heart.

Two rose colored hands closed around hers and the Dragon's stormy blue eyes stared into Arianna's goggles. They were open, unfiltered. The moment before death could only beget clarity.

"What *are* you?" the Rider rasped.

"The White Wraith." Arianna twisted her dagger and felt the last of the Dragon's heartbeat fade against the blade.

She pivoted. Her golden line wrapped itself around the neck of the Dragon approaching Florence in a rage, no doubt from the shot she'd just landed and which his skin was still knitting to repair. Arianna pulled her hands back, yanking on the line. Her magic did the majority of the work, but the physical movement was instinctual, like a mother wolf defending its pup. She wanted to feel the tension in the line, the closing of the loop around the Dragon's neck.

The refined steel cabling was nearly unbreakable, and though the Rider clawed at his skin, seeking purchase on the slowly tightening tether, it was futile. She felt his magic pulse against the line; it shuddered, the tempered gold refusing his command. Arianna pushed her magic a little further, dredging it up from her toes and drawing it out through her hands. The loop closed, decapitating the Rider cleanly.

With a flick of her wrist, the dagger at the end of her cable twisted and reared back, stabbing into the Dragon's heart for good measure. Severing the head from the body was good enough to merit a kill, but anyone who attacked Florence earned death twice over.

Florence missed no opportunity. Arianna wanted to be proud, but the girl was worrying her half to death with this sudden bout of recklessness. It reminded Arianna of herself in the worst of ways. Flor popped open the hinge of her revolver and decided on a new canister with expert ease. She was a Rivet through and through, no matter what was tattooed on her cheek.

Arianna had found the best teachers for her, and it showed. Despite having never been in a fight, Florence moved with the precision of a trained Revo. She kept only one revolver chamber loaded at all times so she could hand select each canister based on the changing needs of the conflict.

Tracking the muzzle of the gun over the Rider that was still engaged with Cvareh, Florence planted her feet and pulled the trigger. It was a smaller version of the canister she'd given Arianna on her mission at the refinery—small enough that it required no extra magic besides what Arianna had stored in the gun with a flare of Alchemical runes. A beam of pure magic shot straight and true, punching a hole through the shoulder of the Rider that loomed over a bloody Cvareh.

She stumbled, dazed. Arianna knew that look: glazed, dull eyes sent reeling from a sudden surge of foreign magic. She'd inflicted it on enough people to know it well and had seen it in Cvareh's eyes when he'd imbibed from her.

This was their chance.

Arianna sprinted over to Cvareh, pulled him off the floor and wrapped his arm around her shoulders. The man was built like a bag of bricks and even Arianna's muscular legs strained against gravity, pulling him to his feet. If she could run against the slowing of time, she could run and support him—or so she told herself repeatedly. With a magical command, her line retracted, the gears in her winch box whirring.

"Time to go!" she called to Florence.

Her apprentice nodded. With a jerk of her hand, she snapped her revolver closed, another canister loaded in the chamber. Florence looked at the Rider, nearly recovered from her last shot.

"Filthy Fen," she sneered.

Florence lowered her gun slightly, her aim changing from the Rider's heart to her feet. Arianna gave an approving nod and

Florence pulled the trigger. They had no canisters on them that could sufficiently destroy a Dragon's heart. Their chest cavities were practically made of diamond. And even if they did, it would need to be Arianna shooting it in order to give the canister enough magic to be lethal.

The explosion was small by Florence's standards. Enough to stun, but not enough to hinder. Its real purpose was obvious as the reaction of the chemicals plumed thick purple smoke into the room. Remaining Fenthri coughed, trying to blink through the smog. Florence pulled up the goggles that sat around her neck and settled a mask around her nose and mouth.

Arianna gave her an appreciative once-over as they sprinted out into the sun. Florence panted softly, but returned the gesture in kind. The girl was brilliant for thinking of practical, multi-functional disguises. Flor's planning and foresight had bought the three a few precious seconds. Now, it was up to Arianna to figure out how not to waste them.

FLORENCE

I t felt like the side of her face had been pistol-whipped.
Florence's cheek had swollen to twice its size, pressing her
eye half-shut uncomfortably. It was true what they said
about Dragons, that their bones were twice as dense as the
average Fenthri's. No wonder the lone resistance on Loom had
been squelched effectively the moment it had sprung up. The
Dragons were superior in nearly every way.

Her eyes drifted over to Cvareh. The Dragon stumbled
along with Arianna's help. If the Rider had messed him up that
badly, Florence couldn't even fathom how strong she'd really
been. The Dragon hadn't even fallen after being shot through
with a magic canister.

"Where are we headed?" Florence dared ask the
question. Arianna had that faraway look that always overcame
her when she was thinking.

Arianna snapped back to reality. "The port."

"There's no way we can board an airship now. If they
had a customs line in the train terminal, they'll certainly have
one on any airships—especially those headed for Keel."

"We'll see when we get there. I'm just hoping to use all
the people to mask our trail." Arianna glanced at Cvareh. His

wounds had nearly healed, but it was taking a magical toll on him and he bumbled along, exhausted. He looked like Ari did after a particularly rough mission. Healing might be in Dragon blood, but it certainly wasn't without cost. "Flor, you did well."

The statement came like a rogue beam of sunlight breaking through the clouds. Florence had never seen such a thing happen, of course, but she'd heard it was possible and if it did happen, she imagined the encouraging smile Arianna was giving her would feel the same. She'd been terrified. Rushing in headfirst with reckless abandon was more Arianna's mode of operation. But she'd take the praise in duplicates if Arianna was the one giving it.

Arianna stopped suddenly, pulling into a sidewall. Florence didn't question and followed suit. They crouched next to a rubbish bin that reeked of spoiled fish and sour milk. Florence was grateful that Dragons didn't seek out blood trails entirely with their noses; otherwise they might have had to bathe in such a foul concoction.

The cause for Arianna's wariness became clear as the unique cry of a Dragon's glider echoed across the clouds. Both women turned their eyes skyward, seeking out the ominous rainbow trail—but neither saw it. With a dull thud, like a metal spoon hitting the bottom of a pot filled with water, the Dragon crossed through the clouds that separated Nova from Loom.

"I've never seen a Rider retreat before." Cvareh frowned, massaging his shoulder. It had hung at an odd angle previously, but was now almost right again.

"Maybe it's a good sign?" Florence was hopeful.

"Never." The Dragon squelched her optimism on the spot. "She's going back for reinforcements. She has our scent now."

"Dragon—" Arianna started tensely.

"Am I back to Dragon now? I thought I had been upgraded to 'Cvareh' on the train."

If Florence had been in his odd, supposedly fashionable shoes, she wouldn't have been trying Arianna's patience at that exact moment.

"If I call you mongrel you'll answer, after that stunt you pulled," Arianna snarled.

Florence expected Cvareh to rise in kind, as he usually did. But the man tilted his head back, exposing his neck and chest. Florence was oddly reminded of a dog exposing its stomach to the leader of the pack.

"You're right. It was stupid of me."

Arianna clearly didn't know how to handle this sudden subservience, and Cvareh's out-of-character actions seemed to annoy her all the more. Florence leaned against the rubbish bin, too tired to care about the smell and already getting used to it. Ari grabbed the Dragon's face, pulling it toward hers.

"Can Dragons track blood or magic across water? How well?"

Cvareh considered this for a long moment. "We don't have large bodies of water on Nova like on Loom—and nothing salty. If we could scrub the trail of our scent before getting on the water and kept the magic to a minimum, it could cover the smell enough—better than the open air would."

"Do you think you can keep the magic 'to a minimum'?"

"Yes." Annoyance at Arianna's tone and manhandling was beginning to creep into Cvareh's words. Florence shifted, preparing to put herself between them like she had back in the bunker.

"You're sure? No more running off and attacking Riders for no good reason?"

Cvareh finally jerked his head from her grasp. He swatted her hand away with a glare and the two locked eyes. They were like counter-weights on either side of the scale. Different, but painfully similar—more so than they wanted to admit.

Florence could see them from a step away, and that step was a half a world of perspective. He was the sugared art on a cake and Ari was the plate and utensils. They saw an enemy in each other, mortal opposites, form versus function. Florence saw two things that were undeniably different, but surprisingly complementary.

"If you knew what they'd said you wouldn't—"

Ari rattled off a string of guttural sounds that echoed up from the back of her throat. Florence knew that Ari could understand Royuk, but she'd never actually heard her teacher speak it. The sounds were perfect, nearly identical to the accents the Riders used.

It was perhaps too similar; Cvareh's talons were unsheathed in a second. He lunged for her and Ari released him to grasp for her dagger. The sharp points of each of their weapons pressed into the other's throat, their noses almost touching.

"I don't give a damn about your House," Arianna growled. "When you are traveling with me you put it aside, and you do as I command."

"You ground-born, soot colored *Fen*," Cvareh snarled in kind, his lips curling back to expose his elongated canines.

Florence placed a hand on both their shoulders, trying to ease tensions. She had worked so hard to make her hands conjure explosions that it was odd to use them to diffuse. "Both of you, stop. What's done is done. This isn't helping." Eventually, Florence had no doubt that appealing to their mutual sense of reason would fail. But for now it seemed she had yet to reach that point. "Ari, you are clearly working on a new plan."

"I am." The taller woman stood. Florence noticed a small slash in her coat, but miraculously, no black blood stained the white. Now that Florence thought about it, she'd never seen Arianna bleeding at all... But perhaps that was a given since the woman healed as fast as a Dragon. Arianna distracted Florence from her thoughts as she continued, "But you're not going to like it."

"Why?" Creeping dread crawled up Florence's spine at Arianna's tone. If the woman said Florence wouldn't like it then Florence had no doubt whatever it was, she'd absolutely hate it.

"I'll tell you when I decide it must be done." Arianna glared back at Cvareh, still heaping mountains of blame on his shoulders for what had happened with just her eyes.

Florence looked hopelessly at the Dragon and stood as well. He was clearly no more pleased with himself than Ari was. Dragon or Fenthri, the look of guilt seemed to be the same. Still, he pulled himself to his feet with them and stood on his own. He didn't do the one thing Arianna would find even more intolerable: give up.

Ter.5.2 was the primary port for the Revolvers' territory. It served both air and sea, a relatively short distance from the land terminal the three of them had entered in on. High above, at the tops of skeleton frameworks and spiraling iron staircases, were the airship platforms.

Large cruising vessels boasted over-sized balloons strapped atop tiny but luxurious passenger cars. Men and women dressed in bright jewel tones that matched the few Dragons they walked alongside. There were smaller, more practical airships parked alongside the opulent dirigibles. They had wings shaped like fish, finned rudders and arcing bodies. Gold glinted on them, magic enabling journeys by air.

The Dragons had brought the sky to Loom.

Below were seafaring vessels. Giant freight cruisers stacked with crates fought against their roped tethers. Ore overflowed from cartons as men and women bearing Rivet tattoos argued with those bearing symbols of the Revolvers. Once in a while, Florence caught sight of a circled master, but the majority were journeymen with filled marks.

But the most common mark was what set Florence's blood to churning beneath her granite colored skin. *Ravens*. For every one Dragon there were three Fenthri in the port, and for every one Fenthri with any other mark there were three Ravens. Florence blended in perfectly; no one looked at her mark twice, and no one questioned the trio. She looked like she belonged. And that was the worst part of it all.

"Flor," Arianna spoke gently but Florence still spooked, pulled from her thoughts. "In here."

Arianna had quite the taste in lodging. The bar stunk of stale vomit and sea scum. There wasn't a single patron and Florence had no doubt it had as much to do with the overall atmosphere as it did the fact that they had just opened.

"You have rooms?" Arianna asked the barman.

"For a price." The man targeted his eyes right on Florence's mark. "Traveling?"

"I'm their escort." She felt as awkward as she sounded trying to play the part.

"Right." The man believed her as much as if she had said she was a Dragon. "Forty dunca, one room, eight hours starting now?"

"Why eight?" Florence couldn't help herself.

"I'm not used to people wanting to stay around for all that long." The man grinned. Half his teeth had rotted out.

"Eight will be plenty." Arianna fished trough her bag. Thankfully, the satchel was designed for being turned up-side-down in all of Arianna's various scuffles and the dunca hadn't been lost in the station. "Eighty dunca."

"Two rooms, or sixteen hours?" the man asked, running the bills through his fingers.

"One room, eight hours, and forty dunca for you to forget we were ever here," Arianna clarified.

"Mum's the word." The man snickered and waved them toward a back hall.

Arianna picked a room, seemingly at random from the doors that were slightly ajar. She locked it behind them with a begrudging pause. Florence knew her teacher was mentally taking apart the lock several times over, scowling at its simplicity.

"You know he'll sell us out to the highest bidder." Cvareh pulled off his goggles as if he needed unhindered sight to stare disapprovingly at the room.

"I know." Arianna leaned against the door like a guard, leaving Florence to take the small stool. None of them was brave enough to try the palette intended to be a bed. The floor was likely cleaner. "But it'll spare him from running his mouth at the very first opportunity that there was a Dragon traveling with two Fenthri staying in his back room."

"How would he know I was—"

Arianna stopped Cvarch by pointing to his hands. The bandages had ripped off when he'd used his talons in the fight. At best he could pass for gray, but there was no denying the shape of his nails, even retracted.

The Dragon spat a word in the heavy tones of Royuk. "So what do we do now?" He sighed heavily and slid along the wall to the floor.

"We wait for nightfall and stow away in one of the cargo ships."

"Cargo ship for where?" Florence still remembered Arianna's promise that she wouldn't like her plan. For emphasis, the woman's stare was openly apologetic. It only made Florence more worried.

"Why a *ship*? Wouldn't an airship be faster?" Cvareh asked.

"It would." Arianna ignored Florence's question completely. "But that's also what they expect—us to take the most direct route."

"They're going to be canvassing everywhere we go, every major city, every major transportation line," Cvareh said. "Even if they weren't, there's the matter of their ability to track my magic."

"And I'm still very curious as to the exact *why* surrounding their motives in tracking you down." Arianna gave Cvareh a penetrating stare. The Dragon set his chin and met it. He was the only person Florence had ever seen challenge Arianna. Then again, Florence didn't exactly see Arianna with very many people.

"I've told you all you need to know."

"Yes, yes, that you're working to overthrow the Dragon King." Arianna snorted, showing how much she believed that particular bit of information.

Florence wasn't as convinced of Cvareh's lie. The Dragon was certainly going to great risk to get to the Alchemists. It was the guild that stood the furthest from being under Dragon control, hiding behind their insistence on secrecy for their experiments. It had been the home of Loom's original resistance.

But even the Council of Five—those foolish few who had attempted to fan spark to flame and free Loom from under the Dragon King in those early days—had perished to the might of the Dragons. The Fenthri stood no chance, outclassed as they were in strength and magic. Florence had grown up hearing the tales of the Council of Five, but as a child's cautionary tale against being too bold. The Council was not spoken of lightly, and never with praise.

"But I don't disagree with you, Dragon." Arianna sighed, continuing, "The Riders will be canvassing every major hub, and an airship is very noticeable if it is not traveling between those hubs. Not to mention your scent is notable."

"So then how will we move?"

"We'll take the Underground." Arianna turned to Florence, and it was suddenly clear.

"No," Florence breathed. "I won't go back there again."

"Flor—"

"You promised me!"

"Then stay here." The words were said gently, but they hurt more than Arianna intended.

Florence fidgeted on the stool, shifting her feet, trying to catch her breath and her balance at the same time. *Tunnels*, endless tunnels that turned the underbelly of Ter.4 into a rat maze. It was known as "the Ravens' playground" by bold new initiates, and "the Ravens' folly" by the far more sensible masters.

When she had escaped those tunnels, she vowed to never enter them again. She had gone in one of ten and come out one of three. The unending blackness had taken its toll on them. They had paid their dues for her freedom many times over.

"I can't lead you through them." Florence shook her head violently. "I wasn't leading last time and I don't remember."

"I know, Flor, I know." Arianna's hands smoothed over Florence's shoulders. The motion did little to soothe her racing heart or calm her nerves. "But we must use them. They're the only straight shot from Ter.4.2 to Ter.4.3 that assures no chance of anyone sensing Cvareh's magic or picking up his scent. From there we can cross to Ter.0."

She wants to cross the wasteland. Florence shook her head. It was clear this was a Rivet making a traveling plan, because no Raven in their right mind would suggest such a dangerous and backwards journey to Keel.

"That still doesn't solve your problem of navigation." Florence was grasping at straws, anything to make Ari reconsider.

"I'll have help." Arianna's eyes told Florence she had yet to reach the worst of it. Those wretched, expressive Dragon's eyes suddenly looked so foreign. This woman, this woman who had pulled Florence from the shadow of death, would now plunge them willingly back under that shade.

"Who?" Florence asked, though she already knew the answer.

"Your friends."

Florence's mouth dropped open. Arianna was reckless—that much Florence had always known. But never once had she thought the woman was stupid enough to break out two inmates from the floating prison of Ter.4.2.

LEONA

S unset was Leona's favorite time of day. The blinding light began to diminish, turning the sky the color of summer cherries. The world was awash in a pale red haze, sparking the accents on the Rok estate as though everything was graced by tendrils of flame.

Leona basked in the warm glow, the last fading heat before the chill of night tainted the world. Too fitting that House Xin would be done in blues that mirrored her least favorite hours. She opened her eyes, staring at the archways curving over the balcony's entrance.

House Xin. The name alone put a foul taste in her mouth. There had not been a whisper from Sybil in four days since she descended to Loom. What was taking her so long to find the boy?

Yvaun Dono grew more impatient by the hour, and Leona couldn't really blame him. She turned her head and looked into the room beyond—his drawing room. The King sat atop a raised dais. Behind him was an identical circle embellished with a gold band and even more circles ringed in gold. He looked as though he sat atop the earth, and the moons and suns rose at his back. Her King could pass for part divine.

"You seem cheerful," his voice rumbled from across the room out to the wide railing Leona had made her perch.

"Dono?" She sat straighter, draping her legs on the inside of the balcony.

"You're not one often caught smiling to herself."

Leona pressed her fingertips into her cheeks, catching the offending emotion spread across her lips. Thankfully, it was just the two of them present, and she had no secrets from her sovereign. "I was thinking that it is a lovely evening."

The King paused, looking out over the veranda where Leona sat. He considered the sunset as though he hadn't even noticed the passage of time over the past few hours. His face relaxed, just a fraction. There were only a handful of people Leona suspected would notice the subtle shift in his brow that occurred when the King transitioned from their supreme leader to just a man.

"I suppose it is a nice evening."

Leona averted her eyes, focusing on the horizon once more. Her magic flowed hot through her veins at the King's agreement; it churned in delight, sparking against his as he suddenly appeared at her side. He moved as effortlessly as the wind, as soft footed as starlight.

Her eyelids felt heavy as he ran a claw up the line of her spine. They were so close she could feel the air shifting from the movement, a hair's width from her flesh. He still withheld his touch from her. *They* were nothing. But he was her everything—and what made them dangerous was that he knew it. His breath was warm on her cheek, the only thing he let touch her skin as his face hovered over her shoulder.

She waited for him to say something more. The silence held ciphers of truths that lingered between them, written in a script that neither knew yet how to decipher. This would not be the moment they were given sound.

Yveun Dono pulled away and returned to his desk. Leona continued to stare at the horizon. Neither said anything further until night had begun to overtake the sky.

"I think it's time to dress for dinner," he announced.

Leona rose to her feet a moment after her King stood, then crossed the balcony and fell into step just behind him. They left the room and she saw him to his chambers. His manservant took over and Leona was dismissed from her post.

She started for the dining room, taking back halls to avoid any other House Rok nobility. Coletta'Ryu would be about to dress as well, and Leona's feet purposefully avoided the walkways the queen was known to haunt. It wasn't hard. Yveun Dono's sickly mate didn't wander far from her bed or gardens.

She was halfway to the dining room when she heard the crack of a glider breaking through the clouds below. Leona rushed to the window and scanned the darkening sky. There was the telltale glitter of magic fading on the wind...

A single ribbon where there should be several.

Cursing, she made her way to the landing platform. All the while, Leona was waiting for the sound of more gliders, but none came. A total of five Riders had descended to Loom and only one had returned? Something was off—and Leona, as head of the Riders, would find out.

The platform was a wide, open expanse of cement. Ironwork weaved against tall grasses and wild flowers on the perimeter. The manor opened like the mouth of a fish gasping for water and Leona was equally hungry for information.

The Rider eased their glider onto the platform. It looked lonely as the sole vessel returning, its wide, golden wings dwarfed by the potential capacity of the landing pad. Leona raised a hand to her forehead, pulling away stray bits of garnet colored hair. A familiar woman released the pulleys on the back of the glider and hopped off with an exhausted sway. Bruises from the exertion of flying the glider quickly faded from her skin.

Leona crossed over to her. The Fen slaves stayed behind, waiting to service the flying contraption. They knew their place well and wouldn't interrupt.

"Sybil." Leona dragged her thumb across her palm. Her sister copied her, cutting a golden line into her flesh. The two clasped hands, gold smearing against gold before it could dissipate on the air.

"Leona To." Her sister never forgot Leona's proper title.

"You are...alone?"

"There has been trouble."

Sybil—sweet, nervous, uncertain, aspiring Sybil. The girl nearly stuttered over her words. That was the moment Leona knew there would be no helping her from what awaited. Leona didn't have to know what 'trouble' her sister was speaking of. This was supposed to have been a straightforward mission, simple enough that even a novice should have been able to complete it.

"Say no more. It is not me you will need to answer to this night."

Sybil's face paled at her sister's severity; Leona could practically smell the fear radiating off her. She turned and started for the red room. It was the room Yveun Dono preferred for meetings he wasn't looking forward to.

The King was waiting for them, dressed in the rich velvets and heavy fabrics of his evening garb. His chest was bare from the opening in the middle of his sleeveless robes. They spilled over the edge of the chair and pooled around his feet. A wrapped belt held up wide-legged pants that swayed slightly as he shifted his feet.

"Sybil, you have returned to me." The King smiled wide, displaying his canines.

Leona stopped at the door. She couldn't help her sister now. Sybil walked to the center of the room alone. Whatever awaited her, she had brought upon her own head. There was no helping it.

"Yveun Dono." Sybil sunk to a knee. "No half measures in my love for your rule."

Leona rolled her eyes. Yveun Dono's attention shifted slightly, his mouth twitching in genuine amusement. Sybil never learned, no matter how many times Leona explained. Yveun Dono didn't have time for needless praise and pomp from his loyal lowers. There was only one thing he wanted from them: results. Everything else was just a cheap excuse that disgraced the true meaning of their House.

"Yes..." the King drawled. "Sybil, why are you alone? I sent you with Riders and then granted two more at your sister's suggestion to seek you out after you had not returned in two whole days. Now, you stand before me alone."

Leona could smell her sister's rising panic.

"Tell me, are my other Riders waiting on Loom in dramatic suspense, holding Cvarch in chains until you summon them up here?"

"Not quite, Dono...." Sybil faltered

No one spoke. The silence grated on Leona's ears. Sybil was failing test after test. She had crossed the threshold of incompetence and was now flirting with suicidal foolhardiness.

"Sybil, you were asked a question," Leona pressured.

"He landed in New Dortam, but eluded us. We found him among the scum in Old Dortam, but then he escaped—"

"How does Cvareh *Xin*, a man not known for his prowess in duels or particular cunning, escape *five* of my Riders?" Yveun Dono flexed his hands, his claws extending just barely from his fingertips.

"He has help."

"Help? From who? Only one glider was stolen from the Rok estate and no other Houses are permitted the technology."

"A Chimera," Sybil clarified. "And another Fen."

"A black-blooded monstrosity, and a Fen." Yveun Dono ran his fingertips over his lips. "You're telling me *that* is what has made fools of my Riders?"

"They killed the rest."

Leona wanted to throttle her sister. The details were obvious; saying them did nothing to help her case. But blended with her annoyance was intrigue. As impossible as Sybil's claims seemed, the fact remained that four Riders were dead. Even with incompetent leadership, that shouldn't happen.

"Where is Cvareh now?" Yveun Dono asked.

"He escaped us in the port city of… Territory 5?"

Ter.5.2, Leona thought to herself. It had taken months for her to memorize the various cities of Loom. Numbers on numbers. Ridiculous. Someone had explained the logic of it to her, but it was all dull and gray and forgettable, just like the Fen themselves.

"Cvareh Xin escaped you? A lowly Xin, a Fen, and a dirty Chimera not only evaded but killed my Riders, *twice*?"

Sybil lowered her head, and her silence was sharper than any executioner's axe. Leona shifted, blocking the room's only exit. Yveun Dono stood.

"Sybil, look at me." Magic lapped against the King's lips as he spoke. It radiated off his tongue, slithering into Sybil's ears. "Tell me, what hand do you favor the most?"

Her sister was frozen on the outside, unmoving, barely breathing. But Leona knew that inside, she was waging a futile mental war. The King's magic was strong and undeniable. His influence couldn't be ignored, not when he threw that much power behind it.

"Tell me, Sybil." The tone Yveun Dono took as he softly beseeched Sybil would've been enough to make Leona do his bidding, no magic required.

"M-my right." The magic won out. The second her head snapped up to meet his, Yveun Dono shifted his magic.

His eyes seemed to glow in the dimly lit room as they met Sybil's. The faint taste of blackberries filled Leona's mouth, flowing in from her nose. The King's magic had a sweet palate, but almost too much so. Like something that had been left on the vine for too long and was one day from rotting.

"Right it is then," Yveun Dono whispered. "Give me your hand."

His magic reduced Sybil to a puppet with invisible strings. As long as the King's stare was unbroken, she was his.

Her right hand rose up from where it rested on her knee and extended to the King. Yveun Dono took it with grace, all the while his eyes locked with Sybil's, holding his magical control of her mind.

The moment his magic shifted and Sybil regained command of herself, it was too late. The King's onyx claws were out, magic and pure rage woven between them. He brought them down on Sybil's right hand, where they punctured through tendon and bone, ripping meat and flesh and stringy ligament as he shredded the offending appendage.

Her sister cried out in pain as the King twisted his wrist. He rendered Sybil's fingers to nothing more than pulp, her palm in shreds, before cutting her hand off at the wrist. Leona stared darkly at her younger sister as she nursed the stub at the end of her arm. She could feel Sybil's magic trying to regrow the appendage, but to no avail. Dragons could regrow almost anything if their hearts and heads were intact—and if a stronger Dragon wasn't committing himself to blocking the magical healing process.

"Dono, Dono," Sybil wailed. "Forgive me. Spare my life."

Yveun Dono looked down at the bloodied mass of what he had hailed as one of his Riders in disgust. His magic was still locked with Sybil's, stopping hers from healing the wound. He started back for his throne.

"Very well. *I* will spare your life." The King sat. "And I will defer to your commander, my Master Rider, for administering any remaining discipline."

Leona met her King's red eyes, still glowing with magic in the near darkness of the room. He radiated effortless authority. She dissected his decree, looking for the scrap of his true will in it. If there was one, he was hiding it. The King appeared to be giving her a genuine choice.

She met Sybil's eyes. Her sister was still huddled, wounded. Pathetic tears streamed over her cheeks and soiled the floor upon which their King walked. *No half measures.* Sybil had given the King her word and failed time and again. Now her eyes had the audacity to seek forgiveness in light of her shame.

Her sister clung to the desperation to live more than she sought the glory of their house.

Shameful.

Leona wouldn't explain her actions. If her sister had any sense left in her, any pride remaining as an Anh of House Rok, she would know. They were one body, and they worked to serve one mind—Yveun Dono's. Any who didn't were a cancer ravaging the system, leeching resources for their own selfish gain. There was only one course of action when a tumor had grown.

Sybil's eyes went wide in shock the second Leona's hand plunged into her chest. The sharp edges of ribs raked against her fingers and wrist. Her blood mingled with her sister's for what would be the last time. Leona held Sybil's frantically beating heart in her palm. Golden blood dribbled from the younger Dragon's mouth.

She stood over her sister's corpse, the heart still twitching in her fingers with the dying pulses of Sybil's magic. She offered the organ to the King.

Yveun Dono turned his head in a slow, deliberate side-to-side. "It was your kill."

Leona raised the heart to her mouth, tearing into it with her teeth. Her canines rendered the tissue into thin strips that were palatable on her tongue and easy to swallow. Power surged through her; Leona's head swam. She gorged herself on magic and meat until her vision blurred and her stomach felt fat.

"Imbibe her strength. Take her magic." Somehow Yveun Dono was right before her. She hadn't even heard him move. "Take your trusted two—Andre and Camile."

His hand was lacing around hers. He was touching her. The King was touching her. Leona's whole body flushed on a high she had never felt before. Magic mingled with hers, filled her, overwhelmed her.

Golden blood slicked between their fingers, the sticky liquid fading in the air. Leona looked up at her sovereign and breathed the taste of blackberries. If she was ever to die, she would want it to be by his hand; she would want him to be the one to feast on her heart and engorge himself with her essence. She would want her magic to cloud his head and make him feel heavy. She would want him to be drunk on her as she was drunk on Sybil.

"Take your fastest glider and make your way to Loom." He lowered his chin and met her eyes.

"I will take back what is rightfully yours," Leona uttered.

The King's other hand snaked in her hair, under her braid. It tensed, claws scratching against her scalp, hair tangled and pinched between his fingers. The mostly-eaten heart fell to the floor with a dull, wet *splat*. Leona locked eyes with Yveun Dono, giving him the ability to take over her mind if he so desired. He could take whatever he wanted from her. There was nothing she wouldn't give.

"Not quite," he rasped. His voice consumed her, his magic thrilling her to the bone. Leona's chest swelled to press against his, as if she was offering him her own heart—everything she ever was and would be. "You will act as my hand. For I am the only one to *take* what is *mine*."

Yveun Dono yanked her head back. Leona hissed, more in delight than pain. His canines raked against her bottom lip. The kiss exploded violently, smearing across their mouths with the bright sharpness of heavy summer berries, as the King used Leona's body for vindication of every heated truth he breathed into her exposed skin.

CVAREH

Florence hadn't said a word for two hours. She'd argued with Arianna for a short five minutes, then slumped against the wall on her stool, staring at nothing. Cvareh might only have known the girl for about four days, but it had been a long four days mostly spent in close quarters. He could read her, if only just.

Cvareh had studied the people of Loom all his life. He'd learned of the Five Guilds and the specialization of each of them. He'd studied Fenish, the language of the people. But being on the ground itself was a surreal experience. It was like he knew the notes, but he couldn't hear the melody that was being sung. He could say "Rivet," but he didn't understand what that really meant—and every look from Arianna over the past few days had confirmed as much. But nothing made it clearer than Florence's expression.

The girl was in distress. A line marred the space between her brows, her young face twisted in a scowl. Cvareh understood the plan Arianna had laid out—more or less. He knew of Ter.4.2, and the Underground seemed like a logical enough choice to move quickly without being discovered. He understood the word "prison" in the sense that his mind could come up with a definition, the equivalent word in Royuk, but somehow he wasn't speaking their language yet. The gravity he felt at the idea of a prison break was a weightless cloud compared to the lead in Arianna's eyes and, so plainly, Florence's heart.

He wanted to help. Petra had made him smile thousands of times when he was sad. His sister knew exactly what to say to encourage him. But he only had four days of knowledge to draw from when it came to the young Fenthri.

"Florence?" Arianna gave him a cautionary look the moment her pupil's name crossed his lips. The girl was oblivious to her teacher's protective urges, but her eyes came into focus slowly at the sound of her name. Cvareh put his pride aside and sought an absolution from his ignorance from someone who was twenty years his junior. "Can you explain to me how your revolver works?"

"What?"

"Your revolver. I watched you oil it on the train, and then you used it in the scuffle. I know you're not a Chimera and don't have magic… So how did you manage a shot like that?"

"You want to know about guns?" she asked timidly.

"If you'll teach me." Cvareh prayed he hadn't misread the hopeful note in her voice incorrectly.

Florence was moving again. Spurred back to life, she rummaged through her bag on the floor, pulling from it a small red tin that Cvareh recognized instantly as her gun care set, another medium-sized box where she kept her powders, and her weapon. She moved off her stool to sit in front of him on the floor.

Cvareh lusted after the empty stool that would insulate him from the grime and dirt, but he made no motion. His clothes were ugly and dirty, and the stool was really no cleaner.

It certainly wouldn't be comfortable. Plus, Florence had already set up shop in front of him, and this was for her.

"Well, it's not *that* complicated." She put the revolver between them, pointing to different parts. "You have the hammer, the cylinder, the trigger, the barrel and the muzzle. The hammer cocks back, engaging the trigger when you're ready to fire. It strikes against a canister in the chamber and that exchange of force causes a chemical or magical reaction—a small explosion." Her voice lifted on the last word. "That explosion is sent through the barrel and out the muzzle, propelling a bullet. Or whatever else is in the canister."

She held up a small chunk of metal. It was pointed on one end and flat on the other. Cvareh accepted it from her to inspect, pleased the action delighted her.

"The bullet sits on this end of the canister, near the primer—that's what the hammer hits." She produced a long hollow tube that, sure enough, the bullet could be fitted into. "What I fill the canister with, and how much, determines the type of shot."

"But how does magic come into play?" Cvarch passed back the canister and bullet to Florence and picked up the gun. The hammer and muzzle were gold. Poured into the side of the barrel were golden shapes he vaguely recognized, but couldn't place. He peered down the barrel and noted the inside was gold as well.

Florence's fingers wrapped around the barrel, pulling it away from him. "Never point the muzzle of a gun at something unless you're ready to shoot it."

"But it's not loaded." Cvareh didn't appreciate being treated like a child.

"It isn't now. But it could've been. It's just good practice. Every young Revolver learns that."

"Ah, Flor, if he wants to point guns at his face, why don't we let him? It's not like the shot would kill him. Maybe he should learn the hard way and have to sit around a few weeks like a blob while he grows back part of his brain," Arianna quipped unhelpfully.

"If he wants to learn, he should learn the right way." Florence turned to look at her master and Cvareh followed the girl's stare.

He opened his mouth to retort with equal sarcasm, but the look on Arianna's face stilled him. She looked past Florence, who continued on about something, and stared straight at him. Her rounded face was relaxed, her lips forming a thin line that he would almost dare call an appreciative smile. Cvareh gave her a small nod, swallowing down the bitterness her verbal jab had filled his mouth with. Arianna shifted her eyes to Florence, and made him question entirely if he'd read the expression wrong.

"In any case," Florence continued, turning back to him, "the magic lies in the runes. It's something the Alchemists developed, similar to tempering metal. A Chimera, or Dragon I suppose, charges the metal with magic. Different shapes hold different types of magic."

She cocked the hammer back, showing him the striking point. Sure enough, there was a rune there that mirrored a similar one etched onto the flat end of the canister. Cvareh turned the canister over once more, staring in wonder. *Magic that could be used to manipulate the physical world.* For half of his life, for centuries on Nova, it was something that couldn't be done. Magic existed only in the mind, the realm of the ephemeral. It couldn't be used to make explosions, lift gliders, turn wheels or do half the other things the Fenthri had been able to devise. For as strong as the Dragons were and had always been, there were things that eluded them—things the Fenthri could do and they could not.

He passed the canister back to Florence and his hand fell to the folio around his waist. That was why he was on Loom. It was that power he sought, to change the natural order and challenge the laws of the world. The power Cvareh hoped could build an army and lead his family to victory.

"But," Florence continued, "as time goes on the runes can lose their magic, or get worn down."

"They need to be recharged," Cvareh reasoned.

"Which is where Arianna comes in." Florence directed the tiniest of smiles at the gun, rather than her teacher.

Arianna looked weary as she echoed a similar expression, unbeknownst to the girl. "I think I'll go and work a bit. And figure out what ship is headed for Ter.4.2, and how we're getting on it."

Florence didn't acknowledge Arianna for the first time. She didn't even turn. The older woman stood, waiting, crumbling under the weight of the silence from her pupil.

Here it is, then. The one thing that could break the White Wraith.

Catching his eyes, Arianna's face transformed. She shot him a nasty look and stormed out the room. It was a glancing blow, a warning. They both knew the longer they stayed around each other, the more familiar they would become. No matter how hard she tried, he would learn her secrets, at least some.

But that would come in the days leading to the Alchemists' Guild. For now, Cvareh focused on one task at a time. And there was still unfinished business sitting before him.

"Flor." He tried out Arianna's familiar name for the girl. She looked up in surprise, but didn't scold him for using it. "Why don't you want to go to Ter.4.2?"

Her fingers ran over her gun kit, as though she couldn't decide what tool she needed to solve the problem presented to her. When that proved futile, she moved onto her powder box, shifting through the various tins. But Cvareh knew her answers weren't in there either. He was patient, and waited for her to come to that conclusion on her own.

"I was born a Raven." Her fingers finally stopped moving when they rested on her cheek. "But I wasn't any good at it—useless, really..."

"You got a mark," Cvareh pointed out.

"And I *barely* passed that test." She shook her head. "I shouldn't have. I had help."

"Your friends?"

"My friends." Florence dropped her hand with a heavy sigh. "I wish I could've been like Arianna and escaped the mark entirely."

"Why?" Cvareh didn't understand. At every opportunity, he donned the symbol of House Xin. It was as much a part of him as his skin color. It signified who he was, where he belonged. No matter how far he went in the world, being Xin would always be etched upon his identity. Who wouldn't want that?

"Because then I could've been truly free." She sighed wistfully. "People wouldn't look at me and see a Raven, they'd see *me*."

"You mean you could be a Revolver."

"I could be anything I desired," she corrected.

Loom had a backwards system before the Dragons. People going wherever they wanted, doing what they wanted.

For a society that Cvareh had been always taught favored logic, it didn't seem based on reason.

"When it came time for the second test, I knew I wouldn't pass. Half of us wouldn't. But we knew more then. We knew there were days before the Dragons when people studied as they wished. When you could be more than where you were born and what you were born into. So we escaped."

"Anyone caught running from the guild can be put to death." The laws the Dragons put into place suddenly seemed less sensible when he stared in the face of someone perfectly capable who would be lost from the world were they strictly upheld.

"Anyone who fails the first or second guild test is put to death with certainty. If you run, they may just jail you in an effort to persuade you to come back before killing talent… That's what happened to my friends."

"But you're not dead or imprisoned."

"I'm not."

"How?"

Florence was silent for a long time. She focused on selecting canisters from the ones she had made, and made one or two new ones. From time to time, she'd look at him from the corner of her eyes, expectant. Cvareh rested the back of his head against the wall and waited. He wouldn't repeat himself, and didn't need to. He just needed to be patient enough that she'd be out with it on her own.

"My friends and I escaped through the Underground," Florence said briskly. "Seven died, three of us made it out. Two were caught in Ter.4.2."

"How did you—" Cvareh already knew the answer to his question. He knew who got Florence the rest of the way into obscurity: the only woman in the world who seemed to evade all capture, all pursuit.

"She saved me." Florence smiled, seeing him put it together. "I wouldn't be alive if Arianna hadn't smuggled me with her onto that freighter."

Dots connected, one after the next, forming a time line that spanned across blanks in history. Arianna met Florence, took her to Ter.5. They made their way to Dortam and she set up a name for herself as the White Wraith, enemy of all Dragons. But why? Everything before her meeting Florence was still wrapped in the enigma of chaos.

"Was she living in Ter.4.2?" he ventured.

Florence shook her head. "I don't really know. And before you ask, I don't know where she may have came from. I don't really know much more than you do. She's a Master Rivet—"

That was news. He hadn't known she was a master.

"—and she hates Dragons more than anything. Her first rule in taking me with her was that I would never ask anything else."

"And you never did," he observed.

"And I never did. It doesn't matter who she was. It matters who she can become..." Florence's hands paused on one of her boxes, pausing mid-close. She spoke only for herself, barely more than a whisper. "If only I could make her see that."

ARIANNA

Arianna was a stone gargoyle atop one of the spires surrounding the port of Ter.5.2. Magic pulsed through her fingertips, wrapping around the cabling and clips, making its grip on the ironwork surrounding her sure and strong. She watched men and women go about their business.

Dragons walked with guild masters on and off airships. The sight alone made her want to retch in disgust. Fenthri—no, not just Fenthri, *guild masters*—fraternizing willingly and openly with Dragons. She remembered a time when guild masters embodied everything pure and true in the academic world, when they were the pillars of guilds. Now, they spilled their secrets for their oppressors like dogs returning a fetched ball.

The world had changed in the nearly three years she had sequestered herself in Dortam. Every day, it slipped further and further from the land Arianna had been born into. Now, it seemed to race toward a future that cared little for the past.

The line nearly cut into her flesh, she held it so tightly. She was no better than those she judged. She worked with a Dragon, harbored a Dragon; she'd let a Dragon imbibe from her. The line finally bit into the same hand Cvareh had, drawing blood. Her mind betrayed her, filling her with thoughts of the way he looked at her while he consumed her.

Arianna snarled at the memory, scaring it into the recesses of her awareness. She uncurled her fingers and watched the wound on her hand heal slowly. She was part Dragon, too, more than she would ever admit to anyone.

"Eva…" She touched her wrist and the tension faded from Arianna's shoulders. "I'm headed back. I'm going back, finally. I will finish what we started."

That was what separated her from those she watched fraternize with the Dragons below, from the Chimera who prided in being part Dragon. Arianna did not act for herself. She hadn't taken on Dragon organs for pleasure or self-centered power. She didn't help Cvareh for his own sake, or to use his boon for personal gains. She'd done it for her mission, for Loom, but most of all for her vengeance.

Arianna waited for darkness before moving. Three freighters remained docked after the sun set and she already had her eyes and suspicions on one being their best chance for getting to Ter.4.2. But there was one place that would have all the information. Before leaving, and just after docking, Arianna had watched the captains of each of the vessels make their way into a building across from where she perched. She saw them through the third floor windows as they talked with a portly man. This same stout man locked up his business only after the port had gone quiet and the last of the light had diminished from the sky.

She leapt off her ledge, the cord pulling taught and spool whirring as she dropped in free-fall. Kicking her legs in front of her to swing, Arianna set her second line flying toward a crane that loomed high above the docks. The cable clipped to itself, locking with magic. As soon as the new line was fastened, the first unwound and retreated back to its spool.

Changing lines and cabling with her winch-box was mindlessly simple. Her hands knew how to move, her magic operating on instinct. She soared through the night unhindered. No barrier, no watchmen, could keep her out.

The wind howled in her ears and her nose singed with the smell of the sea. She was weightless as she soared high above the port. She was well out of the glow of the lamplight below, and the creaking and clanging of vessels against their tethers with the shifting tides masked the sounds of her lines and winch-box.

Arianna kept her knees loose, bending and curling her body inward to help absorb shock and sound as she landed against the building's exterior. She cast a cautionary eye across the docks. A few sailors and pilots milled about, attracted to the glow of smoking parlors and bars.

Letting out the line, she lowered herself to the third floor windows of the port authority. Her goggles enhanced her Dragon sight, rendering the darkness a mere annoyance rather than a hindrance. The windows opened at the halfway point, no doubt to let in cool sea breezes during warmer months. Simple locks, nothing that would pose a real problem...

She fished through one of the smaller bags on her belt. She could just break the glass and be done with it. But Ari didn't want to do anything that could raise suspicion before the ship they were on was well out of port. Her tool looked almost like a ribbon of gold, flat and hard, it didn't bend as she shoved it halfway through the window jamb.

Arianna shifted her weight on the line, allowing tension and physics to hold her in place more than magic. With her mental capacities freed, she applied them to the strip of gold. It wiggled to life, working its way into the room. At her command, it wrapped itself around the lever of the lock and pulled. The window clicked open, and Arianna slipped effortlessly inside.

The office was well lived in. The leather wing-backed chair was cracking in places of heavy use. The desk had dimples from where forearms had rested for years.

You could learn a lot about a person from their home, and offices were nothing if not second homes. The man was a creature of habit. He paced when he was nervous—judging by the threadbare tracks in the carpet—and he never missed a day. His records had been methodically checked every morning and night for the past year.

Arianna flipped through the port manifest, the record of every vessel, its contents, and its crew. The cargo ship she'd selected for them was named *Holx III*. She suspected that a ship named after the capital city of Ter.4 would be headed in that direction. She slowly flipped through the papers, careful to do so in such a way that she could return them exactly as she found them.

"*Holx III*, cargo… Textiles, safe enough," she mused aloud. "Arrives and departs at night." There wasn't much time; she flipped the papers back in place.

By ship, it would take just under twelve days to travel to Ter.4.2. The *Holx III* was a simple freighter and would likely cruise around 27,800 peca an hour—or 27.8 veca an hour. Arianna breathed a sigh of relief when she saw it ran with a refined engine. Most of the regular runners were outfitted with engines that could run on magic or steam to help save on coal. There would always be room for another Chimera on board a magically-propelled vessel.

Her fingers paused over the ledgers she had been returning in order. Her eyes narrowed and Arianna skimmed the records, trying to put her finger on what her mind was telling her wasn't quite right. She flipped the page, then the one after, and the one after that. That's when she found it—or rather, didn't find it. Not one vessel had headed for Ter.2.3, the main port of the Alchemists' territory, in nearly a year.

Arianna hunted like a Dragon on a blood scent through the port authority's records for evidence of even one vessel headed for Ter.2.3. Sure, it was a far voyage and likely to only be made once every few weeks, even months. But to have *none*, in or out? That made no sense.

It had been the Alchemists who developed the first Chimera. The Rivets were the ones who'd soused out the refining process in their steel mills and all the applications for gold. The Revolvers were close behind, eagerly finding further uses in their guns and explosives. It was the Harvesters who supplied them all with their base materials and the Ravens who moved the entire world—people and goods. Yes, the Five Guilds of Loom were a connected system, a chain in which every Guild formed a link.

So why was one being cut off?

Arianna's hands rested on the file drawer as she closed her eyes in thought. The Revolvers needed Alchemical runes for their weaponry and refining. The Alchemists' Guild hall was in the city of Keel, nestled in the center of The Skeleton Forest, where they needed weapons to fend off all manner of beast. Stopping all trade from the Revolvers would basically be a death sentence for a city that lived in constant fear of wolves, bears, and the endwig.

Cries of reverie from the street brought Arianna's attention back to her purpose: get them out of Ter.5. She'd let the anomaly surrounding the trade routes remain just that, simmering in the back of her mind until she had some explanation for it.

The port authority safe provided a sufficient distraction, pulling her mind fully back into the present. It was complex enough to be a challenge, but not enough to annoy—ideal, really. She lifted some of the tariff and taxes funds. Not so much that it would be immediately noticed or prove detrimental to the running of the port, but a tidy amount sufficient to grease a captain's gears enough that he'd take on three extra crew.

Locking the safe behind her, Arianna scanned the room, comparing it to her mental image of its appearance when she entered. One or two things showed small signs of having been moved, but only to eyes that were looking for inconsistencies. People only saw what they wanted, and there should be no cause for suspicion until their vessel was well out to sea.

She closed and locked the window, slipping back into the night through the front door. Come morning, the port authority would be none the wiser of their late night guest.

When she returned to the inn, there was talking on the other side of the door; Florence's laughter gave her pause. Arianna had felt guilty the moment she'd proposed the notion of navigating through Ter.4 with Flor's old comrades. The young woman's mental collapse had been poison more potent than any Arianna had ever drank. So to hear laughter now… it fit a gear in the mechanics of her heart back into place.

Her expression fell at the resonance of Cvareh's voice. "I can tell you that Dragons wear much less than even that on Nova."

"What about modesty?" Florence asked.

"What about it?"

"Having everything so… on display all the time. Wouldn't that make people nervous?" she ventured timidly.

"Why would it? If anything it displays our physical prowess and discourages duels."

Arianna opened the door with a disapproving glare in Cvareh's direction. He looked up at her, barely stopping short a dramatic roll of his eyes. Arianna's fingers twitched for her daggers but remained at her side.

"You're corrupting my pupil with your tales of Nova," she seethed. Florence had a clever mind, too curious for her own good, and she always saw the best in people. Arianna knew that just a taste of Nova was likely to leave the girl wanting more, no matter how many times Arianna told her that Dragons were not to be mingled with.

"I think it's fascinating." Flor smiled.

And that was what kept her from sewing Cvareh's mouth shut. He had begun to endear himself to Florence. No matter how much Arianna hated him, she wanted Florence to smile even more. So she would do as she'd always done with Florence. She'd linger in the shadows, hovering in a place not even the girl could see her. She'd give her pupil the freedom to spread her wings, fly, be curious and inquire, experience the thrill of feeling on her own. Florence would work with the fear of falling because Arianna believed that fear was necessary to grow, but she'd always be hovering nearby, ready to pick up the girl if necessary.

"If architecture and fashion are corruption, perhaps Loom could use a bit more corrupting." Cvareh's mouth curled upward and his lips spread.

The expression was strange. He wasn't baring his teeth at her. Their points remained hidden behind his bottom lip. It was…a smile. A *Dragon* smile. It unnerved her endlessly.

"We need to move," Arianna announced. "First, Flor, I need the grease pencil."

"You're going to do it?" Florence blinked.

"I'm out of options. Our prior disguises aren't going to work where we're going."

Florence was clearly curious, but she produced the grease pencil kit from her bag. Arianna sat at the stool, passing the tin to Flor to hold like a mirror. Florence stood patiently while her mentor collected herself. The mark would wash off; it was not a tattoo. But every time she put it on her cheek, it felt like forfeit.

Arianna shifted her feet, her coat draping over her thighs. She swallowed the lump in her throat, pulling her cheek taut with her left hand and steadying her right. Her hand was skilled from thousands of hours of schematic creation, and it moved smoothly over her ashen colored skin as she penciled in the symbol of the Rivets.

Coat and harness resumed, she was again the White Wraith: more than Fenthri, more than Chimera, more than Dragon. She cast aside ethical whims and personal grudges. She was the extension of her benefactors' will, and she would work for them even after they were long dead.

LEONA

Leona let out a rallying cry as her magic surged through her palms, into the golden handles of the glider, and across the golden accented wings to propel the contraption upward.

The wind bit her cheeks and whipped her braid behind her. The brisk morning air tasted like freedom, a new dawn heralding a new day—*her* day. She had no choice but to scream and cry and shout and snarl, because she was the Master Rider. She was a dog let off its chain. She was the untamed storm. And she had been unleashed upon Loom below.

Bending her knees and leaning forward, Leona banked her glider, casting a glittering rainbow across the Rok Estate. She wanted to give Yveun Dono one more taste of her magic. To write it across the sky like a promise that she would not fail him.

Her cries were echoed by the two Riders just behind her on either side. Their screaming vessels tore through the air in formation as they banked heavily down off the side of one of the floating islands of Nova. The Rok Estate dominated the top of Lysip, its main hall and gardens expanding out in all directions as far as the eye could see. At its edge stood smaller buildings of state, chambers provided for Rok'Kin and Rok'Da.

Further still were accommodations for To and Veh in society. They all basked together in the sunlight like jeweled turtles on river rocks.

Beneath, the island extended downward. Society's lower rungs lived in the shade of their uppers. Leona had been born in one of those suspended towers, reaching for the clouds rather than the heavens. She'd played in the honeycombed parks between them and worked her way up to the sunlight above. With Sybil dead, the only time Leona would see this shade now was when she descended to Loom.

Sybil. Her sister's magic had been strong and Leona could still feel it in her veins, burning through her. It was fading quickly, but she'd relish in the ghostly resentment that tried to turn her stomach sour. But nothing could spoil this day, for it was the first day that dawned after she had known Yveun Dono.

The King had not explained himself—not last night, not with the dawn. She suspected he never would. He didn't have to. He had made it apparent that he would take what was his. And Leona was nothing if not that.

She adjusted her grip on the handles, the clouds nearing. Throwing a look over her shoulder, she checked that Andre and Camile were still with her. Camile had the face of a cat; her curious amusement at Leona's mood was apparent. Andre wore a grin that was half snarl. This man and woman were more her blood than Sybil had ever been.

Lysip was shrinking further and further behind them. When she returned victorious, she would seek Yveun Dono's blessing to duel Coletta'Ryu. The woman was sickly, and would prove an easy kill. But to challenge a Ryu required the Oji's blessing. After last night, and after she brought home Cvareh's head, she suspected she may have that unprecedented blessing.

Before the first Fenthri broke through the clouds, the Dragons had called the seemingly impenetrable barrier the Gods' Line, as it separated their world from the next. Boco, the bird-like creatures they used to fly between the islands of Nova, lost control of their wings as they neared the speeding winds that always wove through the clouds. Every Dragon who tried to descend on the back of a Boco fell violently through the line and was never seen again.

Certain death by falling into the afterlife had made attempts to descend unappealing. And for hundreds of years, no Dragons tried. When the Fenthri barely broke through the clouds, only to be shortly torn asunder by the winds themselves, Nova learned that it was not the afterlife on the other side of the line but another world entirely. Curious Dragons—fools—attempted to cross once more at the site of the first breach, but fell to their deaths. It was their corpses that provided the organs that led to the first Chimera being pieced together by the Alchemists.

Once the Fen had magic, the God's Line was nearly obsolete. They still struggled, scraping together enough power to cross. But the technology they developed was finally in Nova's grasp—a technology Dragons had been meant to have in their talons all along.

Leona re-centered herself on her glider, the bottom of her boots connected to the platform with magic and sheer will. She had descended a few times, though it never gave her much cause to be fond of the process. The wind was deafening, the clouds blinding. She pointed her glider nose down and plummeted forward.

Gravity was her friend. It fought vertigo and, in free-fall, she didn't need to exhaust magic on keeping herself airborne.

That magic was better spent holding a thin corona around her and the vessel to protect herself from the winds. Her fingers froze; her braid felt like it would rip from her scalp.

Magic cracked, reaching a crescendo as she pushed through, parting the clouds and opening Loom to her like an abysmal present.

The echoes of two more descents reverberated through the mountaintops that surrounded Dortam. Leona trusted Andre and Camile to be where they were supposed to be. If she couldn't count on them to make a descent, she had brought the wrong Dragons as her left and right.

The blackened, pointed rooftops of Dortam reminded Leona of a porcupine's spears. It was a sad, stinted world beneath the clouds. The people were smaller, the plants brittle and hard compared to the lush greenery of Nova. Fen were made of the rocks they cherished so much. Whereas Dragons… they were made of life itself.

"There!" Camile called over the wind.

Leona followed her finger to a broken rooftop. The second they got close, Leona could smell it. She could practically see gold on the ground.

"Xin are built like porcelain dolls. Little Cvareh bleeds from falling off his glider," Camile jabbed.

Leona let her subordinates put down the annoying Dragon House. She even partook from on occasion, delighting in the verbal jabs. But this time, she stayed silent. The smell of blood was faint. It had long since disappeared on the wind. The trace that was left was little more than enough to make a mark.

She hated Cvareh. She hated House Xin. And she still fantasized about all the ways she could pull out Petra's lying teeth one by one. But Leona wasn't going to let it blind her. Sybil had underestimated her foe. Petra was nothing less than a monster, and if Cvareh was cut from the same cloth, he shouldn't be written off lightly. All his appearances at the Crimson Court could be just that—appearances. Who knew what truly lay beneath.

"The trail goes cold," Leona noted. Tracking Cvareh wasn't going to be that easy, or even someone as incompetent as Sybil wouldn't have failed. "We head for Mercury Town."

"Oh, gross," Andre balked. "It smells rancid there."

"And where else do you think we'll find talk of Cvareh?" Leona grinned. It was intended to be playful, but her smile was wide enough to show her teeth. She was the leader and it never hurt to reinforce that fact.

"Lead on. If we are to dredge up the worst, we must go to the worst." Andre motioned a cherry colored hand for her to continue and Leona spurred forward.

If there was a Dragon in Dortam, talk of it would get to Mercury Town. Leona didn't think for a second that Cvareh would get very far before a harvester set eyes on him. It seemed her sister had the same idea.

"I think it's an improvement." Andre tilted his head to the side, assessing the rubble and carnage that was left to rot.

Leona sighed, lowering her glider to the ground, crushing dead Fen underneath. Sybil had no tact, no reason. She reaped chaos, but it was too easy for things to be lost in chaos.

"Anything would be an improvement." Camile toed one of the fallen Fen's heads, rolling it from side to side. "They're at least quieter when they're dead."

"That's part of the problem. Dead Fen don't talk." Leona looked through the silent streets. The usually busy Mercury Town had been reduced to death and stillness. She tried to think like her sister, wild. If she landed in Mercury Town with Sybil's disposition... She'd reap destruction wantonly. "Camile, with me. Andre, that way."

"Follow the trails of destruction?" The man preempted her expectations.

"See what you find," Leona affirmed. "Whisper to Camile if there's anything."

Andre and Camile faced each other, cheek to cheek. They each spoke a series of sounds, nonsense with no meaning, into the other's ear. Leona felt the whisper link establish between them. Now, the moment one of them said their activation word, they could speak with the other across any distance—as though one was whispering in the other's ear.

"So I set the whisper link, *hmm*?" Camile hummed as they began to follow the trail of destruction that wound in the direction opposite Andre.

"I have a whisper link back to Lysip to report." Leona barely contained a smirk. Yveun Dono's activation word had been a flesh chilling, guttural growl that she would gladly scream to have echo through her again.

"I wonder with who? You're quite cheerful for someone who just killed her sister."

"Don't play me for a soft fool. I am not Tam." She brushed off Camile's not-so-subtle inquiry. Whoever the woman suspected, she was wrong.

"That you are not." Camile grinned gleefully. "Tell me, how did her heart taste?"

"Like a cherry, and it exploded much the same in my mouth." Her triumphs were never something she would hide.

"Sybil would—"

Leona held up a hand and Camile was instantly silenced and on alert. The wind had picked up for just a moment. On it she had caught the hint of a familiar scent.

"This way."

Camile kept up easily with her bounding strides. The further they got from the epicenter of Sybil and the prior Riders' destruction, the more Fen were about. They scattered like rats, not one putting up a fight before the Dragons once more in their midst.

The smell nearly overwhelmed her as Leona rounded an alleyway. To the eye, there was no sign of the fight that had taken place, but it had surely been bloody. Camile's talons unsheathed slowly.

A Rider had died here. They both recognized the scent. Layered atop it, almost triumphantly, was the brisk smell of wood smoke, a distinctly Xin smell. *Cvareh.*

Leona walked through the empty dead end. Magic burned under her feet and hung in the air. A silent memorial for months to come to the Dragon who had lost his life in the spot. She knew the essence of the Rider, Cvareh was easy enough to take note of… But there was one more.

"The third, what is it?" Leona asked Camile.

"It's…floral? House Tam?"

"Not quite…" There was a heavy floral note, almost like honeysuckle on a hot summer night. But mingled with it was a sharper smell of cedar, like one of House Xin.

Sybil had mentioned Cvareh had help, but she said nothing of another Dragon from House Tam or Xin. That would make this a very different hunt. Leona continued to try to dissect the smell, fighting to peel back its layers. But there was only a trace amount, and the heavy rose smell of the House Tam rider who had perished overpowered the rest of them.

Her sister said there'd been a Fen and Chimera helping him. Leona had smelled Chimera blood thousands of times from the slaves at the Rok estate. Their blood was black for a reason—it was dirty, muddled, rotten. This was clean and sharp, but unlike anything she'd ever inhaled before.

"Leona, this way." Camile interrupted her thoughts.

Leona followed, giving up the strange third scent for now. Camile was on the trail of the fallen Rider, no doubt picked up by Fen vultures that were already picking the carcass clean. It led them through winding, narrow back passages into the depths of Mercury Town—into the beating heart of the muddled, rotten blood Leona had just been comparing against.

The Fen man who waited at the door didn't seem surprised to see them. They made him uneasy; she could hear his heart racing in his chest. But he didn't run from his post, didn't avert his eyes. Instead, he greeted them.

"We are expecting you." He opened the door.

Leona strode in fearlessly, claws out and gleaming. Some Chimera and Fenthri guns posed no threat to two Dragon Riders. The only thing that could bring down a Dragon in Dortam was another Dragon.

"Welcome, ladies!" A tiny man clapped his hands. His white skin stretched over his bones, giving him a disturbing similarity to a walking skeleton. Beady eyes appraised them as though they were meat. "When I heard the glider, I just knew you would come and investigate your fallen friend. I just knew." He waggled his finger in the air. "You see, the most terrible thing happened. I caught two men dragging the corpse of our King's noble Rider off for harvesting. Now, I tried to get the corpse from them, but they overpowered my men and used this room to—"

Leona hovered over the weak little man, moving with Dragon speed to clamp her hand atop his mouth. Blood beaded around where her claws dug into his cheeks. She could kill him in seven different ways right now and each seemed more delightful than the last. But that would be the course Sybil would've taken: kill first and ask questions later. As tempting as that approach was, it had yet to yield results.

"I am not interested in your lies," she growled. The alabaster-colored wretch's men seemed to be caught in limbo, unsure if they should engage or leave their master to fend for himself. Leona peeled away one finger at a time before removing her hand. She sheathed her claws and dragged her fingers across the man's bloody cheek, drawing lines of crimson across the nearly glowing white of his flesh. "You seem like a smart man."

She was lying.

"Tell me what you know, and I'll let you keep every last organ you illegally harvested, and all your lives. A fair deal, no?"

"Quite fair." His voice trembled slightly as she dragged her knuckles up and down his neck.

"How did the Dragon die?" Leona asked.

"His heart was ripped out."

Cvareh then, without doubt. "Who did it?"

"I hear talk of a Dragon running through Mercury Town, blue."

Cvareh again. This wasn't new information. Leona's fingers walked around his tiny neck, ready to throttle. "Where was he headed?"

"No one could find him." Leona's hand tensed, causing the man to wheeze. "But I have a theory."

"Is it a theory you'd stake your life on?" She curled her lips as she spoke, showing her teeth. Her patience was about to run out.

"I hear word of a fight against Dragons at the Ter.5.2 station, three days after your friend died."

"*And?*"

The man spoke faster at Leona's urging. "It takes three days to reach Ter.5.2 by train from here."

"I already knew he was seen in Ter.5.2. Tell me something I don't know."

"What do you know about the White Wraith?" The man smiled at Leona's immediate reaction.

Now *this* was certainly new information. The infamous White Wraith of New Dortam had been an annoyance for over a year. They had tried to send Riders down, but one ended up dead, and the rest were made fools of. Yveun Dono eventually deemed it a waste of time to fight an enemy that would not stand up for a duel and only fought from the shadows.

She pulled her hand away for him to continue.

"People say your Dragon ran with the White Wraith through the streets here." The man adjusted his velvet vest.

Something didn't add up. "Why would the Wraith help a Dragon?"

"That, I cannot tell you." The man held out his hands hopelessly. "Have I earned my harvest?"

"Keep your pilfered magic," Leona sneered, starting for the door. Camile was silently in step, her claws still extended.

"Oh, I almost forgot." Leona paused. "You see, I happen to be the main contractor of the White Wraith. So I know a few things you may want to hear about how he conducts his business."

Leona squinted at the hustler. She would be impressed if he wasn't a Fen. "Name your price."

"I want a living Dragon."

"Too steep," Leona scoffed. She knew what men like him would do. They would chain up the Dragon and pick them apart slowly, slow enough that the Dragon would re-grow flesh and organs to be harvested again indefinitely.

"Then another corpse—a strong one."

"If your information is worthwhile." Leona could think of a few members of House Xin she'd like to throw down to Loom for this scavenger to lick clean. And there were always those with no rank—they were practically born to be organ fodder.

The man sat in his chair, a tiny throne for the pitiful king of a worthless scrap of dirt. "The first thing you must remember is the name Florence."

CVAREH

He had always been taught that Fenthri didn't have magic. Dragons turned up their noses at the plain creatures of Loom, the hardened, stony residents of the rock below who lacked raw power surging through their veins.

It was the Dragons that had been the fools.

Cvareh had never seen a Fenthri work. The few Chimera that had been brought up to Nova to maintain imported golden machines were kept almost exclusively at the Rok estate; he who held the gold held the power in the sky world above. The Chimera slaves were kept out of sight, trusted to do what they must to keep the devices that had become so integral to Nova running.

On the third day into their voyage, the *Holx III* had suffered engine troubles. Problems with the pistons set the crew to scrambling, and Arianna stepped in. The woman hoisted wrenches as large as his calf, sweat rolling lines through the soot and oil caked on her flesh. She worked tirelessly through the night, changing out lines, welding, creating tools from scratch.

Cvareh was only below decks to support with his magic as needed. Arianna had been reluctant to ask him, but Florence was insistent after the fifth hour. Cvareh knew why the second he arrived.

Arianna's strong shoulders were beginning to sag and her posture was slacker than the normal board-straight height she usually carried herself with. Running back and forth between drafting tables in the small cabin attached to the engine room and maintaining her patches while she rambled off numbers in search of a permanent solution had taken its toll. Arianna didn't have energy to expend on magical pursuits. So when something golden needed to be lifted, or turned just so, Cvareh was there.

Arianna stepped away from the iron, brass, and gold monster she'd been wrestling with all night. The ship's Rivet handed her a soiled cloth, which she uselessly wiped her hands with. The woman was absolutely filthy.

"Cvareh," she summoned him without turning. "Strike the flywheel."

Cvareh stared at the tube of gold attached to the shaft of the mechanism. With a mental command he drove down its weight. It pushed against the shaft, turning the flywheel to life.

"All right, Pops, try the combustion pistons now!" Arianna had to practically scream to be heard over the sounds of the engine groaning to life.

The ship's Rivet—Pops, as everyone called him—raised his thumb in the air as some symbol of affirmation. With the help of another crewmate he engaged a different set of machines. Somehow, despite all the noise, Cvareh heard Arianna's sharp intake of breath. She held it, waiting with as much tension as a harp string.

After a few minutes, the woman put her hands on her hips triumphantly. She curled her lips in a flat-lined smile of admiration at the engine. Cvareh didn't find it beautiful, not compared to the breathtaking aesthetics of Nova. But there *was* something…lovely, in her admiration of the thing she had created.

The flywheel spun, pistons fired, and the noise increased until Arianna finally turned. She rested an oily palm on his shoulder. *Another shirt ruined.*

Her lips moved, but he couldn't make out the sound over the cacophony of the engine.

"What?" Cvareh tilted his head, shouting in her ear. His eyes focused on the patch of skin at the corner of her jaw, usually hidden by her thick hair. The white strands were clumped with sweat and clinging to her neck. A faint scar ran around the base of an ear that had been capped with steel to prevent it from re-growing pointed — an ear that was a dusty sky color. *A House Xin shade of blue.*

"I said let's get above decks." She slapped his shoulder, unaware of his revelation, and led the way.

Cvareh was a step behind, not wanting to make his sudden discomfort obvious. It was only logical that, as a Chimera, she could have some parts from a Dragon that belonged to some rung of his House. He knew she engaged in organ trafficking. So why would it suddenly bother him?

Pops met them topside. "I don't know what we would've done without you."

"You would've figured it out, I'm sure." Arianna rubbed sweat from her face with the back of her hand.

"I'm not certain about that." The weathered sailor's dark leathery skin folded around his smile. "I've been on this ship for twenty years now, making these runs. We've only had people ask to work aboard in exchange for passage thirty or so times... But not one has been a master."

Arianna stilled. Cvareh felt her muscles tense. She fought the instinct in her wrists to seek out her daggers. The longer he spent with the woman, the easier she was to read.

"Your mark is washing off, miss," Pops clarified.

Arianna brought her hand to her cheek, recognizing that not all the grease on her hands was from the engine. "What will the captain do?"

"Cap is a fair man. He won't throw an illegal on a dingy to row back to Ter.5 after she just saved us from being trapped behind schedule." The old man buried his hands in his pockets, more amused than anything. "You're young for a master. Who was your teacher?"

"Master Oliver."

Cvareh hadn't heard the name before. He wondered if she still realized he hovered. And then put a quick stop to the wondering; Arianna was a keen woman, constantly aware. He wouldn't discredit her by thinking she could have somehow forgotten her surroundings like that.

"Master Oliver." Pops shook his head, humming quietly over the name. "One of the best."

"He was the best," Arianna corrected adamantly.

"What ever became of him?" the older Rivet inquired.

"He died."

"I assumed..." Pops's words faded into the silence, inviting Arianna to continue. She didn't. "Well, he passed on his learning to hundreds, and his mastery. Those are the marks of a good life."

Arianna nodded her head a fraction. Pops walked in one direction, she in the other. The woman started up a narrow metal stair for the walk above the engine room, around the smokestack.

Cvareh followed.

"What do you want?" Arianna placed her elbows on the metal of the deck rail, rested the small of her back against it, and looked up toward the sky.

"You must be exhausted. Why not go to bed?"

Arianna snorted in amusement, arching a curious eyebrow at him. It clearly conveyed the weight she placed on his supposed concern for her wellbeing. Cvareh rolled his eyes, leaning on the railing as well, and looked out to sea instead.

"I'm watching the smokestack." Her voice was void of any bite. It was almost the same tone she reserved for Florence. "I want to make sure we're up and running again before I go collapse."

"Good of you to do for people who could turn you in for being unmarked the moment we dock."

"*Ooh*, cynical. You've been around me too long." There was an almost Dragon-like wildness to her grin. Cvareh chuckled and shook his head. "But they won't turn us in."

"How can you be so certain?"

"They're honest men and women." She shrugged. "I believe what Pops said about the captain."

"A thief concerned about honor." He laughed.

"Honor is what I fight for—honor, justice, freedom, and above all, Loom."

"I didn't take you for such an idealist." Cvareh shifted to face her, resting his hip against the railing. Arianna's eyes fell from the sky, where they'd been following the trail of billowing smoke, to meet his. Neither said anything for a long moment.

"You never asked."

He contemplated it. Somewhere, in the week they had spent together, he was certain he had. But he would give her this. For the first time, Cvareh yielded to her. Because she was fundamentally right. If he had asked it had certainly been defensive or insulting. He hadn't asked to know. He hadn't asked in such a way that implied he would listen.

"Why did you take my offer of a boon?" Cvareh dared appealing to her logic. "You're clearly well learned, and you use it to your advantage to get what you want. You're a Chimera, so you can use magic. What does a boon give that you don't already have?"

"The one thing I truly want," she whispered, not looking at him.

"Arianna, what is that?" He shifted closer, to hear her over the sea wind, to not miss a word that fell from her lips. His fingers brushed against her elbow.

Arianna's head snapped down, looking at the offending contact. She pulled away with an expression of horror, laced with confusion. Cvareh tried to make sense of how that touch had elicited such a reaction.

"I want Nova to burn." Arianna looked him right in the eye and Cvareh couldn't find a trace of lie. "And I will use your boon to help me do it."

Cvareh didn't back down. He curled his fingers into fists to keep his talons from unsheathing out of instinct when she threatened his home. "Why?"

"For what you have done to Loom."

"What *we* have done?" he balked. "We have given you magic, we have gifted you with progress. We have imposed logical systems of government, a hierarchy in which everyone knows their place and how they fit."

She began to laugh, though he failed to see how what he said was funny. Arianna grasped her stomach and her shoulders trembled with barely containable, malicious mirth.

"You—*you* gifted *us*, with progress?" She shook her head. "Dragon, check your history. Your people fell from the sky. We were the ones to give you wings, to make your magic useful."

"It was quite useful to begin with."

"And we knew how we fit together before. We were a chain, every Guild forming a link that supplied the next, which made Loom work." She prodded a finger in his chest. "Then you came, and put gates on the system. You tried to turn links in a chain into rungs of a ladder, one atop the next. Our trade has yet to recover, our output is only half of what it was, without the Vicar council the Guilds do not communicate, and that's not even touching on problems with educating our youth now that they are trapped within your asinine notion of 'families,' condemned to their guild only to be killed off if they don't make the cut."

Cvareh didn't know where to start, didn't know if he should engage physically as she encroached on his space. He didn't know if he should try to correct her. Or if there was something to be understood in everything she was telling him.

"Dragon." He had been demoted again. "I do not presume to know your ways. I have studied them, but I do not *know* them. Frankly, I don't care. Keep your Nova logic up in your sky world and leave us alone."

Arianna eased away slowly. If looks could kill, Cvareh would be dead a hundred times over. She panted softly from her tirade. When she took another step, Cvareh's hand closed around her wrist before he could think to arrest it.

He stopped her.

Why did he stop her?

Frustration knitted his brow. This woman was going to drive him mad long before they ever saw the Alchemists' Guild. She had her prejudices and Cvareh knew that she would keep them no matter what he said, but that didn't stop him from speaking. "You're right, Arianna. You don't know anything."

"Unhand me," she snarled.

"I listened to you." He released her. "Now listen to me."

Miraculously, she stayed. Perhaps it would've been better if she'd left.

"The Dragon King kills your people, just as he kills mine. The hierarchy he is imposing upon your world, service and servitude at the cost of well-being, is the same as he imposes on ours. I want to see him dead. That's why I'm here."

The blood rushed into his ears, deafening all sound other than the echo of his confession. He'd never said such treasonous words aloud before. That had always been Petra's role. She was the brave one, and he was just her right hand.

"I want Yveun Dono dead," Cvareh said again, just to prove to himself he could. "And I want a new world order too. For Nova *and* Loom. The Alchemists hold the key to making it happen. Once we're there—"

"—we will find the power to change the world?" she finished, her flat tone deflating him to match. "Everyone on Loom knows of the Council of Five. But that resistance died long ago, and their hopes for the future with them."

"I will build a new hope. My family will, Loom will, and you can too."

"I gave up building hope long ago." She sighed and looked out to sea. Her face was soft, still a mess of soot from her earlier work. It looked more right on her than any powdered makeup Cvareh had ever seen coloring the cheeks of the women on Nova. "It relies too much on trust that is too easily broken."

Arianna did turn then. Cvareh watched her go, a strange ache growing with every step. He hadn't expected to lighten the load of his heart upon her. Even less had he thought doing so would begin to bridge the harrowing gap of the past she lived in, and the future he wanted to build with her help.

FLORENCE

erritory 4, home of the Ravens. It was an ugly blemish on the horizon until it grew large enough to consume the sea whole. Just the sight of it turned her stomach sour and her palms clammy. She had sworn she would never return. She had been happy in Dortam with Arianna. There shouldn't have been a reason to come back.

Florence's focus shifted from her teacher to the man standing at her right. Things had been changing between those two. Arianna seemed more relaxed around Cvareh, just when Florence's resentment was beginning to peak. If it weren't for him they would be back in Dortam. She would be sleeping late with Arianna in their giant bed, scolding the woman for taking unnecessary chances, and keeping the house tidy between private lessons in back rooms of Mercury Town with some of the best teachers in the Revolvers.

To think, she had even been excited by the notion of the journey when Arianna had first suggested it. Now Florence would give anything to rewind the clocks and beg for a different decision to be made. Or at least beg to be left at home.

The buildings were similar, almost identical to those in Dortam, just as the structures in Ter.5.2 had been. No matter what city she went to in the world, the same, gray, towering spires would meet her with their black shingled roofs, stone awnings, and exposed clockwork. The Rivets were Loom's primary architects, and once they had perfected designs that worked in nearly every climate with most available building supplies, they were copied and repeated across the map whenever a new city needed to be constructed.

It wasn't at the cost of foolhardiness. They'd made use of the natural quarries and mountains when building Dortam. Ter.5.2 had seen more windows on coastal facing walls to let in sea breezes. And here, in Ter.4.2, buildings were wound up with the bridges and tracks running at three different levels of the city. They spanned canals and roadways with graceful arches. The buildings themselves moved to meet the Ravens' innate and insatiable need to spread their wings.

"Flor, it'll be okay." Arianna's hand clasped around hers.

Florence turned away from the city and looked into the lilac eyes of her teacher. Was the woman ever afraid of something? Was there nothing that could turn her insides into a squirming pile of grub-worms?

Even Dragons—who Arianna hated—she did not fear. She challenged them with open eyes and broad shoulders. Florence never wanted to meet the thing that brought Arianna to the quaking precipice of terror.

"We will move fast." Arianna's encouragement meant nothing other than good intentions. Even if they moved as quickly as possible, Ter.4 was wide. It would take them at least a couple weeks to cross, and Arianna planned on traveling the majority underground to prevent Cvareh's magic from being sensed by the Riders.

"When will you head to—" Florence glanced over her shoulders at the crewmembers preparing to dock. "—to see my *friends*." She almost choked on the word.

Ari turned, and Florence followed her attention out to a distant point on the horizon. Standing against the choppy waters and undercurrents of the inner sea was a rocky outcropping—a desolate, barren island dominated by a single large structure. Sheer walls towered upward, unmarred by windows or doors. Iron spikes lined the ground, as much for intimidation as function. At the building's center, a tall tower rose up like a single guard looking over the highest security prison in the world.

"By tomorrow night," Arianna announced.

"So soon?" Florence looked back sharply at her teacher. Arianna usually took days, weeks even, to prepare for bigger jobs. But she wanted to tackle the floating prison in one day.

"Yes, soon." Arianna had the audacity to smile, as though they were commenting on a mere train delay, or Florence forgetting to buy the necessary powders for a canister. "I promised you we would move as quickly as possible."

That made Florence feel the tiniest bit more at ease.

"Plus, the sooner we get to the Underground, the better."

And that returned Florence's mood to rock bottom.

The ship turned in a wide arc, gliding into its place at the end of a long pier. Sailors and dockhands were there to tie off ropes and secure lines as the gangplank was lowered. Florence gripped her bag tightly, staring at the line where the gangplank met the dock. That was it: her last chance to run. If she crossed that line she would be committed to the rest of the journey. Time was running out to return home. Once Arianna freed her friends and went underground, there would be no going back.

Florence looked at the crew. They'd been lovely people, half Ravens, but none had recognized her. The youngest was Arianna's age and Florence didn't think it likely that she had any real overlap in the guild with them. If she asked, she knew they would let her stay for the ride back. She could work for her passage and head back to Dortam. *Someone needed to look after the flat...*

"Flor?" Arianna noticed she hadn't fallen into step with her and Cvareh. "Are you coming?"

Florence took a deep breath. It expanded her lungs, making more room for the crippling fear that locked her knees in place. Then she exhaled it, and moved forward.

"Yes, sorry."

Luck had brought her and Ari together, and the past two years had been the best of Florence's short life. She'd learned more than she ever thought possible. She'd seen new sights. She'd even met a Dragon and run from Riders. Compared to all that, facing Ter.4 should be nothing.

Gripping her bag tightly, Florence descended the gangplank onto the hard poured concrete and stone of the dock. She didn't look back at *Holx III* once, their business concluded. Instead, Florence looked at the black skyline that zigzagged against a gray sky. The sounds of engines whirring filled her ears with an uncomfortable din, reminding her of futile hours spent in workshops trying her hardest to connect gearshifts, cranks, and Rivet-designed pistons to axles.

Those milling about the pier paid them no mind. The trio didn't carry much, only one bag for each of them that was now lighter in the absence of what they had consumed already on their journey. Cvareh was back to wearing his mask, goggles, and hood, bundled up tightly. Arianna covered her face as well, rather than drawing on a mark with a grease pen.

Cvareh had argued about the necessity of it the night before, given how open they had been with the crew, but Arianna was insistent. The crew had been likely to find out the truths of their identities on such a long voyage in confined quarters; appealing to their honesty outright had earned them some endearment even. But people on the street needn't be the wiser. Furthermore, while the occasional Dragon could be seen in major cities across Loom, it was incredibly uncommon and would attract immediate attention.

The streets of Ter.4.2 were set up in a grid pattern. Much like the naming system of cities across Loom, they were numbered based in the order they were built. It was simple, straightforward, and easier than remembering unnecessary names. The only named streets or cities were the very first, and that was always after the founder of the city or, in the case of Guild cities, the first Vicar of the Guild.

The smell of burning oil was so thick in the air it was heavy on the tongue and the revving of engines echoed off buildings as three-wheeled trikes tore through the streets at breakneck speeds. Ravens shouted and hollered to each other, trading jests and challenges as they wove through the narrow alleyways and slid around turns. Florence was older now than the first time she'd seen the gangs that dominated Ter.4. As a child, she'd been fascinated with the pitted bronze bodies and curving handlebars that wrapped around the leather seats of the trikes. That fascination still existed, alongside her apprehension.

The motor-trikes moved without rails, at speeds regulated by single riders. It was a rite of passage in the Ravens to build your first bike, win your first race, and join one of the gangs that prowled the streets. It had seemed foolish then, the idea of riding such a tiny machine at speeds so fast it could wipe tears from your eyes. She'd seen what accidents had done to riders.

But, *then again*, now that she was a bit older she could see it was no less reckless than deciding to play with explosives for a living. Adulthood just meant finding the variety of crazy that resonated the most with you and doing it until you died or it killed you—whichever came first.

"Where are we headed?" Florence asked as they wound up an iron spiral stair to the narrow pedestrian catwalks suspended between the ground and the bridged rail above.

"To my place."

Ari's words froze Florence mid-step. To *her* place? Wasn't their flat in Dortam her place?

"Keep moving, Flor." Arianna glanced over her shoulder and Florence took the steps two at a time until she was right behind Cvareh again.

"What do you think?" she whispered to the Dragon.

"Me?" He seemed surprised she engaged him.

"Who else?" Florence put on a brave grin, trying to imagine how the city might look to someone who didn't have the same history with it that she did.

"It's quite unlike Nov—anything I've ever seen before." He caught himself mid-sentence, giving a quick glance to the crowded walk around them. "Why is it so different from Dortam? Or Ter.5.2?"

"Every territory has evolved to fit the needs of its guild. Dortam and Ter.5 have much more condensed cities, usually protected by mountains, to make use of flatter land for explosive testing." Talking about Ter.5 and the Revolvers, even for a moment, made her feel worlds better. "Whereas Ter.4 is the home of the Ravens. The ground is reserved for experimental vehicles. Trains run above. Airship platforms are up top. There are also the walkways we're on now that kind of weave between all of them."

"And the Underground?"

"*Shh*," Florence hissed. She glanced at the group of vested men who had walked by. Only one glanced back at them. "You don't speak about it."

"Why?" Cvareh obliged, but seemed honestly confused.

"Because of what happens there." Florence gave him a small grin. "Because it's difficult to regulate and that means that we don't want Dragons to know about it."

Cvareh snorted in amusement.

Arianna led them to a quieter section of town. The closest station was far enough away that the train whistle had to echo to get to them. The alleyways below were too narrow for even a trike. It was purely residential, which meant that most people weren't milling about during normal working hours.

Florence knew they'd arrived the moment she saw the lock on the door. It was handedly Arianna's craft, though it was less sophisticated than the turning locks she was used to from her teacher. This had a series of dials in which Ari entered a four-digit pass code.

She couldn't help but notice that Ari entered the code with them both watching. The woman didn't rest herself against the wall between them, or quickly turn the tumblers to prevent her or Cvareh from seeing. 1-0-7-4. Florence remembered the number. Ari either placed little value in the abode, or she wanted Florence and Cvareh to feel as though they had the ability to come and go easily. It was a notable shift from the Arianna Florence had first met, who had made her earn the ability to know the key into their flat in Dortam.

The flat was small—one room with a heavy layer of dust atop everything. The air was stale and the curtains had been shot through by time, small holes in the threadbare fabric letting in winks of light from the outside.

There was one large daybed, pushed against the far wall. A drafting table was squeezed in at its foot. Schematics done in Arianna's hand had been pinned up all around. To the right, by the small galley kitchen and only separated room— the bathroom—was a long workbench. Empty shelves lined the wall above it. The wood grain showed remnants of chemical burns and stains.

Ari's eyes went there first, and time seemed to stop for the woman. Cvareh poked his nose around, curiously drawn to the faded schematics and blueprints. Florence remained by her teacher.

"You never told me you had a place in Ter.4.2." She closed the door gently behind her.

"There wasn't a need. I never thought I'd be returning to it." Arianna shrugged half-heartedly.

Florence took in the one-room flat again. It wasn't much, certainly. But owning property—any property—in the major cities of Loom wasn't easy. You had to be a graduate of a guild, at least, and usually preference was given to masters. Of which Ari was one, Florence reminded herself. But the woman was young, unmarked, and had to have achieved her mastery after the Five Guilds fell to the Dragons—meaning there hadn't been much time for her to secure her own living arrangements on the merits of her guild rank.

"We'll only be here briefly." Florence didn't know who Arianna was struggling so hard to convince. "By tomorrow nightfall, we'll be moving again. By the dawn we'll be gone."

"How do you expect to break into the floating prison?" Florence crossed over to the bed and flopped down on it. Stale smelling and worn, it was far more comfortable than her bunk on the ship, and she instantly felt tired.

Cvareh wandered to the opposite side of the room, running his hand along the workbench. Ari turned and Florence expected a thrashing, given her look. But she kept it to herself, letting Cvareh continue to explore. The self-restraint was new.

"I'll go to the port tonight, find a boat worth stealing. I imagine the guards of the prison do leave it now and then. If they go anywhere, it's likely they'll haunt the bars and parlors dockside, close enough to leave if they want to."

"Information gathering." Florence knew Arianna's process. She just wasn't used to the woman only taking a few hours to do it.

"Then, tomorrow, when it's dark and quiet, I'll head out to the fortress. Use my line to get in." Arianna leaned against the door. Despite being in her own home, she looked incredibly uncomfortable.

Florence blinked, trying to fathom the logic. It seemed remarkably clumsy for the woman whose moniker was the White Wraith, and she'd say as much if it kept Arianna from rushing to her death to save two people whom Florence felt no urgency to see. "The walls of the floating fortress are at least three hundred peca tall. You don't have a line that long."

"I'll have to combine two," Arianna agreed, clearly having already given the matter thought.

"Even if you can use your magic to do that, and the line is strong enough to hold, *and* you still have enough magic to work your winch box... It would take you almost a minute to travel that distance. How can you possibly think you'll go unnoticed from the guards for that long?"

"It'll take me twenty-five seconds, actually, to travel the distance," Arianna corrected.

The woman and her numbers.

"And I'm not worried about the guards noticing me."

"Why?" Florence knew Arianna wouldn't make the statement unless she truly believed it.

"Because time will be on my side." Ari gave Cvareh a pointed look.

All color seemed to drain from the man's face. He scowled and balled his hands into fists. "You cannot possibly be serious."

"But I am." Ari grinned madly.

And Florence jumped to her feet as the Dragon lunged for her teacher.

LEONA

The very air itself was different on Loom. It was heavier, as if it carried the essence of the rocks and metals that the people themselves placed so much value in. It was warmer also, and Leona was certain that it made every Fen certifiably mad to wear so many buttons and layers and ruffles.

She wore tight bindings around her hips and chest, petals of decorative fabric floating around her hips. Camile also wore a fitted top, tight to her breast, her stomach bare. Andre had forgone a shirt altogether.

The more clothes one bundled themselves in, the harder it was to move and fight. The Fen gave up practicality for the sake of an insane notion of modesty. Leona could understand the argument for *some* extra clothes for the fragile race; even without coronas, their skin was thinner, their blood cooler, and they had less resistance to wind and cold built into their bodies. But she thought three shirts were excessive by any stretch.

Leona watched the gray people as they moved through the train station, utterly oblivious to the rank smell of Dragon blood that wafted up from the ground under their feet.

"You are the master of this station. You must know what transpires between its walls." A dull thud scattered some of the more skittish Fen as Andre slammed the small frame of a man against a wall.

"I-I was not—" The man gasped for air, Andre's hand tightening around his throat. "—here that day."

"Then you are useless." Andre's hand tensed, his claws punching through the man's neck on both sides. Crimson blood ran over his fingers, preparing the floor for where the lifeless body fell.

"That's going to stain, you know." Camile kicked her feet from where she sat at the ticketing counter. "Their blood isn't like ours."

Andre looked at where the blood had spattered his trousers with a grimace. Leona smirked at how he could always forget that fact. Bringing the hand to his mouth, he took a timid lap of the blood.

"Hanging stars! You actually ate it!" Camile howled with laughter at Andre's offended scowl.

"What did you think it would taste like?" Leona drawled, crossing over to the counter. A small woman quivered behind it, ordered in place by Camile. "Were *you* here when the King's Riders fell?"

The woman blubbered for a minute before collecting her words. "I was not." Leona sighed heavily and Camile swung her feet over the desk. The woman held up her hands, backing against the wall. "But I know what happened. The woman who works the desk on even numbered days of the month was here and she's my friend and she told me everything. I'll tell you what I know."

Leona and Camile exchanged a look.

"Can't we just kill her and be done with it?" Andre spoke in Royuk. "She's clearly going to be useless."

"Let her speak." Leona stopped him with a palm. She spoke in Fenish so the gray woman would understand her calling off Andre.

"You're too nice, Leona To." Andre pouted against the wall. "You never let me have my fun."

"I let you have too much fun," she replied in Royuk. "Plus, you can kill her once we have the information we need." Leona turned back to the woman, shifting her language again. Fenish was soft and delicate, just like the people who it originated from. "Now, what do you know?"

"A Dragon attacked the Riders."

"Blue skin, orange hair?"

"I think so... He wore a hood, goggles, and mask. But that sounds right." The woman's heart raced so loudly, Leona could hear every beat. She was lying through her ugly flat teeth, but Leona knew the Dragon could only have been Cvareh.

"And he had people traveling with him. Tell me about them."

"Two." The woman nodded frantically. "A girl—a Raven—with a revolver. Standard issue for initiates in Dortam. I don't know how she got it."

That would be Florence. Leona kept her thoughts to herself. But the pasty little Mercury Town man's information continued to hold up, affirming that the decision to barter with him was a wise one. "And the other?"

The Fenthri looked around nervously. Leona tilted her had to the side in interest. No matter how afraid of them she was, she was more afraid of uttering this one name.

"I can't say for certain… But the rumor I heard is that it was the blight of New Dortam."

"The blight of New Dortam?" Leona knew exactly who the woman spoke of, but she was going to make her say it. She wanted to watch this Fenthri squirm, to understand the root of the fear.

"The White Wraith." The Fenthri's eyes flicked around like beady little flies, as though the criminal could be summoned with just an utterance.

"Why do you think it was this… *White Wraith*?" Leona asked coyly. She had her own reasons to think it was the infamous organ thief. But she wanted to hear the woman's logic.

"Three days ago, the harbor master reported a break in. A theft. He discovered the funds missing in the middle of the day, in broad daylight! Now the whispers from the station… everyone knows it must be the Wraith. I don't know how he's expanded his territory so widely, but we are all in danger if it is the case."

"Do you fear the White Wraith?" Leona asked loudly.

"Everyone in Ter.5 does. And you should do the same. The Wraith is infamous for a—"

The woman gurgled blood from her flooding lungs. She looked down in shock. She never even saw Leona move over the counter to thrust her razor sharp claws into her chest. Leona leaned forward to whisper in the woman's ear. "There is only one in this wide world whom you should truly fear. And that is your King."

Leona held her hand in the woman's chest cavity until the last muscle spasms faded from her heart. Withdrawing her hand, Leona wiped it on the woman's shirt, taking a page out of Andre's book. It worked to an extent, but she'd want to wash it sooner than later.

"Isn't she cute when she defends her mate?" Camile teased to Andre.

"If only the Dono was here to witness it," he joked back.

"Now, don't be jealous. I would kill Fenthri for your honor too." Leona grinned, flashing just enough of her teeth to caution them to tread lightly when it came to her fondness for their sovereign.

"I'm not sure if that's really a compliment..." Andre folded his hands behind his head, falling into step with them.

"Given the high regard you hold Fenthri in," Camile finished.

"But defend us to, *hmm*, a member of House Tam? Then maybe we'll think you care." The man grinned.

Leona laughed. "Your laziness knows no bounds. You just want me to fight your duels for you."

"No one can tear out throats—" Camile started.

"Or hearts—" Andre jumped in.

"—or maim like you. Just look at how long your beads are compared to ours." The other woman ran her fingers over the strand that ran down from Leona's right ear.

"Flattery will get you nowhere." Leona batted her hand away.

"Not unless you're Yveun Dono," Andre muttered.

"Enough." Leona would only let their jokes go so far. They were her friends, but she was their leader foremost. If she didn't exercise the fact now and again, they would fall out of place and she'd never wrangle them.

"So where are we headed?" Camile asked as they strolled through the streets of Ter.5.2. "Or are we just taking an afternoon walk?"

Leona extended and retracted her claws. "I want to speak with this Port Master."

The man proved to be relatively useless, imparting no additional information than what the woman at the station had already delivered. Leona milled about his tiny office, almost hitting her head twice on the lamp that hung from the ceiling. She'd begun to tune him out, letting Andre and Camile deal with his ramblings so her mind was free to wander.

She didn't much care *how* the White Wraith had infiltrated the man's offices. For all Leona cared, the Wraith could actually be a specter from the other world. Perhaps that would explain the strange blood smell she picked up in Dortam and again in the station. Perhaps it would actually give Leona a challenge to look forward to on the barren rock known as Loom.

But specter or mortal, there was some logic around how this person was moving. The little man in Dortam would have Leona believe so, and Leona was actually inclined to trust his word after so much else had proved true. She looked out the windows at the harbor.

"Give me the logs of the ships that were here the day you discovered the theft, and a day before." Leona interrupted suddenly. The harbormaster blinked at her. "*Now.*"

He rummaged through his office, fat little fingers wiggling over files to find the documents she requested. He laid them out across the desk in batches.

"Information on all these ships." Leona pointed to the ledgers.

"Yes, right." The man repeated the process until she had all she needed.

"Now, get out. You reek of Fen, and if I am forced to smell it for another second I will eat your throat."

The man fled the office in a sweat, only exacerbating the problem. Leona sighed heavily the second the door slammed behind him. The air was heavy enough as it is; she didn't need the Fen to make it worse.

"Would you really eat his throat?" Andre leaned against the desk next to her.

"Twenty gods above, no." Leona grimaced at the idea. "But he certainly doesn't know that."

"You're thinking Cvareh is on a ship?" Camile rounded the other side of the desk, scanning the documents.

"The Wraith broke into the harbormaster's office, not the air admiral's," Leona reasoned aloud.

"His scent will be harder to pick up the closer he is to the salted sea." Andre followed her logic.

"I can't decide what's more impressive, the idea that the Fen helping him would know that, or a Xin who's never set foot on Loom could." Camile hummed in thought.

"I don't think we're facing an ordinary Fen," Leona finally confessed aloud.

"You can't believe this 'Wraith' nonsense." Andre rolled his eyes dramatically. "Lord Xin would let none escape the afterworld."

"A true Wraith, no," Leona agreed, "But there is more to this. I can *smell* it." She didn't tell them about the strange blood scent she'd picked up twice now. If they couldn't figure it out, they didn't deserve to know.

"Which ship do you think he's on?" Camile asked

Leona looked over the ledgers. Five ships had left the port in the two days around the theft. She pushed the two that sailed the day before aside. The harbormaster collected taxes and tariffs daily—meaning he'd notice a safe discrepancy quickly. The Wraith would have left before the harbormaster really began work for the day. That narrowed it down to two ships. One had left in the night and the other in the early dawn.

She straightened, looking at the big picture and weighing her options. "We ride for Ter.4.2 and will swing the wide route across the coast."

"We're not going after a ship?" Andre asked.

"There are two possible options, but it doesn't matter which one Cvareh is on. Four out of five ships, including these two, were headed for Raven territory. That's our best chance." The reasoning was sound, and her gut corroborated the fact. Still, something was off.

The schematics Cvareh had stolen for the Philosopher's Box would need a Rivet to interpret and complete. One vessel had headed to Ter.5.4, the last city in the Revolver's territory that was the closest to the Rivet's. Leona pursed her lips. Perhaps they had just wanted to leave Ter.5.2 quickly after the commotion at the station. Once in Ter.4 it was easy to get anywhere with the help of the Ravens and all their moving machines.

"When we find Cvareh, what are we doing with him?" Camile asked.

Leona thought about it a moment. Yveun Dono had never much specified what he wanted done with the traitor, only that he wanted the schematics back. She could whisper and ask him, but saw no need to bother her King.

"Well, Petra has assured us that he's not even on Loom— that he is praying to Lord Xin high in the mountains."

Andre snorted, showing how much stock he put in the claim.

"So we're hunting a Wraith, a Fen, and a man who was never even here." Leona's lips curled into a malicious grin.

"So no one will care if such creatures were to, say, vanish." Camile wasted no time on the pick up.

Andre laughed aloud. "Very cloak and dagger. What are we, assassins now?"

"I don't think we can assassinate someone who isn't here." Leona started for the door. "And don't act like you've never cleaned up a mess before. I know how many invisible beads you both wear."

They all flashed their teeth madly. The Riders were the King's men and women, the Dono's most loyal warriors. If they were to be thieves, nothing would keep them out. If they were to be advisers, none would give better counsel. And if they were to be assassins…

Then let the scent of blood put a gnawing hunger in their stomachs.

ARIANNA

"Because time will be on my side." Ari looked to Cvareh for confirmation that he understood her meaning. A dark shadow passed over the man's face. *Good. He understands perfectly.*

"You cannot possibly be serious." He shifted as he spoke the words and Ari did the same. Barely perceptible movements braced them both for the storm that was on their horizon.

"But I am." She welcomed the lightning that sparked in his eyes.

He moved on the crack of thunder that heralded the tempest that had been looming between them. His long fingers scooped up the neckline of her coat, tensing. His claws shot out, ripping holes through the otherwise well kept garb of the White Wraith.

"Are you mad?"

"Maybe." Arianna gave a quick look to Florence for the girl to ease away, she could handle herself. She also didn't know what Cvareh was about to do. If Flor got wrapped into the scrap, she'd never forgive herself for it.

"You know how well that went last time. It set the Riders right on our tail," he snarled, his nose nearly touching hers.

"And if I recall correctly, you were fine. We killed one Rider and evaded the others." Her hands were at her side, ready to grab for her daggers if need be. "And we would've lost them entirely if you hadn't gone rogue at Ter.5.2."

"Don't make this out to be that I owe you." Cvareh's tongue was heavy with the sudden spike in his magic. "If anything, you owe me for giving you the opportunity of a boon."

Ari laughed off the influence he was trying to synthetically apply on her. She threw her own magic behind her words, just to make a point that they seemed to be too evenly matched to sway each other falsely. "Hardly. But you must do this for me if you hope to see the outcome of that boon. I cannot get you to the Alchemists' Guild otherwise."

The Dragon threw her away. Ari shifted her weight from the balls of her feet to her heels, stabilizing quickly. He looked at her with a fearsome sort of wrath.

Good. She wanted to see his true colors. She wanted him to see hers. She wanted to smash down the foolish walls they'd allowed to go up between them on the ridiculous notion of etiquette.

"If you cannot, then relinquish the boon contract. You've met your match. Forfeit gracefully."

"Forfeit is something I don't know how to do." Ari advanced on him this time. "I do not give up. I do not relent. I will have my boon or I will die."

"Arianna!" Florence's concerned interjection was lost.

Arianna's world had been reduced to Cvareh. Their magic pressed against each other. Their muscles rippled with palpable conflict over fight or flight.

"Yield, Dragon, and do this for me," she whispered, as quiet as a knife through skin.

"You…" His slitted pupils dilated and thinned. "You insult me at every turn. You shame my name knowingly. And then you expect to use my magic as you need without recourse? Like I am some mule at your beck and call?"

He was angry. But he was equally hurt, and that was compelling. "My, you taste your own kind's medicine and discover it too foul to be palatable? How unbecoming."

"What?"

"To insult someone at every turn, to demean and degrade them, and then to expect them to give up their knowledge, their skill, without recourse? Does that not sound like what the Dragons have done to Loom since our worlds crossed?"

"Don't try to make this the same."

"Isn't it, though?"

"It's not and you know it."

"Do I?" Arianna insisted.

"We are people, not worlds. And *you* commit the faults you blame me for. You judge me for the actions of my entire race. You see me as a Dragon before you see me as a man. You ignore my good will and attempts at peace, only looking for banners of war between my words. And when you find none, you invent them, so that I better fit your expectations."

Her hands found no life, and her tongue refused her mental quips.

"Silence? The great and infallible Arianna has finally been silenced? Finally."

Arianna studied the man. His broad chest rose and fell steadily in time with the deep breaths that were failing to keep his anger at bay. He was genuinely offended. She searched his face and eyes for a trace of deceit.

She found none, though she hadn't seen any all those years ago, either.

"What do you want at the Alchemists' Guild?"

He huffed in exasperation at the inquiry—he'd already answered that question and they both knew it. So she braved an honest question: "How do you think the Alchemists will help you overthrow the Dragon King?"

"I stole something from him, something that could give Loom a fighting chance." His hand moved subconsciously to the folio he never let leave his sight. Arianna had suspected its contents were essential, but now he confirmed it openly.

"And you need an Alchemist to interpret or make that 'something'?"

He nodded.

Arianna sighed heavily. "If all is as you say, if you are Loom's ally, then help me do this. Show me that you are not my enemy, that you are the bigger man you claim to be. Prove to me that I can trust you by trusting me first."

"I have no reason to trust you at all."

"That's rather the point." Arianna eased away from the man, leaning against Eva's old workbench. The wood was familiar under her fingers, soothing. She knew every burn mark and acid splash across its surface.

"You walk us to certain death." There was resignation in his tone.

"I do not."

"Arrogance and confidence are not the same, but both will get you killed."

The words were louder than the crack of a foreman's bell, echoing through her ears with the same mind-numbing resonance. Ari looked at the man before her, gripping the table to brace herself against the torrent of emotions that ripped her from toes to ears. His statement had unleashed a ghost within her. Not the Wraith she claimed to be, but a genuine shade from a time long past. Arianna didn't like believing in things she couldn't quantify. But she'd always believed in that woman.

"I will put my trust in you, if you put your trust in me." The mechanisms of her mind were slow and squealing in warning. "And we'll both make it through this."

It was quiet for a long moment, neither of them seeing the present. Cvareh sought the future that was just beyond the horizon, as she drowned in the past.

"I don't have much of a choice, do I? And we're wasting time arguing about it."

Arianna nodded and set herself to organizing their supplies across the table. She needed to be as prepared as she could in the short time she had. She needed to be over-prepared, because the last time she had made such a declaration, it had turned out to be a lie.

CVAREH

They stood in complete darkness at the end of a dinky pier. His Dragon sight pierced through the blackness, enhanced by the goggles Arianna had upgraded him to. The world was reduced to a reddish filter over shades of gray, but he could see clearly enough to move without hesitation.

The woman was nothing if not meticulous. She waited for the boats around them to creak with every small wave before undoing another knot or line. She was dressed once more in her full regalia as the White Wraith: a pistol on her thigh, canisters around her waist, her winch box and spools of extended line on her hips and strung through her harness.

His attire wasn't much different. It had been strange to be outfitted by the two Fenthri. Foremost, because it had been the most attention they'd paid him his entire time on Loom to date. But mostly because he'd not the foggiest idea how the guns and canisters strapped around his hips worked.

Florence did her best to explain them, but the girl went into far too much enthusiastic detail about alchemical runes, stored magic, latent power, adding will to the shot, and different types of powders for Cvareh to make sense of it. Arianna's explanation made a lot more sense: point one end at the enemy, pull the trigger, and hope they die. The longer he spent around her, the more he saw Petra in her. The two had undeniable similarities in the way they approached the world. Things fit neatly into binaries defined by "that which would help them achieve their goals," or "that which would hinder them." He smirked privately, amending the last: That which had to be eliminated. He wondered if they would get on well, or be two strong personalities repelling, if they ever met.

Which really was a foolish thought, because there was no way Petra could come down to Loom—that was why he was there in the first place. As the Xin'Oji, Petra had too many eyes on her; navigating the Crimson Court for potential allies and enemies was too necessary an occupation to leave. No, the only way Ari and Petra would ever meet would be if the Fenthri traveled to Nova, and that was a trip he couldn't imagine her taking.

Finally finished with the ropes, Arianna nimbly boarded the rocking vessel and held out a hand for him. Cvareh blinked at the gesture. She extended her arm a little further, impatiently.

He didn't want her help; he wasn't a soft House Tam. He was House Xin. He was sharp of claw and mind, and something like boarding a skiff wasn't going to—

The boat rocked unexpectedly. With one foot on the pier and one foot on the vessel he was sent stumbling forward, arms flailing. Between the waves and his balance issue, the floor beneath him heaved back and forth, leaving him straining to find footing.

Two strong hands gripped his shoulders and Arianna virtually shoved him into the front seat. She set her feet wide, her knees bending with each wave to keep her balanced. Her face dominated his field of vision as she encroached on his space, their noses nearly touching.

"We don't have room to be proud," she hissed. "I must accept your help tonight when I need it. You must do the same. Or we will die here."

All her pride, all her hatred for him and his people—however unjustified—she had put aside. Cvareh felt as though his slate had somehow been expunged of the crimes she had chiseled in from before they had even met. This was a woman on a mission: the White Wraith, free of the prejudices her alter-ego carried like armor.

"Do you understand?"

"Yes." He admired her resolve. For all her faults, this was a side of Arianna he could appreciate. If they failed tonight, it would not be because of him.

"Good. Now no more talking. Voices carry over water." She eased away and sat in the back seat. Keeping the small sail furled, Arianna began straining against two oars, pushing them through the choppy inner sea.

Her warmth retreated with her, but her scent remained. He smelled her keenly over the salty sea. They both knew what was going to happen, but hadn't talked about it much from the start. He would imbibe from her again before the night was out. He would taste her power once more.

Cvareh's eyes dilated in the darkness.

The floating prison of Ter.4.2 grew in size. What had been nothing more than a black silhouette breaking the horizon on their way into port was now an ominous colossus of woven metal and impenetrable stone. Arianna had gone over its basic structure with him three times over: an outer ring of cells, an inner guard tower from which guards could observe their tenants at any point without the convicts being aware of who was where. As a result, the prison needed fewer guards. The idea of being watched proved a stronger deterrent against unwanted behavior than the actual, physical presence of someone watching.

From Arianna's limited time to research, she had come to the conclusion that there were between five and fifteen guards on staff at any time. But they were all heavily armed and well trained—trained to kill before asking questions.

She pulled the oars a short way out from the rocky island, allowing them to coast toward the shore. When they were within a stone's throw, she stood, easing herself out of the boat and into the water. Arianna held onto the skiff, inspecting the walls, waiting.

She extended her hand and he took it. It was like a dance, and she was leading. Everything Cvareh had been taught screamed against letting another be in control. It was opposed to the dominance structure of Dragon society. But with Petra, obedience spun from loyalty was a familiar feeling for Cvareh—a feeling that Arianna was slowly stealing for herself as well.

Arianna pulled him from the boat with the crash of a wave. He tried to nimbly exit the skiff and was met with mixed success. Luckily, his flailing was kept to a minimum this time, and Arianna didn't feel the need to have another heart to heart.

She unclipped a small disk from her harness, settled it into the boat, then waded into the water far enough that she could free the vessel from the tug of the waves. They walked together up the shoreline with cautious stares trained at the dark guard towers. Four towers, and only two were ever manned at once. His eyes darted between the three corners he could see, fighting for some sign of where the guards might be. It was his first taste of the harrowing feeling of possibility being watched without knowing by who or from where.

They slunk between spikes of all sizes, erected to ward off ships that would ram the prison for a mass breakout, to the base of one of the towering walls. Without hesitation, Arianna's hands adjusted the cabling through her harness and freed her clip. She spared one glance for him. That was all the confirmation Cvareh knew he would receive.

She closed the gap between them, her hips flush against his, her abdomen pushing into his body as she bent backward, seeking space to navigate the cabling around them. Cvareh swallowed, wondering if she could hear his heartbeat when she leaned into him like that to tether them together. Life and power surged through her, a blend unlike any he had ever known. Knowing that he'd soon have it again made him crave it all the more. It made him want to cling to her until he had bled her dry.

His arms snaked around her back, holding her to him. He was slowly going mad, and she couldn't be calmer; he couldn't even hear a whisper of her heart. Arianna gave a small nod and Cvareh braced himself against the howling winds of time.

He breathed it into him, letting his lungs become a cocoon for the sands of the hourglass. It burned instantly, all the way down his throat. Like a flock of birds, they fought and scratched against his insides, seeking freedom from their unnatural cage. The world slowed as he gained dominance over the minutes of the clock and in seconds that felt like eons, he won control over time itself.

Arianna was moving. He felt her magic clearly through the vacuum of space he had created. As his magic encased her, her magic ensnared him. They were their own world and Cvareh was barely aware of movement. He focused only on keeping control as time fought for freedom from his lungs.

It shredded his insides, filling him with blood. His lungs began to decay, becoming necrotic in mere moments due to magical exhaustion. The world shuddered. He wouldn't be able to hold his breath for another second.

She slammed him against the wall. A scream tried to escape his throat, but all that was there was blood. It poured down her shoulder in the darkness. Arianna pushed herself against him. She clutched his waist, her feet planted.

"Do it."

He was too happy to oblige.

Cvareh yanked on the back of her hood, catching hair with it. Her head twisted backward and pulled her face into a grimace, exposing the one part of her body that wasn't covered in layers of fabric. Magic faltered within him, struggling and failing to heal his ailing lungs.

He sunk his teeth into her eagerly. He fought to keep himself from tearing out strips of her neck in his zeal for her power. Cedar and honeysuckle flooded his mouth, mixing with the smoky musk of his blood spewed on her shoulder.

It was pure power. It was the essence of life. More than anything, it was her.

He invaded her through her magic, pillaging and rummaging through every dark corner. He could smell the tang of regret harrowing her behind every shadowed awning of her memories. He could hear the echoes of longing crying out through the lonely hallways of her daily consciousness. He could feel the heat from the flames that consumed her waking moments whole, a pyre in the lighthouse of her wayward morality that burned for one thing alone: vengeance.

She was an enigma, a strange creature of contrasts. And, for the briefest moments when he imbibed off her living flesh and blood, she was his.

Arianna pulled herself from him, and he barely relinquished. Drunk off her power, his mind swam, clouded. Her hand flew up to her shoulder, smearing the blood from where his lungs had failed and come up golden, covering her wound until it healed. Their eyes met and he felt the same urge as he had last time—the want to drown in her.

She lowered her hand, her stare wavering but not breaking. Her eyes challenged him to say something, to move for her again, to do anything. She threatened the same in kind. He could read every twitch of her muscles. She wanted to level the score, to put him in as vulnerable a position as he had just had her.

What was equally terrifying and thrilling was in that moment, he would have let her.

ARIANNA

There was nothing like this feeling. She had experienced much in her twenty-two years of life. But the sensation of someone stripping her down to an essence that even she couldn't describe was incomparable to any other situation she had found herself in.

Arianna had devoted herself to person and cause. She had wholly and completely loved as a friend, as a lover. But this was something entirely different.

And utterly terrifying.

Once more she was caught bare before him and she hadn't even scratched his surface. Her hands twisted in his clothing, ill-fitting and basic as it was. She wanted to rip it off and push him down. She wanted to sink her teeth into him and show him that their world moved on her terms.

It had only been seconds since they ascended through the empty window of the guard tower. But time falling back into place had made it seem like an eternity. The nagging sensation of things moving once more brought her attention back to the present. The sound of footsteps nearing reminded her of where and who she was, what she was doing.

She was Arianna. She was the White Wraith. And she had a job to do.

Her fingers relinquished him, quickly working to unstrap his body from hers. The cabling retreated into its spool with a thought. She kept her eyes from his until the effects of the imbibing wore off both of them. She had no interest in making herself vulnerable again before him. He had already made her feel that way without even knowing it.

The only way arrogance and confidence are similar is that both can get you killed, Arianna. The words echoed back through her mind from a woman long dead. This man, this Dragon—he was nothing like her Eva. Arianna refused to accept it.

Arianna pulled out a token. On it was an alchemical rune. Florence said the range wouldn't be terribly far, but exactly how far "terribly" was, she couldn't quite say. Ari pressed her thumb into the rune and pushed her magic through it, willing heat. It shattered under her fingertips and, at exactly the same moment, an explosion cut chaos into the quiet night.

The bomb on their skiff drew the attention of the exterior guards and Arianna bounded through the interior door of the tower. A long tunnel connected the outer wall with the guard tower, one of four. Through the window slits on either side, Arianna got her first glimpse of the floating prison. Concrete and steel fitted together to construct a grim image of desolation. Every cell had an open barred wall facing a narrow walk that spiraled around the entirety of the prison—the only way up or down.

On the edge of the walk, facing the inner tower, were painted the numbers of each cell. Arianna quickly made a note of the highest and lowest. Once she knew that, she could calculate approximately where any cell was using basic estimations of height and spacing. The largest variable remained finding what numbers she needed.

The door at the end of the suspended, tunneled bridge opened. A circled Revo leveled a gun with a golden barrel at them, his vermilion eyes nearly glowing in the darkness. She didn't even miss a step. She kept charging down the stretch head on.

His wrist tensed and Ari slammed herself against the right wall. Cvareh moved in lockstep, pressing himself on the opposite wall as she had hounded him to do—when in doubt, she went right, he left. The gunshot was louder than an engine's piston firing and she was certain her ears were bleeding, though her magic worked immediately to repair the damage.

Cvareh winced, covering his ears. But Arianna had a different kind of instinct. Her gun was already drawn. The trigger was pulled before the Revo had time to lower his.

But he was well trained, and he predicted her shot, falling to the ground at a diagonal. Arianna dropped her gun, reaching for her daggers. The man stood, bringing a fist covered in brass knuckles into her gut. Her stomach collapsed, expending the air in her. She curved forward and used the momentum to bring the dagger into his throat, tearing through his windpipe.

"Grab my gun!" she shouted to Cvareh, pushing through the door to engage with the other guard at the top of the Tower.

The woman knocked the knife from Ari with the side of her revolver, then grabbed for Ari's wrist, holding it away as she tried to lock the muzzle of the gun onto her face. Ari spun, slamming her opponent into the wall, the other dagger in her hand. The woman twisted her grip.

Gunfire echoed through the small, barren room, a pockmark steaming in the ceiling from an incendiary round that narrowly missed Arianna's head. The woman slammed her foot into Arianna's heel, trying to trip her. Ari held fast with a grimace.

A steely blue hand jutted over her shoulder, grabbing the woman's neck. Ari felt the heat from her Dragon at close proximity. She watched the muscles in his forearm tense as they pushed his claws through the woman's throat, killing her instantly. He withdrew, shaking the red blood off his hand with a grimace and then held out her gun.

"Thank you." Arianna accepted her weapon from the man and trusted he'd hear the words in more ways than one.

"Lead. I'll have your back." He glanced back toward the hall. Both their sets of Dragon ears were picking up fast-running footsteps, men and women alerted to their presence by the commotion.

"I'll trust you with it, then." The words were cumbersome. Her lips didn't want to form them, but Arianna discovered that something could be right and uncomfortable at the same time. Her footsteps stalled as she rounded the staircase leading down the central watchtower.

He looked at her in confusion. That same emotion was reflected in her every thought. She had left someone behind before. She had done so knowing they would die for her sake, for the sake of their mission.

Arianna held up an accusatory finger. "Dragon, don't you dare die on me."

Cvareh was visibly taken aback at the proclamation.

"I want my boon," she added hastily, and disappeared further down the Tower.

There were five guards, of this she was now certain. Two sets of footsteps from watchers in the Towers. The two they'd killed in the central guard tower. And one below her still.

But time was still of the essence. The explosion from their skiff was likely to draw attention on the shore, assuming none of the guards had fired some kind of signal flare she and Cvareh missed from being indoors since time stopped. Logically, reinforcements were coming, and Arianna gave them six minutes across the stretch of water between the floating prison and the mainland, and perhaps another ten to get themselves and a boat in order—she'd round down to fifteen.

It meant she had ten minutes left to kill the remaining guards, find the cell she needed, break out Florence's friends, steal a boat, and evade any pursuers on the water. Ari grinned wildly, flashing her teeth as a volley of gunfire rang out between her and the guard before her, echoed by shots above. Plenty of time.

The man ahead used a single round shotgun, powerful but slow. He knew it too as he reached for the saber strapped to his hip. Swords. Now there was something she didn't mess with. Swords were archaic and only two types of people used them as a result: arrogant newbie Revos who wanted to show off, and masters. Since the man bore a black circle, she wasn't betting on the former.

The slightly curving blade echoed against its scabbard, its single edge gleaming wickedly in the lamplight. Arianna grabbed for her cabling, quickly clipping her dagger to it. Her weapons wouldn't stand up; she knew when she was bested. So it was time to throw a skill of her own into play. Magic.

Her dagger fluttered around him like an annoying fly. He batted it away with his sword, dodging and half-stepping closer. Arianna tuned out the sounds of the battle above her and targeted the Revo. Malice burned through her, ignited by frustration. She didn't want to kill this man or his allies, she had no delight in it. Their deaths were a means to her end, more bodies sacrificed upon the altar of the lost future she had been striving to build alone in the years following the collapse of the last resistance.

He didn't stand a chance against the beam of pure energy that fired right through his chest.

Ari holstered her gun and leaned against the wall, catching her breath. She was killing Fenthri for a Dragon. It was a truth so insane she had no other option but to believe it was real. Yet she couldn't muster the same hatred for Cvareh. There was a desperate sort of survival in him too.

She shook her head with a breathless laugh at herself. *I actually believe he's fighting against the Dragon King. What was the world coming to?*

The commotion above quieted as Arianna reached the central office of the prison. A shelf of large ledgers directed her to exactly what she needed to know. There were only a few things to monitor in a prison, after all: the scheduling of the guards, general maintenance, food, and who was where.

"Glad to see you could manage two Revos," she remarked as a familiar set of footsteps treaded down the stairs.

"Did you have any doubt?" He wasn't even winded.

"When it comes to you, I have nothing but doubt." Ari glanced over her shoulder. He had a few cuts that were already healing and half his sleeve seemed to have been blown off, exposing cut muscle beneath. "Did you shoulder a shot straight on?"

"They weren't expecting it." Cvareh stood at her side, looking at the ledger she was assessing. She was impressed, but he saved her from saying so when he pointed at the list of names. "Shouldn't we just call out and ask for them by name?"

She rolled her eyes dramatically. "Yes, because no other prisoner would claim to be someone they're not at the prospect of escape."

"Point taken." He turned, leaning against the table and closing his eyes. "Sounds like we're alone."

"For now," she agreed. "Though more will be here soon." Her eyes fell on the names she had been searching for. Arianna dragged her finger across the page, checking the dates they were imprisoned against when she met Florence. It matched. "But we have who we need."

The floors of the tower that were eye-level with the cells had only slats for windows. The wider ones were at the top, where a guard could survey both prison and sea without being visible. Arianna looked out over the compound. Shouts and calls were starting to rise from inmates who realized something was amiss.

"There." She pointed at an enclosed tunnel on the ground. Bloody everything was enclosed so the guards were never visible to the prisoners. "Run down the Tower and get halfway through that tunnel. Use this."

"How?" Despite his confusion, Cvareh accepted the disk she passed him.

Arianna ran his fingers over the alchemical rune Florence had etched onto the surface of the bomb. "Here, focus your magic here. Imagine it heating, melting."

"Right." He bolted for the stairs.

"And make sure you're a good distance away when you do!" Arianna called after him.

"Count on me!" he shouted back.

Arianna gripped her golden line tightly. That was the dangerous thing. The longer they spent together, the more she thought she could.

Hopping up on the windowsill, Arianna glanced down, finding numbers 127 and 138. Unfortunately, the prison was too well run to put partners in crime next to each other. But they were at least close. She set her sights on the higher of the two, her line shooting out and latching to the bars of a cell just above.

The shouts of the offended prisoner whose cell she used as an anchor point were drowned out by the rush of wind in her ears as she leapt into the open air. Her winch box whirred, pulling her up as she arced across the length of the gap between the inner tower and the cells. Kicking out her feet, Ari tumbled onto the narrow spiraling walkway, her cord unhooking and retracting into its spool.

"Falling airships, woman!" the girl behind the bars exclaimed. "The Vicar Raven know you got that setup? Because I'm thinking she may want a schematic."

"Do I look like someone who'd work with the Vicar Raven?" Arianna turned her cheeks.

"Unmarked? Be careful or they'll lock you in here too. You've too much talent for them to just kill. They'll try to break you first." The girl grinned madly. She folded her hands behind her back, swaying from toe to heel.

"Dead men don't lock doors, Helen."

"Guard killer and you know my name? Aren't you just the epitome of mystery?" The girl laughed and shook her head.

Hair that Arianna presumed was once the color of snow hung in dingy, matted chunks around her face. No one ever praised the floating prison for its treatment of inmates.

"Add, 'the woman who broke you out' to that list." Arianna unrolled a strip of tools attached to her hip, setting on the lock. She whistled to herself. "Now, what Rivet built this?"

"A master, I think." Helen watched in amusement. "Some of the other Rivets here have tried. You have tools, but I don't know if..."

Arianna tuned her out. The lock had a closed front, no keyhole. All screws and connectors were concealed within, making disassembly difficult. The key slot was thin and flat, which Ari presumed to mean the keys were like cards embedded with a series of notches that depressed tumblers at the opposite end of the lock box.

She had two more explosives on her, but she really didn't want to waste them. It was likely that she wouldn't have another opportunity for Florence to restock before they fled into the Underground. And using a bomb assumed it would damage the lock enough to crack it without injuring the prisoner within.

First things first, she had to get into the lock to disengage it. Fortunately for her, this wasn't a job that required discretion. She ran the pads of her fingers along the seams, searching for a weak point in the welding. The prison's inners had been exposed to the sea and salt air since its construction in the early days of Ter.4, and if there was one thing metal didn't like, it was the combination of time, moisture, and salt.

Her nails fell into a hairline groove on the side—a fatigue failure. She went for her thinnest golden tool, driving it into the crack and twisting the flat head, widening the gap. Keeping one pin in place, she reached for a second, repeating the process hastily until the front was halfway off. Unfortunately, the top part of the weld proved to be much stronger.

She needed more leverage.

There was enough space now for her slimmer, sharper dagger to fit. Arianna inwardly winced at the idea of sacrificing the edge of her blade like this and made a mental note to sharpen it later. She twisted it, grunting with the strain. The cover bent just enough for her to get a look under.

It was as she suspected: several pins at different intervals, waiting to be lined up. That was the design flaw. Unlike a normal lock that required pressure on the pins throughout a turn to disengage, this only required the pins to be engaged correctly at the same time for the bolt to be pulled back. Ari could see why it was effective given the circumstances—mostly enclosed design, unique key to discourage people from trying to pick it, unconventionally shaped access to the pins. But once it was cracked, it put up no fight.

"What in the Five Guilds are you, lady?" Helen asked as Arianna pulled open the door.

"Someone who's looking for a favor from you."

"Get me out of here, I'll do anything you want." The girl grinned, taking Ari's invitation and strolling out of the cell onto the landing. She took an instinctual breath of air. Though it was chemically no different than what she had been breathing through the bars for two years, Arianna could only suspect that it was a little bit sweeter in that moment.

"I need you to take me through the Underground."

"Tall order," the girl hummed.

Ari smirked, admiring her cheekiness. She was negotiating with the woman who had freed her as though it were nothing. "Florence is waiting for you now at its entrance."

Helen froze. "Flor? She made it?"

Ari nodded. "Now, run down. Head for the tunnel out."

The girl stared skeptically for one long moment, but she didn't have many options—linger and be jailed again, or flee and trust Arianna at face value. Ari greatly appreciated that she was the sensible type. As Helen ran, Ari hooked herself into the bars and jumped over the ledge down to the landing below.

She ignored the calls of inmates pleading for their freedom. There were real criminals mixed among those who had been jailed for failing to follow the Dragon King's mandates, and she had no record of who was who. For all she loathed the Dragons, Ari wouldn't spite them at the risk of putting someone actually dangerous back on the streets of Loom.

Helen was slow, and by the time she had made it around the large loop of the walkway Ari had finished unlocking the door of Will's cell, explaining the same overview of the situation in the process. They were just starting down when the explosion she'd been waiting for rattled the enclosed hall below, blowing out chunks of stone and cement. Dust plumed skyward and Ari looked for a certain blue shadow to emerge from its curtain.

Coughing, Cvareh didn't disappoint her.

"Took you long enough!" she called over the increasing volume of shouts from the other prisoners.

"It's not like you were waiting," he noted as they reached the cement floor at the ground level.

"I can still judge you for taking that long to figure out a simple bomb." The corner of her mouth twitched upward in what could dangerously be called a grin.

"Bent axles, what in the five is a Dragon doing here?" Will blubbered.

"He's a friend," she answered without a thought, stepping into the hall.

Cvareh's golden eyes squinted at her. Arianna didn't even need to turn her head to know his expression. She was just as shocked as he was. The word slipped out before she'd had time to think it through. He is nothing more than the Dragon who offered you a boon, Ari insisted privately.

A well-kept speedboat was docked in one of two open slots protected either side by rocky outcroppings. Arianna looked to her companions. "I trust one of you can captain this thing."

Will and Helen's heads snapped to face each other.

"Helm?" Will asked.

"You get engine." Helen grinned in reply.

The two sprinted up the gangplank, assessing the ship as quickly as Ari did a clockwork machine. She had no doubt they already knew the top speed, drag, handling—everything about the vessel. Florence might not have been a born Raven, but from what she'd said of her friends, they were. And these were things that, once trained, were never forgotten.

"You sure it's safe?" Cvareh followed her aboard. He took a step closer, adding softly, "To let them drive?"

"Safer than my doing it." If there was one thing no one wanted, it was Arianna behind the wheel of any vessel that was more than a rowboat or paddle trike.

"If you insist, I'll trust you." He shrugged and situated himself against the railing.

The words turned over in her head. But before Arianna had a chance to dive into the depths of their implications, a distinct rainbow streak blazed a trail through the darkness over Ter.4.2.

LEONA

*S*he had him.

It was faint and distant, but even a tiny spark of magic in this desolate industrial wasteland felt earth-shaking. This was more than a spark, though. This was magic she didn't even know Cvareh had. This was as powerful as a Rider's would be.

She bared her teeth in malicious glee, knowing she had him, and would soon kill him for Yveun Dono.

Leona sprinted to where she and her riders had landed their gliders on one of the flat rooftops of the port three days ago upon arriving to Ter.4.2. It had been three horrible days of waiting and debating that now came to a satisfying conclusion. They would take to the skies once more and she would hunt down Cvareh like the Xin dog he was.

Magic wrapped around her feet, holding them to the platform of her glider. She pushed power under the wings, drawing it upward, overflow glittering off like fireworks in the night sky. Andre and Camile were close behind, moving without need of instruction.

It didn't matter if they were there or not; the Xin fool was hers anyway. Leona wanted to bathe herself in his blood. She wanted to return to Nova and have there be no doubt as to whose flesh had torn under her fingers.

Loom was darker than Nova. It lacked both starlight and moonlight due to the God's Line that always obscured the sky. She pushed magic into her sight—not enough to blind her, but enough to pierce through the blackness, looking for the source of the magic.

A signal flare drew a line into the sky as if to point an arrow in the right direction. *The prison?* Leona didn't waste thought on why Cvareh would head to such a place. She didn't need to know the method to his madness. She only had to put a stop to it.

She was closing in and fast, close enough to hear the echo of an explosion over the water. Leona gripped the handles of her glider more tightly. It was an island, which meant there would be only one way off of it. Arcing around the prison, she scanned for a port of some kind. It wasn't until her second loop that she saw it.

"There!" she screeched to Andre and Camile, directing their attention to her discovery. "You two kill any Fen and Chimera. Cvareh is *mine*."

Her comrades bared their teeth in understanding, pitching their gliders forward. They shot down toward the boat as it raced out of the harbor. Leona laid her eyes on him for the first time.

His blood orange-colored hair tousled around pale Xin flesh, whipped by the wind off the sea and the speeding vessel. He was short for a Dragon, Leona noted, a pitiful looking thing that didn't radiate half the power of his sister. The Fen in white standing next to him was nearly the same height.

A Fen in *white*.

No, no that wasn't a Fen. That was a Chimera of a different variety. That was the source of the odd blood smell Leona had been tracking across two territories. The woman had a strange and cataclysmic sort of power about her. The madness and blood lust that surged through Leona's veins seemed to cry out in recognition of an equal. An instinct that, even despite being faced with a Chimera, Leona heeded.

The White Wraith—*a woman was the White Wraith*—calmly loaded a small tube into the pistol at her hip. Andre sped toward her, claws out, ready to make a killing blow. The woman reached out her spare hand in a confident gesture and Cvareh took it. Chimera and Dragon, the strangest unified front she'd ever seen.

Magic surged over Leona, splitting her skull from ear to ear. The world blurred and she lost focus and seconds. She blinked rapidly, trying to ground herself once more by pushing aside the strange sensation of lost time. Her eyes scanned the boat in an attempt to pin down what had just occurred.

Andre was no longer on his glider, no longer boasting the upper hand. He was on the deck of the ship, a hole shot through his chest. Cvareh was doubled over, coughing blood as he stumbled toward the corpse of the felled Rider. The ship lurched as the empty glider crashed into the sea next to it.

That was how he'd gotten so far. Leona banked once more through the sky, circling like a bird of prey. The bastard could stop time. Only one in a hundred Dragons were born with that ability and Cvareh Xin was one of them. There was truly no justice in the world. She looked in disgust as he consumed Andre's body. Talent worthlessly fed to the lowest House in Nova.

"Push, don't stop," the Wraith screamed to the helm of the boat.

They were halfway between the prison and the mainland. Leona scanned the horizon. *Where were they headed?*

The vessel was cutting a diagonal path through the water, away from the main port and the second boat of Fen attackers coming at them. The stretch of land at the end of their trajectory was dim and black, little waiting for them. Leona growled. Too much thinking, not enough doing.

"Camile, fly ahead, cut off the boat. When it dodges, I'll flank."

Her remaining Rider nodded affirmation. Camile's focus remained steadfast in the wake of Andre's death. They were the King's Riders and that meant that, if they were lucky, they would die serving their sovereign. Andre had merely reached the logical conclusion of his duty.

The rush of the chase was beginning to get to Leona's head. She wanted to run down her prey. There was no darker glee that lit up her heart than the notion of a well-earned kill. And now she had two, Wraith and Dragon.

Camile did exactly as Leona had instructed, charging the ship head on. The Wraith sprinted to the bow to meet her, gun drawn. She had a steady draw and sure aim, but with the moving of the waves and Camile's evasive bobbing, her shot missed. Without time stopped, they were a lot more difficult to hit. Leona seized the opportunity, heading toward the rear side of the vessel where it banked, the deck tipping toward her as the driver turned wildly.

She found herself face-to-face with the second unexpected discovery of the evening. Cvareh was holding a gun. The born and bred Dragon noble was holding a crude Fenthri weapon. It looked awkward in his hands, but he tracked it on her anyway.

Glyphs on the exterior of the gun flared bright enough that it lit up the entire deck and surrounding sea. It fired at twice the size, speed, and power as any Chimera's would, forcing Leona away. The weapon cracked and crumbled under the strain, falling to pieces in the Dragon's hand.

So, Petra had been hiding this unpolished gem all along. Cvareh was rough, untrained, and generally timid. Underneath it all was true power. The closer they neared land, the more she realized her grave error in underestimating him. He was the younger brother of Petra'Oji and Houyui To, *of course he had strength.*

Camile rejoined her in the sky as Leona let out a cry of frustration. She was done toying with them. "We head to land," she declared. "Cut them off there."

Pushing her magic under her, Leona sped ahead of the boat, keeping in line with its course. She was done fighting over the salted sea and its dangerous depths. On land, she would have the upper hand. She wouldn't underestimate them a third time.

The secondary boat was close enough to open fire, but Cvareh's crew seemed uninterested in engaging. They pushed onward, ignoring all other distractions and opponents. Like a beam of sunlight, they penetrated the inky blackness with speed and certainty. But nothing was ahead of them. A wall of tall bars connecting the sea with the Underground canals and sewers blocked their path.

They were going in hot and fast on a straight collision course for the giant grate, suicidally determined to outrun their pursuers to their deaths. Leona pulled back, unwilling to follow to that watery grave. If Cvareh wanted to kill himself, she'd let him.

The White Wraith turned, watching Leona as she fell away. Leona could feel the woman's eyes on her from underneath the gleam of her magically enhanced goggles. She raised an empty hand and gave a wave, as though bidding farewell to the world.

An explosion ripped the sea apart. The boat turned and zigged, fighting against the currents and waves that pushed against its bow—keeping on course in a display of driving mastery. The rusted iron bars of the grate shattered into pieces, hot molten metal glowing like the jagged teeth of a giant beast in the darkness.

The ship allowed itself to be swallowed whole by it.

"Where are they going?" Camile called. "What do they hope to find under the city?"

And then it hit her. Leona screamed as she realized she'd been thwarted again. This Chimera was making a fool of her. The woman was two steps ahead, preempting Leona's every movement. Leona thought House Xin exhausted the depths of her hatred. But no, this was a rage unlike anything she'd ever felt. It was bitter and rough and raw, and coursed through her like swallowed rocks.

"The Underground," she snarled, panting, worked into a frenzy. "We pursue!"

The moment they crossed into the back thresholds of the Underground, they would be lost. Leona knew better than to follow into that tumultuous blackness, a place where the sun had never shone and true wretches made their home. Even as a Rider, there were some things she had to admit bested her.

The tunnel was narrow and getting smaller by the second. The boat was forced to dock inelegantly, as half its side was smashed in against a narrow walk. Leona skidded her glider against the surface of the water, evading a shot from the Wraith.

"Go!" the Chimera called to her companions.

Leona's eyes fell on a Fen girl with long black hair. She was just as the tiny man in Ter.5 had described. Tiny enough for Leona to pick her up and snap her in two as though she were a wooden doll.

She jumped onto the walk, letting her glider sink into the water. She'd recover it with magic later. Stable ground had never felt so good, and Leona wasted no time in launching herself for a deadly attack. The Wraith thought she'd be aiming for her, but Leona's claws sought a different foe.

The woman in white was fast. She changed from bracing herself to charging forward in a mere instant. But she wasn't fast enough. Leona's claws sunk into the tiny Fen's shoulder, ripping through muscle and sinew. They missed the lethal mark, but the message was clear as the Wraith threw her away with a cry of rage.

"Flor!"

Yes, yes that sound of anguish was what Leona lived for. It sent the previously calm Chimera into a frenzy. The woman charged Leona in a blind rage.

"Arianna!" Cvareh called after her, as he locked claws with Camile.

Leona dodged as the woman threw a golden dagger at her, then ducked when the Wraith pulled it back, hearing it whistle by the side of her head. This "Arianna" was a force unto her own. Like a thorny whip, a second dagger shot out from her hand, tethered to a golden line. Fearless, with complete disregard for her own well being, she launched at Leona headfirst.

"We have to go!" A man's voice—not Cvareh—called from farther down the hall. "We can lose them in the Underground!"

The flurry of attacks didn't stop.

"Arianna!" Cvareh kicked Camile in the chest, sending the other woman scrambling to avoid landing in the water.

Arianna ignored the Dragon. She continued, relentless. Leona grinned at her, and grabbed the dagger rather than dodging. Golden blood streamed down her wrist and elbow.

"If you don't kill me now, I'll hunt down your little pet. I'll kill *Florence*," Leona swore, wriggling as far as she could under the woman's skin.

The Wraith inhaled sharply the instant she heard the name. The Chimera's attacks were becoming sloppy, worked into a fever pitch. It was only a matter of time before—

Leona saw her opening. Her fingers tensed, and she jabbed her hand forward for the Chimera's chest.

And they sunk into the side of Dragon flesh. Cvareh's arms wrapped around the Fenthri woman as he grimaced aloud in pain. Arianna screamed at him in frustration and the sound was cut short as another piercing flare of magic assaulted her mind.

When the haze from magically stopped time cleared, Leona was left with nothing more than Cvareh's blood on her hand, the echo of a collapsed wall, and the rage of an unfinished fight.

FLORENCE

The only thing that made Florence ignore the pain in her shoulder was losing sight of Arianna with the Dragon Rider still attacking. Will planted the charges as Ari had no doubt instructed, as Florence had been told was the plan from the start. She sagged against Helen, trying to hold in the crimson waterfall that poured relentlessly between her fingers on a march to drag her down the river of death.

"We can't—Ari— we have to go back for her." The panic of seeing her friends again was replaced by a greater, more pressing fear of her teacher, her friend, being trapped on the other side of the wall. It pushed aside all reason and logic surrounding Ari's competence.

"The Riders are distracted with them," Will shot back. "We can lose them here."

"I'm not leaving them behind!"

"Yes you will." Helen's words were cold, Helen, her *first* friend, the *first* person Florence had left behind for her own sake.

"No, I won't," Florence insisted. She wasn't the girl she'd been then. She was sixteen now, nearly middle-aged. She was a woman who would stay with the people she loved even if it meant death.

The debate ended in a blink. Cvareh appeared seemingly out of nowhere, collapsing to the ground, and Arianna with him. Blood poured from his mouth and from the wound on his side, but Ari seemed blissfully unharmed.

"Flor!" Her teacher scooped her up in her arms. "Flor, we need to stint the bleeding, now."

"Cvareh—" Florence swayed from blood loss.

"We need to keep going!" Helen interjected frantically.

"Heard." Will ran back to join them, firing at the planted charges.

The explosion sent them all flying, rolling head over heels. Florence cried out in pain as the wound on her shoulder tore further from the force with a violent *rip*. The wall collapsed between them and the Riders, heralding a silent aftermath and pitch blackness.

She blinked into the darkness, creeping panic raising every hair on the back of her neck. She was back in the Underground. One extreme emotion after another was the only glue holding her together, but even that had its limits. Pain was beginning to dot stars against the void and Florence blinked frantically, her senses ringing.

Arianna pulled the cap off a torch, bathing the passage in a faint reddish glow. Helen and Will were finding their breath again, coughing through the dust, rolling to their feet. Cvareh wasn't moving.

"Flor, let me see it." Her teacher moved for her.

"Will can help me." Florence continued to apply pressure on her shoulder. It hurt, but she'd been trained by Ari for years in "what if" scenarios.

"Me?" Will balked.

"Ari, he's not moving," Florence insisted at her hesitation. "What's the point of all this if you lose your boon?"

"Boon?" Helen repeated in a sudden moment of clarity.

Ari scowled at her. It was a face Florence didn't get to indulge in often because it was one she only made when someone else was right and had bested her with the fact. Florence smiled tiredly.

"Pack this into the wound, and then stitch it up with this." Ari shoved some supplies into Will's hands.

"Do I look like an Alchemist?" He regarded the medical tools with skepticism.

"If you haven't learned this yet, learn it quickly: I do not like to be crossed or questioned," Ari growled. "I'm leading this trip and you would still be rotting in that cell if it wasn't for me. I will put you back there personally if you don't help Flor."

Will laughed with a shake of his head, moving over to her. He set down the supplies in the flickering light of the torch that burned harmlessly on the ground between the five of them. "You made a scary friend, Flor."

"I did…" Florence watched Ari as Will began to pack her wound. Her teacher flipped over the prone Dragon, regarding him thoughtfully. There was a softness to Ari's brow that Florence hadn't seen her adopt around the Dragon before. She had been Ari's first priority, but there was genuine concern for Cvareh alighting the woman's violet eyes.

Ari ran her hand over the oozing wound on his side, bringing her fingertips to his face. Florence watched as she pried the Dragon's mouth open. Her teacher opened her mouth a fraction and bit down with a grimace.

Blood, Florence realized. Ari was a Chimera and that meant her blood had magic in it, and the magic that lived in blood had the power to heal. She was giving the man her strength, literally forcing life down his throat.

Arianna knelt at the Dragon's side, bringing her face down to his. Her body blocked the act, but Florence didn't need to see the details to know what was happening. Ari pulled away, waiting a moment before leaning forward again and repeating the process, slowly dribbling blood into the Dragon's mouth from her own.

Helen sat opposite Florence. "So, who's your new friend?"

"She's not really a 'new' friend."

"I was being relative." Helen knew just how to twist the knife. She and Will were her first friends; everyone would be new compared to them.

"Arianna, she's my teacher. She found me when I emerged from the Underground and took me to Ter.5 to learn from the Revos." Ari glanced over her shoulder at the mention of her name, but continued to focus on a slowly stabilizing Cvareh.

"So you made it to Ter.5 then?" Will had almost finished his sloppy attempt at stitches. Turning to look at him was a mistake. It hurt her shoulder the second she moved her head and it made her catch sight of her ravaged flesh.

"Only with her help." She would've never made it anywhere without the help of others.

"I'm glad one of us made it." Helen leaned back on her arms. She was scrawny, thin—all leathery flesh beyond her years stretched across brittle looking bones. Will had clearly passed his days keeping active, but Helen had never spent much time on physical pursuits to begin with. She'd shrunk drastically in the time she'd spent in the floating prison.

"I should've stayed with you. I panicked, and I ran when the constabulary came. I didn't raise the signal and—"

"We know what happened," Helen interrupted.

"We were there." Will wore a tired but coy grin.

"I'm trying to apologize," she floundered.

"We know you are." Helen didn't miss a beat.

"We're not cross with you." Will ruffled her hair.

"Well we *were*," Helen corrected. "I ranted at length about you to him through the cracks in my floor... But we'd be pretty awful friends if we held a grudge for two years over an honest mistake. Even if it was one that landed us in jail."

Tears had boldly ventured down her cheeks from pain and fear, but now they fell in earnest. She'd been so afraid of seeing her friends again. Florence had relived the moment of their capture countless times over the past two years. Will and Helen had been exploring a safe route up to Ter.4.2. The moment Flor had seen the men and women of the law rounding the corners with their torches, she panicked. She knew if she'd been caught she would've been killed or worse. She wasn't like Will and Helen; both had been candidates for a circle. She was a failure of no merit, and the law wouldn't have wasted time trying to "reform" her through a prison sentence. She'd fled.

Again and again she'd asked Ari why, when nightmares had woken her in the dead of night. And time after time, Ari explained the fight or flight reflex, and the training required to control instinct—training that Flor had never been given.

"Chin up, little crow." Will smiled one of his infectious smiles.

A groan interrupted their discussion. The Dragon winced and his eyes pried themselves open. Ari stood, wiping her mouth with the back of her hand.

"How much farther can we move tonight?" Arianna asked Helen and Will, moving away from Cvareh with surprising speed.

"I'm knackered." Helen flopped back onto the rough hewn floor of the tunnel.

"She does have a point." Will motioned to the group. "We're all a bit beaten up."

"We're too predictable in our location right now. I don't doubt for a moment that a caved in wall won't discourage the Riders for long. And even if it did, they'd find another way in."

"You never mentioned anything about *Riders*." Helen squinted at Ari from her place on the floor. "Who are you, lady?"

"I'm the White Wraith." Arianna folded her arms over her chest. "And once we're in the depths of the Underground, we won't have to worry about the Riders any more."

"We won't because they're not foolish enough to traverse a labyrinth of Dark Hands, Golem, and the Wretched," Helen shot back. "You didn't flee into a safe zone."

"No, but I fled with the right people to make it safe." Ari turned her gaze to her student. "Flor, can you travel a little further?"

"A little," Florence insisted bravely, mostly to herself. Truthfully, she never wanted to move from the spot where she'd fallen. But Ari knew what she was doing and more than anything, Florence trusted the woman's instinct. She pulled herself to her feet.

"This is going to be one of *those* trips, isn't it?" Helen groaned.

Florence could already tell her friend was getting on Ari's nerves. And, while she didn't relish it, she was happy enough to have Helen back in her world that all she wanted was for Ari to accept and endure Helen's dry brand of cheek. "Come on." Florence held out the hand on her uninjured side.

Helen stood indignantly, glaring at the offered palm. Florence withdrew, wondering if she'd somehow misread their relationship. "Even if you give me your good arm, my weight will just tear your stitches. It's not like they're particularly good."

"The only thing I've ever stitched is a sailcloth," Will said defensively, standing as well.

"As long as they hold." Ari cast a concerned eye over his work.

"I'll be careful," Florence assured, earning a nod of affirmation from her teacher.

"Well, then, should we head to the terminal?"

"That's too predictable. Let's find a nook on the outer rim." Will hadn't asked her, but Florence felt the need to interject anyway. She knew if Ari understood what Will was proposing, she would've done the same. "Helen, do you remember where one is?"

"Please, to whom do you speak?" the girl scoffed.

The girl who should have been circled for her cartography skills scooped up the torch and started boldly into the waiting darkness. Behind her was the captain, followed by the White Wraith and a Dragon in tow. It was a very different party from the first one she had entered the Underground with, Florence thought optimistically.

But the darkness that pressed in around her, eager to cut her off already from the light of the torch despite being only a couple peca behind, was hungry. It was cruel, and it didn't have the sentience to know mercy. The only things that thrived in it were creatures who cast aside everything but the will to survive.

CVAREH

The three Fenthri passed out almost instantly. They looked like kittens, huddled together and curled in on each other. Cvareh was forced to remind himself that these frail looking children were already well into their prime on Loom. He was entrusting his life to three whom, were they Dragon, he wouldn't even trust to fly a boco alone to deliver a message.

The "nook" they had holed up in was a small connecting hall between the Underground and the steam systems that fueled Ter.4.2. The door to the proper tunnels had been welded shut from the other side. It was barely large enough for the five of them, but the radiant heat and soft breaths of sleeping bodies battled the oppressive darkness with coziness.

Arianna stretched out in the narrow entry, her eyes staring into the void of the silent tunnels. He didn't know what she sought, but he was now familiar enough with the woman to recognize the look of focus on her face. The torch had long run out and they didn't spark a second while the three Fenthri slept. Their Dragon eyes could make sense of the darkness with the help of a little magic.

She turned as he shifted, padding across to her nimbly as to not disturb the slumbering children. Cvareh sat opposite her, resting his back against the roughly carved wall. They matched stares for a long second through their augmented goggles.

"How long will you let them sleep?" he breathed. They both had Dragon ears; to them, the faintest whisper across the silence could be heard as clearly as if one of them were speaking normally.

Arianna produced a worn watch from her inner breast pocket. "Maybe another hour or two?"

"Will you sleep?"

She shook her head. "Someone needs to keep watch."

Cvareh's mouth pressed into a tired smile. She was insistent on her grudge against him past the point of foolishness. Arianna had never even considered him a potential candidate for the task. He had every reason to let the woman exhaust herself if she was too proud to ask for help.

"We can take turns," he suggested. Cvareh could read her whole expression from her mouth alone—he didn't have to see her eyes to know she squinted at him with skepticism. He shook his head with a laugh. "You still don't trust me? You default right, I default left." He pointed out their positions. "I did as you asked. I stopped time without you commanding me to do so."

The expression fell from her face and Arianna pulled off her goggles. He knew she wouldn't see him better without them. So, he did the same. He wanted to see her as she saw him, with his naked eye, no other filters applied.

"Why did you save me?"

He was actually impressed she asked. Cvareh had been expecting her to handle it with the same grace she seemed to muster for all things she didn't like—meaning, shoving it into a corner and disregarding its existence. But there she waited silently for an answer.

Cvareh closed his eyes and thought about his reasoning for the first time—since he certainly hadn't thought about it in the moment. He'd just moved. The King's Bitch was going to kill Ari, and every instinct screamed in harmony for him to prevent it. In a singular breath, he'd put his life, and his mission, as secondary to her. It was a truth that he could never set free, because words would cement the fact to him for gods knew how long.

"Because I need you to take me to the Alchemists' Guild."

"You're lying."

He indulged a short, frustrated sigh. "You're the ringleader of this merry band. If you died, Florence wouldn't carry the torch onward."

"She would've in my name." Arianna's tone left no room for uncertainty. "She sees the best in people, and believed in you before I even wanted to fully admit I was to be saddled with you across the world."

He huffed in amusement. She certainly had a glowing opinion of him, this coarse and cunning woman he'd chosen as his guide on Loom.

"You have everything you need to get to the Alchemists now without me. Guides, weapons expert… You could've done it without giving up a boon, and cleanly at that. So *why*? Why save me?"

"You're relentless." He sighed. He didn't have a succinct answer. Arianna, the almighty and infallible, was, indeed, correct.

"Why?" she pressed.

"Because I want you around." The words were a whip hewn from his annoyance. It cut through the air, and split sound itself in two with a crack. The silence that followed carried the sting.

Arianna didn't know how to react. The woman who always had something to say was at a loss for words. For the first time, he'd gained mental ground against her and pushed onward.

"Why did you save me?"

"I didn't." She tore her eyes from his, looking down the hall as though the beast of offense lurked in its depths.

"You did." His hand curled around his side, touching the site of his most foolish act since he'd been on Loom. He'd risked the schematics being torn at the least, and death at the worst. Cvareh debated which would have actually been more terrible. He could be selfish and say his own death. But if he did say that, even to himself, the words would be hollow and lack conviction. In the scheme of Nova, Loom, and House Xin, the highest purpose he had was to see the schematics for the Philosopher's Box to the rebels building a new resistance in the Alchemists' Guild. That would be a catalyst for far greater and lasting change than him haunting the halls of Xin manor. "Leona's claws pierced my heart."

Arianna was visibly surprised by the news. She mulled it over for a long second. "So the red bitch is named Leona?"

Cvareh couldn't stop himself from laughing. "You pick up fast. Though we call her the 'King's Bitch' in House Xin. My sister invented the short name."

"I can get behind it." Ari grinned, and her flat teeth didn't bother him in the slightest.

"I'm not surprised. I could imagine you both getting along. You're similar," he confessed.

Ari huffed in amusement at the notion. "I doubt there could be more than one woman like me. Otherwise I'd fear for the future of the world."

"Luckily for us all, then, she's not of *this* world."

Arianna actually laughed. It was soft and breathy so as not to wake those sleeping. It wasn't a pretty sound by any stretch. But it was genuine, and that added a sort of spark to it that reminded Cvareh of the Arianna he saw when he imbibed from her. Potent and heady and sparking with life at the corner of every movement.

"I like the attempt at wit, Cvareh. Don't abandon it."

I've been upgraded from just "Dragon" again.

"You still haven't answered my question." He braved exhausting her good will toward him.

"I haven't," she agreed softly. "I was more worried about Flor than I was for you. She was the one who insisted I focus on healing you rather than giving my attention to her."

He shouldn't have expected any different. Their relationship had been set in stone from the start. He would orbit wildly around her hatred for Dragons, her emotions preventing him from crossing her inner threshold. His path would be set by the perfect tension her moods, her eyes, her face, her mouth, *her very existence* held him in.

"But I'm glad she did."

The statement was so faint that he almost asked her to repeat it. As delicate and pure as the lake waters of Shina, it was something he never imagined could come from her. He wanted to hear it again. He instantly desired to know what would make her speak like that in perpetuity. So enamored by it was he, that Cvareh didn't even question why.

"Now, take watch, and wake me if you hear anything." Arianna rested the back of her head on the wall, closing her eyes.

"You can trust me."

"So it seems."

The words should've made him elated. But there was a heavy note of skepticism that weighed them down from having the same effervescence as her prior declaration. It echoed in the heart she'd saved, and cast a shadow of doubt on everything that was building between them.

LEONA

"So, what's the plan?" Camile kicked her feet off the edge of the rooftop where they had decided to land their gliders. She picked her teeth with one of the tiny finger bones from the Fen they'd taken their frustrations out on.

"I'm still working that out," Leona confessed, much to her displeasure. The whole night had been one catastrophic failure after the next. Leona was proud enough to feel an insatiable desire to rectify the events with the sweet solution of a vengeful rage. But she wasn't foolish enough to run in headfirst at the next possible opportunity.

This was the White Wraith's home. She had every advantage of skill and allies. Leona had researched Loom in depth, as had been her duty. But practical application of knowledge was always harder than attaining the knowledge itself.

"Why is she helping Cvarch?" she mused aloud.

"Who?" Camile reminded Leona that she couldn't read her mind.

"The White Wraith." Leona began to think aloud. "She's the self-proclaimed enemy of all Dragons. The pale man in Dortam said she'd take any job if it hurt a Dragon or Dragon interests in some way."

Camile hummed in agreement, rubbing her bloated stomach. The Fen flesh wasn't sitting well with Leona either. Though the killing had been satisfying; at the very least the gray people were good for that much.

"So why help Cvareh? He's certainly a Dragon—"

"Undeniably so."

"—and he's acting only in the interest of his Dragon House."

"Could that interest overlap with her interests?" Camile mused. The woman was smart. The details of their mission were on a need-to-know basis, and Camile didn't need to know every fact that Leona was privy to. But she could work well enough around the blanks. "What does Xin want more than anything else?"

"Power, their 'ends before ideals,' the throne."

"But to do that they'd need to overthrow Yveun Dono. And that's certainly not happening as long as House Tam keeps 'all things equal,'" Camile said with an arrogant huff.

House Rok had been in power for hundreds of years. It would take an army to stand up against a House with the amount of manpower and resources Rok had amassed in that time. Xin may be able to take them to task if they had the support of House Tam. But Tam and Rok made cozy bedmates, leaving Xin short of the manpower they'd need for a civil war.

And if they couldn't find an army on Nova... Leona bolted upright.

"I've an idea," Leona said. "But it's still hazy at the edges."

"Going to disappear for a chat?" Camile turned her attention back up to the sky. Boring and gray every hour of the day, just like the rest of Loom.

"I'll be back." Leona waved the other woman's inquiry off. She wasn't in the mood to field any comment on who she was talking to.

She rounded down the quiet stairs into the living quarters—or maybe they were working chambers? Seriously, the Fen had no sense of originality; every room looked the same. Crimson blood still stained the floor from where her and Camile had violently redecorated.

Leona raised a hand to her ear and whispered, "*Tarukun.*"

The word had no meaning. It was a series of sounds she'd strung together when she'd first learned how to whisper and stuck with ever since. But that was the way it should be to avoid random conversation as a result of saying a common word.

Magic tingled between her fingers and her ear. There was a faint pulse along a thin, invisible tether, a line that connected her all the way back to Nova.

She waited, knowing that it was possible she was waking her King. But as loath as she was to do it, Yveun Dono would want an update. Though waiting for him to activate his end of the whisper nearly killed her.

"Leona," he very nearly purred her name. "Tell me good news."

"Regretfully not." Leona made no excuses. As much as she despised having to admit her shortcomings, hiding them would be far worse. Yveun Dono was silent as she recounted the events of the night prior, and that silence stretched toward infinity after she finished her retelling.

"I know you did not wake me merely to report failure. You are far too savvy to my will to do such a thing."

Leona's heart soared. Even in the wake of shame, he put faith in her. Rather than lashing out, he gave her another opportunity for redemption—one she would not squander.

"Yveun Dono, I know what Cvareh—all of House Xin—is after."

"Do you?"

"They want to make an army of perfect Chimera to stand against you," she declared boldly, praying her logic was sound. "If they managed to create a working Philosopher's Box and solve the issue of forsaken Chimera, they would be able to make Fen as strong as Dragons."

His silence told her everything.

"Dono, my sovereign, I have put this much together on my own... But I cannot decide upon a heading. Would they travel to the Rivets to find an engineer who could solve the riddle of their box? Or would they head to the Alchemists, to put it in the hands of those responsible for splicing Chimera into existence? Has there been word from those loyal to us in the Rivets' Guild since I left?"

Yveun Dono rightfully preferred his inferiors to be able to reach their own conclusions; he didn't have time for nor interest in holding their hands through every decision. But this was a risk Leona deemed worth taking. At worst, she would upset him marginally now by asking for guidance, rather than enrage him later with another failure.

"The watchers you appointed in the Rivet guild have been silent. And they would report immediately should Cvareh appear. If he goes there, let him be lulled into a false sense of security until you arrive for his heart." Yveun Dono's voice shifted into the cold and calculating tones of a commander—the true and cunning nature he masked under the charm he applied for his Crimson Court. "However, the Alchemists prove... resistant, even still. It has been merely two years since their last petty uprising was squelched, but they remain obstinate in their tiny corner of the world. They hide much behind their veils of secrecy, so much so that even my eyes are blurred. I would not find it surprising if they felt inclined to harbor a Dragon like Cvareh, given his desired ends."

"All else aside, perhaps my presence may remind them that no guild operates in half measures when it comes to loyalty to their King." Leona grinned faintly to herself, savoring the idea of having an entire guild under her boot and hanging on her every beck and call.

"Indeed."

"Then I make my heading for Ter.2," Leona declared. "And this time, I will not fail you."

"See that you don't."

Magic popped and the link between them fizzled. Leona lowered her hand from her ear. They would move a lot faster with their gliders than Cvareh would be able to travel in the Underground, even with two renegade Ravens. She had time before he would emerge again—if he emerged again. Though, Leona knew if he were lost to the creatures of the depths of Loom, she would be disappointed at fate for stealing her kill.

Yes, she started up the stairs, *Cvareh and the Wraith will be mine.* But she wasn't going to be made a fool a second time, and she was no longer going in blind. Leona now knew what type of forces she was up against.

"You look surprisingly chipper," Camile assessed as Leona returned to her prior place.

"We're heading back to Ter.5."

"Oh?"

"We need to pay the Revos a visit." Leona flexed her fingers, sheathing and unsheathing her claws. They were trusty, reliable weapons. She hadn't been like her sister, adopting every new killing tool that came into existence; she'd favored the tried and true methods of slaughtering her enemies for years. But that was up on Nova, and here on Loom the fights were different. "Cvareh had a pistol."

"A fragile one," Camile scoffed.

"So let's get some better ones." Leona bared her teeth, showing that the matter wasn't up for discussion. The Revos would give her something the world had never seen before, something so powerful that it would slay even Wraiths, and Dragons who could manipulate time.

ARIANNA

From the brief and tumultuous explanations of Florence's last time in the Underground, Ari understood why it was called "The Ravens' Folly." The Guild wasn't known for their building skill or logical city planning—however good they were at cartography and public transportation. The Underground was mazelike at best, hellishly backwards at worst—from all the different "builders" adding on at their own discretion. If that wasn't enough, the deepest parts were said to be occupied by some of the most wretched creatures found anywhere on Loom. And, unlike the Harvesters who occupied the mines of Ter.1, the Ravens who ventured into the Underground were not outfitted regularly with weaponry from the Revos to keep such monsters at bay.

It wasn't until Arianna was grasping onto the side of a strange mine cart-like transportation machine, with two Ravens laughing gleefully at every pitch-black corner they took at break-neck speed, that she grasped the concept of the Underground also being described as the "Ravens' Playground."

"Is this it?" Helen called back to Will. "This is the best she has?"

"Rusty!" Will replied with a shout, pulling another lever on the contraption housed in a back compartment of the vessel.

Arianna focused on it—trying to figure out how it worked—rather than the mind-numbing feeling of being hurled through the unknown while trusting the most annoying girl she'd ever met at the wheel and the clinically insane at the engine. "Flor, you have any grease?"

"When have I *ever* carried grease on me?" Florence couldn't plaster herself any tighter against the side of the cart if she tried.

Ari hated seeing her distressed. But there was something about the girl's fear she found the slightest bit endearing. Despite Flor's Raven tattoo, she was a wrench in a toolbox of screwdrivers here. Ari had only ever known her pupil as a Revo in training. But now she saw clearly why Florence had felt the need to flee the Ravens. There would be no way the girl could pass the mandatory Dragon tests imposed on Guild initiates to cull out those who lacked talent and manage the population they'd sent into a spiral when they'd removed Loom's breeding policies.

"You *had* to pick this cart. Didn't like the other rider," Will huffed.

"We'd need two riders and only one of these," Helen answered. "Stop complaining and just manage my speed!"

It wasn't long before Cvareh was emptying the contents of his mostly empty stomach over the railing. Ari laughed with the rest of them at his expense and he alternated the rest of the day between fuming and panting softly, muttering prayers under his breath to Nova's endless pantheon. At least, Ari assumed it to be the rest of the day.

Hours were lost to the darkness of the Underground. She'd originally tried to keep up with her timepiece, but quickly abandoned the idea. They pushed every hour they were awake at her behest, moving as fast and as far as they could beneath Ter.4 before exhaustion took over.

Cvareh and she alternated watches. They needed less sleep. Having magic in the blood that constantly healed their bodies and kept them in shape increased their ease of survival tenfold. It also made the fading conditions of the Fenthri in their party all the more obvious. Living creatures weren't meant to make these halls home for extended periods of time. The strange sleeping schedule and hours upon hours of darkness took a toll on the body as much as the mind. Laughter faded from the group first, talking second, and soon the only sound that filled the air was the screeching of brakes and the clacking of metal wheels on veca after veca of track.

They were four days into their journey and somewhere around Holx, according to Helen, when the last of their rations ran out. The empty bag stared back at Arianna, more vacant than every tunnel she had faced during the hours of their travel. They weren't going to make it to Ter.4.3 without additional supplies.

"What are you going to do?" Cvareh watched her thoughtfully as she retreated away from the last of the diminished supply bags. The other two mostly empty sacks were in the cart with the sleeping trio.

"I don't know yet." Her mind had yet to work out the best solution. It was strange to admit it, however.

She never confessed to Florence when she needed time to work through a plan, or operated with less than one hundred percent certainty. The girl was someone Arianna wanted to look after, care for—someone whose well being Arianna wanted to ensure into eternity. And, while Arianna could see the woman she had become in the past two years, part of her still clung to the idea of protecting the shaking, scared little crow who had run lost through the streets of Ter.4.2.

"They're not going to last long."

"No, they won't, not at this pace anyway."

"Is there something down here you could hunt?" He was making an effort, she'd grant him that much. But the effort was ill placed; he just didn't know enough about Loom.

"Not down here." Rather than taking the easy insult, Ari explained: "The softest things are glovis grubs. But they feed off rocks, so they're filled with corrosive acids. The people who do eat them... don't last long."

But those people didn't die. The chemicals in the glovis ate away at their bodies and corroded their minds until what was once Fenthri became something between man and monster. The Wretched were worse than forsaken Chimera. At least the forsaken had a timer on their lives. If the Fenthri body managed to adapt to consuming the glovis' flesh, they could survive indefinitely, haunting the tunnels.

"Up then?" he reasoned.

"I seem to have no other choice." She adjusted the strapping on her harness. As much as she didn't mind wearing it, she was ready for a reprieve that would let her take it off.

"When are we going?"

She laughed with a shake of her head. "There is no *we* on this trip. Alone I can navigate whatever streets or plains wait above us effortlessly. If I'm looking out for everyone, it'll slow me down."

"I can look out for myself, and you know I'll help look after them," he insisted defensively.

"I know," she confessed. A similar sensation to the one she'd felt a few days ago washed over her, and Arianna assessed the Dragon in the darkness. Without light, he looked the same as any Fenthri would—save for the black slits of his eyes and his physical size. Perhaps that was why she was beginning to feel easier around the man. But that didn't quite make sense, as Arianna didn't find relief, but rather a small disappointment, in not being able to see the colors she knew him to be. "And I will trust you to do it."

"What?"

"I'm going alone. I'll only be gone an hour, and I'm certain they'll sleep the entire time and then some ... But I'm trusting you to look after them." The words still made her uneasy because it meant that she really was daring to put her faith in another Dragon. But they came more smoothly than she expected.

"Be careful, Ari. First you trust me, then you may actually like me." He leaned against the wall with a smug grin.

Her emotions ran wild. Arianna tried to get them back under control but didn't know where to begin. Correcting him on his use of Flor's shortened name? The ease by which he assumed her trust? The implication that she might actually enjoy him and his company?

Or perhaps it was the fact that, yet again, he reminded her of a woman who was long dead.

"Don't push your luck." It was a weak return, and she knew it. But she wouldn't be too hard on the man, she insisted to herself; she told him she'd liked his newfound sass and it would be contradictory to squelch it.

His eyes followed her as she woke Helen softly, helping the girl out of the cart without waking Will or Florence. She could feel his attention prickling at her magic until she disappeared around a winding tunnel, Helen leading the way. And yet, she still felt his presence long after. It was a shadow connected to her heels, waiting on her as her footsteps echoed through the caves, no doubt audible to his Dragon ears.

That sensation faded away as a hazy dawn faded into view. Helen blinked blearily at the light, the small amount nearly blinding after spending five days trekking with nothing more than torches and the faint glow of glovis eyes lining the tunnel walls. Fresh air kicked the dust around, making no effort to pierce the depths of the Underground. Nature heeded the lines between above and below; it was the boldness inspired by steam and guns and magic that inspired Fenthri to blur it.

"You're going to make it back?" Helen yawned. "Do you need me to wait here?"

Arianna made a show of pocketing her grease pen. "I can follow the line." She tapped the mark she'd drawn while walking.

"You're sure? If we get separated, there's no hope of finding each other down there," the cartographer cautioned.

"So go back and sleep, and don't move for a while—if you can manage that."

"Sleep, yes, understood." Helen's dramatic salute quickly deteriorated into another wide-mouthed inhale of air. She passed the hardened eye of a glovis from hand to hand. It still emitted a faint glow even after the creature's death, and Ari watched the speck of light as Helen traveled back into the depths.

The fog embraced her as Ari emerged, breathing fresh air for the first time in what felt like forever. Standing *alone* for the first time in weeks. She wasn't accustomed to traveling in a pack.

She looked over the dusty plains of Ter.4, a steam engine rolling across the ocean of tall grasses in the distance. Master Oliver had taken her under his wing when she was still so young. They had traveled the world together, just the two of them. And then the Dragons had come to ruin it all. To confine guilds to their territories and initiates to textbooks rather than true learning.

Still, when she watched the sky lighten over the plains, the quiet dawn on a mostly barren land, it looked as it had then— smelled as it had then. Arianna stepped forward, putting Wraiths and Dragons and boons and misplaced Ravens behind her. For a brief hour, she navigated the world as nothing more than a Fenthri woman.

Three hare and a bag full of edible plants later, she returned to the world below. Escapes were wonderful, but impermanent and shallow. She was made of stronger mettle than those that fled into the warm bosom of nostalgia.

The fingers of her left hand trailed through the grease line, following it down and through the winding passages. Silence flooded her, and it wasn't until Arianna was nearly to their resting place that she realized the source of her unease.

It was *too* quiet. She heard no breathing, no discussion, no clanking of the cart over the rails as its occupants shifted in their sleep. Her pace quickened and Arianna sped to meet the last corner, already knowing what would greet her.

Nothing.

Her line ended where it had begun in a spot she knew she could not be confusing for any other. Panic swelled to a crescendo and Ari forced it down with a hand on her dagger, as though she could ward off her emotions with golden blades and lock them away behind spools of wire. She stretched her hearing, but stillness greeted her in all directions.

Wherever they had gone, it was far and fast—enough that even her Dragon ears couldn't pick up the faintest squeal of wheels on rails. Her breathing quickened as the options unfurled before her, and Arianna picked up a faint scent.

It was one she'd come to know on their travels—the crisp, fresh smell of burning wood. *Cvareh.* Her eyes drifted over to the wall, led by her nose, and Arianna ran her fingers along the fresh scratches in the rock. He had bled here.

Balling her hand into a fist, Arianna screamed, punching the rock so hard blood exploded and her bones snapped. Her anguish echoed through the caves uselessly, the ears she wanted to hear were too far away. But there were more things to hear her than a Dragon and a few misplaced Ravens in the Underground.

She drew her daggers, her bones already knitting, the pain sharpening her mind. A primal hiss echoed up to her, followed by the clicking of pincers. Ari placed the tip of her dagger in the wall, slowly walking backward.

"That's it…" The sound of metal on stone grated through the tunnel like an alarm for any in the vicinity. "Follow me."

Helen's words were still fresh in her mind: *no hope of finding each other once separated.* Arianna watched as the darkness melted around the shape of a Wretched, lean ropes of muscle suspended over bones and wrapped in the thinnest of pale gray skin. Useless eyes—white and beady—were placed behind the gaping orifice that was once a Fenthri mouth. Acidic saliva glowed faintly, oozing between pincers that clicked in excitement, tracking her movements.

A second emerged in her field of vision, followed by a third. Arianna slowly pulled her dagger away from the wall. At the least she'd draw them off Flor, or try.

"Right, then." She flipped her grip on her dagger, clipping in the second. "Who's first?"

The beasts hissed the moment she started to speak. Their long claws scraped against the stone, charging for her with gurgling madness. Arianna let out an animalistic roar in reply.

Wretched and Chimera lunged for the kill.

FLORENCE

The Wretches chased them on all fours down the tunnel. They hissed and clicked, moving unnaturally fast through the darkness, dotting a trail of glowing saliva that steamed pock marks into the stones behind them.

Florence's shoulder ached and burned as she struggled to keep her balance in the jostling cart. Will strained against the levers in the back. Helen was rigid at the wheel, trying to keep them on a course she could track in her mind.

"Ari. What about Ari?" She grabbed for Cvareh. He was the only person she could distract with her panic, the only one of the three she could lose her head around. Helen and Will had their hands full enough trying to keep them from dying in a swift and terrible crash.

"We can't go back that way." He bared his teeth in a fearsome snarl at the creatures in hot pursuit.

Florence's hand shrunk away from him on instinct at the terrible look that overcame his face, wild and savage. It was the face of the Dragons Ari had filled her head with over the past two years and one she hadn't witnessed with her own eyes until that moment.

"Those things are exactly what I'm worried about! Ari's alone with them!"

Ari, her teacher, her friend, a woman who was a shining and steady light in Florence's otherwise gray world. She had left someone precious behind in the Underground. Again.

"At this exact second, I think you should be more worried about *us* being alone with them!" Cvareh shouted.

A Wretch dove from a side tunnel. Cvareh instinctively placed his body between its sharp pincers and Florence. He grunted in pain as he slashed into the creature and acidic blood poured over his hand. With an aggravated roar he threw the body away, and it bounced limply down the cart path.

"Can you not get acid on our only means of transportation?" Will scolded, motioning to where erosion was already weakening the side of the cart, boring holes in the rusted metal. "We're pretty far from the Holx yard and I don't think we'll stumble on another this deep."

"Why don't you ask the monsters? I'm sure they'll be happy to oblige. Or should I just let it into our cart next time?" Cvareh growled in reply, rubbing his knitting flesh.

"Can you all not talk so much? It's taking a lot of focus to keep us on track!" Helen's words had both a literal and figurative meaning.

Wretches on their tails, Arianna nowhere to be found, and the only thing separating them from being lost in the Undergound forever was the map that spun madly inside Helen's head. They were falling apart at the seams, cracking under the pressure. Florence swallowed.

Fight or flight.

The instinct rose up in her, hot and searing under every nerve. She dropped her bag, falling to the floor of the cart with it. Flight after flight, she'd run through life. From avoiding responsibility in the guild, to running out on Will and Helen, to letting them leave Ari now.

"What are you doing?" Cvareh asked as she frantically tried to make sense of the state of their current supplies. It wasn't much. She couldn't restock with everything she'd needed in Ter.4.2—there was no substitute for Mercury Town.

"I'm trying to get us out of this mess." She passed Cvareh her revolver, loading it with three canisters. "Hold this."

He took the gun skeptically and turned back to the Wretches.

"No, you're not shooting them. Don't fire a shot." Florence dumped one canister over the side of the cart, the precious gunpowder lost to the air whipping around them. It hurt her very soul to see it wasted, but she didn't have anywhere else for it to go and she needed a blank vessel of some kind.

While she was up, she tried to assess how fast they could be going, but the numbers all blurred in her head. *Ari would know what to do*, a voice in the back of her mind nagged. But Ari wasn't here. She was, and someone had to think of a solution, however wild and reckless.

"Helen, when's the next downhill?"

"Uh…"

"Helen."

The other woman spun the wheel frantically.

"Helen! Log it aloud, recount later to figure out where we are, and take the next downhill." Florence demanded.

"Understood." Helen began muttering to herself, a method Florence knew the girl used to help commit things to memory.

Florence's hands shook as her brain replayed chemical after powder, reaction after reaction. She shuffled the deck of everything she'd been taught from Ari, from her Revo tutors, from books. She threw out every ounce of conventional wisdom on explosives and bombs; she needed the most unstable reactions. The world was upside down, and the only way it was getting righted was with an explosion that would shake the foundation of the earth itself.

She cradled the canister in her hand, trying to counter the sudden movements of the cart so nothing would be set off prematurely. Helen was finally able to fulfill her request and the cart tipped forward. Will frantically twisted and pulled, trying to temper their fall.

"Let it go, Will!" Florence demanded. "Let it all go."

"But if we gather that much sp—"

"Just do it!" Her order didn't vibrate with the same resonance as Ari's would have, but it carried equal weight.

He flipped a few levers, and the cart became a bullet barreling down the darkness. The sound of the Wretches grew distant and Florence exchanged the pistol for the canister in Cvareh's hands. The faint glow of the glovis eyes they'd harvested rattled around the bottom of the cart, illuminating his confusion.

"I'm going to shoot three times. On the second, you throw that and wait for the third shot before you push every ounce of magic you have into that gold pin." She manually placed his thumb over the pin at the end of the canister, the spot where the golden hammer of a gun would strike.

"You got it."

"Flor…" Helen had stopped muttering.

"Ready?" Florence raised the revolver.

"What do you think you're doing?" Will shouted.

Florence spared him a brief glance before curling her finger around the trigger. "What Revos do best."

She fired. The first shot exploded against the ceiling. On the second shot Cvareh threw, and rock began to collapse in place. On the third shot he did exactly as she had instructed, and the three, their cart, and everything in it were sent flying forward by the shock wave.

The earth groaned and Florence groaned with it. She instantly panicked, thinking she'd gone blind somehow, only to remember that she was working with nearly no light. The tunnels rumbled with shock waves. Large chunks of rock began to fall and Florence heard the first satisfying hiss of a Wretch crushed beneath one.

Another set of spider web fractures cracked across the ceiling above them. Florence pushed herself to her feet, running on pure adrenaline as the world spun. "We have to move."

She wrapped her arms around Will, hoisting him to his feet with all the strength she possessed. Her left arm couldn't get a good grip on him, and just as she nearly lost her ability to support his weight, he found his balance.

"Helen?" Florence called further up the tunnel, scattered glovis eyes gave them barely enough light to see by.

"I have her," Cvareh called. Helen was cradled in his arms; Florence suppressed her panic at the sight. If their navigator died, they would be stuck forever. "Hurry!"

They sprinted forward through the dark tunnels. Florence and Will led with a glovis eye each. It wasn't until the last echo of the cave-in that they all collapsed at once, chests heaving, exhaustion crushing their shoulders.

Florence and Will crumpled to the floor. Cvareh gingerly laid a moaning Helen next to them. He squinted into the blackness beyond their tiny fragments of light.

"Hold your breaths, for just a moment." He motioned, and they obliged. "I don't hear anything…"

"We either scared them all off, cut them all off, or told them exactly where we were with that." Will rubbed his ears. "Next time you feel like going explosive crazy, warn us?"

"I did. You just—" she interrupted herself with a hiss of pain as she shifted.

Florence looked down at her arm. Will's clumsy stitches had been ripped wide open. Blood poured from the wound, merging with blood from a secondary location where the bone in her forearm protruded from her body. She felt faint almost instantly.

"Flor, Florence." Cvareh was at her side, propping her up, supporting her as Ari would. "Hang in there."

Hang in there for what? she thought grimly. They had no food, were down to two canisters and one pistol, their medical supplies were depleted, and they'd lost their transportation. No one was coming for them. Even if Arianna tried—and Florence found herself hoping her teacher wouldn't do something so foolish—she'd never find them. Even if she somehow knew the right path, she'd never make it to them now with the cave-in.

Florence tilted her head back and rested it on the rock, panting softly, unsure how much of the darkness at the corners of her vision was due to blood loss and how much was just lack of light.

"It's like then," Helen whispered.

"We'd pushed the cart too fast, we'd made too much noise." Will's eyes glossed over, looking at the past they were all reliving.

"Drew them right to us." Helen turned her head, staring at Cvareh. "I thought with a Dragon, we were nearly invincible."

The expression that briefly overtook his eyes was heartbreaking. He felt guilty for their situation, despite having no real obligation to. They had thought him near invincible, a god among them, as if by virtue of his blood alone he could be their savior.

And that was the thought that sparked an explosion of possibility in Florence's mind

"Helen, how long to Ter.4.3?"

The other woman sighed heavily, looking up at the nothingness that coated the rocks above them. She muttered under her breath, and every second she took doing so oozed another bit of life from Florence's veins. "We'll have to loop back toward Holx, maybe not. Depends on how fast we can find another vehicle. Accounting for us going *all* the way back to the higher levels right beneath Holx...maybe four or five more days?"

Longer than she wanted, shorter than she'd thought. Helen and Will were beaten up, but their wounds looked superficial enough. Food would be an issue, but if they had to go that close to Holx anyway, they may find someone they could trade with or one of them could brave sneaking up. Then again, there were always the glovis... Ralph made it through three of them the last time they were all in the Underground before he died.

So there were options for all of them; they could make it to Ter.4.3 safely underground and keep Cvareh's magic hidden from the Riders. Florence knew Arianna would head there eventually.

That left the matter of Florence.

She would not make it, and they had no supplies to mend the amount of blood she was losing, even if they somehow managed to set the break. Florence pressed her eyes closed, turning to Cvareh. By the time she opened them, she had made up her mind.

"Cvareh, have you ever made a Chimera before?"

CVAREH

I f he never went underground again, it would be too soon. The journey underneath Ter.4 had been one harrowing moment after the next that he was sure did nothing for the luster of his skin or wrinkles around his brow. They surfaced from the quagmire bloody, beaten, thinning, and blinking against the faint twilight of sunset in Ter.4.3. But emerge they did, in one miraculous piece, and thanks in no small part to the dark-haired girl at his side.

Cvareh had a whole new appreciation for the girl—no, woman. She was sixteen, barely more than a *toddler* by the lifespans on Nova. But, for a Fenthri, it made her almost middle aged. This was a woman who was coming into her prime and knew what she wanted.

At least, that's what he had to believe. Because he'd been feeding her his blood for five days now. The magic had a strange affect on the not-yet Chimera Fenthri. Without a proper transfusion of blood she couldn't be made into a full Chimera, so his magic didn't take hold like a proper imbibing would. It also began to work away at her stomach and mouth, creating bloody sores that would be aggravated with every feeding, heal as a result of the magic, and then be made worse again as the magic faded.

Imbibing like this would eventually kill her. But she maintained both their spirits by reminding him that they were already headed to the home of the Chimera—the Alchemists' Guild. Once she had been given the blood properly, gold mingled with red to make black, she would rebound stronger than before. Such was the way of Chimeras; Florence should need no more living proof than the woman she had made her teacher.

That particular woman was elusive for two days after they emerged from the Underground. They holed up in squalor, but it was far safer than the depths they had endured and even scraps were better sustenance than what they'd had available previously. Cvareh began to fear that perhaps Arianna had not escaped. That she had gone back and was met with an ill fate of pincers and the Wretches they had left behind.

If she died, would he know? Was there something about the magic of the boon contract that would alert him to its dissolution? He had no idea. She'd been an enigma from the start and the woman was content to remain such even when she wasn't around to give him a hard time.

For two days, Florence went and sat at the port of Ter.4.3. She had an unending belief that Arianna would somehow know to find her there. Where it stemmed from, Cvareh wasn't quite certain. But she was resolute enough to kill herself for it.

On the third day, he walked with her, bundled and hidden. It was taking longer and longer for her to traverse the area from their hideout to her waiting spot and, after fearing she wouldn't return yesterday, Cvareh had made up his mind to go with her from then on. He could do little more than give her blood, but that he would do... even if the idea of piercing his flesh above ground settled restlessly across his consciousness. But if he didn't, eventually, the girl would die. And he'd promised Arianna he would keep her safe. More than that, he wanted to see her safe for himself.

A pop sounded in his ear, echoing from a great distance away with the closeness of someone clicking their tongue by the side of his face. He looked out over the port, feeling the tether form between him and his sister, tugging at his ear. Cvareh rose slowly, giving Florence a reassuring squeeze.

"I'm going to take a short walk."

"I'll wait here." The girl gripped the bench seat for support. He would have to let her imbibe tonight or else she would certainly be beyond help.

"I'll be right back," he promised.

Cvareh strolled away, at least until he was out of eyesight. His pace quickened and he ducked into a side alley, wedging himself between some shipping crates. With a quick glance, he rose his hand to his ear, magic crackling into his skin and across the void that separated him and Nova.

"Petra," he whispered.

"I was beginning to wonder, little one." Genuine relief flooded her voice and Cvareh felt instant guilt at the idea of making her worry.

"I haven't been in a position to talk."

"Yveun Dono sent Riders after you. But I heard no word of capture or kill and I know he would boast of it had his red bitch been successful." She was utterly triumphant at the sound of Cvareh's voice, knowing they had so far thwarted the best efforts of House Rok. "Still, with your silence—"

"I move slower than expected, but safer than we predicted." It was irony to say given all he had faced, but with

Arianna he had been far safer than he would've been venturing out on his own. Though his luck might be thinning on that front.

"You have made an ally?" Nothing escaped his sister.

"I have."

"Who?"

"She is—"

"*She?*" Petra's expression was readable through the word. She'd heard the shift in his tones, the note placed under the pronoun at the mere thought of Arianna.

"—the White Wraith," he finished determined.

"My brother has befriended the infamous White Wraith?" The echo of Petra's chuckle whispered back to him. "You're certain she's on our side?"

"I am," he affirmed.

"She has quite the reputation. I don't know if I would trust her."

"Then trust me. There's nothing she would do that would hurt me." Why was he so confident? She'd spent days illustrating how little she thought of him. She'd spent hours annoying him for the sake of it.

"What have you done to tame this beast?"

"Just trust me that I have this under control."

"Do you?" a voice spoke from above him.

Cvareh's head snapped up to the top of the pile of crates he'd been hiding between. There, perched at their top as though she had materialized out of thin air itself—like a wraith—was the woman in question. The connection with his sister fizzled from lack of focus and his hand fell from his ear.

"Tell me what control you're exercising." With the grace and nimbleness of a cat, she dropped before him, rising slowly. "You know what hangs on your response."

"Florence is safe." It was mostly true, at least.

Arianna visibly relaxed, leaning against the crates with her arms lazily folded over her chest.

"How did you find me?"

"I've been waiting for you to mess up and use enough magic to leave a trace in the air." She reached forward and he expected her to grab him, to smack him, to grab her dagger and hold it to his face in an instant. But her hand wrapped around his shoulder in an almost reassuring manner. "I'm glad you're all right as well."

"You just want your boon." He laughed nervously, not even knowing why he was nervous, not knowing why he was so eager to write her off.

"Oh I do." She didn't waste breath on denying it. "But I'm still glad to see you in one piece." Arianna stepped away and, for the very first time, he wished she hadn't. "Now, take me to her."

Cvareh led the way, though his relief at seeing the white-clad woman faded quickly. Florence's shoulders sagged as she continued to clutch at the bench, waiting diligently for her master's return. Waiting even if it meant her death. It was a loyalty that could not be bought and in that brief moment, he wondered if it was a loyalty Arianna had actually earned.

Arianna stopped in her tracks a few steps away from the young woman. She spun on Cvareh and he was surprised she didn't burn her cheeks for all the fire that sparked from her eyes underneath her goggles. *She knew.* He could sense it with every move she made.

"What did you do to her?"

ARIANNA

"Now listen—" The Dragon held up his hands, pleading for something she wasn't about to give him.

"What did you do to her?" she repeated, her voice rising. She didn't care if the world heard her, if they all watched as she tore the man limb from limb.

"I didn't—"

"He didn't do anything I didn't expressly ask for." Florence was on her feet. Arianna watched her fingertips track along the bench, keeping her steady. The girl looked frail. Her steps were small, her ankles threatening to revoke their support at any moment.

"Flor... You..." She didn't have words. The world had fallen away, crumbling into a vortex of emotions. The anger, confusion, rage, and panic she'd felt for days not knowing if she'd ever find her Florence again vanished. Pure relief flooded the vacant hollow in the center of her chest. Ari scooped her up, holding her, stabilizing her. "I'm so relieved."

"I am too." Flor's arms snaked around her waist, holding her in kind. Arianna sighed softly into her hair, content to know the most precious person in her world was safe once more. Both their hands pressed into the other's left shoulders for a long moment.

But there was a *smell* that interrupted her bliss, that tainted and changed it. Ari finally pulled away, bracing herself to handle the truth that was already apparent. "You reek of him."

"Arianna," Florence spoke firmly and evenly. "There was no other way. If we hadn't made the effort, I would've died. There was an accident after the Wretches—we're lucky to be alive at all."

Ari chewed over her tongue to keep it from spitting venom. She had never wanted Florence to endure the pain and danger of becoming a Chimera. She had never wanted the girl to feel the draw of magic, the lust of possibility for one more organ, one more scrap of stolen power.

"I had been thinking about it for the past year." Florence squeezed her forearms. "As a Chimera I can do more; I can make my own weapons better than with your help. Not that your help isn't marvelous, but it's that—"

"I know, Flor." Arianna smiled tiredly and squeezed the girl's arms in reply. She wasn't sure if Florence was trying to convince her, or herself. But what was done was done.

If she could smell Cvareh on her, the girl had already ingested quite a bit of his blood. Florence's body would go into full rejection if they didn't complete the transfusion sooner rather than later. There was no going back.

"But this does change things." Arianna thought aloud, looking between Florence and Cvareh. "I've been here for five days now, no sign of the Riders, so I'll trust we lost them in the Underground. Cvareh, did they know where you were headed?"

He shook his head. "Most would reason I'm headed to the Rivets, I would think." He patted the folio strapped around his waist.

The Rivets? *What exactly does he have?* Ari regarded him skeptically for a long moment.

"Then I think we should risk an airship, instead of traveling on foot across Ter.0," she decided aloud.

"Are you sure that's wise? We'll be easier to find in the air."

"We will be." There was no point denying or disagreeing. "But if the Riders have headed down to the Rivets in Ter.3, they won't be anywhere close enough to smell you."

"Still…"

"You're *sure* they don't know where you're headed?" she pushed at his indecision.

"They shouldn't know."

It wasn't the answer she was looking for, but it would have to be enough. Florence wouldn't—couldn't—make the trip on foot. She needed a transfusion within the week, and an airship would guarantee their arrival well before then.

"Don't do this on my behalf," Florence interjected quickly. The girl was too smart. Of course she put together the reason for their change in plans. "After all we've been through to get this far, if we're caught now because we take a risk just for me, I would never forgive myself."

"And if we let you die what was the point of making the effort to save you at all?" The Dragon clad in grubby Fenthri clothing crossed over to Florence. Ari watched as he patted her pupil on the shoulder in admiration.

Despite his face being almost entirely covered, Ari knew clearly what his expression was. She could almost feel it. She didn't want to allow the fractures shaped like his face upon her heart. She didn't want this Dragon to cut down the measuring stick she used to keep the world at length with his tenderness toward Florence.

"You made your decision, and it seems we have as well." She never thought there was a space for her and the Dragon between the two letters of the word "we". "We'll get on an airship tonight. Most of the vessels here seem to be headed for Faroe, but we should be able to find at least one to Keel."

"Ari, most of our supplies..." Florence shifted uneasily from foot to foot. "I lost them in the accident in the caves."

"We didn't have that much anyway." She brushed off the girl's concerns, focusing on what was important—the fact that she was all right. "Plus, I've had five days here waiting for you. What do you think I've been doing?"

"I should've never doubted you." Florence laughed, but it was a hollow sound that served only to hide a wince.

"No, never," Ari teased. The world was right with Florence at her side again. She'd spent most of her life without the girl. But now she couldn't imagine a world that didn't have her in it, and she would fight tooth and nail to keep her there.

Cvareh led them back to the place they had made their home. It was a small stretch of fabric suspended between some crates that offered little protection from the elements. Curled underneath it were her two filthy prison birds—thin, worse for wear, but in one piece. Helen's eyes rose and grew wide as she realized who she was looking at.

"Oh, you made it," she said dryly.

"You should've never had any doubt," Ari proclaimed, heaping on an equal portion of her own brand of arrogance. Doing so made her guilt potable. Florence had been forced to stay in this squalor for days while she had been sleeping in relative comfort in the abandoned store she'd broken into.

"Well, now that our little family is finally back together, what's the plan?" Will looked at Arianna.

"You did your part." She wasn't going to bury the lede. "As far as we're concerned, your freedom has been earned and you owe me nothing further." Boon aside, she didn't actually enjoy the feeling of people owing debts to her. She didn't want anything from anyone.

"We're leaving for Keel on the next airship we can find," Florence explained.

Her two friends shared a look.

"You are," Helen agreed. "But we've been talking, and since your teacher will not be hunting us down, we're going to head back into the Underground."

"What? Why?" Florence looked frantically between her friends.

"We're not bad at this whole 'moving people' business," Will started.

"And we think it *can* be a business," Helen interjected.

"Minus dealing with the Wretched." Arianna couldn't stop herself.

"Yes, well... When we're moving things—people— we'll do so on our own terms. We've learned every time we've maneuvered down there."

"You're not joining us?" Florence couldn't seem to process it.

Will shook his head. "Flor, we've always ridden in separate trikes. Sometimes we can ride side by side, but our destinations are different."

"Unless you want to join us, instead?" Helen asked hopefully. "We need a Revo for protection, just in case. You really are brilliant with gunpowder."

Florence fought to hide a smile at the well-deserved flattery.

"Plus, you could help ferry more people out of the Guilds, just like you, to live a free life doing whatever they choose."

It would be a noble cause, Arianna admitted. One that would resonate strongly with Florence as someone who had used that method herself to avoid the fatal outcomes of failing the Dragon tests. Florence had every reason to say yes.

And yet, Arianna desperately wished she wouldn't. If Florence disappeared with these two, she would likely never see her again. Florence would become her own White Wraith, operating outside the law and in the greatest secrecy possible. She would be at constant risk.

Arianna wanted to be happy for the girl. She wanted to support blindly. But the panic the very thought put in her made her tongue act differently.

"You could stay," she said softly. Florence looked at her in shock—shock Ari hoped wasn't stemming from excitement and relief. "But you should come with us to the Alchemists first. You won't last long without being transitioned to a full Chimera, even less without Dragon blood."

If the girl leaves these two, the chances of her ever rejoining them decreases greatly, a nagging voice in the back of Arianna's mind assured her. She only wanted what was best for Florence. She hadn't lied.

Florence looked between Ari and the two Ravens. She desperately wished she knew what was going through the girl's head.

"I can't." Florence shook her head. "Will, Helen, I can't go with you."

"You're sure? Will you meet us after you become a Chimera?" Helen squinted at Ari skeptically while the Wraith fought to keep a triumphant smile off her lips.

"I don't know... But Arianna is right. I need to go for that, at the very least." There was no room for hesitation in Florence's words and Arianna was pleased to note that her student clearly thought of the whole matter as her idea. "I've come this far. I need to see Cvareh through to the Alchemists. And even after that, who will make Ari's canisters for her?"

"She can always buy them." Arianna was going to sew Helen's mouth shut. She did not want to lose Florence to these people. She felt like the girl had only just entered her life and now they were trying to take her away.

"The canisters they sell in Mercury Town are wretched." Florence shook her head firmly. "I'd never let her have those."

"I'm lucky to have a Revo like you looking out for me." Arianna nudged Florence's shoulder with her own, satisfied it seemed she had no intention of leaving her side anytime soon. It wasn't every day you had the opportunity to meet another gear that fit so well against your own.

She mused on the fact as she led them all to where she had been holing up, promising Will and Helen some supplies to get them on their way. Meeting the two Ravens had proved to Ari how special Florence was, how unique it was that she had slotted nicely into Ari's world. But it equally illuminated something else she never expected. Everyone she'd met in her life could be organized into two categories: those who fit in seamlessly, and those who didn't.

She never expected Cvareh to fall in with the former, rather than the latter.

CVAREH

O f all the ways to travel, the airship was the one Cvareh liked the best. *Anything* was better than the Underground— he'd consider diving head first into the Gods' Line before venturing down into those forsaken depths again—but it wasn't the most recent harrowing experiences that colored his opinion on the matter. They had traveled decently well on the train, and he had traversed skies and land alike on the backs of boco on Nova. But this, *this*, was something completely different.

The ship was hoisted on magic and mechanics. A giant balloon, filled and strapped into the top of the airship, supplied the majority of the lift. The rest was seen in the faint trail of magic that glittered off from the propellers on each of the golden-tipped wings, fanning out widely. The front of the airship was pointed and drawn up like the bill of a fish eating water bird. But the back was open. Multiple tiers of viewing decks connected in to the dining room, the gaming parlor, and at the end of the residences that filled the top deck entirely.

Everything was done in pale woods and iron, accented with other dark and light stones like marble. As pretty as it was comfortable, it was the closest to home he'd felt the entire time. And that was no small wonder, as Dragons seemed to be regular patrons on airships. There were aesthetic elements the Fenthri regarded as fascinating marvels—like the curling vine-like banisters, or the wave embellishments around the cabin windows—but for a Dragon, they were nothing more than calls to the aesthetic that surrounded them on Nova.

Even now, as he stared down at the lower observation balconies, he could see the inspiration of some Dragon designer at work in the way the tile was laid and the arcs were off-set slightly. Cvareh rested his elbows on the wooden railing and watched the faint trails of magic spiraling in the wind before disappearing. It had been such a wonder, the first time he'd seen magic manifest itself in the physical world. Now it was commonplace, so much so that he didn't even think about it. And, if he *did* think about it, it was associated with Yveun Dono's Riders and their gliders. It was something that brought grief, not wonder. *Yet another thing the Dragon King has taken from us all.*

"What's so fascinating out there?" Arianna rested her elbows next to his. For a whole day, she had worn proper clothing. The coat of the White Wraith had been safely tucked away and forgotten about.

Now, her coat was of a military-inspired sort, intricate roping braided down her chest, knotted on either side and tied over clasps in the middle. The design was mirrored on the sleeves and collar. He particularly appreciated the designer's choice to add a similar embellishment right at the small of the back, though he said nothing about it.

He didn't want to admit that he had studied the taper of her trousers or the shine of her shoes. He would never confess to admiring the elegance with which she could tie her cravat to emphasize her Rivet pin. And he didn't even dwell too long on how aware he was that the roping on her jacket brought out the purple of her eyes.

"Nothing." He answered her question before his silence brought her eyes to his. "And there's actually something rather blissful about that fact." It was nice not to worry about Riders, or the Wretched, or anything else Loom had on it.

"I'm glad you find it blissful." Her tone had become bitter in an instant when her initial question had seemed so light and harmless.

"What have I done to upset you *this* time?" he asked with a sigh. She gave him a look. The more he acted like he didn't care about her moods, the more bothered she became. Cvareh savored it guiltily.

"Do you know why there's nothing out there?" Her voice had gone soft again. It was an odd contrast that Ari pulled off easily as the woman who could wear men's clothing and look wonderfully feminine while doing so.

"Because we're flying?"

She looked at him like he had just made the most idiotic statement she'd ever heard. "I mean why there's nothing on the ground beneath us. No lights, no ports, black above and black below."

"We're over Ter.0, aren't we?" It clicked for him.

She nodded, turning her attentions to the darkness once more—both within and outside.

"You were born in Ter.0, weren't you?" If she remembered the time of the Guilds before the Dragons, then she was born before Loom knew what families were. Back in the primitive days when they rounded up men and women of breeding age to reproduce on the island of Ter.0—a place owned by none of and all of the guilds.

"And I spent my first ten years studying there," she elaborated willingly.

"Then you were initiated into the Rivets after formative education?" he probed gently. It was the most personal information she had ever disclosed at once and he didn't want to say or do something that would bring it to an end.

"'Formative education.'" She repeated with a grin. It was coy and arrogant on the surface, but it had the same undercurrent that tugged down her shoulders. "*Oh-ho*, you have read about the history of Loom."

"I have." Cvareh shifted closer to her, keeping their conversation just to themselves and not speaking loudly enough that the few others milling about the deck could hear. "At least what's been written on Nova about it."

"Which I'm sure is mostly slander and propaganda."

He couldn't argue. "And the other third is just incorrect, I'm coming to find."

"Are you?" Arianna turned to look at him. She'd grease-penned in the symbol of the Rivets on her face again to avoid questions. Cvareh found the mark clashed with the curve of her jaw and the cut of her cheek. It was somewhere it didn't belong, and he suppressed the urge to take her face in his palms and rub it off with his thumb. "What else were you taught about Loom?"

"That its people are weak," he answered easily. "All my life, I've been told the Fenthri are pitiable creatures. That they were simply roaming around in a barren world, barely surviving by trying to establish an order they couldn't maintain—hence no king or supreme ruler—and that the Dragons were their saviors."

She snorted in amusement.

"The Dragons have done nothing for Loom but cause disruption in a system they shouldn't have touched because they didn't understand it."

"Help me understand it?" He wanted to know more. Cvareh mentally insisted it was a result of spending time on Loom, and that was certainly a part of it. But he wanted to know about her. What had made Arianna into the woman she was. A woman who outclassed Dragon and Fenthri and Chimera alike.

She said nothing—barely moved, barely breathed. Her silence made him hang on her every action all the more. He waited for what was percolating in the back of her mind to bubble forward.

"What will you do, Cvareh, after you make it to the Alchemists' Guild and deliver what it is you've carried so far, so diligently?" Arianna stared him down, pinning his toes to the floor with the weight of her interrogation. In her mind, she drew honesty from him like moisture from a cool stone on a hot day.

"I don't know," he confessed. "I may return to Nova to help my sister. She's lied for me, I believe, making up some story about where I am to prevent my arrest."

"What do you call the King's Riders then?"

"Think of them more as assassins than knights while they're here." He shrugged. "I'm not supposed to be on Loom, so they're not technically hunting me. Being here is all one big gray area."

She snickered. "I'm not sure if you intended that as a pun, but it was rather funny."

Her joke was so foreign from her usual seriousness that Cvareh had to stare and process it for a long moment before he realized it had been sincere. Arianna had found humor in what he said. Not only had she not immediately assumed the worst possible implication for his words, but she had found *humor* in them. It was a far cry from the woman who'd held blades against his tongue, threatening to cut it out if he bothered her.

"I hadn't." He laughed lightly. "But it is amusing in hindsight."

"You seem close with your sister," Arianna mused after a long moment. "I'm not surprised you have a whisper link with her."

He almost asked her how she knew about the link. But for someone who never seemed to miss a thing, it was simple to see how Arianna had arrived at the conclusion. He'd mentioned Petra fondly before, and he'd told Ari he had magic in his ears. She'd seen him reporting in.

"It would make sense that you would want to go back to her," Ari whispered so faintly that he almost thought the wind was playing tricks on him. But his hearing was too good for that. He knew exactly what she'd said, and the quickening of his heartbeat knew it too.

"I could stay." They were the only words he could say that would offer a brief respite from the pressure that had been building in his chest.

"What?" She straightened, her arms sliding off the railing. One hand rested on it as Arianna turned to face him.

The look she gave him almost made the feeling worse. Did she realize how her eyes pleaded? Was she aware of the softness in the slope of her shoulders, or the way her hand had crept closer to his on the railing? Cvareh instinctively responded in kind, his body language unfurling to meet hers, to face her chest to chest as they had so many times.

"For a little, I'm sure I could stay, or I could leave and come back quickly." His words were making no sense. His mind was making no sense. Nothing about them had ever made any sense and yet…he thrived off her. Her blood, the way she pushed those around her, her sharp mind and sharper blades.

"Why would you do that?" Fear penetrated her stare. She was nervous of his answer, which made it all the clearer that she was becoming aware of what was happening—what had been happening—at the same time he was.

This woman had become something more to him. He didn't know what quite yet. But he wanted to find out.

"Because I have work I can do with the rebels at the Alchemists' Guild. I can help them," he lied, mostly. Her lips pressed into a small frown; she knew it, too. Before she could press him on it, however, he changed the direction of the wind that blew between them. "What will you do after you have your boon? What do you even want your boon to be?"

Arianna fought a war against his words. She struggled to such a degree that the pain from the battle made it onto her face. Why did she fight so hard to keep him out?

"All my life, well, almost… I wanted the Dragon King dead," Arianna breathed. "But I know your boon won't be strong enough for that. I know asking for that would solve nothing. Overthrowing one tyrant only makes room for another. So, if I am selfish, I would ask for something simple: the death of a Dragon."

"Who?"

She shook her head.

"*Why*, then?" He didn't want to let go of the connection they had found between them. Not when he was finally seeing the true colors of the gray woman who had enchanted him.

"Because the Dragon betrayed us all. He was responsible for the death of the last rebellion. The deaths of my teacher, my friends, and the woman I loved."

The woman she loved. He knew Fenthri didn't share the Dragons' concept of family. He knew they had structured breeding before the Dragon King took over and reorganized their guilds and society. He knew that, despite the fact they could not reproduce and therefore the union could bear no true meaning, the Fenthri would couple with the same sex if it suited them to do so.

He knew that. But now it stood before him and he suddenly had to pass an opinion on it. And the only emotion he found was disappointment. Heartbreaking disappointment.

He scolded himself internally. Even if she had been the slightest bit sweet on him, what did he think could come of any type of relationship with a Fenthri—a Chimera? There was almost no point in exploring it.

"I have told you of my heart." Arianna leaned against the railing, folding her arms over her chest as if to guard the remaining details she hadn't shared. "Tell me of yours. What makes you so convicted to reach the Alchemists?"

Cvareh sighed softly, other matters still clouding his mind. It wouldn't hurt to share the schematics with her. She might know what it was, but that could only prove his sincerity for her cause at this point.

Unfastening the folio on his hip, Cvareh pulled back the top flap and selected one of the smaller pieces of schematic. He didn't know what it detailed, some inner working likely. He passed it over to her and she stilled instantly, taking it.

"They're schematics for the Philosopher's Box. With this—"

"Where did you get this?" she uttered, deathly quiet. Arianna remained focused on the paper in her hands. Her fingers tensed, crumpling the edges. "Where did you get this?"

"I was told that—"

"You were told?" Her jaw thrust forward as her eyes rose to scrutinize him. He could practically hear the grit of her teeth. "Told what? Told by who?"

"I was told this was what the rebellion had been working on after the One Year War. That the Dragon King thwarted the possibility of creating a perfect Chimera army. We knew if I had it, I could earn the trust of the Rebels and we could continue work."

"You could earn their trust," she repeated mockingly. "No, now I see what this really is." Arianna crumpled the paper in her fist.

"You can't do that!"

She prodded him in the chest. "I will never take you to the Alchemists. I will never let you close. If you get off this airship and even think about heading to the Guild, I will cut you down where you stand. Crawl back to Nova, Dragon scum."

Arianna stormed past him, the paper still in hand.

Cvareh was left to catch his balance as her shoulder clipped his. He was left wondering what he had done, how his branch of peace had been turned into the first shot fired in a new war between them. He turned to call after her and, as if sensing his intention, she spun in place.

"And don't you think about coming near Flor or me ever again," she snarled, then continued in toward the cabins.

The other patrons of the ship whispered to each other, tittering as though they had just witnessed a scandalous lovers' quarrel. Cvareh didn't know what they had seen. Because this wasn't the Arianna he knew. At every turn the woman seemed like she was someone different. Every bit of clarity he'd gained into her true nature only served to confound him further.

FLORENCE

Ari slammed the door behind her so hard the desk that was bolted to the wall next to it shook, a small tool rolling off its surface. Both Arianna and Florence paid the out-of-place screwdriver no mind. Ari looked at anything else but the paper she'd left on the table with a shout. She set to pacing the narrow cavern, her feet quickly forging ruts in the plush carpet.

"What's gong on?" Florence finally asked, when it was clear the woman had no intention of doing or saying anything more than fevered mutterings.

"I knew it. I should've known all along," Ari seethed. "He was never our friend, Flor. He's a Dragon and a King's man in his own way. He works for the King himself."

"What?" The machine in Ari's mind had jumped three gears and Florence couldn't figure out how she'd gotten from one spot to the next.

"This whole time, he's been working for the King. It's been a ploy to get us to trust him. It's just like last time. He came down and he's convinced us that he can be trusted, never mind what his real motives are."

"Ari, stop." Florence grabbed her friend by both shoulders, which trembled slightly under her fingers—a feeling

Florence had never felt from Ari before. Fear and rage mixed potently, bleeding into her veins.

She kept herself calm. It would do no good if Florence blindly agreed to what Ari was claiming. One of them had to keep her head and sort through this as logically as possible. Florence tightened her grip. "Arianna, take a deep breath and get a grip on yourself."

"Flor, you have no idea—you, you bled so much for this man, you put yourself in a position of being forced to become a Chimera—" The word still brought ample shame to Arianna's face. "And he was playing you all along."

"I don't believe you," Florence declared. Her head was getting fuzzy from standing so long. She was practically bedridden all the time now from the effects of Dragon blood without being a proper Chimera. It had only taken one day on the airship for Florence to realize that Arianna had made the right decision in taking the risk, at least when it came to her own wellbeing. She would've never made it in a trek across Ter.0.

"You have no idea what he's done. What he intends to do."

"Then tell me." Florence sat, finally. Her hands fell from Ari's shoulders to grip the woman's fingers. She pulled Ari down toward her. Arianna reluctantly obliged, falling onto the narrow bed they'd been sharing for the journey. "What happened that has you in such a state? You and he were fine over dinner."

Better than fine, actually. It had been slow coming, but in the weeks they'd spent together, Arianna and the Dragon seemed to have found a kind of mutual peace. After the floating prison and the Underground, that peace blossomed into appreciation. Florence had watched it grow all along, two people determined to hate each other realizing just how much they could complement each other.

Florence knew why she liked Cvareh: He reminded her of Ari. Certainly, they weren't identical. But they were both driven, both determined; they both set course for something only they could see on a distant shore. She suspected Ari saw much the same in the man, that he sparked memories within her. But now, those memories seemed to be rife with pain.

"He wants to see Loom forever under the thumb of the Dragon King. He wants to keep us under the Dragon's control for eternity," Arianna repeated her earlier words, unhelpfully.

"If you want me to believe you on this, Ari, you'll have to give me some better proof," Florence encouraged gently.

"My word isn't good enough?"

Florence gave her an encouraging smile, and shook her head. "Not this time, I'm afraid. I know Cvareh. I've already formulated my own thoughts and opinions on him. This is not a story of times long gone that you recount for me and I must take at face value. This is a situation in which I have my own empirical evidence to support what I believe to be true. If you want me to change my mind, you must present new evidence."

Arianna stared at her for a long moment. Something in Florence's words had penetrated through the mindless aggravation and hurt. Ari shook her head, laughing bitterly.

"Since when did you become the scientist?"

"I have a good teacher," she replied easily, nudging Ari with her shoulder. "Now, tell me what's happened."

The other woman sighed heavily, running her hands through her cotton-colored hair. Indecision didn't fit Arianna well, and she struggled every second she spent thinking about

Florence's request. But finally, Ari stood, walking over to the slip of paper she'd discarded with such passion earlier.

Just looking at it brought a scowl back to Ari's face. Florence had to brace herself once more for the torrent of emotions that ripped through Ari and broke over her shoulders.

"This. *This* is what he's been struggling to deliver."

Florence examined the paper closely, leaning forward to get a better look. Parts were done in pencil, and those had been smudged by Ari's treatment. The darker lines done in ink over top persevered, however. It looked like some kind of pumping mechanism? Or perhaps an engine? It wasn't something designed to explode, of that much she could be certain.

"What is it?" She failed to see how this tiny bit of a Rivet's sketch had upset Ari so much—even if Ari, as a Rivet, could decipher its intention. It was next to useless in its current state. She knew schematics required dozens of drawings, often of the same thing, to make assembly and creation expressly clear.

"It's a sketch detailing a part of the Philosopher's Box."

"What?" Florence had only heard of such a thing existing in theory.

It was regarded as a clever exercise for students of all ages. What if a perfect Chimera were possible? One who could possess all the powers of a Dragon and not become forsaken from the stress of the magic on their body? How would that change Loom? How would it make things different?

Most knew the answer: It would make everything different. With access to that much magic on Loom, they could create larger, more intricate machines without the need of backup mechanics to run them. They could successfully fly their own gliders up as high as Nova without losing control. They would need less food, so the Harvesters could spend more effort on deeper mining of rarer minerals. And they could stand a fighting chance against Dragons.

The Philosopher's Box would change everything, and that was why no one believed it could ever be real.

"This is meant to be a Philosopher's Box," Ari insisted again. "You can see it in the casing, the way it opens and closes in place of heart valves here, right here."

"In place of heart valves?" Florence repeated, confused. She'd always imagined the Philosopher's Box to be a sort of Chimera-making contraption—like a golden coffin.

"Yes, it's obvious by the tension in the springs and the way this is drawn to have a circle stopper."

Florence would have to take her word for it.

"Let's say for a minute that I believed you on all this." Ari looked instantly hurt that she would imply any differently. Florence continued, determined. "That this is a part of a schematic for an actual Philosopher's Box. Why would Cvareh bring it to Loom, to the resistance? Doesn't that seem like he's trying to help us?"

Arianna didn't miss a beat. "He's doing it to earn their trust. He wants them to think they can trust him."

"And what if he wants them to think that because they actually can?" Florence shook her head. "If he just wanted to try conning them into belief, couldn't he have brought anything and said it was a piece of an unfinished Philosopher's Box? By the time they finished investigating, he could have what he wanted."

"It's more realistic if he brings them the real thing." Ari set the paper back down on the table with a sigh.

"You don't quite believe yourself..." She stood, taking a step toward her teacher. Florence wrapped her arms around the woman's waist, resting her cheek in the center of Ari's back. "You want to, you're trying to, but you don't believe the words you're saying, either."

"I do."

"You don't."

"How can you say that with such certainty?" Arianna grumbled.

Florence laughed softly. Her teacher, the brash and beautiful. "Tell me this: Does Cvareh still have his head and heart intact?"

"He does." Though Ari's tone implied it was a fact she might regret. An error she might be inclined to remedy sooner over later.

"Since when have you spared a Dragon's life when you thought he was guilty of crimes against Loom? Or even the sincere possibility of committing crimes against Loom?" Florence waited a long second, giving Arianna a chance to grab for straws at an answer she knew she didn't have. "That's right, you don't. So somewhere in you, you must be questioning this. You must be wondering if what he's saying is true. His actions must have spoken to your heart clearly enough that you know he is not the evil you're painting him to be."

"You don't know him," Arianna whispered.

"After all we've been through? I think I have a pretty good idea. And I think you do too." Florence rounded Arianna, leaning against the small table for support. The older woman looked down at her tiredly. "Ari, I don't know what demons you face. I know they're there, but I promised you I would never ask. Don't let the shadows of the past smother the possibility for a bright future."

It looked as though she was going to triumph. Arianna's face relaxed, but the older woman's eyes pressed closed, and she took a deep breath through her nose as though bracing herself.

Arianna opened her mouth to speak, when the airship lurched violently. Florence stumbled, off-balance and too hopelessly weak to correct herself. Arianna grabbed her, supporting her as a primal cry rose from outside. They heard the sound at the same time and it washed the gray from both their faces—the magical *zip* of a Dragon Rider's glider.

"Bloody cogs." Arianna was tearing off her clothing, throwing it about the room in a sprint for her harness and coat. "They weren't supposed to have any idea where we were headed. Do you see now, Flor? The man lies! He's in cahoots with them."

"Then why are they hunting him?"

"It's all a ruse!"

The ship jostled again. Florence gripped the table for support. "This is a pretty deathly ruse."

"You just stay here." Ari tightened her harness, feeling for her daggers, running some line through her winch box. "Stay here for now, and don't be anywhere I can't find you. I have a feeling we'll be needing to make an exit before we reach port."

Florence nodded, looking about the room, already making a list of what she needed to pack. "But find Cvareh too."

"Oh, I will." Arianna left with murder in her eyes.

She sighed heavily, leaning against the table. If she could go her entire life without ever seeing another King's Rider, that would be ideal. Florence leaned back, wondering for a brief moment how she would make that come to pass. Her hand rested on the paper and Florence brought it up for inspection with a sigh.

Such a tiny thing had caused so much drama in what had been going so smoothly.

It was then that she noticed a small area that Arianna's fingers had covered the first time she'd shown the page to Florence. Her eyes looked over it once, twice, three times. A few notes were scribbled on the paper, ripped off in the corner where the drawing had been taken from a larger schematic.

Florence didn't even read what they said. She was too obsessed with the way the 'h' curved in the script, the weight of the 'a', the overall slant and clarity of the letters. The penmanship was unmistakable.

It answered the question of why Arianna had been so upset—how she had known so much about the paper—at least enough that Florence could now make educated guesses. But those only created deeper questions. Questions she had sworn never to ask. Questions about Arianna's history.

Why was the woman's handwriting on a schematic she claimed Cvareh had acquired with malicious intent? Why was her penmanship on *anything* that could even closely resemble the Philosopher's Box?

LEONA

They had been zipping across Loom for weeks now. By all measure Leona should be exhausted. But the moment the airship had emerged from the starless sky, like a shining beacon heralding her triumph, there was nothing but power under the wings of her glider. There was nowhere for them to run. No sea to mask their scent, no Underground to crawl into like rats.

She had been expecting to face them in Keel. After all the Wraith's precision and care in their travels, Leona expected them to think of some other way to cross the last of the distance to the Alchemists' Guild. Some way that wouldn't trail their scent through the air in all directions.

She didn't rule out the possibility that it was some kind of trap or attack. After all, the Wraith could make seemingly any situation work to her advantage. If she could turn a prison break into a victory against three of the King's Riders, she could somehow turn an airship into a floating fortress.

So Leona wasn't taking any chances. She wasn't interested in being elegant or tactful in her approach. She wasn't going to imagine herself above the Wraith. She was going to fight in the most underhanded ways she knew how. And she was going to finally bring victory for Yveun Dono.

Strapped over her back was a large weapon. It was cumbersome to wield and awkward to feel, but the Revolvers had assured her it was capable of an explosion like no other. Leona stabilized her glider and planted her feet. She looked over to Camile who did the same without needing to be told.

"Let's clip its wings." Leona reached for the weapon.

"Leona'Kin, there *are* members of House Rok on that vessel." Leona smelled them, too. Not many, but a few mixed among the bland stench of Fenthri and haze of other Dragons.

"No half measures, Camile." She tracked her weapon over the wing. "If they are strong enough, they will survive."

It wasn't too tall of an expectation. Dragons were hearty and House Rok was the strongest of them all. If any emerged, Leona would see them to whatever business they had on Loom personally.

Camile did the same with her gun. Leona had to hold in laughter at the sight. Her companion looked ridiculous with a weapon in hand. Though the same could be said of her. It had been Sybil and her pack that ran with guns. Leona and her acolytes always preferred the Dragons' traditional means of destruction: claws.

Still, when on Loom she would fight as the Fenthri did if it served her means. The thinking was a very Xin approach. But to kill a Xin, she conceded, one needed to think like a Xin. Terrifying as that might be.

Leona leveled her weapon and gripped the trigger. The Revos had given them only one canister each, insisting they wouldn't need more. When Leona pushed back, delicately and not so delicately, they still did not come up with more canisters, saying that the chemicals and powders required simply weren't kept in stock.

Leona forced her magic into the long gun. The second she did, runes lit up along the handle and barrel. Once activated, she had no choice but to keep feeding it. They leeched magic from her hungrily, siphoning it out through both hands. The runes glowed in the darkness so brightly they drew their shapes with beams of light in the hazy night air around her. The last rune on the barrel sparked, joining the rest.

Leona wasted no time and pulled the trigger.

A bolt of magic shot forward in a straight line and missed the wing by a small margin. Leona screamed in annoyance. She was sure it was her sister's heart that lingered somewhere in the depths of her magic that cackled hellishly, scolding her for all the times she'd skipped shooting practice.

The magic ray continued forward, striking the ground far below. In a reverse chain reaction, the beam exploded backward, fanning out in all directions. The edge of the magic clipped the wing she had been aiming for, which had already moved well ahead, and disintegrated the edge of it on contact. At least she'd taken out some of the gold helping keep the airship aloft.

Leona threw away the weapon and grabbed the levers of her craft with a heavy sigh. The Revos hadn't been lying to her. Despite all her boasting and arrogance, it had taken a lot out of her to make such a shot. Bruises dotted her skin where blood vessels had broken. She focused on nothing more than keeping her glider aloft, letting her magic slowly replenish through the fatigue.

Her attention was pulled left as another shot exploded from across the airship. Camile's magic burned a slightly different color from Leona's, but it was just as large. Even better, it hit its mark. Leona howled with bloodthirsty joy at the sight of the beam of magic cutting through the wing of the airship.

Magic glittered across its surface, hungry for sustenance. It consumed the wing whole, and the side of the airship when the beam expanded. Even better, the shockwave clipped the delicate balloon helping hold the ship aloft. It expelled air with a mighty wheeze and the vessel lurched through the air, swaying and dropping precipitously with only one wing to support its flight.

Leona looked at the triumphant smile Camile wore and rolled her eyes. "Don't you start bragging."

"The one thing Sybil was good for!" Camile called back.

"You practiced shooting with Sybil?"

"Someone under you needed to know a little about Loom's weaponry. I thought it would pay off eventually." Camile winked.

Pay off it did. Leona vowed that when they returned to Nova, she would see Camile rewarded handsomely by the Dono. She would figure out later what that reward would look like. For now, she would remain focused on what would get her back to Nova: killing Cvareh.

Men and women ran around the airship, shouting and screaming. Just a tiny little act and their peaceful night was thrown into delicious madness. Leona rounded the airship, watching them sprint to the back balconies in confusion. She caught glimpses of crowded hallways and utter chaos within.

But she didn't see Cvareh or the Wraith.

She would remain on her glider until she had visual confirmation of them. And, if she must, she would hand-pick them from the airship's rubble. On the lowest balcony in the back, a crowd was beginning to amass. They tripped and stumbled over the pitching of the airship as it continued to fall through the sky. Small gliders were being loaded frantically. Dragons stepped forward to man each of them, their magic more certain to provide sustainable lift or flight than any Chimera's.

Leona made an involuntary gagging motion at the sight of it. Dragons helping Fenthri. It was disgusting. She wanted her kin aboard those tiny fliers, certainly. But Fenthri? Let them all die; there were far too many of them anyway.

Still, she hung back. She waited. She would not charge in hastily. She would let her plan unfurl like a banner of victory on the winds she had called up beneath her wings.

Leona was taking another loop toward the front of the airship when she felt the characteristic snap of magic across her mind. Time resumed itself normally—there had been only a second of stillness. The Fenthri moved as normal, completely unaware of what had happened. But the Dragons all looked at each other blearily.

She frantically searched the decks for the source of the time-stop. A commotion summoned her attention, men and women shouting in panic at a group of three that had pushed their way onto a tiny emergency glider. The young Fenthri Florence—shouted at her master, who was fending off others from getting on their emergency escape. In the back was Cvareh, looking like the complete idiot he was behind the relatively simple handles.

This was what she'd been waiting for. Leona dove, landing her small vessel hard atop the heads of Fenthri, crushing them into a bloody smear on the deck beneath her. The other Fen scattered and pushed on all the edges of the deck in panic. More rescue gliders launched. The Wraith's girl pulled a few others onto the platform where she and Cvareh stood.

Leona charged.

"Cvareh—go!" the Wraith screamed.

"Ari!" Florence cried.

"Go, go now if anything you ever said to me was true." There was a bitter pain in the Wraith's voice that hadn't been there before.

"I'm not letting you go anywhere!" Leona lunged.

The Wraith spun and met her, blade to talon. Leona bared her teeth and the woman did the same. She was truly hideous, flat teeth and gray skin clashing with bright Dragon eyes. But she moved with the speed of a Dragon, and responded with the strength of a Dragon, and she had no hesitation in any of it.

The small glider carrying Cvareh and the Wraith's girl dropped away. Leona turned her head skyward. She didn't see Camile, but she trusted the other Rider to respond. "Camile! On Cvareh!"

"Oh, she won't be," the Wraith announced triumphantly. "Canisters that can take down Dragons in one shot are rare. I'd been holding onto that one... But I was hoping for you."

Leona roared, pushing off the Wraith. The woman slid as the deck tilted, the captain struggling to keep the airship as level as possible. She spun in the crimson blood of her fellow Fen that oozed from under Leona's glider.

She was expecting the Wraith's barbed whip. And rather than dodging it like a fool, she snatched it from mid air, her hand on the hilt of the golden dagger. It struggled against her fingers, like a bird trying to break free. Leona held it all the tighter. She yanked, trying to catch the Wraith off-balance.

But the Wraith jumped, and the winch box on her hip propelled her to Leona. She stepped off the ground on her toes, twisting in the air over the line to bring her heel across Leona's face. Leona reeled, releasing the dagger to free her hand. She slashed and the Waith dropped backward, rolling away as Leona tried to shatter her bones with a mighty step.

They matched blow to blow, dodge for dodge as the failing airship plummeted through the sky. Leona knew they were nearing the ground when the Fen began to take their chances jumping for trees rather than meeting the earth with the airship. She growled and threw the Wraith off her, leaping for her own glider.

"I'm not letting you go!" The knife on the end of the Wraith's line looped around her neck, forcing Leona to fall backward or be choked into submission.

Free of the cable, Leona gasped for air, the bruising in her neck quickly healing.

"If I'm going down, you're coming with me," the Wraith declared.

"You'll die, and I'll be unscathed, ready to skin your little pet and Dragon alive." Leona snarled, still sliding her feet back to her glider. Even if there was a chance for her to survive the carnage, she didn't want to risk a stray beam or spear of wood carving her through the heart. Not when her glider rested right next to her.

"I don't think so," the woman grinned madly. The wind howled through her words, across the deck littered with bodies and carnage from their fight and the chaos that had erupted from the falling airship. "I have a boon to collect. And I'm not going to die before I get it."

"We'll see about that." Leona began sprinting for the woman and, this time, the Chimera didn't even flinch, boldly standing her ground. There wasn't another second to be wasted as the airship reached its terminal destination. The Wraith waited for her charge.

They both half sidestepped in weak attempts at dodges. Claws cut through gray Fenthri skin. Daggers tore through Dragon bone and muscle.

And *gold* exploded on both sides.

Where Leona had expected a heart, her fingers landed on something metallic. All training faded in utter confusion as she ran the pads of her fingers over its square shape. She gasped, blood bubbling up her throat from the dagger in her chest.

"What are you?" She whispered, staring at the place where her fingers protruded from the other woman's chest.

Gold blood streamed down the Wraith's garb, identical to Leona's. She tried to look over the woman's face time and again. Was she somehow a Dragon in disguise? No, an illusion would've faltered by now.

"*What are you?*" Leona repeated. Her ears howled as she tried to piece together what she had been fighting the whole time she'd been hunting Cvareh on Loom.

"I'm *perfect.*"

The woman twisted her dagger, once, twice. She spun it in place, pulverizing Leona's chest cavity. She felt bone shatter under the blade, sinew stretch and snap against its edge. The Wraith stepped away, reaching for Leona's chest.

She was going to eat her heart.

Leona wheezed. She clung to life, clung to her duty. It was the best death a Rider could hope for, a death while serving their King. She clung uselessly and weakly to the woman's forearm as the White Wraith ripped the remnants of her heart from her chest, bit into it, and ended the life of the King's Master Rider.

CVAREH

He had flown a sum total of one other glider in his life. That time it had been in a rush as well, stolen. He'd barreled down toward the Gods' Line in utter terror, gripping the handles with all his might, pushing as much magic as he could into his feet and around the body of the glider.

It had been how he'd started his journey. And now it seemed it would end much the same. He had no idea what was below him. The faint glow of lights dotted the fast-approaching horizon, winking in and out from the trees that swayed, blocking their path.

"Ari's still up there!" Florence's eyes were glued to the smoking remains of the airship, plummeting down to earth like a swan at the end of its song, taking one last dive.

He gripped the handles tightly. After what she'd said to him, he shouldn't care. She'd stolen his schematic, she'd cast him aside, she'd shown him exactly how little he meant to her. And now...now he should shrug her off like she was nothing. He should focus on the final sprint of his journey. If she wanted to deal with the Riders for him, he should take the gift without a second thought.

But he strained his neck, looking over his shoulder. She was still up there, headed toward death on his behalf. It tied knots in his stomach. It flipped his heart up-side down. It broke his resolve.

Pantheon above save him, he might care for the woman more than he'd ever bargained for. That brash and unfashionable Wraith had lived up to her word from New Dortam. She had stolen his heart after all.

Cvareh looked forward again, grimacing inward. Yes, let the first woman he'd developed any kind of confusing but substantial feelings for be a Fenthri. Not just any Fenthri, but *that* Fenthri.

"We have to go back for her." Florence grabbed his arm, pleading.

"Flor, I'm trying to prevent us from dying right now. It's what she wanted. It's what Arianna wanted," he repeated uselessly, as if that would absolve him of his frantic worry for the woman. "She's stronger than any Chimera I've ever met. She's stronger than most Dragons I've known. If anyone will survive, it's her."

"She's as mortal as you or I! She only dons that illusion because it suits her."

"You think I'm not aware of that!" he snarled. Florence looked at him in surprise. "You think I am not aware that she is just a woman underneath that white coat? I assure you, I am painfully, frustratingly, confusingly aware."

The girl stilled. Her hands fell from his person to grip the railing of the oddly shaped glider for stability. She was still weak, he noted. She would continue to decay until she had her transfusion and made the transition to the halfway state of existence known as being a Chimera.

"When did it happen?" Florence whispered.

Cvareh looked at her, cursing her for being so astute. But if anyone were to notice, it would have been Florence. After all the time she'd spent with him and Arianna, she would sense the subtle changes with even the most cursory observations.

"I'm figuring that out myself." He didn't mince words. "But now isn't quite the time."

Three Fenthri huddled in the front of his glider, clinging to the railing for dear life. Florence had insisted the three join them. The girl refused to take a whole glider to herself despite Arianna's goals and worries. Her good nature even in the face of danger and death shined through.

"Brace yourselves," he shouted as the first tree scraped the bottom of the glider.

Controlled falling he could barely manage. But the amount of magic required to keep the wings aloft, descend evenly—they were skills he'd never learned or even thought to work on. The added difficulty of dodging the silent sentinels of the dark forest made the idea of a smooth landing impossible. He just hoped he wouldn't kill everyone before they touched the ground.

Branches scraped at them as they broke through the tree line. Cvareh's right eye was gouged out by a rogue wooden hook and he cried out in pain, fighting to keep his focus on the task at hand while his eye slowly regrew. He swung right and left, pulling on the handles, his magic straining to keep them aloft and avoid the thick trunks of the trees.

They came in hot and fast, crashing against the ground and sending a tidal wave of brush, leaves, and dirt scattering away in all directions. Two people up front were thrown off, and Florence nearly was as well. Cvareh grabbed for the young woman, pinning her against his chest as he grabbed the railing with his other hand. The glider finally slammed into a fallen tree, tipping forward and purging the last of its contents.

Cvareh twisted in the air, placing himself between Florence and the ground. He had all the wind knocked out of him and his back was shredded from a twig or ten as they skidded to a stop. He panted for air, not moving for a long moment.

Florence did the same before rolling off him with a groan. They both let the world spin and slowly settle into place. The high canopy of the forest was thick, not allowing any of the ambient light from the moon above the clouds that coated Loom through. It wasn't much better than the Underground.

Loom was a dark world of gray people and horrors. It was full of struggle and nine-hundred and ninety-nine reasons to die. The Fenthri were the people who found the one reason to live, time and again.

As if to prove the point, Florence sat with a groan. The girl, for all her bruises and exhaustion, moved before he did. He watched her blink, trying to process in the darkness.

She jumped when a large rumble shook the earth, followed by the boom of an explosion through the trees. The airship had finally joined them. Florence grabbed her shirt over her heart, struggling to her feet, pushing herself forward, stumbling, getting up again, striving to get to her teacher.

Cvareh wouldn't let her struggle alone. He stood as well, crossing to her front and kneeling with his back to her.

"We'll move faster if you let me carry you."

Understanding, Florence wrapped her arms around his shoulders, letting him grab her thighs. She weighed next to nothing. He suspected her long raven colored hair was half of her overall mass. He knew where they were headed, and started in that direction.

"Where are you going?" one of the other Fenthri called to them. "We should stay with the glider. They'll send search parties from Keel."

"You can wait. We had someone on the airship we're going to find," Florence replied.

"No one survived that. And going wandering in the Skeleton Forest alone is just inviting the endwig to attack," the man cautioned.

"You don't know the woman we're looking for. There's no way she'd let a little airship crash kill her."

"Suit yourselves." The man shrugged. He pulled a signal flare from the compartment of the glider and shot it up into the air.

Cvareh and Florence walked in the opposite direction. He set a sustainable pace, quick but not fast enough to exhaust him before they reached their destination. Florence's small head rested on his shoulder, her breathing consistent in his ear.

"Thank you for going back for her," she whispered.

"You never had any doubt I would." He smiled tiredly at himself.

"It's in the opposite direction of where you want to go."

"No." He shook his head. "This is the exact direction I want to go."

The three of them had set out for the Alchemists' Guild together. They would make it together, he resolved. He wasn't leaving Arianna behind. He still had a lot to learn about the woman. He wanted to understand every flavor he'd ever tasted of her. He wanted to know what made shadows cloud her eyes in broad daylight. He wanted to know what made her different from anyone he'd ever met.

They arrived at the crash site without incident. Panting, Cvareh eased Florence to the ground. He took gulps of air, trying to split through the scents.

"Ari!" Florence called. "Arianna!"

Smoke, oil, coal, grease, steel, iron, wood, bronze, pine. They filled his nose, lit up like a giant candle and the twisted airship was the wick. He walked in a circle, inviting every scent.

Then he got a waft of strawberry. Cvareh looked around him in panic for the light, out-of-place scent. *Leona.* Where was she?

His talons shot out from his fingers. A growl rose in his throat. If the King's Bitch survived at Arianna's expense, he would switch them personally in the chambers of Lord Xin. He would steal his Fenthri's soul back from the gods themselves.

The scent led him to a sight he wasn't expecting. He should've known what it meant when it didn't move. Leona's body had been thrown from the airship and lay face-first in the pine needles not far off, her ruby-colored skin illuminated by the orange flames. Cvareh knew she was dead before he flipped her over and saw the hole in her chest.

Arianna had done it. She'd killed the King's Master Rider. Cvareh wanted to cheer, but a sort of quiet fear underscored the thought. This was Leona, a woman with more beads than any other Rider. She was known for being equal parts ruthlessness and loyalty. And she'd been felled by a Chimera.

The wind shifted, and his nose was no longer cluttered with the smoke and flame.

"Who is that?" Florence called nervously, seeing the body he was crouched over.

"We're safe, for now. She's dead." Cvareh stood, sniffing the air. It was clear and fresh, just the heady scent of pine riding the wind. *Had he imagined it?*

Another gust, and the rogue scent of cedar cut through the trees, accented by honeysuckle. It brightened the night and restored his every sense. His feet found strength, his heart beat harder, his mouth watered. Even his magic pulsed outward, an automatic reaction to the magic he had imbibed.

It was like smelling his favorite meal when he hadn't eaten for months. It was like finding the accent to a fine coat. He didn't need her, but gods he wanted her.

Arianna lay prone a short distance from Leona's glider. She'd been trying to fly it away, he realized. Magic that most Dragons struggled to muster, she'd tackled when presented with no other choice.

"Ari! Is it Ari?" Florence was slow behind him. He heard her curse under her breath as she collapsed against a tree to regain her strength before continuing forward again.

"It is." He fell to his knees beside the woman.

"Is she alive? Is she breathing? Will she be all right?"

"She's alive." He didn't know the answers to the rest of her frantic questions.

The woman's magic was weak and struggling to repair the internal bleeding that was drowning her. Her left arm was twisted and her foot was snapped. Cvareh popped them back into place so they'd heal right.

Even unconscious, the pain of it brought a moan from Arianna's lips.

"Can you give her your magic? Like she gave you?" Florence asked.

It would certainly help. But he'd never let anyone imbibe off him before. It raised warning flags, despite the fact that she'd let him consume her magic.

Scowling at himself, Cvareh bit his tongue. Blood filled his mouth from where his canine had pierced the muscle. His hands grabbed her cheeks gently, situating her face upward. He couldn't stop his thumb from smearing away the remnants of the drawn Guild Mark. It was nothing but a blemish on her beautiful face.

Gently prying open her lips, Cvareh leaned forward. He felt her breath on his cheek as his face neared. His own lips parted slightly, letting the blood drip into her mouth. He waited, mouth on hers, for her reflex to swallow.

For a woman who looked like she was made of stone and steel, she was soft and warm. She was strong, and yet in that moment seemed so fragile under his hands. He opened his mouth again, letting more blood—more magic—seep into her.

He didn't like this delicate Arianna. He wanted the woman he knew back. He wanted the woman who would challenge him at every turn. Drive him crazy. Push him to the edge that made him want to cling harder and beg for more. He wanted it all. He wanted her to always be at his side, threatening to cut him if he was stupid.

His magic began to grow in her. He felt the connection of warmth it sparked from his body to hers. Like an ember fanned to a flame by both of their lives. They were entwined, slowly, surely, certainly. As long as he lived, she would. He would see to that much.

He opened his mouth again and her tongue pressed against his, her mouth moving to fit his hungrily. Her teeth raked against his lip and blood smeared between them.

Cvareh's fingers pressed around the back of her neck, and he almost held his breath. He wanted to stop time for her, with her, so that he could savor her shamelessly for another long moment. But he pulled away, meeting her open eyes—they glowed the color of lavender in the night, heightened by the flood of his magic.

She didn't push him away, she didn't scold him, she didn't reach for her daggers—if she even still had them. Arianna stared up at him, and he stared down at her, holding her face, holding her in the small corner of the world in which they existed. And if he were to exist nowhere else, ever, he would be content.

"I finally know what you taste like," she whispered.

If she had asked, he would've let her have a second chance at the flavor.

ARIANNA

A cool gust rushed through her veins. It was crisp and fresh, like winter air across a frozen lake. Shocking to her system, but not in a way that slowed her down. Rather, in a way that reminded her what the reason was for her very existence.

Hovering within the sensation, encased in the taste of cold, was the earthy smell and flavor of wood smoke. Comforting in the most basic way possible, Arianna imbibed it hungrily. Her mouth was eager to consume the sensation, to consume *him* before her mind caught up with the conscious awareness of who *he* was.

She fished gently with her tongue, then not so gently with her teeth. The technical term for the act would, without doubt, be imbibing. But all Arianna could think of was how long it had been since she had last been kissed. She didn't *need* sensual pursuits. If she did there had been ample opportunity throughout the past two lonely years to find some at various parlors in Mercury Town.

But needing, wanting, and enjoying when presented with such, were all different. And in that moment she enjoyed the weight of his mouth on hers. She savored the slickness of his blood, the icy rush of his magic, the crisp, heady flavors of wood smoke. She enjoyed it all shamelessly until he pulled away.

Until she was faced with reality once more.

Fire lit up the side of his face, the smell of actual smoke flooding her nose. Her mind began working instantly, figuring out the who, what, where, and why of her situation. She was alive, which must mean she'd managed to fly the glider long enough to ease her landing.

But underneath her mind, a different sort of machine purred. It was the one in her chest that occupied the place of her heart, and it hummed in a way she'd never heard before. Well, it didn't *actually* hum differently. She knew better than to think emotions could change clockwork gears and screws. In fact, she was glad emotions couldn't. But she heard it differently. She heard the world a little differently. She'd had her first glimpse into the truth of the man that was encased under his pale azure skin and it resonated deeply with the memory of another woman she once loved. It was no wonder she'd been able to grow any fondness for the Dragon. She just hadn't been willing to see it until that exact second.

"I finally know what you taste like," she breathed in relief. It was like finally cracking into a safe that had been driving her mad with its contents for weeks.

"Ari..." Florence whispered weakly.

Arianna was pulled upright at the sound, nearly hitting Cvareh in the face with her forehead. She looked frantically for her student. The glow that had surrounded her from the imbibing slowly faded into the harsh detail of reality.

"Flor!" She held out her arms and the girl came crashing into them. Arianna held her tightly with all her might. "You're all right. Grease every gear, you're all right."

"I should be saying that to you." The girl hiccupped and tears came.

She pressed her eyes closed, pressing her nose into Florence's hair. Her darling Florence was in one piece. Arianna could sense the growing decay in her, but that was no better or worse for the fall. She opened her eyes, looking at Cvareh.

Without the haze of the imbibing, she remembered the tension from the last time they had spoken and it seemed he had as well. He regarded her cautiously, his expression searching. Arianna wished she could give him what he searched for. She *wished* she could—that was a scary thought. But she couldn't. No matter his nature to strive for a better tomorrow, his perseverance in the face of no natural aptitude, or his ability to see right through her reminded her of Eva…

He was not Eva.

He was a Dragon. A Dragon who had her schematics for the Philosopher's Box from years ago. Schematics that, the last time she had seen them, were in the hands of a Dragon who had betrayed them all.

"Thank you," Arianna forced out through her confusion. "For keeping Florence safe."

"You don't need to thank me for that." He shook his head. "I wanted to. She's my friend too, after all."

Florence pulled away to smile at Cvareh. No matter what Arianna said, she would believe until the end he was sincere in his desire to help them overthrow the Dragon King. The girl was young, and she could afford the indulgence of hope.

"Well, I don't see the point of wasting further time…" Arianna stood. "Even though it's not in Keel proper, the Guild will still be a long trek on foot."

"At least we won't have any more Riders after us," Cvareh pointed out optimistically.

"How do you know?" Arianna was skeptical. The notion seemed too good to be true.

"I'm fairly certain the Dono doesn't have many more Riders on retainer. And he may not risk them after how many he's lost."

"I remember the last time you were fairly certain about a Rider," she snapped bitterly.

"Ari, don't be mean," Florence scolded.

Arianna squinted at the girl. Florence had taken his side a few times over the past weeks, and it was becoming a trend she didn't enjoy.

"Cvareh has only been helpful."

"Yes, well…" Arianna had no interest in arguing with Florence. Not when they had somehow made it all the way across the world in one piece despite Riders, prison breaks, and Wretched. "We should get this helpful one to the Alchemists. It's not far now."

In the dim light of dawn they set out through the forest. She and Cvareh took turns carrying Florence on their backs. Florence would insist she could walk on her own and they'd let her, but she tired quickly and began to lag behind within minutes.

Words were scarce between them. They each nursed their thoughts and still-healing wounds before conversation. Arianna would glance at Cvareh from time to time out of the corners of her eyes, but she never caught his.

He still carried the folio on his hip, a hand covering it protectively. It was worn and weathered now from their journey, the leather scratched and curling from wear. When he took his hand away there was an outline of where he usually placed it from fretting so much about its presence.

She could kill him now. She could strike him down before they ever made it to the Alchemists' Guild. Or she could spare him, and merely rip up the schematics.

But that was a painful idea. Arianna had only ever torched her work once, and it was like cutting off her own arm. Progress was never meant to be stinted, and even failures weren't to be destroyed. That was how she'd been raised; that was what her teacher had instilled in her. So even then, in the final hours of the last resistance, it took the dying wish of her late master to force her hand in doing what must be done.

Even then, some of her research escaped.

She navigated the Skeleton Forest on memory. She had run through its trees as a girl. She had spent years of her life in this territory. Now, she walked with the ghosts of her memories. She had returned, but there wasn't any more closure waiting for her here than there had been in Dortam. There was no balm to the wound that ached in her chest. It would bleed eternal, unhealed by any magic or medicine.

The heart of Keel was still a good two days off on foot, but Arianna knew when their journey was nearing an end. The Alchemists were reclusive, protective of their research. The Guild itself was offset outside the outer walls of the city to discourage any from entering its grounds by accident.

Magic sparked from golden stakes driven into the trees. They glowed faintly in warning. Arianna continued, unbothered.

"What was that?" Cvareh rubbed the back of his neck in the same spot Arianna had felt the pressure. Even Florence seemed more alert, despite not yet being a true Chimera.

"The door bell of the Alchemists' Guild," Arianna replied grimly.

She could leave him now, leave him here. She could give up on her boon, or cash it in much later when she hunted him down again. The Alchemists were on their way through the forest to see what magical creatures had crossed through their line. Arianna knew how they worked and she knew it would be less than an hour before their trikes came humming through the trees, billowing steam and sparking with magic.

But Arianna continued forward. She insisted that Cvareh had nothing to do with her decision; it was entirely based on Florence. The girl needed the attention of an Alchemist and Arianna would never leave her alone or settle for less than the best care.

It took a little bit longer than expected for the hum of the engines to be heard through the trees, but Arianna knew the sound. Florence and Cvareh looked on with curiosity and almost excitement at the prospect of finally being at the end of their journey.

The trikes were a larger version of the ones the Raven gangs rode around on. They could sit three people apiece, five if they had a platform suspended between their two gigantic back wheels. Guns were mounted on their fronts, flanked by spikes. The Alchemists took the endwig and the other rare—but deadly—creatures that lived in their forest seriously.

Their eyes were a rainbow of colors. And if they didn't have Dragon eyes, the Alchemists sported Dragon ears or hands. Every one of them was a Chimera, a requisite at a certain level of the Guild.

"You're survivors of the crash?" one of them asked.

Arianna didn't miss how most of them kept their hands by their weapons. But if what she had learned in Ter.5.2 was true, they didn't have enough ammunition to shoot first and ask questions later.

"More or less," she replied. "We seek the Guild."

"The Guild does not take visitors," another replied.

"I have a delivery," Cvareh spoke. Arianna resisted the urge to throttle him. She didn't know what was more annoying, the fact that he was about to say something stupid, or the fact that she could sense he was about to say something stupid. "I come bearing help for the rebels against the Dragon King."

The Alchemists exchanged a look and burst out laughing.

"No rebels here, Dragon." The lead rider leaned back in his seat, folding his arms. "We're all happy to follow our King's decrees."

Arianna snorted softly in amusement. But as much as she enjoyed seeing Cvareh put in his place, it wouldn't solve their predicament of getting to the guild. "He speaks true. Bring us to the Vicar. If there is no new resistance brewing, harvest him for wasting your time."

"Ari!" Cvareh hissed.

"What?" She arched her eyebrows at him. "You're certain there is a resistance, and you're certain that what you carry will help it. Right?" He said nothing, silently fuming. "If you are, there's no real risk to you."

The Alchemists looked at each other, silently debating it. The leader gave a nod to one on the wings and the girl touched a hand to her ear, covering her mouth with her hand, muttering under her breath. They were used to being around people with Dragon hearing, because she spoke so softly that not even Arianna could make out the words.

After several long minutes, she straightened, giving a nod of affirmation to her leader.

"Very well, then." He shrugged. "Onto the trike at the end with the three of you."

They obliged, and the vehicles were speeding through the forest at speeds befitting a Raven. Still, Arianna sat calmly. She knew these drivers had ridden through here countless times to fend off the endwig attracted to the scent of blood and carrion that always lingered around the Alchemists' Guild hall as a result of their studies.

Her eyes drifted over to a far point, invisible through the dense forest. She wondered if the place that had been their laboratory was still black and gray, a dark spot on the living forest of magic gone wrong. Or if the Alchemists had rebuilt, and were working there anew.

She wondered, but she prayed she would never find out.

FLORENCE

The wind whipped through her hair, knotting it even further than the airship crash had. It licked moisture from her eyes as she blinked into the reckless speed that would've made Will and Helen proud. *Perhaps they should've come along after all.*

One of the trikes to their right pulled ahead. Magic flashed around the man's fingers, sparking flares on the ground in reply. *Traps,* Florence realized. Their curving and illogical route was suddenly making more sense. The ground leading up to the guild hall was riddled with traps, discouraging man and monster from wandering too close.

They crossed through a tree line into a scorched and salted section of earth. Nothing grew and dust drifted across the ground. High above, on a lower wall, men and women watched them from behind the barrels of guns.

Florence found it ironic. The guild that made the guns allowed anyone to walk through one of its six main arches that connected its sprawling campus with the city of Dortam. But the guild that merely bought the guns put the weapons to more use.

A hulking portcullis with bars four times her height rose slowly. They rode under, and through a set of metal doors that

were nearly a peca thick. Dust swirled up from under the tires
of the trikes as they rolled to a stop in a small inner yard. What
Florence had thought was merely an outer wall proved to be a
solid structure connecting to the inner tower. The inner tower
rose upward beyond the edge of what Florence had perceived
as a wall and then tapered off again, with the final thin column
stretching high above the tallest trees in the Skeleton Forest.
It reminded her of a many-tiered cake; the thought instantly
made her mouth water for something sweet.

They were led through a second set of metal doors,
gold lining their edges. The core of the guild was hollow.
Florence couldn't suppress a gasp as they entered the central
atrium that stretched all the way to the rooftop.

Golden lifts lined the circumference, whizzing silently
on the magic of their riders. It was well illuminated with the
ghostly pale glow of electric lighting. With an endless supply
of magic to run generators, Florence suspected that outfitting
the guild for electric hadn't been hard. But it had been recent,
judging by the wires that were tacked up along the walls like
copper ribbons.

"We'll need you to leave your weapons here," the man
who had been leading them instructed.

Arianna and Cvareh exchanged a look.

"Suit yourselves." Surprisingly, Ari didn't put up a
fight.

Florence watched as she and Cvareh passed over their
pistols. Ari was out of canisters, so the weapon was useless to
her. Cvareh maybe had one left, but his claws were ten times
as deadly as his shot. She was surprised when Ari passed over
her blades. But no one made any motion for the winch box on
her hip or the spools of cabling.

Arianna's motion gear was unorthodox even for a Raven. Rivets had a hard time deciphering it at a glance without a background of who she was and what she did. None of the Alchemists seemed to even consider the fact that she walked with a noose that could move on its own.

"If you could sharpen my blades while you have them, that'd be great." Ari smiled cheerfully, patting the Alchemist on the shoulder. The girl who was taking their weapons rolled her eyes.

"Hurry up, then." The leader was impatient, ushering them toward one of the lifts.

The gears under the platform churned to life against the pitted tracks that ran up the wall. The Alchemist was silent, focus clouding his eyes. Arianna folded her arms over her chest. She gave the appearance of being nonchalant, but Florence could feel the tension radiating off her. Then there was Cvareh. He didn't even bother with appearances, fumbling relentlessly with the clips of his folio.

For Florence, despite all her exhaustion and her slowly waning strength, she stared in wonder at the world around her. She was getting a glimpse of the most secretive Guild in the world. These were the hallways in which Loom had been changed, the place that had cultivated the scientists who uncovered the ability to refine metal into gold, the doctors to make the first Chimera; some of the greatest thinkers of the ages had lived in these rooms.

Within them, she felt for the first time what Arianna had been telling her all along: the Loom she knew was the shadow of something grander. Every Guild was told by the Dragons what they would be. The students were told what to learn. The people were told where to study. They were kept sequestered like livestock and expected to produce, yet a mind imprisoned was not a mind that could think great thoughts.

The other Guilds regarded the Alchemists with skepticism and jokes. They were either perceived as being mad hermits, hiding in their corner of the world, muttering over their vials and experiments. Or as mad scientists, muttering over their vials and experiments. They might be a bit of both, she decided.

But if they were mad, they were mad because they kept dreaming when the rest of Loom merely slept in stasis. They pushed out others to preserve their way of life. And it was here that a rebellion could be born.

The elevator stopped at the very top of the tower. Florence stared down at the atrium. On the floor was the symbol of the Alchemists: two triangles, one pointing up and one pointing down, connected by a line—symbolizing earth and sky.

The landing led to a set of wooden doors emblazoned with the same symbol. Their guide knocked, but let himself in after only a second. Florence's heart raced as they entered the office. The room was littered with workbenches made out of metal. Vials and beakers cluttered their surfaces. Tubes connected them, transporting bubbling liquid throughout the cluttered lab. The concrete floor was stained in some places, rough in others from various chemical spills.

"Just a second," a woman's voice called from somewhere in the back corner. "I'll be with you in just one second!"

Arianna stiffened. Florence watched her hand twitch for a dagger that wasn't there. After being nonchalant through the entire encounter, she was panicking *now*?

"Sorry about that, I had just gotten it to the right temperature..." A woman with coal-colored skin and ashen hair rounded the tables, weaving her way toward them through the lab. She wiped her hands on a stained apron, lifting goggles onto her forehead. They left a ring on her cheeks from having been there for an extended period of time.

The Vicar Alchemist said nothing as she locked eyes with Arianna. Arianna remained tense as well, a scowl fighting at the corners of her mouth.

"It's you," the woman breathed in shock. "You're alive?"

ARIANNA

S he thought she recognized the voice from the first second, but being face to face with the woman was far worse than she'd ever imagined. Arianna wished she were literally anywhere else in the world.

"It's been some time, Sophie." What did one say to the self-centered best friend of the dead woman she'd loved?

"It is you, then?" Sophie repeated in shock, leaning against one of her tables, almost knocking over a pipette stand in the process. "You died, two years ago...You died with the rest of them."

"I have been called a wraith."

"Why are you here? Did you come back to help us? Arianna, this is excellent, together we can—"

She held up her hand, stopping Sophie before she ran away with her thoughts. "I'm not here for you." She pointed to Cvareh. "I'm just delivering him."

"What?" Sophie looked between them in confusion. "Who's he?"

"He's the one we told you about," the Alchemist who had led them there reported. "The one who claims to have a message for some sort of rebellion."

"Drop the pretenses, Derek. These people are friends."

Sophie was getting ahead of herself on that fact, but Arianna held her tongue on the matter. Perhaps the woman had changed with time. Believing in Sophie's good nature and ability to change would be the ultimate proof of Florence's influence.

But she didn't want to think on it. Now that she knew the Vicar Alchemist was someone from the last rebellion, all she wanted to do now was get out of the Guild as fast as possible.

She glanced at Florence from the corners of her eyes. There was still that loose end to tie up. She may have to use whatever good feelings Sophie held for her to get Florence the treatment she needed. Ari would swallow the thought of staying a night or three under the Alchemists' roof for that. But no longer.

"It's not a message." Cvareh stepped forward. "I have something I stole from the Dragon King. I brought it as a measure of good faith from House Xin. We want to align with you. We want to help you overthrow him."

"Large words from a Dragon." Arianna was relieved to see that Sophie could manage some measure of skepticism. "What do you have that you think could sway us in such a manner?"

Cvareh opened his folio and finally produced the stack of papers that had started everything long before they'd even brought him to her. The very sight of them filled Arianna with anger. It was a frustrating contrast, that a man who had come to fill her with an odd sort of curiosity and infatuation could also bear something that turned him into a vision of pure loathing.

He presented Sophie schematics with both hands; Arianna felt sick. She knew all she had done, everything she had put Florence through, was to allow history to repeat itself.

But a different feeling sparked as the documents changed hands. Cvareh looked at her with wide eyes. He'd felt the spark too. The scales had tipped, and the subconscious drive that had pushed Arianna to get him to the Alchemists' Guild now was transferred to him. *He was hers.* The boon contract had been fulfilled.

"Sophie, foremost," Arianna interrupted before the woman could get a good look. "I have a favor to ask."

"For you?"

Arianna nodded. "For old times' sake." She wanted to vomit in disgust at playing that card.

"Of course, anything. What do you need?" Sophie smiled sweetly, but Arianna could practically see her mixing the elements of their conversation to form an imagined debt that Arianna would now owe her.

"Florence was injured en route here. She had to imbibe as a Fenthri." Sophie didn't seem surprised. She could likely sense it in the girl from the moment they walked in the room.

"You want her to be a Chimera?" Sophie clarified.

"She must be, or she'll die. There isn't much time left before her organs are beyond repair. This has been going on for weeks now."

"I see." Sophie grimaced. "Derek, prepare a transfusion room, begin as soon as it and the young woman here are prepared."

"Thank you, Sophie." Arianna didn't need to lie about her gratitude. "If you'll excuse us, we've had a long journey..."

She had to get out of the room. She'd do *anything* to get out of the room.

"You can rest in a vacant Master's chambers. I trust you still remember where they are?"

"I could never forget."

"Help yourselves to whatever you need. I'll find you later and we can discuss further what you can do to help our cause." Sophie smiled and Arianna grated her teeth, trying to smile in kind.

Taking Florence by the hand, she practically dragged the girl from the room. She had to get on the lift before Sophie had a chance to really look at what Cvareh had brought her. But Arianna knew there would only be so long she could avoid *that* conversation.

CVAREH

He watched Arianna go, magic still arcing between his veins like electricity. The desire to not let her out of his sight no longer stemmed only from his growing fondness for the woman, but now from his desire to fulfill her every wish— any wish. All she had to do was ask it of him. He feared the longer she went without demanding the boon of him, the further her very presence would drive him to insanity.

Still, he struggled for focus on the matter at hand instead of the Chimera who had just left the room. The woman was staring wide-eyed at the papers, slowly thumbing through them. He suspected from her expression alone that she already knew what they contained.

"They're for the Philosopher's Box," he announced proudly. "I uncovered that the King had acquired them from a Rivet here on Loom during the last rebellion. I'm afraid I don't know all the details of what or how, but I thought it could be of use."

The woman placed them aside on the table, looking at him skeptically. It was not the reaction he'd been expecting, to say the least.

"I've traveled quite far to bring them to you. House Xin hopes the schematics can be finished and once they are, we will supply the necessary Dragon organs to see perfect Chimeras made," he fumbled over his words. The more he talked, the less she seemed inclined to him. "I know they're unfinished but—"

"You have no idea what you've brought me, do you?" The Vicar placed her hands on her hips.

"I know exactly what they are," he insisted. This was not how it was supposed to go, not in the slightest. At the least he'd hoped for some gratitude for his assistance. All he was getting instead was skepticism and a small dose of amusement.

"How, exactly, did you find out they were there?" The Vicar folded her fingers before her.

"I overheard a conversation in the villa of the Dragon King."

"And why were you there?"

"I'm the Ryu—the second in command of House Xin," he clarified. "It's not uncommon for noblemen and women to be invited as guests of the King." It was a sort-of lie. Noblemen and women from across Nova were invited on various occasions to visit with the Dono or attend his Crimson Court. Members of House Xin, less so, certainly. But that hadn't been why he'd been there that day. Cvareh kept his mouth shut over the true nature of his then-purpose. He didn't want to add to her skepticism by confessing he'd been visiting his brother.

"You're either a well-trained liar, intentionally kept in the dark, or are the most oblivious creature I have ever met." She shook her head, fanning out the papers in the limited space on the table.

"Why?" Horror at the idea that the documents weren't what he'd been led to believe crept over him as if Lord Xin himself had come from the afterworld for Cvareh's immortal soul. "Are they not for the Philosopher's Box?"

"They most certainly are," she affirmed to his relief.

"Then they should be invaluable to the resistance," he insisted. "And the fact that House Xin would risk both our station and the life of their Ryu to deliver them to you should speak volumes of our loyalty. The King's Riders pursued me in a failed attempt at assassination for these. Just confirm with Ari or Florence." He prayed Arianna wouldn't fabricate something else to knowingly spite him.

"Ari? She lets you call her by that name?"

"Well…" He hesitated. He hadn't ever been given express permission.

Vicar Sophie laughed, shaking her head again. "You are oblivious on all fronts, then."

He opened his mouth to speak, but she continued, finally ending their game of cat and mouse.

"You come to Loom seeking our trust for your House. But you don't seem to grasp why we would distrust you in the first place."

"I know what the Dragons have done to Loom. I know you wouldn't have reason to trust me." Being treated like a child was grating.

"You know why any Fenthri might harbor dislike for the Dragons. But you don't grasp why *we* would," she emphasized. "It may be as you say, that you risk your life in trying to bring these to us. But you don't know what you've brought with you of far greater value."

"Stop talking in riddles."

"You thought I would find value in these schematics, when you have brought me the woman who created them?" Sophie smiled as the realization hit Cvareh.

"The-the woman who created them?" he repeated dumbly, at a loss for all other words.

"You call her Ari, like you're close. But you have no idea who she really is, do you?"

No denial could parry the sword of truth the woman brandished. It cut a bleeding line into his heart atop the space where Arianna's name had been etched, and left the wound to fester with the faint smell of betrayal.

FLORENCE

Derek led her into a small room. A chair was in the center of it, restraints hanging ominously off its edges. Florence eyed them with trepidation. But anything would be better than the way she felt now. She was exhausted all the time, unsteady on her feet, and over the past few days had felt strange pains beginning to creep up on her that were becoming worse and worse, and took longer and longer to go away.

"It hurts," Derek explained, seeing her staring at the restraints. "But we can't have you thrashing about when it happens or you may rip out one of the transfusion lines. If you did, that's the end of it."

"I see." Florence was happy to have an explanation, even if it was a miserable one.

"Unfortunately, we can't give you anything for the pain." He motioned for the chair. "Since the blood is being purged and cycled through your body, anything we could give would be out in minutes."

"I understand." She sat down, willing herself to be still as he began working on the restraints.

Derek paused at her wrist. His steam colored eyes drifted up to her. "It's okay to be scared."

"I'm not scared."

"You're trembling." He shook his head, tightening the leather around her wrists. "What made you want to be a Chimera? To propel engines?"

He was taking note of her Ravens' Guild Mark. "I'm actually a Revo."

"Oh? I bet you fool a lot of people then." He accepted her declaration. It was something that Florence wasn't used to.

"I do," she agreed hesitantly.

"If it gets too much, we'll give you something to clamp down on so you don't bite your tongue off." His hands tightened the strap around her forehead.

"Is that a legitimate concern?" If she was only trembling before, she was shaking now. Every muscle in her body was tense. "I don't understand this—what's about to happen?"

Derek paused what he was doing with the brass mechanism at the chair's side. "We slowly begin to take out your blood. I'll monitor your vitals; the more blood we can take out without completely killing you, the better."

"What's the difference between 'completely' and 'incompletely' killing someone?"

He chuckled. "Right, sorry, Revo… 'Completely' meaning that your body has gone far enough into failure that magic alone will not be able to revive you."

She made a noise of comprehension.

"At which point, we begin introducing Dragon blood, slowly. It mixes with what's left of your blood and your body acclimates to the magic."

"That's why Chimera blood is black and not gold or red?"

"Exactly." Derek smiled reassuringly. After the vote of confidence from the Vicar he had warmed up significantly, and

Florence was never more grateful than she was in that second of sitting in the chair waiting.

"So, why does it hurt?" Nothing sounded particularly terrible. Even if he cut her to make her bleed, she'd endured worse pains.

"Fenthri bodies aren't made for housing magic. I'm sure you're familiar with forsaken Chimera?" She nodded and he continued. "When the Dragon blood is first introduced and hits your system, it's...well, for lack of better words, killing you. But it begins to heal you almost at the same time. Since we do it slowly, it doesn't actually result in death." His voice trailed off and Florence's mind treacherously filled in "normally" for him at the end.

"So I'm dying and being revived a bunch, in a row." Florence looked at the ceiling, bracing herself. "Well, I've never died before, so at least I get to cross that off my list."

Derek laughed. "You're an odd one, aren't you?"

"That's what you get for planning to run away from your guild at thirteen, doing so at fourteen, meeting the White Wraith, and becoming her explosives resource in the span of two years."

"Yes, that would do it." He processed her words for a long moment. "The White Wraith, the spurn of Dortam?"

"The same," Florence affirmed.

"Never imagined I'd see a legendary fighter of Dragons keeping the company of one."

"Cvareh isn't like most Dragons." Florence was instantly defensive. She was exhausted on his behalf of everyone assuming the worst of him.

"Oh, I know."

"You do?"

He nodded.

"How?"

"Because not most Dragons willingly offer their blood to make a Chimera."

"What?"

"What do you think we've been waiting on?"

Within the next minute, the door opened and Cvareh appeared. Sure enough, he sat down on a small stool next to her. Florence looked on in shock.

"You're giving me your blood?" She wished she could find more eloquent words, but all else failed her.

"Technically, I've been doing that for some time already."

"But that was necessary."

"As is this." He leaned against the wall. "I'm the one who brought you here, who took you from your home. I feel responsible for the fact that you're in that chair."

"You shouldn't."

"I do."

"Well you shouldn't—" Her reason was interrupted by the needle that pierced the flesh of her forearm. A second punctured her bicep a little further up and the machine at her side began to whir.

"You're going to start feeling sleepy," Derek informed her. "But I need you to stay awake as long as possible."

Florence watched in fascination as a tank of blood began to fill in the machine. The Alchemist walked around the room, puncturing Cvareh's offered arm. Sure enough, her eyelids grew heavy, her head thick.

"Florence, stay with us," Derek demanded.

"Right, right…" she mumbled. Compliance was becoming awfully difficult. Her vision blurred and her thoughts became sluggish. She wanted to talk, but she had reached a point at which she was no longer certain she could say anything at all.

That's when the pain hit her.

A different set of gears was now whirring on the machine. It was pumping blood from Cvareh's veins into hers. Just as Derek said, the sensation was excruciating. Florence tried to avoid screaming, but eventually failed.

"Hang in there, Flor." A large hand closed around hers. "I'm here... It'll be over soon."

"Well, actually—" Derek started unhelpfully but was stopped short.

"It'll be over soon," Cvareh insisted.

She tried to pry open her eyes. She tried to make sense of what was happening. But it felt like knives were being stabbed into her muscles straight to her bones, only to shear the meat from her skeleton.

Florence breathed heavily. She tried to think of anything else, but the pain was blinding and *everywhere*. It flowed from her arm but soon it was behind her eyes, under her heels, in her chest; there wasn't a place it didn't touch.

"Florence." A stern voice cut through the noises of her agony. "Florence, look at me."

She pried open her eyes and her attention drifted from Cvareh to the new voice that had joined them. Arianna's mouth was set in a grim, determined line. The woman's hand was curled around Florence's fingers alongside Cvareh's.

"I made it through this, and you are stronger than me," Arianna declared.

Florence mentally disagreed, but the thought escaped only as a whimper, as if her body wanted to prove her point for her.

"Hang in there, Flor, a little longer."

They both spoke words of encouragement—more like sweet lies—as she suffered for what seemed like a whole week. But, sure enough, it slowly began to pass and the light at the end of her tunnel vision began to sharpen and grow. Her chest heaved. She couldn't get enough air.

Her body transitioned from utter pain to feeling stronger than it ever had. She could *feel* the fatigue leaving her muscles. The strain of tensing constantly while she'd been in agony was smoothed away magically. Despite the excruciating suffering, Florence wondered why she hadn't made the transition sooner. *It felt that good.*

"Looks like she's out of it," Derek noted. "We'll run this for a bit longer, until her blood runs nearly gold."

"I thought my blood would be black?" she rasped. Her vocal chords had yet to knit from all the screaming.

"It will be," the Alchemist affirmed. "But we want as much Dragon blood in you as we can get. And since we have a willing donor, well, let's be a little selfish, no?"

"I don't want to hurt Cvareh," she breathed, her voice slowly coming back. The magic seemed to place priority on what was vital, followed by functions she put demands on— like her sight or voice.

"You're not going to hurt me," he insisted.

"The Dragon is right. His body produces blood much faster than yours does, even as a new Chimera," Derek said. "Your blood will run black when his fades and your body begins producing new Chimera blood on its own. We just reprogrammed your liver, in essence."

Florence nodded and Derek began removing the restraints. He left only the ones on her right arm until he finally turned off the machine and plucked the needles from her skin nonchalantly. Florence watched as she bled a dark gold that was quickly stopped by her flesh knitting.

"Just rest here for a bit. Don't try to get up yet." He started for the door. "I'm going to get some medicine, just to be safe, and some food."

"Then it's to bed with you," Arianna finished as he left the room.

Florence smiled tiredly at her. Ari always had looked out for her, ever since they first met. It wasn't until this trip that Florence really noticed the fact. And her opinion of it shifted colors alongside her blood.

"Did you ever think I would be a Chimera?" She flexed her hand, imagining herself as much stronger than she likely was.

"No, and I wish you didn't have to endure that," Arianna muttered.

"But I'm rather glad I did." She spoke softly, hoping her words didn't upset Arianna too terribly.

"Flor—"

"Ari," for the first time, Florence interrupted her teacher with purpose. "I can be someone now. It didn't hit me until I was here, until we made this journey. But I can do more than just make guns and bombs. I can *use* them. Everyone here is fighting, and I can help them."

"What are you saying?" Quiet panic tinted her voice.

"I want to help the rebellion."

"They haven't confirmed there is one," Arianna pointed out.

Florence gave her a look that she hoped communicated how much she appreciated being treated like she was stupid. "Well, if there is, I want to help."

"Why?" Arianna's arms dropped to her side. Her shoulders fell. Even Cvareh took note of the uncharacteristic change in the woman.

"Ari, you taught me to believe in possibility. I escaped the Ravens not because I truly wanted to find my calling, but because I just didn't want to be killed when I couldn't pass the aptitude test." Florence sat straighter, her back coming off the recline of the chair. "You were the one who taught me to see Loom as it could be. You wanted me to strive to dream, and I thought you were crazy but I did it anyway because you were the person who saved me and because I wanted to appease you. I never saw it.

"But I see it now, Arianna. I see it now, your vision. I want to fight for it with these people. I can make a difference here. I can fight for real, positive change." Florence swallowed, Arianna's stare a black hole that was consuming her optimism and emotions. "Y-you can too. You can do what you always wanted to do. You can really fight against the Dragons. Can we stay?"

"No," Arianna dismissed her outright.

Florence stared in shock. "Why? *Why?* Isn't this everything you ever said you wanted?"

"Flor, we were fine in Dortam, you and I. We can go back, we can live our lives."

"You taught me to see past what Loom is to what it could be, and now that I can, now that I do, you want me to stand to the side?" Florence balked. "What did we do this for? What did you do this for? Wasn't it for a boon to help you change this world?"

Arianna didn't answer, and her silence stung to a degree that was nearly as great as the transition had been. Florence fell back into her chair.

"Do you really want what's best for Loom?" she whispered. "Or do you only want what's best for yourself?"

"Watch your tongue."

"Watch yours, Arianna." Florence was on her feet.

"Should you be standing?" Cvareh had been entirely forgotten.

"Don't lie to me—tell me straight. Did you ever have any intention of really fighting to win back the Loom you claim to love? Or have you only ever fought for the past under the guise of being a champion for the future?"

Arianna scowled down at her and Florence looked up without hesitation or remorse. Maybe it was the new blood in her veins that made her bold. Maybe it was the struggles she'd overcome on the journey. But she was no longer the girl Arianna had found on the streets of Ter.4.2. She no longer needed saving, which meant Arianna could no longer fill the role of savior. Florence was becoming something more, and she needed Arianna to rise to the task and do the same.

The silence stretched on for too long and Arianna stepped away. Betrayal hit her hard in the chest. Her teacher, her friend, the woman who had been her everything, was walking away when the bombs were dropping.

"I hope you decide to grow into your words," Florence said softly. Arianna didn't even turn. "I hope you decide to stay with me, as my friend. I hope you decide you can live up to who you say you are. That you can support me in what I want even if it's not what you wanted for me."

The door clicked closed as her only reply.

ARIANNA

It had been three days since Florence had last spoken to her. Three days of wading through the din of the Alchemists Guild hall, lacking direction and purpose. Three days of watching Florence recover, stronger than ever.

The girl threw herself into acclimating to the Guild. At some point, she spoke with Sophie and the Vicar had agreed to let her join whatever pathetic rebellion was brewing. That, or Florence was even better than Arianna had given her credit for at making new friends—and Arianna had given the charismatic girl a lot of credit.

Cvareh was nowhere to be found, and she insisted to herself that she was glad for that fact. She didn't need the Dragon in her life. In fact, good riddance if he left her. She didn't need him or the Raven-turned-Revo-turned Chimera. She didn't need anyone.

At least, those were the lies she told herself. But as Arianna sat tinkering, building lock after lock and useless trinket after trinket, the loneliness grew. After she'd lost everything in the last resistance, she'd gained Florence. And now she'd lose Florence to the new resistance. Cvareh would likely betray them all and she'd be left with ghosts and enemies anew.

"So this is what the great and charismatic Arianna has been reduced to."

"Go away." Arianna didn't even turn from her workbench. She remained hunched over the tiny springs and dials of a mechanical bird. Getting its wings to flap had been trying her patience all morning.

Sophie ignored her, crossing over to the table. She picked up the wingless body of the bird. "Well, if I ever need to send messages via clockwork pigeon, I know who to turn to."

"What do you want?" Arianna was already spitting venom. She was in no mood and was utterly unapologetic about the fact.

"You know what I want." Sophie put the trinket down.

"I've been wondering when you'd finally start hounding me."

"I'm not going to be a rusty gear about this."

She didn't believe it for a second.

"I'm going to ask you for your help."

"Oh, is that all? That's a relief. No, then." Arianna returned to fumbling with the wing.

"Arianna—"

She made loud squeaking noises, imitating the rusty gear that Sophie had claimed she wouldn't be.

"Stop." Sophie covered Arianna's hands with hers and the watch she'd been using as a distraction. "You're not a child."

"I was never a child."

Sophie laughed. "Well, there we can disagree."

"I already told you no," Arianna reminded her. "I think we're done here."

"Arianna." Sophie sighed.

"Sophie." She sighed dramatically in reply.

"Weren't we friends?" Sophie had the audacity to look hurt.

"No," Arianna was out for blood. "You and Eva were friends."

"You can't be jealous of her and me. Your presence was the thing that reduced us to nothing. If anything I should be the one cross with you. The woman is dead, let—"

"Don't talk about her!" Arianna slammed her fist on the table, suddenly on her feet. She never wanted anyone to make assumptions about the woman she had loved. Least of all Sophie.

"Let her go." Sophie covered Arianna's hand gently with hers. "It's what she would've wanted."

Arianna pulled her hand away.

"I don't even want you to finish the Philosopher's Box. I just want you to help because I thought it could offer you closure."

When did everyone become so obsessed with my "closure"? Arianna thought bitterly. Then the whole statement seeped into her mind.

"You *don't* want me to finish the box?" The words were hard to say, they made so little sense.

"No, we already had a Rivet do it," Sophie announced triumphantly.

This was the competitive, self-centered Sophie that Arianna knew. "Lovely. It won't work."

"As arrogant as ever, I see." Sophie picked up one of the assorted lockboxes, inspecting it more closely. "You do good work—excellent even. But it's wasted if you don't use it for anything."

No one understood. By not using her talents in certain ways, Arianna was trying to protect them all. If the Philosopher's Box went into mass production it was likely to create an endless roulette of power struggles as one army fought against the next, and the next. She'd seen the destruction it reaped first-hand when men tried to get their hands on it.

"I use it for my own purposes." Arianna pulled the lockbox from Sophie's hand.

The Vicar shrugged and started for the door. "We're going to make a perfect Chimera now, if you want to see the fruit of your labor in action."

Arianna stood in limbo as the other woman left. She really didn't want to be involved. She knew there was no way another Rivet had finished her work, not based on the limited notes that had been stolen from her workshop.

But she found herself hastily following Sophie in two more breaths anyway. If nothing else, she wanted to know if the tensions between Nova and Loom were about to get even worse. Because if they were, she'd take Florence by force if she had to in order to keep the girl safe.

The Vicar and Arianna were escorted into a viewing room that overlooked a surgical lab. Within, a Chimera lay unconscious on a table. Alchemists surrounded him, preparing instruments and measuring chemicals. The Chimera had Dragon hands and ears, and that was only what was visible. It was a miracle he hadn't become forsaken yet.

On one table were the new reagents they were going to stitch in: a tongue and stomach were suspended in stasis liquid, condensing in the air and steaming from the temperature difference. Arianna's eyes fell on a new machine. It wasn't much different from the one that had transitioned Florence days earlier. *That* was what they thought the Philosopher's Box looked like.

"Call off the operation, Sophie," Arianna said softly. She wasn't going to openly embarrass the Rivet standing next to her, the man who was likely responsible for the monstrosity that would take another's life.

"You think I'll let you stand in the way of this?" Sophie smiled.

"It's not going to work."

"Oh, Arianna, you can't stand it when someone else does the work you think only you are fit to do."

"This is not personal." Arianna's voice slowly rose. "You are going to kill this man."

She'd gained the attention of those around her.

"Vicar Alchemist?" one of the surgeons called up, uncertain at Arianna's declaration.

"Continue."

"That isn't going to work. He's going to go forsaken the second you disconnect." Arianna spoke over the Vicar.

"I don't know who you think you are, but I built that from sketches drawn by a Master Rivet." The Rivet at her side took offense.

Well, the line's been crossed. Might as well throw etiquette out the window. "And I can tell why you don't have your circle yet, boy. Because that Master Rivet who drew them was *me*."

The Rivet looked between her and Sophie for confirmation. When Sophie didn't object, he suddenly considered his work a second time. "Maybe we should—"

"Start the operation!" Sophie demanded.

"You are condemning him to death."

"Silence, Arianna. You may be a dear friend of mine but this is my Guild, and I will not tolerate such rudeness."

Arianna held her tongue. They were a lot of things, but they weren't *dear friends*. Time and age couldn't change that fact, it seemed.

The operation commenced, and the Rivet at her side paled as they began removing the tongue and stomach of the man on the operating table. Another Alchemist manned the fake Philosopher's Box. Blood spiraled in tubes, filtering out the Fenthri blood, turning it gold. The fact that the machine had that much working terrified her. The boy at her side was smart to have deciphered the filtration system. It wouldn't be a stretch to think he could achieve real success through enough trial and error.

The problem wouldn't come until they sewed the man up, let him heal, and unhooked their cumbersome box. Arianna waited for it, watching for thirty minutes as the Alchemists finished. Emotions drained from her heart.

It was what had made Eva different. She had been an accomplished Alchemist and still held regard for life. She didn't see creatures as her playthings like these people did—as though the world were a large cage that merely housed their test subjects.

The man's eyes opened with a groan. He sat, and the Alchemists all held their breaths. He made it to his feet before he began to howl in pain. His eyes went bloodshot; his mouth began to foam.

"Put him down, Sophie, he's forsaken," Arianna demanded.

"Don't do anything." The Vicar held out her hand to the woman beside her who had reached for a gun.

"Put him down." The man was growling, beginning to lose his mind. Magic was spiking wildly around him. The golden tools that littered the room shook, shuddering to life at his distorted and unfocused commands. "Your Alchemists are about to start dying, Sophie."

The forsaken Chimera roared and lunged for one of the Alchemists who had been operating on him minutes earlier. The fall to forsaken was fast when that much magic was pumped in at once. Arianna's reflexes kicked in, but the gunfire echoed before she could steal the weapon. The Alchemist lowered her revolver. The forsaken Chimera was dead in one shot.

"Well, this was fun." Arianna turned, anger rising in her. Anger at her greatest work being pilfered and treated as though it was simple enough to be figured out in days. Anger at Sophie's disregard for the life of her fellow Fenthri. At the Alchemists' ever-apparent fault—progress without consideration for what that progress might reap for the world.

"Arianna, help us." Sophie stopped her. "You can turn the tides. You can change our world."

"Change it how?" She spun to face Sophie once again. "Do you even know? Have you even thought what a Philosopher's Box might do?" She already knew Sophie had no good answer so she didn't even give her time to offer one. "No, I didn't think so."

"Do you know what Eva told me she loved in you?" Sophie called down the hall after a long moment. "Your vision. Your pursuit of progress."

Arianna stopped, clenching her fists. She took a deep breath and let it go, unwilling to rise to Sophie's goading. Even if what she said was true, the woman Eva the Alchemist had loved died at her side two years ago. That Arianna had not survived her final act: slitting Eva's throat.

CVAREH

Word of the incident with the forsaken Chimera reached Cvareh's ears within the day. He found it odd how no one seemed to mourn the poor soul. Surely, the man had been *someone's* friend or family? But the world continued as normal, so he did as well. There was much work to be done in establishing a rapport between House Xin and the fledgling rebel group. But every time he thought he opened a door or had some stroke of luck, it closed back in his face.

Cvareh sat across the table from the Vicar Alchemist. Sophie was allegedly reviewing the latest schematics from her team of Rivets. But Cvareh sincerely wondered if she could grasp their contents.

"My sister asks me for updates."

"Updates on what, exactly?" Sophie hummed, flipping the pages.

"She wants to know if the rebels will stand with her bid for Nova's throne." He hastily added, "Of course, in exchange, she'll gladly support Loom's interests in her new regime."

"We aren't fit to stand against—or behind—any regime." Sophie finally deemed the conversation worthy of her full attention. "Our 'rebel army' is full of initiates with no experience on just about every front.

"Our supplies are being throttled by the Dragon King. We have to rely on other loyalists of the old ways, and black markets, to get the ammunition we need to merely defend ourselves, let alone stage a rebellion."

"But you have the schematics of a Philosopher's Box…" he offered weakly.

"I have part of the schematics, and the woman who can finish them won't help me. And, even if she did, it would take me years to acquire enough reagents to stitch up that many Chimera."

The ghastly electric lighting cast long shadows on the woman's skin. He wondered how old she was. She couldn't have been more than Arianna's age, which made her less than half of his age. But she handled herself as though she was eighty. The Fenthri lived half as long as Dragons, and aged twice as fast.

She leaned forward, folding her hands before her. "We keep having these meetings, Cvareh, yet they do not yield results. I am left with no Philosopher's Box, no reagents, no supplies. You want us to work with you? Give me results."

"And if I get these results, will you support my sister?" He remained focused on his mission, focused on the one thing Petra had demanded of him: leave Loom with the promise of the army they needed.

"If you get me even half of these results, I will support you or whoever else you want me to," Sophie swore.

"Then consider it a deal." Cvareh stood.

"Really?" She chuckled. "I'll believe it when I see it."

He must be acclimated to Loom, because the rude dismissal only made him bristle so much. The slights against him he could forgive, and he had the feeling he'd need to forgive much more to achieve what he wanted. With that in mind, he headed straight from one room occupied by a sharp-tempered Fenthri to another.

Arianna had made a virtual sundries shop of clockwork items in the workroom she'd stolen. Even as he arrived some Alchemists were leaving, turning over mechanical locks in their hands with fascination, and cackling over the ideas of all the trouble they could use them for. Things were going to be interesting for a bit in the Alchemists' Guild with Arianna's work in house.

Her head jerked up at the sound of him, as though she'd known it was his eyes on her with the feeling of his attention alone. Perhaps she had. He could find her in a crowd by just her footsteps now. Why would it be far fetched to think she would know him by his stare?

Arianna's mouth pressed into a line, and Cvareh was equally talkative. They hadn't said a word to each other since arriving at the Guild a week ago, despite crossing paths. The last time she'd really said anything to him was when he'd let her imbibe from him.

His obsession with the woman was nothing more than an infatuation, he'd begun telling himself. But one look from her had him questioning everything. To say he loved her would be a stretch. To say he wanted her, wanted to understand her? That was much closer to the mark.

"I want to talk to you." He finally broke the silence.

"I figured that's why you were here," she drawled, returning to the little box before her.

He'd spent so much time around her as the White Wraith that he'd forgotten she was a Master Rivet. Her skills with machinery, locks, buildings—they all contributed so seamlessly to her success as a thief and organ runner that he didn't look at them as separate from that chosen profession. There was something almost soothing in the way she tinkered.

Soothing, and restless.

If he shifted his thinking, it wasn't far-fetched to see the reason for her attempts at finding peace in gears and coils. Cvareh sighed to himself, crossed to the worktable and sat in the chair opposite her. She pretended he didn't even exist.

"I came here to ask for your help."

Arianna continued to ignore him, and for the first time he preferred it that way.

"I came to Loom to bring the schematics for the Philosopher's Box to the rebellion here because my sister wanted to use it as a bargaining chip for their alliance. On Nova, our House has been the lowest on the social ladder for centuries. I understand that may not mean much to you. But to us, it's everything. And Petra is the first chance we have at taking the throne. She's young, and strong, opinionated as anyone, and she fights for who and what she believes in."

Ari reached for another tool, working as though he wasn't there.

"I think that's what I see of her, in you." His soft words finally drew her attention and now that Cvareh had it, he wouldn't let it go. He would lay it all out on the table. He would do what he should've done from the start and let her know exactly who he was and what he wanted. "I don't know how the King got the schematics. I know, now, you were the one to make them. So I can't imagine how they fell into the hands of the Dragon King and I can only assume it has *something* to do with your general hatred for my people and the failure of the last rebellion."

Her challenging stare told him he was right.

"But if I had known they were yours... I would've returned them to you, rather than bring them here."

"Liar." Arianna whipped out the word as though she'd been waiting all along for an opportunity to use it. "Why would you sacrifice the bargaining chip that you said yourself means so much to your family, and your sister?"

"Because of the predicament I'm in now," he answered easily. "Partial sketches are almost useless. But the help of the woman who made them? That's worth something far greater."

"Did Sophie send you?" Arianna scowled at the mention of the Vicar's name.

"Not directly," he confessed. "But she has put a high price on the alliance of the rebellion."

Arianna sighed and turned back to her box. She struggled with a tiny gear, trying to force it onto a peg and into place. It just wouldn't go.

"I may have done all this out of order. But I want to earn your trust."

"For your family."

"For my family," Cvareh confirmed. "And because I want to know why I can't seem to stop thinking about you at every turn. Why I find the shade of your skin and flatness of your teeth charming, when a few months ago I found it repulsive."

"What are you saying?" All emotion dropped from her voice. It was virtually unreadable to his ears.

"I don't know what I'm saying." Cvareh stood. "But I want to find out. And I intend to do so."

"A Dragon earning my trust?" she scoffed, back to the Ari he knew. "That could take years."

"Good thing I'm a Dragon. Years are something I have." Cvareh chuckled and grinned. "If I have to, I'll stop time."

That *almost* earned him a smile, and he'd take almost. Cvareh was nearly out of the room, his mission accomplished for now, when something else struck him. He stopped and turned to find Arianna looking up at him in confusion. He would capitalize on whatever good mood he'd earned.

"One more thing. Whatever you think about me… don't believe me, think I'm a total liar, take no heed of my truth." The thought stung him a bit—the idea that after all they'd been through she could still not trust him. "But if you listen, not just hear, but *listen* to one thing I say, let it be this: patch things up with Florence. You will regret it, Ari, if you let her vanish because of your own stubbornness."

ARIANNA

The bed was cold and the room, though nicely sized, felt a million veca wide. There was no rumbling of Cvareh's deep breaths while he slept. Florence's heat wasn't warming her sheets. Arianna was left alone—as she had been for a week now—with her thoughts.

She had almost worked up the resolve to leave the Alchemists' Guild without Florence, when Cvareh had visited her that afternoon. He'd come bearing himself to her in ways she hadn't expected, and didn't want to believe were true.

Because believing would mean trusting a Dragon again.

And then there were all the claims Florence had made against her. Arianna stared listlessly at the ceiling. The girl had seen vision in her, when there had only ever been vengeance. Both drove, both were pursued with all the passion of the soul.

But a soul driven by vengeance was a selfish soul. A soul driven by vision was a generous one—one that bore itself before others and put the needs of the many before the needs of the few.

There was a time that she had actually possessed those traits. A time when they weren't just vacant, labeled pegs on the walls of her personality. She had written them off when the rebellion died. Eva, Master Oliver, and the Arianna they had known died alongside them.

She was nothing now, and that had enabled her to be an extension of her benefactors' will as the White Wraith. What Florence had seen in her was nothing more than a mirror of the potential that lived in the girl herself. Potential Ari eagerly reflected and wanted to grow—as if its vines and roots could curl around the fragments of her heart and pull them back together.

Arianna sat up, rubbing her eyes tiredly. Even Sophie's words about Eva had stuck with her. What would Eva think if they met now? Was Arianna still someone she'd want to love?

Chasing ghosts down empty halls, she stood, padding on silent feet through the Master's passages of the Alchemists' Guild. Eva was dead. Whatever she would or wouldn't love no longer mattered. Now, Arianna had to live for the living—for herself.

Arianna turned the knob of Cvareh's door, letting herself quietly into his room.

Even amid her virtual silence, the Dragon woke. Talons jutted from his hands, ready to ward off a shadowed attacker. She leaned against the door, waiting for him to calm himself, to realize who was there. It only took a moment.

"What are you doing here?" he whispered.

She could hear his quickening heartbeat, feel his magic responding to hers. Arianna crossed over to his bed with purpose. He sat straighter as she made herself at home without his permission, drawing up her legs to sit atop his sheets.

His words about her played relentlessly in harmony with everything else she'd been coming to terms with. Arianna had heard them clearly, but they were so difficult for her to process.

This Dragon and she had embarked on an odd journey with each other. It was a winding path that had taken them across Loom, and what she thought was to be their final destination had turned out to be a resting point before the next, greater trek.

"I want proof," she announced.

"Proof of what?" Cvareh asked skeptically.

"Proof that your sister is who she says she is. That *if* I help this resistance—and her—get their footing, I will not just be replacing one tyrant with another."

The fact was that Loom was headed toward another war no matter what she did. If it was in one year, or twenty, eventually the rebels here would grow enough, become reckless enough, that they would attack. Loom wasn't meant to sustain itself as it was. That Ari believed above all else. Tensions would be omnipresent until things with the Dragons were settled in a far better manner than their current arrangement.

"Whatever proof you want, I'll get," Cvareh said hastily.

"I don't want it from you."

"What then?"

"I want it from *her*."

"Her?" It took him a second to put it together. "Petra? My sister will never come to Loom. She can't. There are too many eyes on her."

"I never said anything about her coming here."

"You want to go to Nova?" Cvareh couldn't process what he was hearing. The idea of Arianna on Nova was preposterous—she could agree with him on that.

"*Want* may be a strong word, yet..." Arianna sighed softly. "I've been standing still for far too long, hiding behind excuses and poor attempts at belief in something, anything."

"Is this because of Florence?"

"Among other things." He may have been ready to bare his soul to her, but Arianna wasn't there yet. They were still too much of nothing and not enough of everything for her to expose herself emotionally.

"So you patched things up with her?" he asked.

"I'm on the way to doing so." Arianna was pointedly ambiguous, and he fell down the rabbit hole of drawing his own conclusions. The Dragon no doubt presumed she'd spoken to Florence about her plans. But Arianna would face Florence again when she could be the woman the girl had seen in her all along. She would apologize with her actions before her words.

"I'm glad." The Dragon genuinely sounded it. *Sincerity, from a Dragon.* The idea was far-fetched in her mind, but Cvareh continued to make a strong case. "I'll speak to my sister, and figure out a way back to Nova for both of us."

Arianna shook her head. "We should go now. The more time you take, the more opportunity I have to back out of this."

"But we have no way of breaking through the Gods' Line…"

"The what?"

"The clouds," he corrected hastily.

"Yes we do," she declared triumphantly. "You didn't think the Alchemists would let a Rider's glider sit in the forest to be picked apart or rusted to dust, did you?"

"Leona's glider is here?" He'd heard nothing of it.

"I found it when I was nipping through storerooms for parts." She stood.

"The nipping around bit I believe. The rest seems suspect."

Arianna grinned and extended her hand to the Dragon. "I like this newfound sass of yours, Cvareh. Don't give up on it."

"As you ask." He took her right hand with his left. It was awkward, but it suited them. She went right, he went left: two halves of the same whole.

FLORENCE

lorence raked her hands through her hair, teasing out the tangles from sleeping. It was nice to finally have a certain level of cleanliness back in her routine. Her hair had been so knotted upon arriving to the Guild that she'd been afraid she'd have to cut it. Luckily, she saved her dark locks with about an hour of careful brushing.

Her morning routine still took some getting used to. All the clothes were in their proper place. There wasn't a Rivet tearing through closets and coming in at all hours from odd jobs, leaving her soiled clothing lying about. Her room was neat and orderly, as she preferred it and as it had been her whole life before Arianna.

But now it seemed sterile.

She hadn't found the courage to talk to her teacher. *Former teacher? Teacher.* Since the day of her transition. It wasn't that she didn't want to, but that she had no idea how.

Arianna wanted Florence to go back to her and apologize. She wanted the girl she'd known in Dortam. But Florence had changed, and she wasn't going to hold herself back for the sake of someone who claimed to want what was best for her but couldn't live up to those words in practice.

Ari was being the fool, Florence was being stubborn, and she wondered how much longer they could both go before something broke. She just desperately hoped that all that gave was the silence, and not her morals, or Arianna's love for her. She pulled on some of her borrowed clothing and started the day.

The connections Florence had gained in Mercury Town and the convenient knowledge of two transporters in Ter.4's Underground was proving more useful than she ever imagined for helping the resource-starved Alchemists. She'd spent most of her days with Derek, working on how to get them more ammunition so they could actually make a stockpile, rather than just using it regularly to fight off endwig.

In the hours she wasn't there, she was helping the armorers see how they could stretch their supplies further. Sometimes, she ran into something that made her wish she was still on speaking terms with Ari—or something that made her wish for the Revo teachers she'd had in Dortam. But Florence was determined to power through it on her own, even if it meant some late nights of trial and error with her newfound magic.

"Good morning," she greeted Derek. He occupied one corner of a laboratory he split with a girl named Nora. She was a late riser due to her midnight bursts of inspiration, and they usually had the desk to themselves.

He stared at her skeptically.

"What?" Florence wondered if she had only thought she brushed her hair and it was still a tangled mess.

"Did you know?"

"Know what?"

"You know what," he pressured.

"Actually... I don't." She hadn't the foggiest what had gotten him so twisted in knots.

"You really don't know?" Derek eased off, sitting across from her.

"I don't know what I don't know?" Florence thought about the self-posed question and struggled to see if she'd said it right. "What am I to know?"

"Your friends stole the Rider's glider we pulled from the wreckage of that airship crash."

"I didn't know you had the glider." *Out of everything to focus on, she picked the fact that the Alchemists had taken one of the gliders?* "Where did they go?"

Florence folded her fingers together, gripping them tightly. They'd left her behind. It was all for what she said. Maybe she'd been right, maybe she'd been justified, maybe she still was, but none of that expunged the pain at the thought of being left alone.

"Well, with a Dragon glider, they could've gone anywhere far and fast." Derek leaned back in his chair, terribly amused by the situation since he lacked all emotional investment. "But the morning watch says they charted a course skyward for Nova."

"Impossible. Arianna would never go to Nova." Florence couldn't believe it.

"Think what you will... But that happens in the dawn, and now, the Vicar tells me that we must increase our preparations. We must remain diligent, she says, because one 'never knows when the resources we need could come."

Florence knew for all the help she'd been, the Vicar wasn't talking about her. It'd take a greater force to sway the tides in the favor of the fledgling rebels. A force that might be mustered by a Wraith, and a Dragon.

"We should get to work then," Florence resolved with a small smile. "There's much to be done—just in case we have the opportunity to overthrow a King."

"Just in case?" Derek grinned. The man clearly believed she knew more than she did. But all Florence had was her intuition. Then again, when it came to Arianna, her intuition was rarely off.

"Just in case." She gave him a small wink and looked over all there was to be done.

PETRA

It was the second time she'd been summoned to the Rok Estate in a few month's time. It wasn't that Petra didn't enjoy inspiring frustration and anger in the man who was supposed to be revered as her supreme ruler, because she did—she enjoyed it a lot. Shameful amount, really. But she just had other things to do.

Running a House, managing nobles, and overseeing the wellbeing her family was enough to fill anyone's plate. Throw on regicide and treason while trying to broker deals with—apparently—the most temperamental Fenthri there were? She barely had time to sharpen her claws these days.

She clicked her tongue off her teeth, pulling lightly at the boco's feathers, guiding it with her knees to bank toward the landing area for nobility. Other giant birds milled about, some saddled, some not. Their iridescent feathers shone in the midday sun.

With the buffeting of large wings, her cerulean mount landed with a dignified caw. At least Petra found it dignified. She didn't speak boco, and some of the other birds ruffled their feathers at whatever it was her Raku had said.

Petra patted him lovingly on the bill. "You annoy the feathers off these gaudy chickens."

She might not speak boco, but she suspected Raku understood her language as he cooed gleefully in reply. Spinning, she adjusted the thick beaded necklace that ran down front and back, sauntering into the Rok estate as though she already owned the place.

"I haven't met you before." She gave a wide smile to the Rider who was escorting her to Yveun Dono's infamous red room. The thought of it made her yawn. He did it to be intimidating, but it made him predictable and dull.

The real way to intimidate people was to capture their imagination. The imagination was far more wicked than anything someone else could think up because it knew every insecurity to play off. Yveun Dono was too overt. House Rok sharpened their blades, but not their minds.

"We have not had the pleasure, Petra'Oji." Nothing about the Rider's tone made Petra think that meeting her was a pleasure. She raked her fingers through her golden curls, drawn back and pinned away from her face.

"You have two whole beads I see." She made a scene of fussing over them. "What an accomplishment."

The man almost swatted her hand away. He might be new, but he was trained enough to avoid making that mistake. If he struck her, she would kill him. Not even Yveun Dono would bother denying her that duel.

"Dono, I have brought Petra'Oji," the Rider announced as they crossed into the threshold of the red room. The man strode ahead of her, assuming the place at the side of the King.

Petra tilted her head. *Now this was too delicious not to comment on.* "Yveun Dono, did you change staff? Or is our dear Leona sick?"

The King's claws dug into the throne. He was on edge. No, not on it—past it. Further than she'd ever seen him before.

Petra drew her magic within her, bracing herself subconsciously against the King's aggression. If he wanted to fight her here and now, that would be fine. In fact, it'd save her a lot of time and effort if he just challenged her to a duel. But she wanted it to be a *fair* duel, one that didn't involve outside interference. And the Riders seemed to have their own definition of fairness when they claimed they were all one to begin with.

"You know what happened to her," Yveun Dono snarled.

He looked like an old man guarding a stupid bone. Petra didn't tell him so. She just continued to play dumb. "Me? My lord, if I knew I would gladly tell you as your most humble servant... But I'm afraid I've been overseeing the smiths lately, working on establishing our own gold tempering mills here on Nova as you yourself requested."

And for every one she set up for the King, she set up one for House Xin.

"You are on your last line, Petra," the King barked. "Leona is dead, and I demand Cvareh's head for it."

He led them down the exact path Petra had been expecting.

"Cvareh had nothing to do with it. He's been praying at the Temple of Lord Xin, as I told you months ago." Petra watered the seed she'd sewn and watched it flower.

"If you're lying to me Petra—"

"See for yourself, Dono," she interjected. "If you are so concerned, venture to the temple. While he is in private mediation, I imagine even the gods would forgive the intrusion of our supreme ruler."

"Perhaps I will." He grinned madly.

Oh, Yveun Dono, you make this too easy. He thought he was calling her bluff while she watched him play right into her palms. House Rok certainly hadn't stayed in power for so long because they possessed the most wit of all the Dragon houses.

"Very well. I will gladly go with you. I haven't seen my brother in far too long." She smiled easily, flashing her canines.

The King stood, furious. "If you are lying, I will kill you."

"I'm not lying."

"Then lead on, Petra'Oji, and we will see where we stand when the sun falls."

She led without hesitation or concern. She'd stalled the King's demands for an audience long enough that Lord Agnedi had turned his lucky eye on her. Cvareh had arrived just that morning. And a few hours was plenty of time to hide a glider, position her brother where he needed to be, and mask the curious scent of the Chimera who traveled with him.

Petra smiled as she mounted her boco, running her fingers through his feathers. She rose to the sky like a proverbial curtain. The stage was set and the actors she'd so carefully selected were in their place. It hadn't all gone according to script, but *oh*, if the climax hadn't proved interesting. She'd sent Cvareh down with schematics of a Philosopher's Box, and he'd returned with the inventor herself.

She would focus on that fact later. For now, she had a King to make her fool.

The story continues in…

ON SALE APRIL 2017

Pronunciation Guide

People

Arianna	Are-E-ah-nah
Cvareh	Suh-var-ay
Florence	Floor-in-ss
Leona	Lee-oh-nah
Yveun	Yeh-voo-n
Louie	Loo-EE
Petra	Peh-trah
Sophie	So-fee

Places

Ter.	(Short for Territory)
Lysip	Lisp

Dragon Houses/Titles

Xin	Shin
Rok	Rock
Tam	T-am (same as 'am' in 'I am')
Oji	Oh-jee
Ryu	Re-you
Dono	Dough-no
To	Tow
Bek	Beck
Da	Dah

The Five Guilds of Loom

Harvesters   Alchemists   Rivets

Ravens   Revolvers

Guild Brands

*Found on the right cheek, tattooed guild brands were
imposed by Dragon Law to designate a Fenthri's rank
and guild membership. The tattoo is elaborated upon as
new merits are achieved.*

Initiate

Journeyman

Master

Dragon Houses

All members of Dragon society belong to one of three Dragon houses. Ties into the House can be by blood, adoption, mating, or merit.

 Rok

 Tam

 Xiu

Dragon Names

All Dragon names follow the structure:

[Given Name] [House Name]'[House Rank] [Societal Rank]

Shortened names are said as one of the following:

[Given Name]'[House Rank]
or
[Given Name] [Societal Rank]

House Ranks	Society Ranks
Oji – House Head	Dono – King/Queen
Ryu – Second in Command	To – Dono's Advisors/High Nobility
Kin – Immediate Family to the Oji/Ryu	Veh – Nobility Chosen by the Dono
	Soh – Upper Common
Da – Extended Family	Bek – Lower Common
Anh – Vassals/Lower Members of the Estate	(nothing) – Pauper, Slave, Disgraced

Acknowledgements

THE GATEKEEPER PRESS TEAM—I recognize it may be weird to start with the team that helped me bring Air Awakens to market, but I wouldn't be here if it weren't for each of you. The fact that I came across Gatekeeperpress.com at the start of my publishing career was downright serendipitous and it was through the experience, exposure, and partnership that I found there that I was able to get to where I am today. So thank you for your continued professionalism and I hope to work with you all again in the future.

ROB PRICE—from the bottom of my heart, I thank you. Our partnership began humbly enough, but look at what it has become! When I had nothing but a story and a dream, you helped me through Gatekeeper Press. And then you and Price World Publishing embarked on this journey with me. I hope to continue working with you and your teams in the future.

MY EDITOR, REBECCA—it has been an absolute joy to work with you. On a nuts and bolts level, thank you for all the insights you gave me and work you put into this manuscript. But, on a higher level, thank you for being the one to encourage me to take my work beyond the scope of Young Adult. I've grown so much as a writer in a short time working with you and I hope we have many more manuscripts ahead of us.

JEFF—it's not easy to find someone who will unconditionally support you in all you do. Thank you for giving that to me. Hearing that you are proud of the work I'm doing is all the motivation I need some days to keep going when it gets hard.

NICK—thank you for letting me be really bad at listening to you when you said you didn't want to help me conceptualize my work and tolerating all the times I forced you to do it anyway. You are the best beta reader an author could want, and the best friend anyone could ever hope for. I hope you can see all the places you helped change for the better in this manuscript. I will always hold it and think of pacing my living room as I prattled off ideas to you.

MY COVER ARTIST, NICK D. GREY—thank you so much for bringing the characters of Loom to life. It's been a pleasure working with you and I can't wait to see how you envision Petra and Yveun! I'm so happy that you drew that Bloodborne fan art.

ROB—I'm not sure if meeting you when I did was a stroke of luck, or fate, but I know better than to look a gift horse in the mouth. Thank you for all the guidance and help you've given me throughout this process. You offer a unique perspective, a sturdy counterweight when I need it, an expert opinion, and a perpetually patient ear. You are truly one of the best people I have ever had the privilege of meeting.

JON—your counsel has been invaluable throughout this process. The guidance you have given me has not only been essential in shaping my publication journey, but also sound life advice in general.

KATIE—I think it's safe to say that you are the first person who has talked about getting a Loom tattoo! I will always remember with fondness reading over your shoulder the first time you experienced this story and playing just the right music at just the right time. Thank you for always being there to go out with me when I'm going stir crazy!

DOUG—thank you for helping me navigate the dollars and cents side of running a business and making sure my books are in order. Your candor and professionalism are always appreciated.

DANIELLE L. JENSEN—our Twitter DMs will live forever in infamy! Thank you for helping me both as an author and as a friend. I can't tell you how much I've appreciated everything from your guidance in why a sentence didn't make sense to you reading the manuscript in advance.

SUAN DENNARD—your title for the world's most supportive author is only rivalled by the title of most awesome friend. Even when you were deep in the writing cave you allowed me to be random at you. Thank you so much for taking the time to read The Alchemists of Loom when you were so, so busy.

L.R.W. LEE, RACHEL E. CARTER, and SYDNEY—for taking the time to read The Alchemists of Loom in advance, giving me your thoughts, and catching the mistakes that fell through the cracks.

VICARS DANI, JAMIE, EMILY, MAUD, and SHANNON— thank you, thank you, thank you, for helping me bring the Guild Games to life. I could not have accomplished even half of what the Guild Games were without the five of you as fearless leaders. Your time, effort, and consistency was not unnoticed nor unappreciated.

MOM and DAD—your love and support knows no bounds. Thank you for being understanding and encouraging of this wild journey your daughter has embarked on.

MER—thank you for constantly expanding my world, pushing me to be better, and believing in this story.

THE CITY OF SAN FRANCISCO—from your floating museums, to your art-deco architecture, to the wooden temple in Hayes Valley, to the ferry terminal, to the tucked away stairways, and more… thank you for existing and welcoming this wayward traveler among your streets. Thank you for inspiring and enriching the world I've made during its conception.

THE TOWER GUARD—even if we are now in a new world, .you will always be my dear guard. Near or far, we take care of our own and no one feels that more than me. Thank you so much for all your help in spreading the word about my works. Each and every one of you are so dear to me. Thank you to…

Tara, Jan, Desyerie, Abigail, Leah, Linda, Iris, Eileen, Sana, Kelly, Erika, Mi-Mi, Anjuli, Michaela, Erin, Bryce, Shelly, Hameedah, Alicia, Kim, Heather, Lola, Lauren, Ali, Jemimah, Betsy, Alex, Rachel, Katie, Emily F., Azazel, Kami, Nora, Kathleen, Tarryn, Aya, Jade, Vanessa, Nina, Cassie, Justine, Annie, Rafael, Christine G., Jaclyn, Karen, Sarah M., Kelsea, Lauren, Theresa, Brittany E. Kara, Suzann, Danielle K., Vanessa A., Teresa T., Shahira, Alexis J., Jessica W., Denise R., Jasmine, Jzn, Cassandra, Rocio, Hadassah, L Manzano, Erin H., Abigail H., Gaby N., Jenna T., Sandra F., Vannah, Royala, Emily R., Sabrina, Book Crazie, Vhiskey, Andrea M., Christine O., Shannon, Lina, Megan J., Alexandra, Melisa, Jamie K., Megan M., Alexis K., Kimberly, Maud, Shara, Jenny P., Mia, Michelle M., Emily G., Jayden, Dani, Joana, Shelly, Johanne, Tracey B., Myranda, Annabelle N., Kathleen S., Heidi, Andrea L., Joanne, Chelsea Q., Parryse, Sophie K., Nadine,Lea, Vandana, Julie, Linda M., Chelsea C., Joselyn, Amanda F., Julianne T., Kass, Aiko, Jessica L., Bingkat, Siomara, Candice, Senan, Logan R., Mariana, Devin F., Ivan, Nicolette, Jess S., Autumn T., Lovelene, Tayla, Carly V., Victoria C., Ashley, Sarah M., Margo, Megan E., Swati, Roshell, Nicola, Alexandra R., Keo, Roz, Ali B., Rehan, Megan M., Maggie W., Nkisu, Avery, Jannin, Gavin, Myrtle, Nichole, Aila, Chelsea H., Winnie, Clare, Ana, Yeechi, Carmela, Robyn, Erin C., Brianna M., Dina, Aentee, Laura S., Jenara, Randi, Brianna, Daphne C., Janine, Lily-Jo, Bre, Emily M., Daniel R., Addison, Amber, Helen N., Cleo, Ngu, Madison W., Janessa, Fatima, Anne, Ciara, Karina, Kaitlin D., Maxx, Liza, Melissa R., Danielle E., Kara,

Vivien, Mara, Meyan, Hoai, Annalisse, Heather K., Duane, Madeline, Misha, Dorothy H., Jordan, Salwa, Monique, Alice W., Meghann, Malene, Natalia, Lisa, Zoe, Jenna R., Raisa, Anna C., Brian G., Grace, Tho, Ellen V. Desi, Alicia S., Amanda L., Denise C., Katelyn, Dianna H., Sokha, Amani, Jennifer, Kristie, Amber, Moa, Wendy, Fiona, Eveline, Merilliza, Vinky, Mary B., Sarah L., Lee F., Karina, Barbara, Bonny, Kate R., Cassidy, Yaprak, Irene, Ana, Raissa, Lauren, Joyce, NeSsa, Alyssa L., Leila K., Jennylyn, Aimee, Pammy, Sophie P., Zoe, Katie G., Jessica N., Angel, Rennie C., Samantha M., Skyly, WanHian, Angelia

About the Author

fantastical worlds. Somehow, she managed to focus on the real world long enough to graduate with a Master's in Business Administration before crawling back under her favorite writing blanket to conceptualize her next magic system. She currently lives in St. Petersburg, Florida, and when she's not writing can be found playing video games, watching anime, or talking with readers on social media.

Visit her on the Web at www.elisekova.com
Twitter (@EliseKova)
Facebook.com/AuthorEliseKova
Instagram (@Elise.Kova)
Subscribe to her monthly newsletter on books and writing at www.elisekova.com/subscribe